MYSTERY
WALK

The most dangerous step you'll ever take.

Also by Robert R. McCammon
Published by Ballantine Books:

USHER'S PASSING

MYSTERY WALK

ROBERT R. McCAMMON

BALLANTINE BOOKS • NEW YORK

Library of Congress Catalog Card Number: 82-15419

ISBN 0-345-31514-6

This edition published by arrangement with Holt, Rinehart and Winston

Manufactured in the United States of America

First Ballantine Books Edition: April 1984
Third Printing: October 1989

To my friends John Scott and John Willis,
who each took a different road

Mystery Walk

Prologue

"Yes," the woman said at last, lifting her finely shaped chin from where it had rested against one thin brown hand, her elbow supported in turn on the armrest of a cherrywood rocking chair. She'd been staring into the fire as the two rawboned men in their patched overcoats and scuffed workboots had been talking. Though she was outwardly thin and fragile, the woman had deep-set hazel eyes that radiated a thoughtful inner strength. Her name was Ramona Creekmore, and she was one-fourth Choctaw Indian; the breed blood showed in her sharp, proud cheekbones, in the lustrous russet of her shoulder-length hair, and in the eyes that were as dark and placid as a forest pond at midnight.

When she spoke, John Creekmore shifted uneasily in his chair across the room. He'd pulled himself out of the way as they'd been talking, wanting to be no part of what was being said. He'd put his dog-eared Bible in his lap and looked into the fire and thought that Hell was all around him now, quickly closing in upon him. He had a long, lean, and weathered face, cracked with lines like a thin pane of autumn ice. His hair was thick and curly and reddish-brown, his eyes a clear ice-blue; Ramona had told him many times that she could see the sky in them, clouds when he was angry and rain when he was sad. Now, if she had looked into his eyes closely enough, she might've seen the approaching storm.

The two men hadn't moved. They were leaning on each side of the fireplace like long blue-jeaned bookends. John placed his hands on his Bible and watched the back of Ramona's head.

"Yes," she said quietly. "I'll come."

"No she won't!" John said harshly. The two men glanced at him, then waited for the woman to speak again. That angered him, and he said, "You two have made the trip up from Chapin for

1

nothin'! It bein' such a cold day and all, I'm sorry for you. I know why you're here, and I know why you think my Ramona can help you, but that's all over now. It's in the past, and we're both tryin' to forget it." He rose to his feet, still clutching his Bible. He stood tall, at six-three, and his broad shoulders stretched the red flannel shirt he wore. "My wife can't help you. Don't you men see that she's eight months along?"

Ramona touched her stomach gently. Sometimes she could feel the baby kicking, but right now he—yes, it would be a boy, it *had* to be a boy, for her husband's sake—lay perfectly still, as if minding his manners because they had company. But she could feel his heart beating deep within her, like the soft fluttering of a bird aching to take flight.

"Mr. Creekmore," the taller man said quietly; his name was Stanton, and he wore a full winter beard flecked with gray. He was pale and gaunt, and John figured he wasn't too far from eating bootsole soup. "We can't go on like this, don't you understand?" The man's narrow face was pinched, as if in pain. "My God, man, we just *can't!*"

"Don't you come in my house and take the Lord's name in vain!" John thundered. He stepped forward, raising his Bible like a weapon. "If you people in Chapin followed the Holy Word like you should, then maybe you wouldn't have this trouble! Maybe this is God's way of lettin' you know you've been sinners. Maybe it's meant to—"

"That ain't the way it is," the second man, named Zachary, said wearily. He turned toward the fire, kicking at errant chips of wood. "Lord knows we didn't want to come here. But . . . it's a painful thing and not somethin' that you want to talk about or think about too much. People know about your wife, Mr. Creekmore; you can't deny that they do. Oh, not everybody, I mean, but a few people. People who've had a need. And now . . ." Zachary looked over his shoulder, directly at the woman. "*We* have the need."

"But you don't have the right!"

Zachary nodded. "Yes, that may be. But we had to come, and we had to ask, and now we have to hear the answer."

"I've given it." John raised the Bible high, firelight licking at the battered leather binding. "What you need is *this,* not my wife."

2

"Mr. Creekmore," Zachary said, "you don't understand, I'm Chapin's minister."

John's mouth hung open. The blood seemed to rush from his face, and the Bible slowly came down to his side. "Minister?" he echoed. "And you . . . you've seen this thing?"

"I've seen it," Stanton said, and quickly averted his gaze to the fire. "Oh, yeah, I've seen the thing. Not too clear or too close, mind you . . . but I've seen it."

There was a long moment of silence between the men. The firewood popped and sizzled quietly, and the November wind crooned across the roof. Ramona rocked in her chair with her hands across her belly and watched John.

"So you see," the minister said, "we didn't want to come. But it . . . it's an unholy thing not to try to do *something*. I've done all I could, which wasn't so much, I guess. Like I say, there are folks who know about your wife, and that's how we found out about her. I prayed to God about this, and Lord knows I don't understand it, but we had to come here and ask. Do you see, Mr. Creekmore?"

John sighed and sat back down. His face was slack-jawed, his eyes grim. "No, I don't. Nothin' I see about it a'tall." But now he'd turned his attention to his wife and was waiting for her response. The Bible felt cool in his hands, like a metal shield. "Ain't no such thing," he said. "Never has been. Never will be."

Ramona turned her head slightly toward him, her delicate profile etched by the firelight. The two men were waiting, and they'd come a long way on a cold afternoon with a real need, and now they would have to have their answer. She said to the minister, "Please leave us alone for a few minutes."

"Surely, ma'am. We'll just go out and wait in the truck." The two men went outside into the deepening gray light, and before the door shut, a cold wind whipped through and fanned the hearth flames into a crackling fury.

She rocked silently for a moment, waiting for him to speak. He said, "Well? Which is it?"

"I have to go."

John let out a long deep sigh. "I thought things were going to be different," he said. "I thought you wouldn't . . . do those things anymore."

"I never agreed to that. I never could."

3

"It's unholy, Ramona. You're in danger of Hell, don't you know that?"

"Whose Hell, John? Yours? No, I don't believe in that kind of Hell. Not at the center of the world, not with devils carrying pitchforks. But Hell is right here on earth, John, and people can step into it without knowing, and they can't get out—"

"Stop it!" He rose abruptly from the chair and strode toward the fireplace. Ramona reached out and grasped his hand, pressing it against her warm cheek.

"Don't you understand that I try to do my best?" she asked softly, her voice quavering. "That's all there is in this world: to try to do the best you can. . . ."

John suddenly sank down on his knees beside her and kissed her hand, and when her knuckles were pressed against his cheek she felt the wetness of a tear. "I love you, Ramona; Lord knows I do, and I love the child you're gonna give me. But I can't say yes to these things. I just . . . *can't.* . . ." His voice cracked. He released her hand and stood up, his back toward her. "It's up to you, I guess. It always has been. It's unholy, that's all I know, and if you want to walk that path then God help you." He winced as he heard her rise from the rocker.

She gently touched his shoulder, but he didn't turn toward her. "It's not that I want to walk it," she said. "It's that I was born to. I have to go with them." She left him, going into the small bedroom where tiny pipings of wind shrilled through minute cracks in the pinewood walls. Just above the bed's headboard hung a beautifully detailed piece of needlepoint showing a forest in the flaming reds and oranges of autumn; it was the view from the house's front porch. Near a large maplewood chest of drawers—a wedding present from her mother—hung a 1951 Sears and Roebuck calendar; the first fifteen days of November had been crossed out.

Ramona struggled into an oversize pair of dungarees—her stomach was so big!—and a heavy brown sweater. She put on thick brown socks and her penny loafers, then tied a pale pink scarf around her head. The weather had snapped after a long warm Indian summer, and rain clouds had tumbled down from the north. Chill Novembers were rare in Alabama, but this one was a gray, hulking bear with a coat of freezing rain. As she struggled into her old plaid coat, she realized John was watching her from the doorway. He was whittling a bit of wood with his penknife, and

4

when she said, "Do you want to go with us?" he turned and sank down into his chair again. *No, of course not,* she thought. She would have to do this alone, as always.

The two men were waiting patiently in their old green Ford pickup truck. Ramona walked to the truck through the swirling wind and saw that most of the dead brown leaves in the elm, ash, and pecan trees around the small farmhouse were still fixed securely to their branches like tenacious, wrinkled bats. That, Ramona knew, and the large number of blackbirds she'd seen out in the barren cornfield, were sure signs of a hard winter to come.

Zachary opened the door for her and she said, "I'm ready now." As they drove away from the house, along a narrow dirt road that cut through the pine forest and connected with Fayette County Road 35, Ramona looked back over her shoulder and caught a glimpse of John watching from a window. A sadness ached within her, and she quickly looked away.

The truck reached the potholed county road and turned north, away from the small scattering of farms and houses that made up the town of Hawthorne. Fifteen miles north lay the booming town of Fayette, population a little over three thousand, and forty miles to the northeast was Chapin, which, with almost four hundred people, was a bit larger than Hawthorne.

Once on the road, Zachary told Ramona the story: It had happened almost two years ago, when a farmer named Joe Rawlings had been driving his wife Cass to a square dance just north of Chapin. He was a good Christian man, Zachary explained, and no one could understand why or how it had happened . . . or why it kept happening. Their truck had for some reason veered off the road and slammed at forty-five miles an hour into the Hangman's Oak. Maybe it wasn't so hard to figure out, Zachary said; it had been raining that night and the road was slippery. Four others had been killed at the Hangman's Oak curve as well, the minister told her; accidents happen there all the time. A couple of months later, some kids driving to a high-school dance had seen it. A state trooper had said he'd seen it, too. So had an old man named Walters and—worst of all—so had Cass Rawlings's sister Tessa. It had been Tessa who'd begged the minister for help.

The miles rolled past. Darkness started spreading. They passed abandoned gas stations and empty houses consumed by dense seas of kudzu. Thin evergreens swayed against a sky seething with the threat of freezing rain. Stanton switched on the headlights; one of them cast a murky yellowish glow, like light seen through a diseased eye. "Mind if we have music?" he asked, a nervous quaver in his voice. When nobody spoke he turned on the radio, and from the cheap Philco Hank Williams was in the middle of singing about those chains he wore around his heart. Gusts of wind alternately pushed and tugged at the pickup, sweeping dead leaves from the overhanging trees and making them dance like brown bones in the road.

Stanton turned the dial, one eye on the snake-spine of the road ahead. Faraway voices and music floated past on a sea of static. And then a solid, burly, and authoritative voice boomed out from the tinny speaker: "*You can't fool Jesus, neighbor, nosiree! And you can't lie to Jesus either!*" The voice paused for a gulp of air, then steamed ahead; to Ramona it sounded rich and thick, like fine close-grained wood, but somehow sheened with an oily layer of shellac. "*Nosiree, you can't make promises that you don't keep, neighbor, 'cause there's a tab bein' kept in Heaven and your name's right there on it! And if you go get yourself in trouble and you say, 'Jeeeesus, you get me out of this one and I'll put five dollars in the plate come Sunday morning,' and you go back on that promise, then . . . neighbor . . . WATCH OUT! Yes, watch out, 'cause Jesus don't forget!*"

"Jimmy Jed Falconer," Zachary said. "That's coming from Fayette. He preaches a powerful message."

"Saw him preach in Tuscaloosa once," Stanton replied. "He filled up a tent as big as a football field."

Ramona closed her eyes, her hands laced across her stomach. The booming voice continued, and in it was a smooth, sure power that made her slightly uneasy. She tried to concentrate on what had to be done, but Falconer's voice kept getting in the way.

In another half-hour they passed through the center of quiet Chapin—like Hawthorne, blink your eyes and you missed it. Then they were curving in the darkness on a narrow road shouldered by underbrush, skeletal trees, and an occasional house fallen to ruin. Ramona noticed that Stanton's hands had clenched more tightly on the steering wheel, and she knew they must be almost there.

"It's just ahead." The minister reached forward and turned off the radio.

The truck rounded a bend and slowed. Ramona suddenly felt the life in her belly give a strong kick, then subside. The truck's headlights glanced off a huge, gnarled oak whose branches stretched out toward them like beckoning arms; Ramona saw the scars in the oak's massive trunk, and the ugly bulbous mass of wood tissue that had grown back to fill in the gashes.

Stanton pulled the truck off the road just this side of the Hangman's Oak. He cut the engine and the lights. "Well," he said, and cleared his throat, "this is where it happens."

Zachary drew a deep breath and slowly released it. Then he opened the pickup's door, got out, and held it open for Ramona. She stepped out of the pickup into a rush of frigid wind that caught at her coat and tried to rip it open; she had to hold it tightly around her, feeling that the wind might lift her off the ground and sail her into the darkness. Beside her, a line of dead trees swayed back and forth like a minstrel chorus. She walked away from the truck into knee-high grass, leaves crackling underfoot, and toward the looming Hangman's Oak. Behind her Stanton got out of the pickup truck, and the two men stood watching her, both of them shivering.

Ten feet away from the Hangman's Oak, Ramona abruptly stopped and sucked in her breath. She could feel a presence in the air: something cold, cold, a hundred times colder than the wind. It was something heavy and dark and very old, and it was waiting. "It's in the tree," she heard herself say.

"What?" Zachary called after her.

"The tree," she said in a whisper. She neared it and felt her flesh break out in goosebumps that ebbed and swelled; her hair crackled with static electricity, and she knew there was danger here—yes, yes, there was *evil* here—but she had to run her hands across the scarred wood, she had to *feel* it. She touched it; gingerly at first, then clasped her palms to the wood; a shiver of pain ran up her spine and centered at her neck, becoming unbearable. Very quickly she stepped away, her hands tingling. At her feet a small white-painted wooden cross had been hammered into the ground; a black-scrawled legend read: SIX KILLED HERE. YOUR LIFE IS IN YOUR HANDS. DRIVE CAREFUL.

"Mrs. Creekmore?" Zachary said, standing a few feet behind her. She turned to face him. "It doesn't happen every night. Is there something you can do right here and now to . . . stop it?"

"No. I have to wait."

"Well, come on and wait in the truck, then. It'll be warmer. But

7

like I say, it doesn't happen every night. I hear it happened twice last week, but . . . gosh it's cold out here, isn't it?"

"I have to wait," she repeated, and Zachary thought her voice sounded more determined. Her eyes were half closed, long strands of her russet hair flying free from her pink scarf, her arms cradling her child-heavy belly. He was suddenly afraid for her; she could get sick out in this cold, and something could happen to the child. He'd thought, from what he'd heard about her, that she could say some Indian words or something and that would be the end of it, but . . .

"I'm all right," Ramona said quietly. "I don't know how long it will be. It may not happen at all. But I have to wait."

"Okay, then. I'll wait with you."

"No. I have to be alone. You and Mr. Stanton can stay in the truck if you like."

Zachary paused for a moment, undecided, then he nodded and, bowed into the wind, started walking back to where Sam Stanton was blowing into his hands and stamping his feet. He turned back after a few paces, his face furrowed with concern. "I don't . . . I don't understand this, Mrs. Creekmore. I don't understand how it could . . . keep on happening."

She didn't answer. She was a dark form staring out into the distance, along the road where it curved beyond a stand of pines. Her coat tortured by the wind, she walked past the oak tree and stood motionlessly at the roadside. Zachary returned to the pickup and climbed in, shivering to his bones.

Full dark covered the forest. Staring into the night through slitted eyes, Ramona had a sense of low-lying clouds running before the wind, just above the swaying treetops. All the world seemed in dark, tumultuous motion, but she had concentrated on rooting herself to the earth, on bending like a reed when the wind swept past so she wouldn't be knocked off her feet. She could feel the Hangman's Oak behind her, its old evil pulsating like a diseased heart. It would have to be cut down, the stump dug up like a rotten tooth, the crater salted. Above her its heavy branches stirred like the arms of a huge gray octopus. Dead leaves spun up from the ground and snapped at her cheeks.

"Do you want some light?" Stanton shouted from the truck. When the woman didn't even move, he glanced uneasily at Zachary and said, "I guess she don't." He fell into silence, wishing he'd brought along a snort of moonshine to keep warm

8

and to keep from thinking about what moved along this road in the dead of night.

Headlights glinted through the pines. Ramona's eyes opened fully. The shape grew nearer; it was an old Packard with an ancient black man behind the wheel. The car slowed enough for the driver to get a good look at her, standing before the Hangman's Oak, and then the car accelerated away. Ramona relaxed again. She had decided she would wait for as long as it took, even though she could feel the life within her aching for warmth. The child would have to grow up strong, she thought, and would have to get used to hardships.

Almost three hours later, Stanton stirred and blew into his cupped hands. "What's she doin'?" he asked, straining to see through the darkness.

"Nothing," the minister replied. "She's still standing there. We were wrong to bring her out here, Sam. This whole thing is wrong."

"I don't think it's gonna happen tonight, parson. Maybe she's scared it off."

"I just don't know." Zachary shook his head in awe and bewilderment; his dark brown eyes had gone softly despairing. "Maybe it's all been talk—probably has been—but maybe . . . just maybe she *can* do something. Maybe if she believes she can, then . . ." He let his voice trail off. A few drops of cold rain spotted the windshield. Zachary's palms were wet and clammy, and had been since they'd brought the woman out here. He had agreed to ask the woman for help after he'd heard the stories, but now he was truly afraid. There seemed nothing of God in what she could do—if she actually *had* done those things—and he felt marked with sin. He nodded. "All right. Let's take her home."

They got out of the truck and approached her. The temperature had fallen again, and frequent drops of rain struck their faces. "Mrs. Creekmore?" Zachary called out. "You've got to give it up now!" Ramona didn't move. "Mrs. Creekmore!" he shouted again, trying to outshout the blustering wind. And then he suddenly stopped where he was, because he thought he'd seen something flicker like blue fire on the road, just beyond the curve through the screen of dancing pines. He stared, unable to move.

Ramona was stepping out into the road, between the oncoming thing and the Hangman's Oak. Behind the minister, Stanton shouted, "I see it! My God, I see it!" Zachary could see roiling streaks of blue, but nothing of any definite shape. He shouted, "What is it? What do you see?" But by then Stanton was shocked speechless; the man made a soft moaning noise from deep in his throat and was almost pitched to one side by a freight-train roar of wind.

Ramona could see it clearly. The pickup truck was outlined in blue flame; it was gliding soundlessly toward her, and as it neared she could make out the windshield wipers going full speed, and behind them the faces of a man and woman. The woman wore a bonnet, her face as round as an apple and beaming with anticipation of the dance. Suddenly the man's brown, seamed face contorted in surprised pain, and his hands left the steering wheel to clasp his temples. Ramona stood at the road's center, the blue-flaming headlights bearing steadily upon her.

Stanton's voice came out in a wild shout: "Get out of the way!"

Ramona held her hands out toward the blue truck and said quietly, "No fear. No pain. Only peace and rest." It seemed she could hear the engine now, and the tires shrieking as the truck slipped and veered across the road, picking up speed for its rendezvous with the Hangman's Oak. The woman in her bonnet was reaching desperately for the wheel; beside her the man writhed, his mouth open in a soundless scream.

"No fear," Ramona said. The truck was less than ten feet away. "No pain. Only peace and rest. Let go. Let go. Let . . ." As the blue flame bore down on her she heard Stanton cry out in terror, and she felt a crushing pain in her head that must've been a blood vessel bursting in Joe Rawlings's brain. She felt the woman's confusion and horror. Her jaw clenched tight to hold back an agonized scream. And then the blue-burning pickup truck struck full-force into her.

What Zachary and Stanton saw, they weren't sure. Afterward, they never spoke of it between them. When that truck hit the woman it seemed to collapse like a balloon exploding, and it was all a hazy blue mist as it lengthened and seemed to soak right into her body like water into a sponge. Stanton saw details—the truck, the passengers' faces—while Zachary was aware only of a presence, a swirl of blue mist, and the strange odor of burning rubber. They both saw Ramona Creekmore stagger backward, blue mist churning before her, and she gripped her head as if it were about to explode.

Then it was gone; all of it, gone. The wind seethed like something darkly hideous that had been deprived of a plaything. But the blue-flaming pickup truck was burned into Sam Stanton's eyes, and if he lived to be two hundred years old he'd never forget the sight of it disappearing into that witch-woman's body.

Ramona staggered out of the road and fell to her knees in the grass. For a long moment the two men were reluctant to move. Zachary heard himself whispering the Twenty-third Psalm, and then somehow he got his legs moving. Ramona groaned softly and rolled over on her back, her hands pressed to her stomach.

Stanton came up behind Zachary as the minister bent over Ramona Creekmore. The woman's face had gone gray, and there was blood on her lower lip where she'd bitten through. She clasped her stomach, looking up at the men with dazed and frightened eyes.

Stanton felt as if he'd been slugged with a sledgehammer. "Sweet Jesus, parson!" he managed to say. "This woman's about to have her baby!"

ONE

Hawthorne

1

Struggling through his arithmetic homework in the warm glow of the hearth, the dark-haired ten-year-old boy suddenly looked up at the window. He was aware that the soft crooning of the wind had stopped and a deep silence had filled the woods. He could see bare branches waving against a gray slice of sky, and a quiver of excitement coursed through him. He put aside his pencil, pad, and book—gladly—and then rose from where he'd been lying on the floor. Something was different, he knew; something had changed. He reached the window and stretched upward to peer out.

At first nothing looked different, and he was mildly disappointed; all those numbers and additions and subtractions were rattling around in his head, clinking and clattering and making too much noise for him to think. But then his eyes widened, because he'd seen the first flurry of white flakes scatter down from the sky. His heart skipped a beat. "Daddy!" he said excitedly. "It's snowing!"

Reading his Bible in his chair before the fireplace, John Creekmore looked out the window and couldn't suppress a grin. "Well, it sure is!" He leaned forward, just as amazed as his son. "Glory be, weatherman was right for once." It rarely snowed this far south in Alabama; the last big snowfall he could recall was back in 1954, when Billy had been only three years old. That had been the winter they'd had to accept charity canned goods from the church, after the stone-scorching summer had burned the corn and bean crops to stunted cinders. Compared to that awful year, the last few crops had been real bounties, though John knew it was never a good thing to feel too blessed, because the Lord could easily take away what He had provided. At least they had enough to eat this year, and some money to see them through the rest of the winter. But now he was infected with Billy's giddy excitement, and he stepped to the window to watch the flurries beside his son.

"Might fall all night long," he said. "Might be up to the roof by mornin'!"

"Gosh!" Billy said, his light hazel eyes—so striking against the darker coloring he'd inherited from his mother—widening with pleasure and a bit of fear too; he could imagine them all getting very cold and hibernating like bears, snowed in until April when the flowers came out. "It won't be that deep, will it?"

John laughed and ruffled the boy's curly, reddish brown hair. "Naw. Might not even stick. The way it's comin' down now, it's just bein' windblown."

Billy stood watching it fall for a moment more, then he shouted, "Momma!" and scuttled across the room, through a short hallway, and into the room where Ramona Creekmore sat propped up on pillows in bed, patiently mending a brown sweater she'd stitched for Billy as a Christmas present. It was less than a month since Christmas, and already Billy had worn the elbows out climbing trees and running wild in the woods. "Momma, it's snowing outside!" he told her, pointing out the small window near her bed.

"I told you those were snow clouds, didn't I?" she said, and smiled at him. There were deep wrinkles around her eyes, and strands of gray in her hair. Though she was only thirty-four, the years had been hard on her; she had almost died of pneumonia just after Billy was born, and she'd never fully recovered. She stayed in the house most of the time, doing her intricate needlepoint, and drank homemade herbal potions to fight off chills and fevers. Her body had gathered weight from lack of exercise, but her face was still fine-boned and lovely but for the faint dark circles under her eyes; her hair was still long and lustrous, her Indian complexion giving her a false appearance of perfect health. "Coldest weather of the year is still ahead, long as those blackbirds perch in the trees," she said, and returned to her work. It constantly amazed her how fast he was growing; clothes that fit him one month were the next ready to put back into the Hawthorne cycle of hand-me-downs.

"Don't you want to come see?"

"I know what it looks like. It's white."

It suddenly struck Billy that his mother didn't like the cold or the snow. She coughed a lot at night sometimes, and through the thin wall he could hear his father trying to soothe her. "You don't have to get up, then," he said quickly. "It's better if you stay right here."

John came up behind him and pressed a weathered hand against the boy's shoulder. "Why don't you bundle up and we'll take a walk."

"Yes *sir!*" Billy grinned widely and hurried to the closet for his battered green hooded parka.

John took his blue denim jacket with the sheepskin lining out of the closet; he slipped it on and then worked a black woolen cap onto his head. In the ten years that had passed, John Creekmore had grown lean and rugged, his wide shoulders stooped slightly from his seasonal labors in the field and the constant work of keeping the ramshackle cabin together through summer heatwave and winter frost. He was thirty-seven, but the lines in his face—as rough and straight as any furrow he'd ever plowed for a crop of corn—made him out to be at least ten years older; his lips were thin and usually set in a grim line, but he was quick to smile when the boy was around. There were those in Hawthorne who said that John Creekmore was a preacher who'd missed his calling, settling for earth instead of reaching toward Heaven, and they said that when angered or antagonized his steely blue gaze could drill holes through barn planking; but his eyes were always soft when he looked at his son. "I guess I'm ready," he said. "Who wants to go walkin'?"

"Me!" Billy crowed.

"Time's wastin'," John said, and reached out to his son. They linked hands and John felt the immediate warm pleasure of contact with the boy. Billy was so *alive,* so alert and curious; some of his youth rubbed off on John when they could be together.

They pushed through the plain pine door and the screen door and out into the cold gray afternoon. As their boots crunched on the frozen dirt road that connected the Creekmore property, all two acres of it, with the main highway, Billy could hear the soft hiss of the tiny snowflakes falling through the dense evergreens. They passed a small round pond, now muddy brown and veined with ice. A white mailbox dotted with .22 holes leaned toward the paved highway, and bore the legend J. CREEKMORE. They walked along the roadside, toward the main part of Hawthorne less than a mile ahead, as the snow fluctuated between flakes and sleet; John made sure the boy's hood was up good and snug, and the cord tied securely beneath his chin.

17

It had already been a hard winter, with January not even half over yet. There had been several freezing rains, and a fierce hailstorm that had shattered windows all across Fayette County. But as sure as day followed night, John thought, spring would follow winter and the real work of farming would start again; there would be corn and beans, tomatoes and turnips to plant. A new scarecrow would have to be put out in the field, but in these troubled times it seemed that even the crows were willful and refused to be bluffed. He had lost much of his seed to birds and bugs in the last several plantings, and his corn had grown weak and stunted. This was good land, he thought, blessed by God; but it seemed that finally the earth was beginning to give out. He knew about rotation planting and nitrites and all kinds of chemical soil foods the county agent tried to sell him, but all those additives— except for plain old fertilizer, which was as basic as you could get—were violations of God's plan. If your land was played out, so be it.

But times were troubled everywhere, John thought. That Catholic was president now, the Communists were on the march again, and people were talking about going up into outer space. Many autumn and winter afternoons John ambled down to Curtis Peel's barbershop, where the men played checkers in the warm wash of a potbellied stove and listened to the news from Fayette on the ancient Zenith radio. Most people, John was sure, would agree that these were the Final Days, and he could point to the Book of Revelations to show scoffers just exactly what evils would befall humanity in the next ten years or so—if the world lasted that long. Things were even troubled right here in the Hawthorne Baptist Church; Reverend Horton did his best, but there was no fire nor brimstone in his sermons, and worst of all he'd been seen over at the church in Dusktown helping the blacks with their potluck supper. Nobody liked to shake Horton's hand anymore after the services were over.

Billy's gloved hand was thrust out, trying to catch snowflakes. He snagged one on a fingertip and had a second to examine it— tiny and as lacy as his mother's Sunday tablecloth—before it vanished. She'd told him about the weather, and how it speaks in many voices when its moods change, but to hear it speak you have to be very quiet and listen. She had taught him to watch the beautiful pictures the clouds made, and to hear soft sounds in the forest that meant shy animals wandering near. His father had taught him how to gig for frogs and had bought him a slingshot to bring down squirrels, but he didn't like the way they squeaked when they were hit.

They were passing the small wood-frame houses outside Hawthorne's single main street. Billy's best friend, Will Booker, lived in a green house with white shutters just up the road; he had a little sister named Katy and a dog called Boo.

There was a light scattering of snow on the road. A black pickup truck came crawling along the highway toward them, and when it reached them the driver's window rolled down and Lee Sayre, who owned the hardware and feed store where John Creekmore worked on weekends, stuck his crewcut head out. "Hey there, John! Where you goin'?"

"Just takin' the boy for a walk. Say hello to Mr. Sayre, Billy."

"Hello, Mr. Sayre."

"Billy, you're growin' like a weed! Bet you'll top six-four before you quit. How'd you like to be a football player?"

"Yes sir, that'd be fine."

Sayre smiled. In his ruddy and slightly overfed face, Sayre's eyes were as pale green as a jungle cat's. "Got some news for you about Mr. Horton," he said in a quieter tone of voice. "Seems he's been doin' more than socializin' with his darky friends. We need to have a talk."

John grunted softly. Billy was entranced by the white puffs of exhaust that were billowing from the rear of Mr. Sayre's truck. The tires had made dark lines in the faint white spread of the snow, and Billy wondered where the air came from that filled tires up.

"Real soon," Sayre said. "You come down to Peel's tomorrow afternoon around four. And pass the word along." He waved to the boy and said cheerfully, "You take good care of your daddy now, Billy! Make sure he don't get lost!"

"I will!" Billy called back, but Mr. Sayre had already rolled up his window and the truck moved away along the road. Mr. Sayre was a nice man, Billy thought, but his eyes were scary. Once Billy had stood in the middle of the Ernest K. Kyle Softball Field on an April afternoon and watched a storm coming over the forested hills; he'd seen the black clouds rolling like a stampede of wild horses, and bolts of lightning had jabbed from clouds to earth. Lightning had struck very near, and the boom of thunder had shaken Billy to the soles of his battered Keds. Then he'd started running for home, but the rain had caught him and his father had given him a good whipping.

The memory of that storm wheeled through Billy's head as he watched the pickup drive away. There was lightning behind Mr. Sayre's eyes, and it was looking for a place to strike.

The snow had almost stopped. Nothing was even white, Billy saw, but instead a wet gray that meant there would be school tomorrow, and he would have to finish that arithmetic homework for Mrs. Cullens.

"Snow's about quit, bubber," John said; his face had gone red with cold. "Gettin' a bit chillier, though. You about ready to turn back?"

"Guess so," he answered, though he really wasn't. That seemed to him to be a matter of great concern: no matter how far you walked the road still went on to *somewhere,* and there were all the dirt trails and forest paths that led off every whichaway too, and what lay at the far end of *them?* It seemed to Billy that no matter how far you walked, you never really got to the end of things.

They walked on a few minutes longer, to the single blinking amber traffic light at the center of Hawthorne. The intersection was bordered by the barbershop, Coy Granger's Quick-Pik grocery store, a rundown Texaco gas station, and the Hawthorne post office. The rest of the town—clapboard-and-brick structures that looked like blocks a baby's hand had strewn into disarray—sat on either side of the highway, which swept on across an old gray trestle bridge and up into the brown hills where an occasional chimney spouted smoke. The sharp white steeple of the Hawthorne First Baptist Church stuck up through the leafless trees like an admonishing finger. Just on the other side of the disused railroad tracks was the jumble of stores and shanties known as Dusktown; the tracks might have been an electrified fence separating the black and white sections of Hawthorne. It disturbed John that Reverend Horton was leaving his rightful duties to go into Dusktown; the man had no cause to go over to the other side of the tracks, and all he was doing was trying to stir up things that were best kept buried.

"Better head on home now," John said, and took his son's hand.

In another few moments they came up even with the small but neatly kept green house on their right. It was one of the newer houses built in Hawthorne; there was a white-painted front porch at the top of a few steps, and white smoke curled from the chimney. Billy looked at the house, looked again, and saw Mr. Booker sitting up there on the porch. The man was wearing his yellow John Deere cap and a short-sleeved blue shirt. He waved to his best friend's father, but Mr. Booker seemed to be looking right through him. He said uneasily, "Daddy? . . ."

John said, "What, bubber?" Then he looked up and saw Dave Booker sitting there like a rock. He frowned and called out, "Afternoon, Dave! Pretty cold to be outside today, ain't it?"

Booker didn't move. John stopped walking, and realized that his old fishing partner was staring out at the hills with a blank, frozen expression, as if he were trying to see clear to Mississippi. John saw the summery short-sleeved shirt, and he said quietly, "Dave? Everything all right?" He and Billy came up the brown lawn slowly and stood at the foot of the steps. Booker was wearing fishing lures stuck in his hat; his square, heavy-jowled face was white with the cold, but now the man blinked and at least John knew he wasn't frozen to death.

"Mind if we come up for a spell?" John asked.

"Come on up, then. Long as you're here." Booker's voice was empty, and the sound of it scared Billy.

"Thanks kindly." John and Billy climbed the steps to the porch. A window curtain moved and Julie Ann, Dave's wife, peered out at them for a few seconds before the curtain closed. "How about that snow? Came down for a few minutes, didn't it?"

"Snow?" Booker's thick black brows knitted together. The whites of his eyes were bloodshot, his lips liver-red and slack. "Yeah. Sure did." He nodded, making one of the chrome lures jingle.

"You okay, Dave?"

"Why shouldn't I be?" His gaze shifted away from John, and he was staring into Mississippi again.

"I don't know, I just . . ." John let his voice trail off. On the floor beside Dave's chair was a scattering of hand-rolled Prince Albert cigarette butts and a baseball bat with what looked like dried blood on it. No, John thought, must be just mud. Sure, that's all it is. He gripped Billy's hand tightly.

"Man can sit on his own front porch, can't he?" Dave said quietly. "Last I heard he could. Last I heard it was a free country. Or has that changed?" His face turned, and now John could clearly see the terrible, cold rage in his eyes. John felt his spine crawl. He could see the wicked prongs of a hook protruding from the man's cap, and he recalled that they would've gone fishing last Saturday on Semmes Lake had it not been for one of Dave's frequent migraine headaches. "It's a fuckin' free country," Dave said, and suddenly grinned viciously.

John was jarred; it wasn't right that Dave should use such a word in front of the boy, but he decided to let it pass. Dave's gaze had clouded over.

The front door opened and Julie Ann peeked out. She was a tall, fragile-looking woman with curly brown hair and soft pale blue eyes. She smiled—grimaced, John thought—and said with tense good cheer, "John Creekmore! What brings you uptown? Billy, you takin' care of your daddy today? Step on in and let me offer you a cup of hot coffee, John."

"No, thank you. Billy and I've got to get on back. . . ."

"Please," Julie Ann whispered. Her eyes were luminous with tears. She motioned with a quick tilt of her head. "Just one cup of coffee." She opened the door wider and raised her voice: "Will? Billy Creekmore's here!"

"KEEP YOUR DAMNED VOICE DOWN, WOMAN!" Dave thundered, twisting around in his chair; he plastered one hand against his forehead. "I'LL STROP YOU! I SWEAR TO GOD I WILL!"

John, Billy, and Julie Ann formed a frozen triangle around the man. From within the house Billy could hear little Katy sobbing in a back room, and tentatively Will called out, "Mom?" Julie Ann's grin hung by one lip, and she stood as if motion might cause Dave to explode. Dave abruptly looked away, dug into a back pocket, and brought out a bottle of Bayer aspirin; he unscrewed the cap and tilted the bottle to his lips, then crunched noisily.

"Strop you," he whispered, to no one in particular. His eyes bulged above dark blue circles. "Strop the livin' shit out of you. . . ."

John pushed Billy toward the door, and they entered the house. As Julie Ann closed the door, Dave said mockingly, "Gonna talk about the old man again, aren't you? You dirty bitch. . . ." And then Julie Ann shut the door, and her husband's curses were muffled, indistinct ravings.

2

The house was dark and oppressively hot, one of the few in Hawthorne that had the luxury of a coal-fed furnace. John saw splinters of glass twinkling in the grayish green carpet; a broken chair sagged in a corner, and there were two empty bottles of Bayer on a lamptable. A framed print of Jesus at the Last Supper hung crookedly on one wall, and opposite it was a stuffed and mounted large-mouth bass, painted in garish blue and silver. In addition to the furnace heat, raw pinewood crackled and hissed in the fireplace, sending plumes of smoke up the chimney and scenting the room with pine sap.

"Excuse the mess." Julie Ann was trembling but trying to keep a desperate smile on her face. "We've . . . had some trouble here today. Billy, Will's in his room if you want to go on back."

"Can I?" he asked his father, and when John nodded he rocketed down a corridor to the small room Will shared with his little sister. He knew the house by heart because he'd spent the night several times; the last time, he and Will had explored the forest together in search of lions, and when Katy had tagged along they'd let her carry their stick-guns for them, but she had to do as they told her and call them "Bwana," a word Will had learned from a Jungle Jim comic book. This time, though, the house seemed different; it was darker and quieter, and might have been scary, Billy thought, if he hadn't known his father was up in the front room.

As Billy entered, Will looked up from the plastic Civil War soldiers he'd arranged on the floor. Will was the same age as Billy, a small thin boy with unruly brown hair plagued with cowlicks, and he wore brown-framed glasses held together in the center with Scotch tape. On the other bed, his sister lay curled up in a ball, her face against the pillow. "I'm Robert E. Lee!" Will announced, his sallow, rather sad-eyed face brightening at the approach of his friend. "You can be General Grant!"

"I'm not a Yankee!" Billy objected, but within another minute he was commanding the bluecoats in a daring attack up Deadman's Hill.

In the front room, John sat down on a rumpled sofa and watched as Julie Ann paced before him, stopped to peer out the window, then paced again. She said in a tense whisper, "He killed Boo, John. He beat Boo to death with that baseball bat and then he hung him in a tree with fishin' line. I tried to fight him, but he was too strong and . . ." Tears brimmed from her swollen eyes; John quickly averted his gaze to a little clock sitting on the mantel. It was ten minutes before five, and he wished he'd never offered to take Billy for a walk. "He was just too strong," she said, and made a terrible choking sound as she swallowed. "Boo . . . died so hard. . . ."

John shifted uneasily. "Well, why'd he do it? What's wrong with him?"

She pressed a finger to her lips and stared fearfully at the door. She held her breath until she'd looked out the window again and seen her husband still sitting there in the cold chewing on another aspirin. "The children don't know about Boo," Julie Ann said. "It happened this mornin', while they were at school. I hid Boo in the woods—God, it was awful!—and they think he's just roamed off somewhere like he does. Dave didn't go to the garage today, didn't even call in sick. He woke up yesterday with one of his headaches, the worst he's ever had, and he didn't get a wink of sleep last night. Neither did I." She put a hand to her mouth and chewed on the knuckles; a cheap but sentimental wedding ring with tiny diamonds in the shape of a heart twinkled merrily in the orange firelight. "Today it . . . it was the worst it's ever been. *Ever.* He screamed and threw things; first he couldn't get hot enough, then he had to get outside in the cool air. He said he was going to kill me, John." Her eyes were wide and terrified. "He said he knew all the things I'd done behind his back. But I swear I never did a thing, I swear it on a stack of Bi—"

"Just calm down, now," John whispered, glancing quickly at the door. "Take it easy. Why don't you call Doc Scott?"

"No! I can't! I tried to this morning, but he . . . he said he'd do to me what he did to Boo, and . . ." A sob welled from her throat. "I'm *afraid!* Dave's gotten mean before, and I never let on to anybody; but he's never been this bad! He's like somebody I don't even know! You should've heard him yell at Katy just a little while ago, and he eats those aspirins like candy and they never do no good!"

"Well"—John looked at Julie Ann's agonized expression and felt a long stupid grin stretch his face—"everything'll be all right. You'll see. Doc'll know what to do for Dave's headaches. . . ."

"No!" she shouted, and John winced. She stopped, frozen, while they both thought they heard Dave's chair scraping across the porch. "Doc Scott said he had a damned sinus infection! That old man ain't got good sense anymore, and you know it! Why, he almost let your own wife just linger and . . ." She blinked, unwilling to say the next word. *Die* is a terrible word, she thought, a word that should not be spoken out loud when talking about a person.

"Yeah, I guess so. But those headaches need lookin' after. Maybe you could talk him into goin' up to the Fayette hospital?"

The woman shook her head forlornly. "I've tried. He says there's nothin' wrong, and he don't want to spend the money on foolishness. I don't know what to *do!*"

John cleared his throat nervously and then rose to his feet, avoiding her stare. "Guess I'd better get Billy. We've been out too long as it is." He started to walk back through the hallway, but Julie Ann's arm shot out and grasped his wrist tightly. He looked up, startled.

"I'm *afraid,*" she whispered, a tear trickling down her face. "I don't have anywhere to go, and I can't stay here another night!"

"Leave him? Come on now, it can't be that bad! Dave's your husband." He pulled his arm away. "You can't just pack up and leave!" He caught the broken chair from the corner of his eye, and the marks on the hearth where Dave had frantically shoved wood and kindling into the fireplace and scraped the paint. He summoned up another grin. "Everything'll be fine in the mornin'. I know Dave pretty good, and I know how much he loves *you.*"

"I can't . . ."

John looked away from her before she could finish. He was shaking inside, and he had to get out of this house fast. He looked into the back room, saw the two boys playing soldiers on the floor while Katy rubbed her reddened eyes and watched. "Got you!" Will shouted. "That one's dead! *Bam! Bam!* That one on the horse is dead!"

"He's shot in the arm is all!" Billy said. "KABOOM! That's a cannon and that man and that man and that wagon are blown up!"

"Are *not!*" Will squawked.

"War's over, boys," John said. The strange ominous feeling in this house lay like a cold sheen of sweat on his neck. "Time to go, Billy. Say good-bye to Will and Katy. We'll see y'all later."

"'Bye, Will!" Billy said, and then followed his father back to the living room while Will said, "'Bye!" and went back to the sound-effects of rifles and cannons.

Julie Ann zipped up Billy's parka. When she looked at John her eyes were full of pleading. "Help me," she said.

"Wait until mornin' before you decide what to do. Sleep on it. Say thank you to Mrs. Booker for her hospitality, Billy."

"Thank you for your hospitality, Mrs. Booker."

"Good boy." He led his son to the door and opened it before Julie Ann could speak again. Dave Booker sat with a cigarette butt between his teeth; his eyes seemed sunken in his head, and the strange smile on his face made Billy think of a Halloween pumpkin's grin.

"You take it easy now, Dave," John said, and reached out to touch the man's shoulder. But then he stopped, because Dave's head was turning and his face was dead-white from the cold, and the smile on his thin lips was murderous.

Dave whispered, "Don't come back. This is *my* house. Don't you dare come back."

Julie Ann slammed the door shut.

John grasped Billy's hand and hurried down the steps, across the dead brown lawn to the road. His heart was beating very hard, and as they walked away he felt Dave's cold stare following them, and he knew that soon Dave would rise from that chair and go inside, and Lord help Julie Ann. He felt like a slinking dog; with that thought he envisioned Boo's white carcass swinging from a tree with fishing line knotted around its throat, bloodied eyes bulging.

Billy started to turn his head, snowflakes melting in his eyebrows.

John tightened his grip on the boy's hand and said tersely, "Don't look back."

3

Hawthorne closed down for the night when the steam whistle blew, promptly at five o'clock, at the sawmill owned by the Chatham brothers. When darkness settled across the valley, it signaled a time for families to eat dinner together, then sit before the fire and read their Bibles or subscription magazines like the *Ladies' Home Journal* or *Southern Farm Times*. Those who could afford radios listened to the popular programs. Watching television was a real luxury that only a few families possessed; reception from Fayette consisted of only one weak station. Several houses farther out from town still had outhouses. Porch lights— for those who could afford the electricity—usually burned until seven o'clock, meaning that visitors were welcome even on cold January nights, but after they went out it was time for bed.

In his wood-framed cot between the front room and the small kitchen, Billy Creekmore was asleep beneath a quilt and dreaming of Mrs. Cullens, who stared down at him through her fish-eyed glasses and demanded to know exactly why he hadn't finished his arithmetic homework. He tried to explain to her that it *had* been finished, but when he was walking to school he'd been caught in a thunderstorm and he'd started running, and pretty soon he was lost in the woods and somehow his blue Nifty notebook with the problems he'd done was gone. Suddenly, as dreams do, he *was* in the dense green forest, on an unfamiliar rocky path that led up into the hills. He followed it for a while, until he came to Mr. Booker sitting on a big rock staring out into space with his scary, sightless eyes. As he approached, Billy saw that there were timber rattlers on the rocks and ground all around him, crawling and rattling, tangled together. Mr. Booker, his eyes as black as new coals for the basement furnace, picked up a snake by the rattles and shook it at

27

him; the man's mouth opened and a terrible shriek wailed out that grew louder and louder and louder and—

The shriek was still echoing in his head when Billy sat up with a muffled cry, and he could hear it fading off in the distance.

In another moment Billy could hear his parents' muffled voices through the wall beside him. The closet door opened and closed, and footsteps sounded on the floorboards. He got out of his cot in the dark, stepping into a draft that made his teeth chatter, and then he was facing the door of their bedroom. He paused, hearing them whispering inside but remembering the time he'd opened that door without knocking and had seen them dancing lying down; his father had been sputtering and furious, but his mother had explained that they needed to be in private and calmly asked him to close the door. At least *that* had been better than when he heard them fighting in there; usually it was his father's voice, raised in anger. Worse than the yelling, though, were the long wintry silences that sometimes stayed in the house for days at a time.

Billy gathered up his courage and knocked. The whisperings stopped. In the distance—out on the highway, he thought—he could hear another shriek like a ha'nt up in the Hawthorne cemetery. The door opened, and standing against the dim glow of a kerosene lamp was his father, pale and bleary-eyed, shrugging into his overcoat. "Go back to bed, son," John said.

"Are you goin' somewhere?"

"I have to go into town to see what those sirens are for. I want you to stay here with your mother, and I'll be back in a few . . ." He stopped speaking, listening to the fading echo of another siren.

Billy asked, "Can I go too?"

"No," John said firmly. "You're to stay right here. I'll be back as soon as I find out," he told Ramona, and she followed him with the oil lamp out into the front room. He unlatched the door, and when he opened it frost cracked on the hinges. Then John was walking toward his beat-up but still reliable 'fifty-five Oldsmobile, made up of different colors and different parts from several wrecked car dumps. Ice crystals seemed to hang in the air like sparks. He slipped behind the wheel, had to wake up the cold engine with a heavy foot on the gas, and then drove along the frozen dirt road to the main highway with a cloud of blue exhaust trailing behind. As soon as he turned onto the highway and started toward Hawthorne he could see the red comet flare of spinning lights. He knew with a sickening certainty that the police cars were parked in front of Dave Booker's house.

He felt numbed as he saw all the trooper cars and ambulances, and the dark human shapes standing out front. The Olds's headlights picked out an overcoated state trooper talking on his car radio; Hank Witherspoon and his wife Paula were standing nearby, wearing coats over their robes. They lived in the house closest to the Bookers. Lights blazed through the Bookers' windows, illuminating the bundled figures who went in and out through the open front door. John stopped the car, leaned over, and rolled down his passenger window. "Hank!" he called out. "What's happened?"

Witherspoon and his wife were clinging to each other. When the man turned, John saw that his face was gray, the eyes sick and glassy. Witherspoon made a whimpering sound, then he staggered away, bent double, and threw up into a steaming puddle on the icy concrete.

The trooper thrust a hawk-nosed face into the window. "Move along, fella. We got more gawkers than we need."

"I . . . just wanted to know what was goin' on. I live right down the highway, and I heard all the commotion. . . ."

"Are you related to the Booker family?"

"No, but . . . they're my friends. I thought maybe I could help, if . . ."

The trooper braced his Smokey the Bear hat to keep it from flying away in the wind. "Move on," he said, and then John's attention was caught by two white-coated men bringing a stretcher down the steps from the house; there was a brown blanket over the stretcher, preventing him from seeing who lay on it. A second stretcher was borne down the steps as well, this one covered with a bloody sheet. John felt the breath rasp in his lungs.

"Bring it on down!" the trooper shouted. "Got another ambulance on the way from Fayette!"

The first stretcher was being shoved into the rear of an ambulance not ten feet away from where John sat; the second, covered with the bloodied sheet, was laid down on the ground almost opposite his window. The wind caught at the sheet, and suddenly a white arm fell out as if trying to hold the sheet in place. John clearly saw the wedding ring with its heart-shape of diamonds. He heard one of the attendants say, "Holy Christ!" and the arm was shoved back underneath; it looked stiff and bloated and hard to manage.

"Bring 'em all down!" the trooper shouted.

"Please," John said, and reached for the man's sleeve. "Tell me what's happened!"

"They're all dead, mister. Every one of them." He whacked the side of the Olds with his hand and shouted, "Now get this damned piece of junk out of here!"

John pressed his foot to the accelerator. Another ambulance passed him before he turned off the highway for home.

4

The coals in the cast-iron stove at the rear of Curtis Peel's barbershop glowed as bright as newly spilled blood. Chairs had been pulled up in a circle around it, and five men sat in a blue shroud of smoke. There was only one barber chair at the front of the shop, a red-vinyl-padded monstrosity. It tilted backward to make shaving easier, and John Creekmore had always kidded Peel that he could cut hair, pull teeth, and shine shoes from that chair at the same time. A walnut Regulator clock rescued from the abandoned train depot lazily swung its brass pendulum. On the white tiled floor around the barber chair were straight brown snippets of Link Patterson's hair. Through the shop's plate-glass window the day was sunny but bone-chilling; from the distance, seeping in like the whine of an August mosquito, was the sound of saws at work up at the mill.

"Makes me sick to think about it," Link Patterson said, breaking the silence. He regarded his cigarette, took one more good pull from it, and then crushed the butt in an Alabama Girl Peaches can on the floor at his side. His smooth brown hair was clipped short and sheened with Wildroot. He was a slim, good-natured man with a high, heavily lined forehead, dark introspective eyes, and a narrow bony chin. "That man was crazy in the head all the *time,* and I saw him near about twice a week and I could never tell a thing was wrong! Makes you sick!"

"Yep," Hiram Keller said, picking at his teeth with a chip of wood. He was all leathery old flesh and bones that popped like wet wood when he moved. Gray grizzled whiskers covered his face, and now he stretched his hands out toward the stove to warm them. "Lord only knows what went on in that house last night. That pretty little girl. . . ."

"Crazy as a drunk Indian." Ralph Leighton's ponderous bulk shifted, bringing a groan from the chair; he leaned over and spat Bull of the Woods tobacco into a Dixie cup. He was a large man who had no sense of his size, and he could knock you down if he brushed against you on the sidewalk; he'd played football at Fayette County High twenty years before and had been a hometown hero until his knee popped like a broomstick at the bottom of a six-man pileup. He'd spent bitter years tilling soil and trying to figure out whose weight had snapped that knee, robbing him of a future in football. For all his size, his face seemed chiseled from stone, all sharp cutting edges. He had hooded gray eyes that now glanced incuriously toward the opposite side of the stove, at John Creekmore, to see if that comment had struck a nerve. It hadn't, and Leighton scowled inwardly; he'd always thought that maybe—just *maybe*—Creekmore had stepped on that knee himself for the pleasure of hearing it crack. "Sure ain't gonna be no open coffins at the funeral home."

"I must've cut that man's hair a hundred times." Peel drew on a black pipe and shook his head, his small dark eyes narrowed in thought. "Cut Will's hair, too. Can't say Booker was a friendly man, though. Cut his hair crew in summer, gave him a sidepart in winter. Anybody hear tell when the funerals are going to be?"

"Somebody said tomorrow afternoon," Link replied. "I think they want to get those bodies in the ground *fast.*"

"Creekmore?" Leighton said quietly. "You ain't speakin' much."

John shrugged; a cigarette was burning down between his fingers, and now he drew from it and blew the smoke in the other man's direction.

"Well, you used to go fishing with Booker, didn't you? Seems you knew him better than *us.* What made him do it?"

31

"How should I know?" The tone of his voice betrayed his tension. "I just fished with him, I wasn't his keeper."

Ralph glanced around at the group and lifted his brows. "John, you were his friend, weren't you? You should've known he was crazy long before now. . . ."

John's face reddened with anger. "You tryin' to blame *me* for it, Leighton? You best watch your mouth, if that's what you're tryin' to say!"

"He ain't tryin' to say anything, John," Link said, and waved a hand in his direction. "Get off that high horse before it throws you. Damn it, we're *all* tied up with nerves today."

"Dave Booker had headaches, that's all I know," John insisted, then lapsed into silence.

Curtis Peel relit his pipe and listened to the distant singing of the saws. This was the worst thing he'd ever remembered happening in Hawthorne, and he was privileged with more gossip and inside information than even Sheriff Bromley or Reverend Horton. "They had to take Hank Witherspoon to the hospital in Fayette," he told them. "Poor old man's ticker almost gave out. May Maxie told me Witherspoon heard the shots and went over to find out what had happened; seems he found Booker sittin' naked on his sofa, and the room was still full of shotgun smoke. Must've put both barrels under his chin and squeezed with his thumbs. 'Course, Hank couldn't tell who it was right off." He let a blue thread of smoke leak from one side of his mouth before he puffed again. "I guess the troopers found the rest of 'em. I liked Julie Ann, she always had a kind word. And those kids were as cute as buttons on a Sunday suit. Lordamighty, what a shame. . . ."

"Troopers are still at the house," Leighton said, risking a quick glance at John. He didn't like that sonofabitch, who'd married a women more squaw than white; he knew the tales told about that woman, too, just as everyone around this stove did. She didn't come into town much, but when she did she walked like she owned the whole street, and Leighton didn't think that was proper for a woman like her. In his opinion she should be crawling to the church to pray for her soul. That quiet dark-skinned whelp of hers wasn't any better either, and he knew his own twelve-year-old son Duke could whip the living hell out of that little queer. "Cleanin' up what's left, I suppose," he said. "What they're puzzlin' over is where the boy might be."

"May Maxie told me they found blood in his bed, all over the sheets. But could be he got away and ran off into the woods."

John grunted softly. May Maxie was Hawthorne's telephone operator, and lived attached to wires. "Thank the good Lord it's over with," he said.

"Nope." Hiram's eyes glinted. "It *ain't* over." He looked at each man in turn, then settled his gaze on John. "Whether Dave Booker was crazy or not, and how crazy he *was*, don't make no difference. What he did was pure evil, and once evil gets started it roots like a damn kudzu vine. Sure, there's been calamities in Hawthorne before, but now . . . You mark my words, it *ain't* over."

The front door opened, jingling a little bell that hung over it. Lee Sayre stepped in, wearing his brown-and-green-splotched hunting jacket with stags' blood still marking it like a badge of honor. He quickly shut the door against the cold and strode back to the stove to warm himself. "Colder than a witch's tit out there!" He took off his brown leather cap and hung it on a wall hook, then stood beside John and kneaded his hands as they thawed. "I hear Julie Ann's mother came to town this mornin'. They let her go in there and she had a fit. It's a shame, a whole family killed like that."

"Not a whole family," John reminded him. "Maybe the boy got away."

"Anybody believes that can whistle 'Dixie' out his ass." Sayre drew up a chair, turned it around so he could rest his arms across the back, and then sat down. "Next thing you'll be sayin', the boy did the killing himself."

That thought caused a sudden shock, but John knew it wasn't true. No, Will was either wandering in the woods or buried somewhere. He cursed himself for not seeing this before, in the rages of temper Dave had displayed sometimes when they were fishing. Once Dave had become infuriated with a tangled line and ended up throwing a perfectly good tackle box into Semmes Lake, then cradling his head and breaking into tears as John had nervously steered their rowboat back to shore. *Lord*, he thought, *she was begging me to save their lives yesterday!* He'd told no one that he'd been there; fear and shame had stitched his mouth shut.

"Yeah, it's a shame," Lee said. "But life's for the livin', huh?" He swept his gaze around at the others. "It's time we talked about what's to be done with Preacher Horton."

"Damned nigger-lover"—Ralph leaned over and spat tobacco juice—"I never liked that blowhard bastard."

"What's to be done?" Lee asked the group. "Are we going to have a regular meetin' to decide on it?"

"Lieutenants are all right here," Hiram drawled. "We can decide now and be done with it."

Curtis said hesitantly, "I don't know, Lee. Horton may be associatin' with the niggers, but he's still the minister. He was awful good to my Louise when her mother took sick, you know."

"What're you talkin' about, boy? Horton's tryin' to get niggers to come to white services! He's been hangin' around Dusktown, and Lord only knows what he's up to!" Lee lowered his voice conspiratorially. "I hear he fancies some black tail, too, and he knows where to find it when he needs it. Are we gonna stand for *that?*"

"Nope," Ralph said. "No way in hell."

"John, you're mighty quiet today. Guess I can't blame you, seein' what went on last night and you were Dave Booker's best friend and all. But what do you say about Horton?"

John could feel them waiting for him to respond. He didn't like to have to make decisions, and he hadn't wanted to be a lieutenant anyway but they'd forced it on him. "I think we should wait until after the funerals," he said uncertainly. He could feel Ralph Leighton's wolfish gaze on him. "Horton's going to conduct the services, and I think we should show respect. Then . . ." He shrugged. "I'll go with whatever majority vote is."

"Good." Lee clapped the other man's shoulder. "That's just what I was going to say. We wait until the Booker family is buried, then we pay a visit to Mr. Horton. I'll get things ready. Curtis, you start callin' everybody."

They talked on for a while longer, the conversation turning back to the murders. When Curtis started going into the details he'd heard from May Maxie again, John abruptly rose to his feet and put on his coat, telling them he had to be getting home. The men were silent as he left the barbershop, and John knew all too well what the subject of conversation would be after he was gone: Ramona. Her name was never mentioned in his presence, but he knew that as soon as he'd gone they would turn their minds and tongues to the subject of his wife, and what they disliked and feared about her. He couldn't blame them. But he was still a son of Hawthorne, no matter who he'd married, and they were respectful in his presence; all except that fat pig Leighton, John thought as he walked to his car.

He slid into the Oldsmobile and pulled away from the curb. Slowing as he reached the Bookers' house—*help me help me*, Julie Ann had said—he saw two state-trooper cars parked out in front; a trooper was walking up in the woods beyond the house, poking a stick into the ground. Two others were methodically ripping up some of the front-porch boards underneath. *Never going to find that boy,* John thought. *If he ran away he's so scared he'll never come out, and if he's dead Dave did away with the corpse.*

Returning his attention to the highway, he was startled to see two figures standing on the roadside staring across at the Booker house. Ramona wore her heavy brown coat and clenched Billy's gloved hand; her eyes were closed, her head tilted slightly back. John screeched the brakes in stopping the Olds, and he had his window rolled down as he backed up and yelled, "Ramona! Come on, both of you! Get in this car!"

Billy looked at him fearfully, but the woman stood very still for a moment more, her eyes open, gazing across the road at the house.

"RAMONA!" he thundered, his face flaming with anger. He was amazed that she'd ventured out from home in this numbing cold, because she rarely left the house even at the height of summer. But here she was, and he was furious because she'd dared to bring the boy. "Get in this car right *now!*"

Finally they crossed the road and climbed in. Billy shivered between them. John put the car into gear and drove on. "What're you doin' here?" he asked her angrily. "Why bring the boy? Don't you know what happened there last night?"

"I know," she replied.

"Oh, so you thought you'd bring Billy to *see* it, did you? Lord God!" He trembled, feeling like the sputtering wick on a stick of dynamite. "Don't you think he'll find out quick enough at school?"

"Find out what?" Billy said in a small voice, sensing the sparks of a fight about to explode into flames.

"Nothin'," John said. "Don't you worry about it, son."

"He needs to know. He needs to hear it from *us,* not from those children at school. . . ."

"Shut up!" he shouted suddenly. "Just shut up, will you?" He

35

was going too fast, about to overshoot his dirt driveway, and he had to fight the brakes to slow the lumbering Olds enough to turn it. Ramona had looked away from him, her hands clenched in her lap, and between them Billy had slunk down low with his head bowed. He wanted to know what those police cars were doing in front of Will's house, and why Will hadn't been at school this morning; he'd heard whispered stories from the other children, stories that made him feel sick and afraid inside. Something bad had happened, but no one was exactly sure just what it had been. Billy had heard Johnny Parker whisper the words *murder house*, but he'd shut his ears and hadn't listened anymore.

"Just can't leave it alone, can you?" John said between gritted teeth. The Olds was racing along the driveway, throwing up rocks and snapping sticks in its wake. "Woman, haven't you had a gutful of death and evil *yet?* Do you want to rub your own son's face in it? No, no, you can't leave it alone, you can't stay in the house where you belong when you smell *death* in the air, can you? You can't act like everybody else, and—"

Ramona said quietly but firmly, "That's enough."

The blood drained from his face for a few seconds, then his complexion turned an ugly mottled red. "HELL IT IS!" he roared. "You don't have to get out and go about the town! You can just stay put and hide, can't you? But what about *me?*" He wheeled the car to a halt in front of the house and yanked the key from the ignition. "I don't want you *ever* goin' back to that house again, do you hear me?" He reached out and caught her chin, squeezing it so she couldn't look away; her gaze was dulled and distant, and that made him want to hit her but he remembered Billy and so stayed his hand. "I don't want to hear any of your damned ravin's, do you understand? Answer me when I speak to you, woman!" In the sudden sharp silence he could hear Billy sobbing. He was pierced with shame, but there was still anger in him and he had to get it out. "ANSWER ME!" he shouted.

She sat very straight and motionless; there were tears in her eyes, and she regarded him for a long time before she spoke, making him feel like a bug that had just crawled from beneath a rock. She said softly, "I hear you."

"You better!" He released her chin, then he was out of the car and hurrying into the house, not daring to look over his shoulder at either of them because anger and guilt and fear were chewing him up inside like a dull plow on wet earth. He had to clench his hands

36

around the Good Book, had to find something that would soothe the tortured ache in his soul.

When Ramona and Billy came in, John was already sitting before the hearth with the Bible on his lap. He was reading silently, his brow furrowed with concentration, but his lips were moving. Ramona squeezed her son's shoulder in reassurance and also as a warning to walk quietly, then she went quietly to the kitchen to finish the vegetable pie—made of leftovers from the last few meals—she was baking for their supper. Billy added another hickory log to the fire and positioned it with the poker. He could still feel the storm in the air, but most of it had already struck and he hoped things would be all right now; he wanted to find out from his father exactly what had happened to Will and the Bookers, and why those men were tearing up the front porch, but he knew it was something very bad and it might cause another fight between his momma and daddy. He replaced the poker, glanced at his father for approval—John was reading in the Book of Daniel and didn't look up—and then went back to the little secondhand desk next to his cot to start on his spelling homework.

The house was quiet but for the soft crackling of the flames and the sounds of Ramona working in the kitchen. Billy began on the words he was supposed to learn, but he kept thinking about something his daddy had said in the car: *death and evil . . . death and evil . . . haven't you had a gutful of death and evil yet?* He chewed on the pencil's eraser and wondered what Daddy had meant by that: did death and evil go together all the time, like the Massey brothers with the same haircuts and same clothes? Or were they kind of the same but somehow *different*, like if one of the Massey brothers was claimed by Satan and went around doing Satan's works, and the other brother turned toward the Lord. He found himself looking in through the short hallway to where his daddy sat reading the Bible, and he hoped that someday he'd understand all these things, just like grown-ups did. He turned back to his homework and forced himself to concentrate, though the image of that dark, silent house and the men tearing up the front porch stayed in his mind.

John admired Daniel's strength. He liked to think that he and Daniel would have gotten along just fine. Sometimes John felt as if the whole of life were a lions' den, ravenous beasts snapping and roaring on all sides and the Devil himself laughing fit to bust. At least, he thought, that's how it had turned out for him. He leaned forward and read Daniel's speech of deliverance to King Darius: "My God sent his angel and shut the lions' mouths, and they have not hurt me, because I was found blameless before him. . . ."

. . . *blameless before him* . . .

John reread it and then closed the Good Book. *Blameless.* There was nothing he could've done about Julie Ann, or Katy, or Will, or Dave Booker. He felt that in his choice of this scripture he was being told everything was all right, he could let the worry melt away from his mind and put it in the past where it belonged.

He stared into the crackling flames. When he'd married Ramona—and God only knew why he had, except that he'd thought she was the most beautiful girl he'd ever seen, and was all of twenty, not knowing anything about love or duty or responsibility—he'd stepped into the lions' den without knowing it, and it seemed to him that he had to guard himself every day to keep from being swallowed whole down the Devil's throat. He had prayed over and over again that the boy wasn't touched by her darkness too. If *that* ever happened, then . . . John was startled, because he'd had the mental image of himself in Dave Booker's place, bursting their heads open with a Louisville Slugger and then putting a shotgun underneath his chin. *Lord God,* he thought, and shunted that awful image away.

Putting the Bible aside, he rose from the chair and went into the bedroom. His heart was beating harder; he was thinking of Reverend Horton, creeping over the tracks to Dusktown. He didn't want to join in what had to be done, but he knew the others expected him to. He opened the closet and took out a cardboard box tied with twine. John cut the twine with his penknife, took the top off the box, and laid his Klan robes across the bed. They were dusty and wrinkled, made of heavy yellowing cotton; he clenched the material in one fist and felt the power of justice in it.

And in the kitchen, kneading dough between her brown hands, Ramona heard the distant call of a bluejay and knew that the cold weather had broken.

5

At the wheel of his racketing old Ford, Reverend Jim Horton rubbed his eyes wearily and tried to focus on the highway ahead. It had been a long and terrible week; tomorrow was Sunday, and he had yet to go over his material for the sermon, which he'd titled "Why Does God Let It Happen?" Tonight he would stay up late again at his desk, and his wife Carol would come in to rub the kinks out of his shoulders and neck before it was time for bed. He felt he'd been a stranger to her lately, but he'd told her a long time ago that being the wife of a country preacher was definitely not going to be a bed of roses.

The Ford's headlights cut white holes in the darkness. The heater chirred ineffectively, though it wasn't nearly as cold out now as it had been a few days before. He remembered how the sunlight and shadows had lain across the Hawthorne cemetery as the bodies of Dave Booker, Julie Ann, and Katy were lowered into the hard red-clay earth. The coffins had been closed, of course, during the memorial service at the Fayette funeral home, and Julie Ann's mother, Mrs. Mimms, had been almost overcome with grief. Tonight Horton had driven the fifteen miles to Mrs. Mimms's house to sit with her awhile, because she lived alone and was getting on in age, and it was obvious that this tragedy had almost destroyed her. He'd offered to have someone bring her in for church in the morning, and as he'd left she'd clutched his hand and cried like a baby.

Sheriff Bromley, Horton knew, was still searching for Will's corpse. Just yesteday the sheriff had poked a stick in the ground and brought up the odor of decaying meat; but when the shovels had finished it was Boo, the Bookers' dog, that lay moldering in the earth. Bromley had told him in private that most probably Will would never be found, that there were too many places Dave might have buried the body. Perhaps it was for the best, Horton thought, because Mrs. Mimms couldn't stand any more strain, and for that matter neither could Hawthorne itself.

He was aware that he walked a dangerous line. Things were changing in the world, due to people like Dr. King, but it wasn't fast enough to help the people of Dusktown. These last few weeks he felt he'd made a little progress: he'd been helping the Dusktown elders rebuild their burned-out box of a church, and he was on a committee to plan a potluck supper, raising money for purchase of lumber from the sawmill. There was still hard work to be done.

Horton was jarred out of his thoughts when a pair of headlights stabbed into his eyes. He instinctively swerved before he realized the headlights had reflected out of his rearview mirror. A red chevy roared past him as though he were sitting still, and he had the fleeting impression of a pale face glaring at him before the car whipped around a curve up ahead. He could hear the Chevy's horn honking—once, twice, three times—and he thought, *Wild kids on a Saturday night.* He would be in Hawthorne in just a minute; he hoped Carol would have coffee ready for him. When he took the curve the Chevy had disappeared around, Horton thought he saw something red flicker on the road before him. A strange thought flashed through his mind: Ramona Creekmore, at the Bookers' funeral, stepping forward from the assembly of people and standing right at the edge of Julie Ann's grave. Her hand had come up and out; dozens of red petals, picked from wild flowers that must've grown in some secret, protected grove of the forest, had floated down into the ground. Horton knew that the woman wasn't well liked, though in the eight months he'd been Hawthorne's minister he hadn't been able to find out exactly why. She never came to church, and he'd only seen her a few times in town, but she'd always seemed pleasant and certainly not a person to fear. . . .

Something moved on the road ahead, just out of range of his headlights. He thought of red petals floating, floating, floating down, and then . . .

The headlights picked out two large bales of hay that had been dragged into his path. He knew with a surge of fear that he couldn't stop the car at this distance, he was going to hit; and then he'd swerved the car to the right, the tires squealing, and slammed into one of the bales with a jolt that cracked his teeth together and struck his shoulder a bruising blow into the steering wheel. The Ford, out of control, left the highway and plowed into deep weeds. The car crashed into a three-foot-deep ditch and hung at an angle, its tires digging into the thawed mud. The engine rattled, and came to a dead stop.

Dazed, Horton touched his lower lip with a trembling hand; when he looked at his fingers he saw bright red petals blooming, and he numbly realized he'd bitten into his tongue. Fireflies were bobbing in the dark around the wrecked car, circling closer.

The driver's door opened. Startled, the minister looked up into the blinding glow of flashlights; behind them were white figures with black, ragged-rimmed eyes. Someone shouted, "Get that shit outta the road! Hurry it up!" He remembered the hay bales now, and swallowed blood. His right eye was swelling, and he was getting one whopper of a headache. A voice beside him said, "He's all bloody!" And another, muffled by a mask, answered, "Ain't nothin'! You ready to heave him out? Horton, you stay real quiet now, you hear? We don't want to have to get rough."

He was pulled out of the Ford by the hooded white figures, a blindfold of coarse burlap slipped around his eyes and knotted behind his head.

The Klansmen hauled him up into the bed of a pickup truck and covered him with gunnysacks. The engine started, and the truck headed for a backwoods road. Horton was held down by several men, and he imagined what they would probably do to him, but he was too weary to try to escape. He kept spitting blood until someone shook him and hissed, "Stop that, you damn nigger-lover!"

"You don't understand," he said with his mangled, bloody mouth. "Let me . . ."

Someone grabbed his hair. From the distance, perhaps at the end of the road, Horton heard a high-pitched Rebel yell. "You think we don't *know?*" a voice rasped into his ear. Horton could almost make out whose voice it was: Lee Sayre's? Ralph Leighton's? "The niggers are tryin' to take over the country, and it's sorry white trash like you that's helpin' 'em! You get 'em in your schools and your cafés and your churches, and they drag you down to where *they* are! And by God as long as I've got breath in my body and a pistol at my side no damned nigger is gonna take what belongs to *me!*"

"You don't . . ." the minister began, but he knew it was no

use. The truck slowed, jarring over a last crater in the road, and stopped.

"We got him!" someone yelled. "Easy as pie!"

"Tie his hands," a harsh voice commanded.

6

Carol Horton knew her husband had probably stayed longer than he'd planned at Mrs. Mimms's house, and might have stopped somewhere else between here and there as well. But now, at twenty minutes before midnight, she was very worried. There might've been car trouble, a flat tire or something. Jim had been tired and disturbed when he'd left home, and Carol had been concerned for a long while that he was just trying to shoulder too much.

She looked up from the book she was reading on antebellum history and stared at the telephone. Mrs. Mimms would be asleep by now. Perhaps she should call Sheriff Bromley? No, no; if the sheriff had heard anything he would've called. . . .

There was a quick rapping at the front door. Carol leaped up from her chair and hurried to answer it, trying to get herself composed. If it was Sheriff Bromley standing out there, bringing the news of an accident on the highway, she didn't think she could take it. Just before she opened the door she heard a truck roar away, and a chorus of male laughter. She unbolted the door, her heart pounding.

In a way, she was relieved to find that no one was there. It was a joke, she thought; somebody was trying to scare her. But then her breath froze in her lungs, because she saw the mottled black-and-white bundle of rags out under the pines, at the edge of the light cast from the front-porch bulb. A few bits of white fluttered away on the chilly breeze.

Feathers, she thought suddenly, and almost laughed. *Now who*

42

would dump a bundle of feathers into our front yard? She stepped off the porch, her gown windblown around her, and approached the mass; when she was five paces away she stopped, her legs gone rubbery, and stared. A crudely hand-lettered sign hung around the thing's neck: NIGGER-LOVER (THIS IS WHAT THEY GET).

Carol did not scream when the eyes opened, wide and white like the eyes of a painted minstrel. She did not scream when the awful swollen face lifted toward her, shining in the light and oozing fresh tar into the grass; nor when the arm came slowly out, gripping at the empty air with a black-smeared hand.

The scream burst free, ravaging her throat, when the thing's tar-crusted mouth opened and whispered her name.

Feathers danced on the breeze. Hawthorne lay nestled in the valley like a sleeping child, only occasionally disturbed by nightmares. Wind moved like a living thing through the rooms of the dark Booker house, where brown blood stained the floors and walls, and in the profound silence there might have been a footstep and a soft, yearning sob.

TWO

The Coal Pile

7

"There she is, Billy!"

"Why don't ya go catch her, Billy?"

"Billy's got a girl friend, Billy's got a girl friend. . . ."

The singing of that dreaded song was more than he could bear. He took after his three tormentors—Johnny Parker, Ricky Sales, and Butch Bryant—swinging his schoolbooks at the end of a rubber strap like a makeshift knight's mace. The boys scattered in three directions, jeering and thumbing their noses at him while he stood sputtering like a live wire, atop the pitcher's mound at the center of Kyle Field, spring's dust rolling around his sneakers.

They couldn't fathom why Billy had started noticing Melissa Pettus. Maybe she did have long pretty blond hair done up with ribbons, but a bird-dog pup was pretty too and you didn't make a fuss about one of those, did you? So today, when they'd all been walking home across Kyle Field beneath a blue late-April sky and they'd seen Melissa walking up ahead through the green weeds, the only thing to do was to have some fun at Billy's expense. They hadn't expected such a violent reaction, but it gratified them, especially since they were aware Melissa had stopped and was watching.

Ricky Sales crowed, "Loverboy, loverboy, Billy's a loverb—" He had to dodge fast, because Billy was suddenly coming at him like a steam engine, swinging his schoolbooks.

Suddenly the strap broke with a moaning sound and books were flying through the air as if fired from a slingshot. They spread open like hard kites and sailed into the dustclouds.

"Oh . . . *damn!*" Billy said, instantly ashamed that he'd cussed. The other boys howled with laughter, but all the anger had seeped out of him; if there was anything Mrs. Cullens hated, Billy knew, it was a dirty arithmetic book, and he was certain some of the pages had been torn too. The boys danced around him for another moment, careful not to get too close, but they saw he didn't care anymore and so they started running away across the field. Ricky looked back and shouted, "See ya later, Billy! Okay?"

He waved halfheartedly, distressed about the battered books, and then began picking them up. He turned to pick up his arithmetic book, and Melissa Pettus, wearing a dress as green as the new grass of April, held it out to him. There were flecks of yellow pollen on her rosy cheeks; her hair shone in the sunshine like waves of spun gold, and she was smiling shyly.

"Thanks," Billy said, and took it from her. *What do you say to girls?* he asked himself, as he dusted the books off on the front of his shirt. Then he started walking for home again, aware that Melissa was walking a few feet to his left. She made him nervous down in the bottom of his stomach.

"I saw your books fall," Melissa said after another moment.

"Yeah. They're okay, though. Just dusty."

"I made a hundred on the spellin' test today."

"Oh." He'd only made an eighty-five. "I missed a couple of hard words."

Yellow butterflies swooped through the grass at their approach. The noise from the sawmill sounded like a big cricket humming up in the woods, interrupted by the chugging of conveyor belts hauling cut lumber. Before them, heatwaves shimmered across the field.

What do you say to a girl? he asked himself again, feeling panic-stricken. "Do you like the Lone Ranger?"

She shrugged. "I don't know."

"Last Saturday night we went to the movie in Fayette and know what we saw? *The Lone Ranger and the Canyon of Gold*, but I fell asleep before it was over. There was too much talkin'. He rides on a horse named Silver and he shoots silver bullets."

"Why?"

He glanced at her, startled by the question. "'Cause silver bullets kill the bad guys faster," he explained. "There were Indians in the movie too, they were 'Patchee Indians. I've got some Indian in me, did you know that? I'm part Choctaw, my momma says; they were the forest tribe that lived around here a long time ago. They hunted and fished and lived in huts."

"I'm an *American*," Melissa said. "If you're an Indian, how come you don't wear war paint and moccasins?"

" 'Cause I'm not on the warpath, that's why. Anyway, my momma says the Choctaws were peaceful and didn't like to fight."

Melissa thought he was cute, but she'd heard strange things about the Creekmores from her parents: that the witch-woman kept jars of bats' wings, lizard eyes, and graveyard dirt on shelves in her kitchen; that the needlepoint pictures she made were the most intricate anyone had ever seen because demons helped her do them in the dead of night; and that Billy, who looked so much like his mother and not at all like his father, must be tainted with sinful blood too, bubbling in his veins like the red morass in a hag's stewpot. But whether all that was true or not, Melissa liked him; she wouldn't let him walk her all the way home, though, for fear her parents might see them together.

They were nearing the place where Melissa turned off onto the path for home. "I've got to go now," Melissa told him. " 'Bye!" She cradled her books and walked off along the path, weeds catching at the hem of her dress.

"Good-bye!" Billy called after her. "Thanks for helpin' with my books!" He thought for a moment that she wouldn't turn, but then she did—with a sunny smile—and he felt himself melting into his shoes like a grape Popsicle. The sky seemed as big as the world, and as blue as the special plates Gram had made for his mother's birthday last month. Billy turned in the opposite direction and walked across Kyle Field, heading homeward. He found a dime in his pocket, went into the Quik-Pik store, and bought a Butterfinger, eating it as he walked along the highway. *Girl friend, girl friend, Billy's got a girl friend.* Maybe Melissa *was* his girl friend, he thought suddenly. The heat of shame flamed his face as he thought of magazine covers he'd seen in the grocery store: *True Love, Love Stories,* and *Young Romance.* People were always kissing on those covers, getting his attention while he paged through the comic books.

A shadow fell across him. He looked up at the Booker house.

Billy froze. The green house was turning gray, the paint peeling in long strips; the dirty white shutters hung at broken angles around rock-shattered windows. The front door sagged on its hinges, and across it was written in red paint, PRIVATE PROPERTY! KEEP OUT! Weeds and vines were creeping up the walls, green clinging vines of the forest reclaiming its territory. Billy thought he caught a soft, muffled sigh on the breeze, and he remembered that sad poem Mrs. Cullens had read to the class once, about the house that nobody lived in; he would have to get his feet moving now, he knew, or soon he'd feel the sadness in the air.

But he didn't move. He'd promised his daddy, back in January after it had happened, that he wouldn't go near this house, wouldn't stop in front of it just as he was doing now. He'd kept that promise for over three months, but he passed the Booker house twice a day on the walk to and from school and he'd found himself being drawn closer and closer to it, only a step or so at a time. Standing right in front of it, its shadow cast over him like a cold sheet, was the closest he'd ever come. His curiosity was tempting him to climb those steps to the front porch. He was sure there were mysteries waiting to be solved in that house, that when he stepped inside and looked for himself all the puzzling things about why Mr. Booker had gone crazy and hurt his family would be revealed like a magician's trick.

His mother had tried to explain to him about Death, that the Bookers had "passed away" to another place and that Will had probably "passed away" too, but no one knew exactly where his body lay sleeping. She said he was most likely asleep back in the forest somewhere, lying on a bed of dark green moss, his head cradled on a pillow of decaying leaves, white mushrooms sprouting around him like tiny candles to reassure him against the dark.

Billy climbed two of the steps and stood staring at the front door. He'd promised his daddy he wouldn't go in! he agonized, but he didn't step down. It seemed to him to be like the story of Adam and Eve his daddy had read to him several times; he wanted to be good and live in the Garden, but this house—the murder house, everybody called it—was the Forbidden Fruit of Knowledge about how and why Will Booker had been called away by the Lord, and where Will had "passed away" to. He shivered on the hard edge of a decision.

Sometimes it seemed that when he'd tried to walk past this house without looking at it he could hear a soft, yearning sound through the trees that always made him look up; sometimes he imagined he heard his name whispered, and once he thought he'd seen a small figure standing behind one of the broken windows, waiting for him to pass. *Know what I heard?* Johnny Parker had asked him just a few days ago. *The Booker house is full of ghosts! My daddy says for me not to play around there, 'cause at night people see funny lights and they hear screams! Old man Keller told my daddy Mr. Booker cut Katy's head off and set it on a bedpost, and my daddy thinks Mr. Booker hacked Will up into little pieces and scattered him all over the woods!* . . .

Will was my best friend, Billy thought; there's nothing in that house that would hurt me. . . . Just one look, his curiosity urged.

He gazed off along the highway, thinking about his father busy at work in the cornfield, tending the new spring shoots. *Just one look.* Billy laid his books down on the steps. He climbed up and stood before the sagging door, his heartbeat quickening; the door had never looked so massive before, the inside of the house never so dark and full of mysteries. The Adam and Eve story flashed through his mind, like one last chance at turning back; *Once you sin,* he thought, *once you go where you're not supposed to, you can never go back to the way it was before; once you step out of the Garden and into the Dark, it's too late.* . . .

A bluejay shrieked, scaring him almost right out of his shoes. He thought he heard his name called in a hushed sigh of breath, and he listened hard but didn't hear it again. Momma's callin' me from the house, he told himself, 'cause I'm already so late. I'm gonna get a whippin'! He glanced to his left, at the ragged hole where the troopers had searched for Will under the porch. Then he grasped the door's edge and pulled it partway open. The bottom of the door scraped across the porch like a scream, and dry dusty air came roiling out of the house into his face.

Once you step out of the Garden, and into the Dark . . .

He took a deep breath of stale air and stepped across the threshold into the murder house.

8

The front room was huge, barely recognizable, because all the furniture had been hauled away. The Last Supper picture and the mounted fish were gone too, and yellowed newspaper pages covered the floor. Vines had crept through the cracks in the windows, snaking up toward the ceiling; Billy's gaze followed one of them, and stopped abruptly at a large mottled brown stain on the ceiling just above where he thought the sofa had been. The house was full of deep green, shadowy light, and seemed a secretive, terribly lonely place. Spider webs clung to the corners, and two wasps flew about seeking a secure place to start a nest. Nature was at work tearing the Booker house back to its basic elements.

When Billy crossed the room to the hallway, his shoes stirred up a few of the newspaper pages, exposing a horrible blotched brown patch on the floorboards. Billy carefully covered the stain back over again. When he walked into the hallway spider webs clutched at his hair, sending chills up his spine. What had been Mr. and Mrs. Booker's bedroom was bare but for a broken chair and more newspapers across the floor; in Will and Katy's room brown flecks and streaks marred the walls as if someone had fired paint from a shotgun. Billy got out of that room quickly, because his heart had suddenly given a violent kick and he'd had trouble getting his breath. The house was silent, but seemed alive with imagined noises: the creaks and sighs of a house continuing to settle into the earth. Billy heard the high whining of the saws at work, the barking of a dog in the distance, a screen door slam shut, sounds carried far on the warm spring air.

In the kitchen Billy found a garbage can filled with an odd assortment of items: hair curlers, ice trays, a reel of fishing line and a snapped pole, comic books and newspapers, brown-smeared rags, cracked cups and dishes, coat hangers, a pair of gray Keds that had belonged to Will, and a crumpled sack of Bama Dog Chow.

Sadness gripped his heart. *This is all that's left of the Bookers*, Billy thought, and placed his hand against the can's cool rim. Where was the life that had been here? he wondered desperately. He didn't understand Death, and felt a terrible sense of loneliness sweep over him like a January wind. The leaves of the snakelike vines that had found their way through the broken kitchen windows seemed to rattle a warning at him—*Get out get out get out . . . before it's too late*.

Billy turned and hurried along the hallway, glancing back over his shoulder to make sure the bloated corpse of Mr. Booker wasn't following, armed with a shotgun, grinning and wearing his yellow cap with the fishhooks in it.

Tears of fear burned his eyes. Spider webs caught at his face and hair, and as he passed the door that led down to the basement, something cracked sharply against the other side.

He yelped and flung himself backward, pressing against the opposite wall and staring at the doorknob, expecting it to . . . slowly . . . turn; but it never did. He looked toward the front door, getting ready to run before whatever haunted this murder house sprang up from the basement after him.

Then: *bump!* Silence. Billy's eyes widened, and he heard a low bubbling of fear deep in his throat.

Bump!

When it happened a third time, he realized what was causing the noise: someone was hitting the door with pebbles of coal from the large mound that lay down there, near the furnace.

There was a long silence. Billy said, "Who's there?"

And then there was a hail of noise, as if a flurry of coal had been thrown in response to Billy's voice. It went on and on, until Billy clapped his hands to his ears; then it abruptly stopped. "Whoever you are, you're not supposed to be in this house!" Billy called out. "It's private property!" He tried to sound braver than he was.

Slowly, he placed his hand on the cold knob; something pulsed into him like a mild charge of electricity, enough to make his arm buzz. Then he shoved the door open and protectively pressed against the opposite wall again. The basement was as dark as a cave, oozing a cold and oily odor. "I'll call Sheriff Bromley!" Billy warned. Nothing moved down there, and now he realized there were no pieces of coal littering the top few steps at all. Maybe they'd all fallen off, or bounced back down to the floor, he reasoned. But now he had the cold and certain feeling that the heart of the mystery—what had drawn him into this house, only a step or so a day for over three months—beat in the silence of the Bookers' basement. He gathered up his courage—*Nothing in here that can hurt me!*—and stepped into the darkness.

A few shards of muted gray light filtered through small, dirty panes of glass. The bulk of the furnace was like a scorched metal Halloween mask; and standing near it was a mountain of darkly glittering coal. Billy reached the bottom of the steps and stood on the red-clay floor. A shovel was propped against the wall near him, its triangular head giving it the look of a snake about to strike. Billy avoided it, and as he walked closer to the coal pile, one tentative step at a time, he thought he could see the faint blue plume of his breath before him. It was much colder here than in the house. His arms were sprouting goose bumps, and the hair at the back of his neck was standing on end.

Billy stood a few feet away from the coal pile, which towered over him by several feet, as his eyes grew used to the dim light. He could see almost all the shadowed nooks and crannies of the basement now, and he was almost certain that he was alone. Still . . . He called out in a shaky voice, "Anybody here?"

No, he thought, nobody's here. Then *who* made that noise on the door? . . .

His brain froze in midthought. He was staring at the coal pile, and he'd seen it shudder.

Bits of coal, a tiny avalanche, streamed down the sides; it seemed to breathe like a laboring bellows. *Run!* he screamed inwardly. But his gaze was fixed on the coal pile and his feet were glued to the ground. Something was coming up out of the coal— perhaps the dark key to a mystery, or grinning Mr. Booker in his yellow cap, or the very essence of Evil itself coming to carry him to Hell.

And suddenly a small white hand clawed itself free from the top of the coal pile, perhaps three feet above Billy's head. An arm and shoulder followed, slowly working out and writhing in the air. Rivulets of coal rolled down and over Billy's sneakers. A small head broke free, and the ghastly, tormented face of Will Booker turned toward his friend, the sightless white eyes peering down with desperate terror.

The gray-lipped mouth struggled to form words. *"Billy"*—the voice was an awful, pleading whine—*"tell them where I am, Billy . . . tell them where I am. . . ."*

A wail ripped from Billy's throat, and he scrabbled up the basement stairs like a frantic crab. Behind him, he heard the coal pile shifting and groaning as if gathering itself to chase after him. He fell in the hallway, struggled wildly up, heard a scream like a neglected teakettle spouting hot steam filling the house as he burst onto the front porch and ran, ran, ran, forgetting his books on the porch steps, ran, forgetting everything but the horror that lay in the Bookers' basement, ran home screaming all the way.

9

John quietly opened the bedroom door and peered in. The boy was still lying huddled beneath the quilt, his face pressed against a pillow, but at least he wasn't making those awful whimpering sounds anymore. In a way, though, the silence was worse. Billy had sobbed himself sick for almost an hour, since coming home twenty minutes late from school. John thought he'd never forget the white expression of fear stamped on his son's face.

They'd put him in the bedroom, since it was much more comfortable than the cot and he could be quiet in here. As John watched, Billy shivered beneath the quilt and mumbled something that sounded like "cold, in the cold." John stepped inside, arranged the quilt a little more snugly because he thought Billy had felt a chill, and then realized his son's eyes were wide open, staring fixedly into a corner of the room.

John eased down on the side of the bed. "How you feelin'?" he asked softly; he touched Billy's forehead, even though Ramona had told him Billy didn't have a fever and didn't seem physically ill. They'd taken off his clothes and checked him thoroughly for the double punctures of a snakebite, knowing how he liked to ramble through dark corners of the forest, but they'd found nothing.

"Want to talk about it now?"

Billy shook his head.

"Your momma's about to put supper on the table. You feel like eatin'?"

The boy whispered something, and John thought it sounded like "Butterfinger." "Huh? What do you want, a candy bar? We're havin' sweet potatoes, will that do?" When Billy didn't reply, but stared straight ahead with such intensity that John was beginning to feel uneasy, John squeezed the boy's shoulder through the quilt and said, "When you feel like talkin' about it, I'll listen." Then John rose from the bed, feeling sure Billy had just stumbled onto a snake up in the woods and he'd be more careful next time, and went to the kitchen, where Ramona was laboring over a woodburning stove. The kitchen was filled with late afternoon sunlight and smelled of fresh vegetables from several pots on the stove.

"Is he any better?" Ramona asked.

"He's quieted down some. What did he say to you when he first came in?"

"Nothing. He couldn't talk, he was sobbing so hard. I just picked him up and held him, and then you came in from the field."

"Yeah," John said grimly. "I saw his face. I've seen sun-bleached sheets that had more color in 'em. I can't figure out what he might've gotten into." He sighed and ran a hand through his hair.

"I think he'll want to sleep for a while. When he wants to talk about it, he'll let us know."

"Yeah. Know what he said he wanted? A Butterfinger, of all crazy things!" He paused, watching his wife take plates out of the cupboard and set them on the small dinner table, and then jingled the few loose coins in his pocket. "Maybe I'll drive down to the store to get him one before they close up. Might ease his mind. That suit you?"

56

She nodded. "I'll have your supper on the table in ten minutes."

John took the car keys from his pocket and left the house. Ramona stood over the stove until she heard the engine start and car pull away. Then she took the pots off their burners, checked the corn muffins, and hurried into the bedroom, wiping her callused hands on her apron. Her eyes were shining like polished amber stones as she stood over the bed, staring down at her son. Softly, she said, "Billy?"

He stirred but did not answer. She laid a hand on his cheek. "Billy? We've got to talk. Quickly, before your father comes back."

"No . . ." he whimpered, his mouth pressed against the pillow.

"I want to know where you went. I want to know what happened. Billy, please look at me."

After a few seconds he turned his head so he could see her from the corner of a swollen eye; he was still shaking with sobs he was too weak to let go of.

"I think you went someplace where your daddy didn't want you to go. Didn't you? I think you went to the Booker house." The boy tensed. "If not inside it, then very close to it. Is that right?"

Billy shivered, his hands gripping at the covers. New tears broke over his cheeks, and like a dam bursting everything came flooding out of him at once. He cried forlornly, "I didn't mean to go in there, I promise I didn't! I wasn't bad! But I heard . . . I heard . . . I heard it in the basement and I . . . I had to go see what it was and it was . . . it was . . . *awful!*" His face contorted with agony and Ramona reached for him, hugging him close. She could feel his heartbeat racing in his chest.

But she had to find out, before John returned. "What did you *see?*" she asked.

"No! Can't . . . can't tell. Please don't make me!"

"Something in the basement?"

Billy shuddered; the illusion he'd been building in his mind, that it had all been just a particularly nasty nightmare, was falling apart at the seams like wet and rotten cloth. "I didn't see anything!"

Ramona gripped his shoulders and looked deeply into his swollen eyes. "Your daddy's going to be back in a few minutes.

57

He's a good man in his heart, Billy, and I love his heart, but I want you to remember this: your daddy is afraid, and he strikes out at what he fears because he doesn't understand it. He loves us; he loves *you* more than anything in the world, and I love you too, more than you'll ever know. But now you have to trust me, son. Did . . . whatever you see speak to you?"

Billy's gaze had gone glassy. He nodded his head with an effort, a strand of saliva breaking from his half-open mouth and trailing downward.

"I thought so," Ramona said gently. Her eyes were shining, but there was a deep sadness in her face too, and a certainty of the trouble to come. *He's only a little boy!* she thought. *He's not strong enough yet!* She bit her lower lip to keep her face from collapsing in a sob. "I love you," she told him. "I'll always be there when you need me. . . ."

The sounds of the sawmill's steam whistle and the screen door slamming came at almost the same time, making them both jump.

"Supper on yet?" John called from the front room.

Ramona kissed her son's cheek and eased his head back down on the pillow: Billy curled up again, staring sightlessly. *Shock,* she thought. *I was like that too, the first time it happened to me.* He would bear watching for the next few days.

John was standing in the doorway when Ramona looked up. He was holding two Butterfinger candy bars in his right hand, and with his left seemed to be supporting himself in the doorframe; Ramona knew it was her imagination, and perhaps a trick of the dusky afternoon light that cloaked his shoulders from behind, but he seemed to have aged ten years since he'd left the house. There appeared to be a sickness behind his eyes. A weary smile worked across his lips, and he came forward to offer the candy bars to Billy. "Here you go, son. Feelin' better?"

Billy took them gratefully, though he wasn't hungry and couldn't figure out why his father had brought them.

"Your face looks like a puffball," John said. "Guess you took a wrong turn in the woods and saw a snake, huh?" He gently ruffed the boy's hair before Billy could reply, and said, "Well, you've got to watch your step. You don't want to scare some poor timber rattler half to death, do you?"

For the first time that afternoon, Billy managed a tentative smile; Ramona thought, *He's going to be all right.*

"I'll put supper on the table now," she said, touching her son's cheek softly, and then walked past John—who stepped suddenly away from her, as if fearful of being contaminated—and into the hallway. She saw that John had left the front door open, and closed it against the evening chill.

And as she turned to go to the kitchen she saw the dusty set of schoolbooks lying on a chair.

10

As the pearly-white '58 Cadillac limousine, sparkling from its showroom wax job, its sharp rear fins jutting up like the tail of a Martian spacecraft, pulled up to the entranceway of the Tutwiler Hotel in downtown Birmingham, an elderly black doorman in a dark red uniform and cap was already coming down the marbled steps, eager to find out just who was riding in the rear seat of that spiffy automobile. Having worked for over twenty years at the Tutwiler—the finest hotel in Alabama—he was accustomed to celebrities, but he knew from a quick appraisal of that Caddy that behind those tinted rear windows was American sugar. He noticed the shining chrome hood ornament in the shape of clasped, praying hands. He reached the sidewalk and thrust out his frail hand to let the passenger out.

But the door fairly burst open before he could get a grip on it, and from the Caddy uncoiled a giant of a man in a bright yellow suit, spotless white shirt, and white silk tie; the man rose to a height well over six feet, his chest expanding like a yellow wall.

"Fine afternoon, isn't it?" the man boomed. At the crest of his high forehead was a curly mass of gray-flecked blond hair; he had the kind of handsome, square face that made him look like a human nutcracker, ready to burst walnuts between perfect white teeth.

"Yessir, sure is," the doorman said, nodding his gray-wooled head, aware that pedestrians on the Twentieth Street sidewalk were turning to gawk, caught by the sound of power in the man's voice.

Realizing he was the center of attention, the man beamed like sunlight on a July Sunday; he said, "Just take it around the corner and park it," addressing the Caddy's driver, a young man in a seersucker suit, and the long sleek car pulled away from the curb like a stretching lion.

"Yessir, nice afternoon," the doorman said, his eyes still jangling from that glowing suit.

The man grinned and thrust a hand into his inside coat pocket; the doorman grinned too—*American sugar!*—and reached out with the obligatory "Thankee, sir!" already on his lips. Paper was put into his palm, and then the giant man had taken two long steps and was moving up the marbled stairs like a golden locomotive. The doorman stepped back a pace, as if scorched by energy. When he looked at what he held gripped in his hand, he saw a small pamphlet titled *Sin Destroyed the Roman Empire;* across the title page was a signature in red ink: J.J. Falconer.

In the dimly lit, luxurious leather-and-wood interior of the Tutwiler, Jimmy Jed Falconer was met by a young gray-suited lawyer named Henry Bragg. They stood at the center of the large lobby, shaking hands and talking about general things—the state of the weather, farm economics, and what the Crimson Tide was likely to do next season.

"Everything ready up there, Henry?" Falconer asked.

"Yes sir. We're expecting Forrest any minute now."

"Lemonade?" Falconer lifted his thick blond brows.

"Yes sir, Mr. Falconer," Henry said. "I've already ordered it."

They entered the elevator and the coffee-colored woman sitting on a stool inside smiled politely and turned a brass lever to take them to the fifth floor.

"Didn't bring the wife and son with you this time?" Henry asked, pushing his black horn-rimmed glasses back onto his nose. He had graduated from the University of Alabama Law School only last year, and still wore the brutal white-walled haircut of his Delta Kappa Epsilon days; but he was a smart young man with alert blue eyes that rarely missed a trick, and he was pleased that J.J. Falconer remembered him from the work his firm had done last spring.

"Nope. Camille and Wayne stayed home, mindin' the store. I'll tell you, keepin' up with that Wayne is a full-time job in itself." He laughed, a bark of muted trumpets. "Boy can run a bloodhound ragged."

The fifth-floor suite, with windows overlooking Twentieth Street, was decked out like an office, containing a few desks, telephones, and filing cabinets. There was a reception area set apart from the workspace, containing comfortable easy chairs, a coffee table, and a long beige sofa framed by brass lamps. An easel had been set up facing the sofa, and on the wall hung a large framed Confederate flag.

A stocky man with thinning brown hair, wearing a pale blue short-sleeved shirt with *G.H.* monogrammed on the breast pocket, looked up from the paperwork strewn across one of the desks, smiled, and rose to his feet as the other two men entered.

Falconer gripped his hand and shook it. "Good to see you, George. How's the family?"

"Doing just fine. Camille and Wayne?"

"One's prettier than ever, the other's growin' like a wild weed. Now I see who the hard worker is in this organization." He slapped George Hodges on the back and slid a sidelong glance at Henry, whose smile slipped a fraction. "What do you have for me?"

Hodges offered him a couple of manila folders. "Tentative budget. Contribution records as of March thirty-first. Also a list of contributors through the last three years. Cash flow's thirty percent ahead of where we were this time last April."

Falconer shrugged out of his coat and sat down heavily on the sofa, then began reading the organizational reports. "I see we had a sizable donation from Peterson Construction by last April, and the April before that too; but they're not on the sheet this year. What happened?" He looked up squarely at his business manager.

"We've contacted them twice, took old man Peterson to lunch last week," Hodges explained while he sharpened a pencil. "Seems his son is in a stronger position this year, and the kid thinks tent revivals are . . . well, old-fashioned. The company needs a tax writeoff, but . . ."

"Uh-huh. Well, it appears to me that we've been barking up the wrong tree then, doesn't it? The Lord loves a cheerful giver, but He'll take it any way He can get it if it helps spread the Word." He smiled, and the others did too. "Seems we should've been talking to Peterson Junior. I'll remember to give him a personal call. George, you get his home phone number for me, will you?"

"Mr. Falconer," Bragg said as he sat down in one of the chairs, "it seems to me that—just maybe—Peterson has a point."

Hodges tensed and turned to stare; Falconer's head slowly rose from the file he was reading, his blue-green eyes glittering.

Bragg shrugged uneasily, realizing from the sudden chill that he'd stepped through the ice. "I just . . . meant to point out that in my research I've found most of the successful evangelists have made the transition from radio and tent revivals to television. I think television will prove itself to be a great social force in the next ten years, and I think you'd be wise to—"

Falconer laughed abruptly. "Listen to the young scholar, George!" he whooped. "Well, I can tell I don't have to worry about how slick your brain gears are, do I?" He leaned forward on the sofa, his face suddenly losing its grin, his eyes fixing in a hard stare. "Henry, I want to tell you something. My daddy was a dirt-poor Baptist preacher. Do you know what *dirt-poor* means, Henry?" His mouth crooked in a savage grin for a few seconds. "You come from a fine old Montgomery family, and I don't think you understand what it means to be hungry. My momma worried herself into an old woman at twenty-five. We were on the road most of the time, just like tramps. They were hard days, Henry. The Depression, nobody could get a job 'cause everything was closed down, all across the South." He stared up at the Confederate flag for a few seconds, his eyes dark.

"Anyway, somebody saw us on the road and gave us a beat-up old tent to live in. For us it was a mansion, Henry. We pitched camp on the roadside, and my daddy made a cross out of boards and nailed up a sign on a tree that said: REV. FALCONER'S TENT REVIVALS NIGHTLY! EVERYBODY WELCOME! He preached for the tramps who came along that road, heading for Birmingham to find work. He was a good minister too, but something about being under that tent put brimstone and fire in his soul; he scared Satan out of more men and women than Hell could hold. People praised God and talked in tongues, and demons came spilling out right there like black bile. By the time my daddy died, the Lord's work was more than he could handle; hundreds of people were seeking him out day and night. So I stepped in to help, and I've been there ever since."

Falconer leveled his gaze at Bragg. "I used to do a radio show, about ten years or so back. Well, those were fine, but what about the people who don't have radios? What about those who don't own television sets? Don't they deserve to be *touched*, too? You know how many people lifted their hands to Jesus last summer, Henry? At least fifty a night, five nights a week May through August! Isn't that right, George?"

"Sure is, J.J."

"You're a bright young man," Falconer said to the lawyer. "I think what's in the back of your mind is the idea of expansion. Is that so? Breaking out of the regional circuit and going nationwide? That's fine; ideas like that are what I pay you for. Oh, it'll happen all right, praise the Lord, but I've got sawdust in my blood!" He grinned. "With Jesus in your heart and your blood full of sawdust, boy, you can lick Satan with one hand tied behind your back!"

There was a knock at the door, and a porter came in wheeling a cart with Dixie cups and a pitcher of cold lemonade, compliments of the management. The porter poured them all a drink and left the room clutching a religious pamphlet.

Falconer took a cooling sip. "Now that hits the spot dead-center," he said. "Seems Mr. Forrest forgot about us, didn't he?"

"I spoke to him this morning, J.J.," Hodges said. "He told me there was an afternoon meeting he might get hung up in, but he'd be here as soon as he could."

Falconer grunted and picked up an Alabama Baptist newspaper.

Hodges opened a folder and sorted through a stack of letters and petitions—"fan letters to God," J.J. called them—sent from people all over the state, asking for the Falconer Crusade to visit their particular towns this summer. "Petition from Grove Hill's signed by over a hundred people," he told Falconer. "Most of them sent in contributions, too."

"The Lord's at work," Falconer commented, paging through the paper.

"An interesting letter here, too." Hodges spread it out on the blotter before him; there were a couple of stains on the lined paper that looked like tobacco juice. "Sent from a town called Hawthorne. . . ."

Falconer looked up. "It's not but fifteen miles or so away from Fayette, probably less than ten from my front door, as the crow flies. What about it?"

"Letter's from a man named Lee Sayre," Hodges continued. "Seems the town's been without a minister since the first of February, and the men have been taking turns reading a Bible lesson on Sunday mornings to the congregation. When did we last schedule a revival near your hometown, J.J.?"

"Four years or more, I suppose." Falconer frowned. "Without a minister, huh? They must be starving for real leadership by now. Does he say what happened?"

"Yes, says the man took ill and had to leave town for his health. Anyway, Sayre says he came to the Falconer revival in Tuscaloosa last year, and he's asking if we might get to Hawthorne this summer."

"Hawthorne's almost at my front door," he mused. "Folks would come in from Oakman, Patton Junction, Berry, a dozen other little towns. Maybe it's time for a homecoming, huh? Mark it down, George, and let's try to find a place in the schedule."

The door opened and a thin, middle-aged man in a baggy brown suit entered the room smiling nervously. He carried a bulging briefcase in one hand and an artist's portfolio clasped beneath the other arm. "Sorry I'm late," he said. "Meeting at the office went about an hour—"

"Close that door and cut the breeze." Falconer waved him in and rose to his feet. "Let's see what you ad boys have for us this year."

Forrest fumbled his way to the easel, set his briefcase on the floor, and then put the portfolio up on the easel where everyone could see it. There were faint dark circles beneath his arms. "Warm outside this afternoon, isn't it? Going to be a hot summer, probably. Can I . . . uh. . . ?" he motioned toward the lemon-ade cart, and when Falconer nodded he gratefully poured himself a cup. "I think you'll like what we've done this year, J.J."

"We'll see."

Forrest laid his half-empty cup on the coffee table, then took a deep breath and opened the portfolio, spreading three poster mockups. Hand-inked letters proclaimed: TONIGHT! ONE NIGHT ONLY! SEE AND HEAR JIMMY JED FALCONER, AND GET CLOSE TO GOD! Beneath the lettering was a glossy photograph of Falconer, standing on a podium with his arms uplifted in a powerful gesture of appeal.

The second poster showed Falconer standing before a bookcase, framed on one side by an American flag and on the other by the flag of the Confederacy; he was thrusting a Bible toward the camera, a broad smile on his face. The lettering was simply blocked, and said: THE SOUTH'S GREATEST EVANGELIST, JIMMY JED FALCONER! ONE NIGHT ONLY! COME AND GET CLOSE TO GOD!

The third was all picture, with Falconer raising his arms and gaze upward in an expression of calm peace. White letters were superimposed at the bottom, and said: ONE NIGHT ONLY! SEE AND HEAR JIMMY JED FALCONER AND GET CLOSE TO GOD! Falconer stepped toward the easel. "That picture is just fine," he said. "Yes, I *like* that one. I surely *do!* Knocks ten years off my age with that lighting, doesn't it?"

Forrest smiled and nodded. He brought out a briar pipe and tobacco pouch, fumbling to fill one from the other. He got it lit after two tries and puffed smoke into the room. "Glad you like that one," he said, relieved.

"*But*," Falconer said quietly, "I like the message and the lettering on the middle poster the best."

"Oh, we can put them together any way you want. No problem."

Falconer stepped forward until his face was only a few inches from the photographed Falconer face. "That's what I want. This picture *speaks*. I want five thousand of these printed up, but with that other message and lettering. I want them by the end of this month."

Forrest cleared his throat. "Well . . . that's rushing things a bit, I guess. But we'll handle it, no problem."

"Fine." Beaming, Falconer turned from the poster and took the pipe from between Forrest's teeth, pulling it away like lollipop from a baby. "I cannot abide lateness, Mr. Forrest. And I have told you again and again how I hate the stink of the Devil's weed." Something bright and sharp flashed behind his gaze. Forrest's struggling smile hung crookedly from the man's face as Falconer submerged the pipe in the cup of lemonade. There was a tiny *hiss* as the tobacco was extinguished. "Bad for your health," Falconer said quietly, as if speaking to a retarded child. "Good for the Devil." He left the offending pipe in the Dixie cup, clapped

Forrest on the shoulder, and stepped back so he could admire the poster again.

One of the telephones rang. Hodges picked it up, said, "Falconer Crusade. Oh. Hi there, Cammy, how are you . . . sure, just a minute." He held the receiver out for Falconer. "J.J.? It's Camille."

"Tell her I'll get back to her, George."

"She sounds awfully excited about something."

Falconer paused, then reached the puhone with two long strides. "Hey hon. What can I do for you?" He watched as Forrest put the posters away and took the dripping pipe from the cup. "What's that? Hon, the connection's bad. Say that again now, I can hardly hear you." His broad face slackened. "Toby? When? Hurt bad? Well, I told you that dog was goin' to get hit chasin' cars! All right now, don't get all excited . . . just get Wayne to help you, and the both of you pick Toby up, put him in the station wagon, and drive to Dr. Considine's. He's the best vet in Fayette County, and he won't charge you . . ." He stopped speaking and listened instead. His mouth slowly opened, closed, opened again like a fish gasping for breath. "*What?*" he whispered, in a voice so fragile the other three men in the room looked at each other with amazed expressions: they'd never heard J.J. Falconer when he wasn't booming with good cheer.

"No," he whispered. "No, Cammy, that can't be. You're wrong." He listened, his face slowly going pale. "Cammy . . . I don't . . . know what to do. . . . Are you *sure?*" He glanced quickly up at the others, his beefy hand about to crunch the receiver in two. "Is Wayne there with you? All right, now listen to me *carefully*. I don't care, just listen! Get that dog to the vet and have it checked over real good. Don't talk to anybody but Dr. Considine, and tell him I asked that he keep this to himself until I speak to him. Got that? Calm down, now! I'll be home in a couple of hours, I'm leavin' as fast as I can. Are you *sure* about this?" He paused, exhaled a long sigh, and then said, "All right. Love you, hon. 'Bye." And hung up the receiver.

"Anything wrong, J.J.?" Hodges asked.

"Toby," Falconer said softly, staring out the window at the surrounding city, golden afternoon light splashed across his face. "My bird dog. Hit by a truck on the highway. . . ."

"Sorry to hear about that," Forrest offered. "Good dogs are hard to . . ."

Falconer turned to face them. He was grinning triumphantly, his face a bright beet-red. He clenched his fists and thrust them toward the ceiling. "Gentlemen," he said in a voice choked with emotion. "God works in mighty mysterious ways!"

THREE

Tent Show

11

Heat lay pressed close to the earth as John Creekmore drove away from the house on a Saturday morning in late July. Already the sun was a red ball of misery perched atop the eastern hills. As he drove toward the highway, heading for his job at Lee Sayre's hardware and feed store, a maelstrom of dust boiled up in the Olds's wake, hanging in brown sheets and slowly drifting toward the field of dry brown cornstalks.

There had been no rain since the second week of June. It was a time, John knew, of making do or doing without. His credit was getting pretty thin at the grocery store, and last week Sayre had told him that if business didn't pick up—which it wasn't likely to, being so late in the summer and so stifling *hot*—he'd have to let John go until the autumn. He was digging into the emergency money to get his family by, as were most of the valley's farmers. Perhaps the most contented creatures in the Hawthorne valley were the local hogs, who got to eat a great deal of the corn crop; happy also was the man from Birmingham who bought dry corncobs at dirt-cheap prices, turning them into pipes to be sold at drug stores.

There was the Crafts Fair, held in Fayette in August, to look forward to now. Ramona's needlepoint pictures sold well. John remembered a woman buying one of Ramona's pieces and saying it looked like something "Grandma Moses" might've done; he didn't know who "Grandma Moses" was, but he figured that was a compliment because the woman had cheerfully parted with five dollars.

Morning heat waves shimmered across the highway, making Hawthorne float like a mirage about to vanish. He shifted uneasily in his seat as he passed the still-vacant, rapidly deteriorating Booker house; it had a reputation, John knew, and nobody in his right mind would want to live there. Only when he had passed the vine-and-weed-grown structure did he permit himself to think about that awful day in April when he'd seen Billy's schoolbooks lying on the front steps. The boy still had occasional nightmares, but he never explained them and John didn't want to know, anyway. Something in Billy's face had changed since that day; his eyes were troubled, and locked behind them was a secret that John found himself afraid of. More than anything, John wished there was a real minister in town, someone who could fathom this change Billy was going through; the whole town was in dire need of a preacher: Saturday nights were getting wilder, bad words brewed into fights, and there'd even been a shooting over in Dusktown. Sheriff Bromley was a good, hard-working man, but Hawthorne was about to slip from his control; what the town needed now, John knew, was a strong man of God.

He had wanted to be a minister himself, a long time ago, but the farming heritage of his family had rooted him to the earth instead.

At a tent revival one hot August night, he'd watched his father spasm and roll in the sawdust as people screamed in strange tongues and others shouted hallelujahs; the unnerving sight of the lanky red-haired man with his face contorted, veins jutting out from the bullneck, had stayed with John all his life. John feared the blue evening twilight, when—his father had said—God's Eye roamed the world like a burning sun, in search of the sinners who would die that night. It was understood that Life was a gift from the Lord, but Death was Satan's touch in this perfect world; when a man died spiritually and turned away from God, physical death was sure to follow, and the pit of Hell yawned for his soul.

His father had been a good family man, but privately John was told that all women, like Eve, were cunning and deceitful—except for his mother, who was the finest woman God had ever created— and he was to beware of them at all times. They had strange beliefs, could be swayed by money and pretty clothes, and they bled once a month to atone for the Original Sin.

But, at a barn dance when he was twenty, John Creekmore had looked across at the line of local girls waiting to be asked to dance, and his heart had grown wings. The tawny-skinned girl was wearing a white dress with white honeysuckle blossoms braided into her long, shining russet hair; their eyes had met and held for a few seconds before she'd looked away and trembled like a skittish colt. He'd watched her dance with a boy whose clodhoppers kept coming down on her feet like mules' hooves, but she only smiled through the pain and lifted her white hem so it wouldn't get dirty. Rosin leapt from the fiddlers' bows, dusting the tobacco-stained air, as the dancers stomped and spun and bits of hay drifted down from the loft like confetti. When the girl and her partner had circled close enough, John Creekmore had stepped between them and taken her hands, spinning away with her so smoothly Old Mule Hoof grabbed for empty air, then scowled and kicked at a clump of hay since John was twice his size. She had smiled, shyly, but with true good humor in her sparkling hazel eyes, and after the dance was over John asked if he might come see her some evening.

At first, he'd never heard of Rebekah Fairmountain, Ramona's mother. Later, he dismissed the tales he heard as idle gossip. He refused to listen to any more wild stories and married Ramona; then it was too late, and he turned alternately to moonshine and the Bible. He could never say, though, that he hadn't been warned about how things were; he remembered several times even Ramona trying to tell him things he couldn't stand to hear. He clung to the Bible, to the memory of his father once telling him no good man would ever turn tail and run from a woman, and to God. And life, like the seasons, went on. There'd been two blessings: the birth of Billy, and the fact that Rebekah Fairmountain, as tough as kudzu vine and alone since the death of Ramona's father, had moved to a house fifty miles away, on land with a better consistency of clay for her pottery.

A man John had never seen before—city man, he guessed, from the looks of the clothes—was nailing up a poster on a telephone pole near Lee Sayre's store. John slowed the Olds and gawked. The poster showed a righteous-looking man lifting his arms to Heaven, and read: THE SOUTH'S GREATEST EVANGELIST, JIMMY JED FALCONER! ONE NIGHT ONLY! COME AND GET CLOSE TO GOD! Beneath that, in smaller letters, was: AND WITNESS THE GOD-GIVEN HEALING GIFTS OF LITTLE WAYNE FALCONER!

John's heart thumped. Praise the Lord! he thought. His prayers had been answered. He'd heard of Jimmy Jed Falconer before, and the tent revivals that had saved hundreds of sinners; he'd always wanted to go, but they'd always been too far away before. "Hey, mister!" he called out. The man turned around, his sunburned face bright red against the whiteness of his sodden shirt. "When's that preacher speakin'? And where's he gonna be?"

"Wednesday night, seven o'clock," the man replied; he motioned with his hammer in the direction of Kyle Field. "Right over there, fella."

John grinned. "Thanks! Thanks a *lot!*"

"Sure thing. Be there, will you? And bring the family."

"You can count on it!" John waved, his spirits buoyed by the idea of taking Billy to hear an evangelist who would really put the fear of the Lord back into Hawthorne, and drove on to work.

12

Standing on the porch in the Wednesday evening twilight, Billy itched in a dark gray suit that was at least a size too small; his wrists jutted out from the coat, and the necktie his father had insisted he wear was about to choke the breath out of him. He'd accompanied his daddy to Peel's barbershop just that afternoon for a severe haircut that had seemingly lowered his ears by two inches. The front was pomaded enough to withstand a windstorm, but a disobedient curly cowlick had already popped up in the back; he smelled strongly of Vitalis, an aroma he loved.

Though the suit made him feel as if bumblebees were crawling over him, he was excited and eager about the tent revival; he didn't fully understand what went on at one, except that it was a lot like church, but people had been talking about it for several days, planning what to wear and who to sit with. As he and his father had passed Kyle Field that afternoon, Billy had seen the huge tent being staked down by the workmen, and a truck filled with sawdust to be used for covering the ground had rolled up into the grass like an enormous beetle. The tent, crisp-looking, brown and peaked at the center, took up almost the entire softball field, its folds stirring in the dusty breeze as another truck with a heavy-duty electric winch played out thick black cables. Billy had wanted to stay and watch, because he'd never seen such activity in Hawthorne before, but John had hurried him on; driving back home, they'd both glanced silently at the ruin of the Booker house, and Billy had squeezed his eyes shut.

A white full moon was rising in the darkening sky, and Billy watched with fascination as a long beam of light swept in a slow circle from the direction of Kyle Field. He heard his parents' voices from within the house and almost flinched, but then he realized they weren't arguing; everything had been fine today, since his mother had agreed to go to the tent revival with them. But when she'd at first refused to go, John had made the flimsy walls tremble with his shouts of indignation. The fighting had gone on for two days, usually with Ramona coldly silent and John circling her, trying to bait her into anger. But now, Billy thought, they were all going to the tent revival together, like a real family.

In another few minutes, John and Ramona came out on the porch. He was wearing an old brown suit and a black bow tie on a slightly yellowed dress shirt. His face and hair were freshly scrubbed. He carried his Bible pressed to his side.

She wore a dark blue dress and a white shawl around her shoulders; her hair had been brushed until it shone and was allowed to tumble freely down to the middle of her back. It was not for the evangelist, or to placate John, that she'd decided to go, but because she'd been in the house so long; she wanted to see people—not that people would be overjoyed, she knew, to see her.

Tonight, she decided, she would make herself be very strong. If she happened to see the black aura, she would quickly look away; but she probably wouldn't see it, and everything would be just fine.

"Ready, bubber?" John asked his son. "Let's go, then!"

They got into the car and drove away from the house. *Won't see it tonight*, Ramona thought, her palms suddenly perspiring; *no, probably won't see it at all. . . .*

Cars and pickup trucks were parked in rows all around the huge peaked tent, and there was a line of cars waiting to turn in beneath a long banner that read REVIVAL TONIGHT! EVERYBODY WELCOME! Men with flashlights were waving the vehicles into parking places, and John saw that school buses had brought whole loads of people. A gleaming silver Airstream trailer sat just behind the tent, separated from the parking lot by sawhorses. The air was filled with dust and voices, and John heard the banner crackle above them as he pulled the car onto the field.

A man with a flashlight peered into the window and grinned. "Evenin' folks. Just pull on over to the right and follow the man who directs you over there." He held up a bucket that was filling up with change. "Quarter to park, please."

"Quarter? But . . . this is a public field, ain't it?"

The man shook his bucket so the coins jingled. "Not tonight, fella."

John found lint and fifteen cents in his pockets. Ramona opened her change purse, took out a dime, and gave it to him. They drove on, following the impatient swing of flashlights. They had to park at the far edge of the field, between two school buses; by the time they'd walked the fifty yards to the tent's entranceway their carefully prepared clothes were scaled with dust. John took Billy's hand as they stepped across the threshold.

The interior held more people than John had ever seen gathered together in his life, and still the folks were coming in, rapidly filling up the wooden folding chairs that faced a large raised platform. Golden light streamed from shaded bulbs hanging in rows from the tent's high ceiling. Over the excited but restrained murmur of voices, a church organ played "The Old Rugged Cross" through two mighty speakers, one on each side of the platform. An American flag and the Stars and Bars of the Confederacy were suspended above the platform, the Old Glory just slightly higher than its rival. A bow-tied usher in a white coat came back to help them find a seat, and John said they wanted to sit as close to the front as they could.

As they walked along the narrow aisle, John was uneasily aware of the stares that were directed toward Ramona. Whispers skittered back and forth, and a whole row of elderly matrons who comprised the Dorcas Society stopped their sewing to stare and gossip. John felt his face redden and wished he'd never insisted she come with them; he'd never expected her to give in, anyway. He glanced back at Ramona and saw she was walking with her spine stiff and straight. He found three chairs together—not nearly as close to the platform as he'd wanted to get, but he couldn't take the gauntlet of stares and whispers any longer—and he said to the usher, "Right here's fine."

At five minutes before seven there wasn't enough room in the tent for a thin stick. The air was heavy and humid, though the ushers had rolled up the tent's sides so a breeze could circulate; paper fans rustled like hummingbirds' wings. The organ played "In the Garden" and then, promptly at seven, a dark-haired man in a blue suit came out from behind a curtain at the right of the platform and climbed several steps up to it, where a podium and microphone had been set up. He tapped the mike to make sure it was working and then surveyed the crowd with a gleeful, toothy smile. "How do!" he said loudly. He introduced himself as Archie Kane, minister of the Freewill Baptist Church in Fayette, and talked about how glad he was to see such a good response, as a choir in yellow robes assembled on the platform behind him. Billy, who'd been growing a little restless in the stifling heat, was excited again because he liked music.

Kane led the choir and assembly in several hymns, then a long rambling prayer punctuated by people calling out hallelujahs. Kane grinned, dabbed at his sweating face with a handkerchief, and said, "Brothers and sisters, I suppose those who know me have enough of me on Sunday mornin's! So . . . there's a gentleman I want to introduce to you right *now!*" Whoops and hollers spread over the crowd. "A fine gentleman and a man of God, born right here in Fayette County! I expect you already know his name and love him like I do, but I'm gonna say it anyway: the South's greatest evangelist, Jimmy *Jed* FALCONER!"

There was an explosion of clapping and cheering, and people leaped to their feet. A fat man with a sweat-soaked plaid shirt rose up just in front of Billy, obscuring his view, but then John was rising to his feet with the rest of them and had swept Billy up high so he could see the man in the bright yellow suit who bounded to the platform.

Jimmy Jed Falconer grinned and raised his arms, and suddenly a huge poster began unrolling down the backdrop behind him, a black-and-white Jimmy Jed Falconer in almost the same pose the real one held. Across the poster's top was the large red legend: THE FALCONER CRUSADE.

Falconer waited for the applause and whooping to die down, then stepped quickly to the microphone and said in a polished, booming voice, "Do you want to know how God speaks, neighbors?" Before anyone could answer, he'd pulled a pistol out of his coat, aimed it upward, and fired: *crack!* Women screamed, and men were startled. "*That's* how He speaks!" Falconer thundered. "The Lord speaks like a gun, and you don't know when you're going to hear Him or what He's going to say, but you'd sure better be on His right side when He does His talkin'!"

Billy watched the blue haze of gunsmoke waft upward, but he couldn't see a bullethole. *Blank* he thought.

Falconer set the pistol atop the podium, then swept his intense blue-green gaze across the audience like the searchlight that still pierced the sky outside. Billy thought that the evangelist looked directly at him for a second, and a fearful thrill coursed through him. "Let's pray," Falconer whispered.

As the prayer went on, Ramona opened her eyes and lifted her head. She looked first at her son, his head bowed and eyes squeezed tightly shut, then directed her gaze across the tent to a small, frail-looking boy she'd noticed even before Archie Kane had started speaking. Her heart was pounding. Enveloping the child was a shiny, purplish black cocoon of malignant light that pulsated like a diseased heart. The child's head was bowed, his hands clasped tightly in prayer; he sat between his mother and father, two thin figures who had dressed in the pitiful rags of their Sunday best. As Ramona watched, the young mother placed her hand on the child's shoulder and gently squeezed. Her face was gaunt, pale, grasping at the last straw of hope. Tears burned in Ramona's eyes; the little boy was dying from some sickness, and would be dead soon: in a week, a day, several hours—she had no way of knowing *when*, but the black aura was clinging greedily to him, the sure harbinger of death that she had feared seeing in this crowded tent. She lowered her head, wondering as always when she saw it: *What should I do?*

And the awful answer, as always: There is nothing you *can* do.

"Amen," Jimmy Jed Falconer said. The congregation looked up, ready for an explosion of fire and brimstone.

But he began softly, by whispering, "Sin."

The sound of his voice made Billy tremble. John leaned forward slightly in his seat, his eyes wide and entranced; Ramona saw the dying child rest his head against his mother's shoulder.

"Sin," Falconer repeated, gripping the podium. "What do you think of it? What do you think *is* a sin? Somethin' you're not supposed to do or say or think?" He closed his eyes for a second. "Oh Lord God, *sin* . . . it's an evil that gets in the blood, gets in our hearts and minds and . . . corrupts, decays, makes rotten . . ."

He looked across the congregation, bright beads of sweat shining on his face. Then, in an instant, his placid expression changed; his lips curled, his eyes widened, and he growled, "SINNNNNN. . . . Can you smell it can you feel it can you see it? Do you know, neighbors, when you've sinned? I'll tell you what sin is, neighbors, pure and simple: it's walking away from God's light, that's what it is!" His ruddy face rippled with emotion, his voice taking the place of the silent organ, flowing up and down the scales. He pointed into the audience, at no one in particular, yet at everyone. "Have you ever stepped out of the light," he whispered, "and found yourself in a *dark* place?"

Billy tensed, sat bolt upright.

"I mean a darrrrrk place," the evangelist said, his voice deep and gravelly. "I mean a place so dark and Evil you can't find your way out. Answer for yourselves: have *you* been there?"

Yes, Billy thought. *And it's still in my head, it comes to me at night when I try to sleep. . . .*

"No matter where the place is—the poolhall, the gamblin' room, the shothouse, or the moonshine still—there's hope, neighbors. Or it might be even darker than that: it might be the Room of Lust, or Envy, or Adultery. If you're in one of those dark places, then you're a guest of Satan!"

Billy's eyes widened, his heart thumping. The last nightmare he'd had, several nights before, streaked through his mind: in it he'd sat up in his bed and seen the black mountain of coal slithering toward him through the hallway, and then the awful white hand had plunged out and grasped Billy's sheet . . . slowly, slowly pulling it off and to the floor.

"SATAN'S GOT YOU!" Falconer roared, the veins of his neck bulging. "That cloven-hoofed, horned, fork-tongued Devil has got you right in his clawwwwws"—he lifted his right hand into the air, contorting it into a claw and twisting as if ripping flesh from the bone—"and he's gonna squeeze you and mold you and make you like he isssss! . . . And if you're a guest in Satan's house and you like the dark, evil place, then *you don't belong here tonight!*" The evangelist's eyes glowed like spirit lamps, and now he lifted the microphone off its stand and paced the platform with nervous, electric energy. "Do you like the house of Satan? Do you like bein' in that darrrk place, with *him* for company?" He stopped pacing, flailed the air with his fists, and raised his voice to a volume that almost blew out the speakers. "Well, I'm here to tell you there's HOPE! You can BREAK OUT of Satan's house! You can FIGHT that silver-tongued Devil and WIN, yes, WIN! 'Cause there's nowhere so dark—not poolhall nor brothel nor Room of Adultery—where you can't find the Light of Jeeeesus! Nosir! It might be just one little candle, but it's there, neighbor! And if you follow that light it'll get bigger and brighter, and it'll sure enough lead you right *out* of that dark place! The light of Jeeeesus will save you from sin and corruption and the everlastin' burning fire of the PIT!" He stabbed his forefinger downward, and someone sitting behind Billy yelped, "Amen!"

Falconer grinned. He clapped his hands together like a second gunshot, and shouted, "Glory be to God, 'cause there's power in the blood!" He lifted his head upward like a dog baying toward the moon. "Praise be the Light! Praise be the Redemption of the Sinnnnner!" Then he was right at the edge of the platform, falling down on his knees with his hands tightly clasped. He whispered, "And do you know how to find that Light, neighbors? Do you know how to renounce your sins and get out of that dark place? You've got to confess those sins!" He leaped up, bounding across the platform. His face streamed with sweat. "Confess! Give it all up to Jeeeesus! You've got to lay that darrrrk place out for the Lord to see!"

Confess? Billy thought, his heart hammering. Is that what I have to do to get it out of me? Around him people were crying and moaning; his daddy's head was bowed in prayer, his momma was staring straight at the evangelist with a glazed look in her eyes. Confess? Billy asked himself, feeling a shiver of terror; if he didn't confess, how would he ever escape the dark place?

"Confess! Confess! Confess!" Falconer was shouting, pointing his finger at random into the congregation. A heavy-hipped woman in a print dress stood up and began shaking, strange gurglings coming out of her mouth as her eyes rolled back in her head. She lifted her fleshy arms, crying out, "Praise God!" through the gibberish. Then a crewcut man in overalls rose to his feet and began jumping as if buck dancing, his boots stirring up clouds of sawdust. "CONFESS! CONFESS!" the evangelist roared. "Get out of that dark, dark place in your soul! Lay it out for the Lord!" He paced the platform, raising people from their seats with broad sweeps of his arms, as if they were attached to him on strings. John stood up and pulled Billy with him. "Glory be to God!" John shouted.

Falconer clutched at the microphone. "Is the Spirit with us tonight, neighbors?"

"YES!"

"Are we gonna lay it all out for the Lord tonight?"

"YES!"

"Praise the Spirit! Now folks, I want you to know that without you, and without the Hand of God moving you as He sees fit, the Falconer Crusade couldn't go on like it does, year after year! We're passin' the collection plates now, and I want you folks to look deep into your hearts! Remember: Satan don't want you to give! Nosir! Ol' Satan wants that money for the gamblin' den and the moonshine still! If you feel the Spirit with us, if you want to confess your sins, then dig into your pockets and give! Hallelujah!"

Organ chords crashed through the speakers. The choir began to sing "Love Lifted Me," and Falconer returned the microphone to its cradle, then clapped in rhythm to the music until everyone in the tent was clapping and singing. The golden light was full of sawdust, the air heavy and sweat-drenched. As the collection plate passed Billy, he saw it was filled with dollar bills.

When the offering was over and the plates had been taken up, Falconer shed his yellow coat and turned his blazing smile on full wattage. His shirt stuck to his back and ample belly. "Folks," he said, "maybe you didn't come here tonight just to hear me preach. Maybe you have other needs that have to be met. Right now I want to introduce somebody who's real close to my heart. You might've heard about this young man. Folks, here's my son—Little Wayne Falconer!"

There were loud whoops and hollers, and a small figure in a bright yellow suit ran up the steps to the platform, throwing himself into his father's arms. The evangelist caught him, and grinning, held him high. Billy craned his neck to get a good look. The little boy in Falconer's arms had a mass of curly red hair, and his smile was even more incandescent than his father's. Staring at him as the people in the audience shouted and applauded, Billy felt a strange stirring in the pit of his stomach. The boy's gaze swept the crowd and seemingly lingered on him for a few seconds. Billy had the sudden urge to race forward to that stage and touch that boy.

"Wayne?" the evangelist asked. "Do you feel the Presence in this tent tonight?"

A silence fell. "Yes, Daddy," the little boy said into the microphone.

"Do you hear the Presence callin' on you to do miracles?"

"Yes, Daddy."

"Miracles!" Falconer shouted to the congregation. "You heard me right! The Lord has seen fit to work through my son! This boy has a power in him that'll shake you to your shoes, neighbors!" He lifted the boy as high as he could, and Wayne beamed. Again, Billy felt drawn toward that boy. "Are there those here tonight in need of healing?"

"Yes!" many in the audience cried out. Ramona saw that the young woman with the dying child—purplish black cocoon writhing, pulsating, sending out oily tendrils—had raised both arms, tears rolling down her face. The child clung around her neck, while the father whispered to him and smoothed his hair.

"Wayne, is the Presence gonna work through you tonight?"

The little boy's eyes glowed with inner fire. He nodded.

Falconer set his son down, then handed the microphone to Wayne. Then he lifted his arms and shouted to the audience, "DO YOU BELIEVE IN MIRACLES?"

The tent was filled with clamorous shouts and cries, and already people were rising from their seats to approach the platform. Electricity sparked in the air. Beside Billy, John was dazed and weak with excitement.

Wayne Falconer took a stance like a fighting rooster at the platform's edge. His jaw was set and determined, though his eyes flickered nervously back and forth across the tent. "Who needs a miracle here tonight?" he called out, in a voice that carried almost as much power as his father's.

People started pushing forward, many of them weeping. Ramona watched the couple with the dying child stand up and get in the line that was forming along the aisle. "Come on!" Wayne shouted. "Don't be afraid!" He glanced back at his father for reassurance, then stretched out his hand for the first person in line, an elderly man in a red checked shirt. "Let the Lord work His miracles!"

The man gripped Wayne's hand. "What's your sickness, brother?" Wayne asked, and put the microphone to the man's lips.

"My stomach's got pains . . . my joints, oh Lord God they're always achin', and I can't sleep at night . . . I'm sick . . ."

Wayne placed his hand on the man's brown, creased forehead

and closed his eyes tightly. "Satan's causin' this sufferin'!" he cried out. "Satan's in you, 'cause people with God in their souls don't get sick!" He clamped his small hand to the man's head. "Come out, Satan of pain and sickness! I command you to come . . . *out!*" He trembled like a live wire, and the man's legs sagged. An usher stepped forward to help him away, but then the elderly man was dancing in a circle, his arms uplifted and a wide grin on his face. "Walk the way of God!" Wayne shouted.

The line kept moving forward, full of people whose knees were aching, whose hearing was deteriorating, who were short of breath. Wayne healed them all, commanding the Satan of bad knees, bad hearing, and shortness of breath to leave their bodies. Behind him, Falconer smiled proudly and urged people to come up.

Ramona saw the couple with the child reach the platform. Wayne thrust the microphone to the woman's lips.

"Donnie's so weak," she said in an emotion-laden voice. "Something's wrong with his blood, the doctors say." She sobbed brokenly. "Oh God sweet Jesus we're poor sinners, and we had to give up one baby 'cause there weren't no food. God's punishin' me 'cause I went and sold our little baby to a man in Fayette. . . ."

Wayne gripped the boy's head. The child began crying weakly. "Satan's in this boy's blood! I command you, Satan—come out!" The child jerked and wailed. "He won't need a doctor again!" Wayne said. "He's healed!"

Ramona reached for Billy's hand. She clenched it tightly, her insides trembling. The black aura around that child had gotten deeper and stronger. Now the parents were grinning and sobbing, hugging the little boy between them. The black aura swelled. She stared at Wayne Falconer, her eyes widening. "No," she whispered. "No, it's not true. . . ."

And to her horror, she saw an aged woman leaning on a cane stagger forward. The black aura clung to this woman too. The woman spoke into the microphone about her heart pains, and she said she was taking medicine but needed a miracle.

"Throw away that medicine, sister!" Wayne crowed as she was helped away by an usher. "You're healed, you won't need it!"

The black aura pulsated around her.

"No!" Ramona said, and started to rise to her feet. "It's not—"

But then Billy pulled free from her and was running up the

aisle. She shouted, "Billy!" but John's hand closed on her arm. "Leave him be!" he said. "He knows what he's doing—finally!"

When Billy reached the front, a grinning usher swept him up so he could speak into the microphone. Up close, the young evangelist—about his own age, Billy realized—had eyes that glinted like chips of blue ice. Wayne started to reach out for him, then stopped; the power of his grin seemed to falter, and there was a hint of confusion in his eyes. Billy could feel the hair at the back of his neck standing on end.

"Sin!" Billy wailed. Suddenly he was crying, unable to hold it in any longer. "I've sinned, I've been in the dark place and I need to confess!"

Wayne paused, his hand out toward the other boy. Suddenly he trembled, and his hand closed into a fist. He stepped back from the edge of the platform as his father quickly brushed past him and took the microphone. Falconer helped Billy up. "Confess it, son!" Falconer told him, putting the microphone to his lips as Wayne watched.

"I went into the dark place!" The loudness of his voice through the speakers startled him. He was crackling with electricity, and he could feel Wayne Falconer's stare on him. Everyone was watching him. "I . . . I saw Evil! It was in the basement, and . . ."

Ramona suddenly rose to her feet.

". . . it crawled up out of the coal pile and it . . . it looked like Will Booker, but its face was so white you could almost see right through it!" Tears rolled down Billy's cheeks. The audience was silent. "It spoke to me . . . and said for me to tell people . . . where he was. . . ."

"*Billy!*" John Creekmore shouted, breaking the awful silence. He stood up, gripping the chair before him, his face agonized.

"I sinned by going into the dark place!" Billy cried out. He turned to reach for Falconer's hand, but the evangelist's eyes were ticking back and forth. Falconer had sensed the gathering explosion, had seen the poisonous looks on the faces of the crowd.

And from the rear of the tent came a voice: "*Demon!*"

Someone else—Ralph Leighton's voice, John realized—shouted, "The boy's cursed, just like his mother! We all knew it, didn't we?"

"He's got the dark seed in him!"

"Like his mother, the Hawthorne witch!"

The tent erupted with ugly shouts. On the platform Billy felt a wave of hatred and fear crash over him. He stood stunned.

"He's a child of the witch!" Leighton shouted, from the rear of the tent. "His mother's Ramona Creekmore, and they don't belong in here!"

J. J. Falconer had sweat on his face. He sensed their mood, and he knew also what he had to do. He gripped Billy by the scruff of the neck. "Demon, do you say?" he crowed. "Are this boy and his mother pawns in the hand of Satan?" The name Ramona Creekmore had struck an alarm bell of recognition in him: Ramona Creekmore, the Hawthorne Valley witch, the woman who supposedly spoke with the dead and weaved evil spells. And this was her *son?* His showmanship went into high gear. "We'll drag the Devil right out of this boy tonight! We'll pull out Old Scratch, a-kickin' and—"

Then there was utter silence. Ramona Creekmore was walking along the aisle, looking to neither right nor left. She said in a soft but commanding voice. "Take your hand off my son."

Falconer released his grip, his eyes narrowing.

Ramona helped Billy down. Behind Falconer she saw Wayne's frightened face, and something inside her twisted. Then she turned to face the mob. "You scared sheep!" she said, in a voice that carried to the back of the tent. "Nobody's been healed here tonight! People who think they're sick are being told they're well, but those in real need are being doomed by false hope!" Her heart pounded. "It's akin to murder, what these two are doing!"

"Shut your damned mouth!" a woman shouted. It was the young mother, still clutching her child.

Ramona turned toward Falconer. "Murder," she said, her eyes flashing. "Because deep in your hearts, you know what you're doing is wrong." She looked at the boy, who trembled and stepped back under her gaze.

The evangelist roared, "Do you know what the Unpardonable Sin is? It's seeing the Lord's Power and calling it the Devil's Work! You're lost to the Lord, woman!" A cheer went up. "You're lost!" he bellowed.

Before the ushers rushed them out of the tent, Billy looked over his shoulder. Behind the yellow-suited man, the boy in yellow stood rigid and frozen, his mouth half open. Their gazes met and locked. Billy felt righteous hatred, bitter and hot, flowing from that boy.

Then they were out in the field, and the ushers warned them not to come back.

They waited for over ten minutes, but John never came out. The congregation began singing in loud, loud voices. When Falconer's voice boomed out, Billy felt his mother tremble. She took his hand and they began to walk into the darkness toward home.

13

"Billy? Son, wake up! Wake up, now!" He sat up in the darkness, rubbing his eyes. He could make out a vague figure standing over his bed, and he recognized his daddy's voice. Billy had cried himself to sleep a few hours earlier, when his mother had told him that John was upset at them and might not come home for a while. Billy was puzzled, and didn't understand what had gone wrong. The power of that young evangelist had drawn him to the stage, but when he'd confessed his sin everything had gone bad. Now, at least, his daddy had come home.

"I'm sorry," Billy said. "I didn't mean to—"

"Shhhh. We have to be quiet. We don't want your mother to hear, do we?"

"Why not?"

"She's alseep," John said. "We don't want to wake her up. This is just something between us two men. I want you to put on your shoes. No need to change clothes, your pajamas'll do just fine. There's something I want to show you. Hurry now, and be real quiet."

There was something harsh about his father's voice, but Billy put on his shoes as the man asked.

"Come on," John said. "We're going out for a walk. Just the two of us."

"Can't I turn on a light?"

"No. Open the front door for your daddy now, and remember to be quiet."

Out in the humid night, crickets hummed in the woods. Billy followed his father's shape in the darkness. They walked down the driveway and toward the main road. When Billy tried to take his father's hand, John drew away and walked a little faster. *He's still mad at me*, Billy thought.

"Didn't I do right?" Billy asked—the same question he'd repeatedly asked his mother on that long walk home. "I wanted to confess my sin, like that preacher said to."

"You did fine." John slowed his pace. They were walking alongside the main road now, in the opposite direction from Hawthorne. "Just fine."

"But then how come everybody got mad?" His father looked a lot taller than usual. "How come you wouldn't go home with us?"

"I had my reasons."

They walked on a bit further. The night sky was ablaze with stars. Billy was still sleepy, and he was puzzled as to where his father was taking him. John had started walking a few paces ahead of Billy, a little more out into the road. "Daddy?" Billy said. "When that boy looked at me, I . . . felt somethin' funny inside me."

"Funny? Like how?"

"I don't know. I thought about it all the way home, and I told Momma about it too. It was kinda like the time I went into the Booker house. I didn't really want to, but I felt like I had to. When I saw that boy's face, I felt like I had to go up there, to be close to him. Why was that, Daddy?"

"I don't know."

"Momma says it was because he's . . . He paused, trying to recall the word. "Charis . . . charismatic. Somethin' like that."

John was silent for a moment. Then he abruptly stopped, his face lifted toward the darkness. Billy had never remembered him looking so big.

John said quietly, "Let's cross the road here. What I want to show you is on the other side."

"Yes sir."

Billy followed his father. His eyes had began to droop, and he yawned.

The concrete trembled beneath his feet.

And from around a wooded curve thirty feet away came the

dazzling headlights of a huge tractor-trailer rig, its high exhaust pipe spouting smoke, its diesel engine roaring.

Billy, caught in the center of the highway, was blinded and dazed; his legs were leaden, and he saw his father's shape before him in the headlights.

Except it was no longer John Creekmore. It was a huge, massive beast of some kind—a seven-foot-tall, hulking monster. Its head swiveled, its sunken eyes burning dark red; Billy saw it looked like a wild boar, and the beast grinned as it whirled into dark mist before the headlights of the speeding truck.

The driver, who hadn't slept for over twenty-four hours, only vaguely saw something dark in front of the truck. Then there was a boy in pajamas standing rooted in the middle of the road. With a cry of alarm, he hit the emergency brake and wildly swerved.

"Billy!" It was Ramona's voice, calling from the distance.

The clarity of it snapped Billy into action; he leaped toward the roadside, losing one shoe, and tumbled down into a ditch as the truck's wheels crushed past only inches away from him. He could feel the hot blast of the truck's exhaust scorching his back, and then his face was pressed into dirt and weeds.

The truck screeched to a stop, leaving rubber for fifty feet. "You little fool!" the driver shouted. "What the hell's wrong with you, boy?"

Billy didn't answer. He lay curled up in the ditch, shaking, until his mother found him. "It was Daddy," he whispered brokenly, as the truck driver continued to yell. "It was Daddy, but it wasn't Daddy. He wanted me to die, Momma. He wanted me to get run over!"

Ramona held him while he sobbed, and told the driver to go on. *Lord God!* she thought. *Has it started already?* She stared into the darkness, knowing what had to be done to protect her son's life.

14

Evening was falling, and still John hadn't come home. Ramona sat on the porch swing, as she had for most of the day, working on a new piece of needlepoint in the lamplight and watching the highway for John's car. The memory of what had happened last night still sent a tremor of terror through her. It had been in the house, she knew, and she hadn't even heard it! It had tricked Billy, tried to kill him.

She felt an undercurrent of evil in the valley, running like silt in a stream. It had been in the Booker house the night of the violence; it had been in John's eyes when he'd come home one night smelling of tar; and it had been in that revival meeting last night, laughing and kicking up its heels as sick people were told Satan was in them and that they should throw away their medicine. The idea that only sinners got sick was ludicrous to her, and yet those two—Falconer and the boy—were trading on that inhuman notion.

She'd realized from the very beginning, when she'd seen a lanky red-haired boy at a barn social and her heart had galloped away with her head, that John should know everything about her. Her mother had urged her to tell him, and several times she'd tried—but John hadn't seemed to want to listen to any of it. Of course he'd found out after they were married. How could she have kept it from him? There were so many people, in little hamlets across Alabama, who'd heard the stories about her mother, Rebekah. For the first few years, John had shown her a gentle, loving kindness—but then it had all changed.

She recalled the day over thirteen years ago when a man named Hank Crotty, from Sulligent, had come to see her, and John, though puzzled, had let him in. Crotty said he'd first gone to see

Rebekah Fairmountain, but the old woman had sent him to Ramona with a message: *It's your turn now.*

Her Mystery Walk called for her; how could she turn away?

Crotty's brother had been killed in a hunting accident two months before. But—and Crotty's face had gone dark with despair as John's had gone pale—some part of the dead man kept trying to get home, back to his wife and children. Something kept knocking on the door in the dead of the night, trying to get in. Crotty had broken into tears and begged for her help.

And that was how John had been made to realize the truth of Ramona's legacy: that in her Choctaw blood was the power to lay the dead to rest.

She'd waited alone at that house near Sulligent for two nights before the revenant came. It was first a small grayish blue light in the woods, and then as it approached the house it was a misty blue shape that took on the appearance of a man. Finally it was the outline of a man in a camouflage hunting jacket, his hands clasped to a hole in his belly. Ramona had stepped between the revenant and the house; it had abruptly stopped, shimmering in the darkness, and Ramona had felt its confusion and agony. It was the essence of a human being, trying desperately to cling to life, not realizing it could give up its pain and confusion and pass on to another, better place. Her mother had taught her what to do, and Ramona had spoken gently to it, calling its name, bringing it closer to her by sheer willpower. It trembled like a small child who sees a lighted doorway but fears traveling through a dark corridor to get there. The entrance was through Ramona, and she would have to take its terror and earthly emotions into her so it could pass on unencumbered.

Finally, after a long time of trying to make the revenant understand it could no longer exist in this world, it had swept toward her as if rushing into her arms. The sheer force of its agony staggered her backward. She felt the bullethole in her stomach, felt the awful yearning to touch wife and children, felt a hundred different emotions that had to be left behind, inside her.

And then she was alone in the dark, lying on the ground, sobbing and full of terror. But the revenant had gone, shedding its pain like a dead old skin.

For a long time, the pain stayed with her. She felt that bullet wound in a dozen nightmares. A package had come from her mother. In it was a needlepoint kit and a note: *I heard you did mighty good. I'm proud of you. But this won't be the last time. Remember I told you that once you'd done it, you'd have to handle the feelings that were left inside you? I recall you liked to sew as a little girl. Make me a pretty picture. I love you.*

John had finally allowed himself to touch her again. But then the next caller came, and the next—and John had withdrawn into a scared chunk of ice. She'd been carefully watching Billy these last few years. He'd had his first contact with a revenant—a strong one, too, who'd needed his help badly. She hoped he'd be spared the ability to see the black aura, a power that hadn't developed in her until she was in her late teens. To her, that was the worst of it: knowing who was going to die, and not being able to help.

Ramona looked up, catching her breath. A car's headlights showed on the highway; the car turned in and started up toward the house. She rose unsteadily to her feet, clutching a porch post. It was Sheriff Bromley's dark blue Pontiac.

Bromley stopped the car and got out. "Evenin', Mrs. Creekmore," he drawled, and walked toward the porch. He was a big man with a large, square jaw and a flat boxer's nose; he wore a CAT cap, a tan shirt, and tan trousers that made his belly roll slightly over his belt. His only concession to the job was a utility belt holding a flashlight, a pair of handcuffs, and a .38 Special.

The screen door banged open and Billy, carrying the oil lamp he'd been reading a Hardy Boys book by, came running out of the house, expecting to see his father stepping out of the Olds. When he saw Sheriff Bromley he stopped as abruptly as if he'd run into a brick wall.

"Hi, Billy," the sheriff said; there was a thin, uneasy smile on his face. He cleared his throat and returned his gaze to Ramona. "I . . . uh . . . was at the tent revival last night. I guess most of Hawthorne was. I'm sorry you were treated roughly, but . . ."

"Has anything happened to John?"

Bromley said, "No. Isn't he here?" He worked his fingers into his belt loops and stared off into the darkness for a few seconds. "No, this isn't about John. I just have to ask Billy a few questions."

"Questions about what?"

He shifted uneasily.

"About Will Booker," he said finally.

"Billy, set that lamp on the table here to give us more light. You heard the sheriff. Will you answer his questions truthfully?"

91

He nodded uneasily.

Bromley stepped closer to the porch. "I have to ask you these things, Billy. That don't mean I *want* to."

"It's okay."

"Well . . . just when was it that you went down into the Bookers' basement?"

"The last part of April. I didn't mean to go in there, I know it was private property, but . . ."

"Why did you decide to go down there in the first place?"

"I heard a . . ." He glanced at his mother, but she was staring out toward the highway, letting him handle this on his own. "I heard a tapping. Behind the basement door."

"Did you go back there again, after you . . . saw what you said you saw?"

"Nosir. I *couldn't* go back to that place again."

Bromley looked into Billy's eyes for a few seconds, then sighed and nodded. "I believe you, boy. Now can I speak to your momma alone for just a minute?"

Billy took his lamp, leaving hers burning on the wicker table, and went inside. Fireflies winked in the woods, a chorus of toads began burping down at the green pond. She waited for him to speak.

"After Dave Booker killed them," Bromley said in a distant, wearied voice, "he stuffed Julie Ann's body beneath a bed, and he locked Katy's in a closet. It was . . . like he wanted to get rid of them, or pretend it hadn't happened. We searched for Will all through that house, up in the woods, under the front porch, everywhere we could think of. We looked for bones in the furnace, got a diver to go down into the well behind the Booker place, even dragged Semmes Lake. We looked through that coal pile, too, but we . . . never dug up the floor *underneath* it." He took his cap off and scratched his scalp. "That's where Will was, all the time. His little body was . . . curled up in a croaker sack. Looked like he might have been beat to death with a shovel or somethin', from the broken bones. Ah, this whole thing has been mighty shitty, 'scuse my French." He worked the cap back down onto his head again. "Link Patterson, Cale Joiner, and me found Will this morning. I've had to handle some bad things in my time, but this is the . . ." He suddenly reached out and gripped a porch post, his knuckles whitening. "Mrs. Creekmore?" he said hoarsely, as if fighting emotions he knew a sheriff wasn't supposed to show. "I'm so sorry about what happened to you last night. I should've . . . done something, I guess. . . ."

"No need."

"You . . . know what kind of things are said about you, don't you? I've heard 'em too, but I never gave them no account." His mouth worked, forming the words that were hard to find. "Are they *true?*"

She didn't answer. She knew he wanted desperately to understand, to know the secrets in her mind, and for an instant she wanted to trust him because maybe—just maybe—there was within this bearish man the spark of his own Mystery Walk. But then the instant passed, and she knew she could never bring herself to trust anyone in Hawthorne ever again.

"I don't believe in ghosts!" the sheriff said indignantly. "That's just . . . fool's talk! But can you answer me this? How did Billy know Will Booker was under that coal pile?" There was a long silence, broken only by the frogs and crickets. And then Bromley said, "Because he's like *you*, isn't he?"

Ramona's chin lifted slightly. "Yes," she said. "Like me."

"He's just a little boy! What . . . what in the name of Heaven is his life going to be like, if he's cursed to see ghosts and . . . God knows what else! . . ."

"Is your business finished, sheriff?"

Bromley blinked uncertainly, feeling a raw power in her leveled stare. "Yes . . . except for one last thing. Jimmy Jed Falconer is a well respected and loved man in this county, and that son of his is a bona fide miracle worker. When you jump up and start yellin' 'Murder' you'd best be standing on solid ground unless you want a slander suit slapped on you."

"Slander? Isn't that saying things that aren't true? Then I've no need to worry, do I? Did that man, or someone from his Crusade, tell you to say that to me?"

"Maybe, maybe not. Just listen to what's said. *Now* my business is finished." He turned and stalked to his car, but paused with the door open. "You know things are never going to be the same for Billy ever again, don't you?" He got into the car and backed off down the road.

Ramona waited until the sheriff's car had gone, then took the lamp and went inside. Billy was sitting in his father's chair in the front room, his lamp and the *Mystery of the Missing Chums* on a table beside him. She knew that he must've heard everything said on the porch. "Sheriff Bromley found Will," he said.

"Yes."

"But how could it be Will if Will was already dead?"

"I don't think it was Will as you knew him, Billy. I think it was . . . some part of Will that was scared and alone, and he'd been waiting for *you* to help him."

Billy frowned, his jaw working. "Did I help him, Momma?"

"I don't know. But I think that maybe you did; I think that he didn't want to be left lying alone in that basement. Who would want to wake up in the dark, without anyone near to help them?"

Billy had thought about his next question for a long time, and now he had to force himself to ask it. "Is Will going to Heaven or Hell?"

"I think . . . he's already spent enough time in Hell, don't you?"

"Yes."

"I'll make our supper now," Ramona said, and touched the boy's cheekbone. He was over his skittishness from the night before, but there were unanswered questions in his eyes. "I'll heat up the vegetable broth and fix some corn muffins, how about that?"

"Isn't Daddy ever comin' home?"

"He'll be home, sooner or later. But right now he's scared. Do you understand that not everybody could've seen what was left of Will Booker, and very few could've helped him like you have?"

"I don't know," he said uncertainly, his face a patchwork of orange light and black shadows.

"I wish I could help you with all of it," she said softly. She gripped his hand and held it. "God knows I do, but there are some things you have to find out on your own. But may-be . . . maybe your gram can help you in a way I can't because there's still so much I don't understand myself. . . ."

"Gram help me? How?"

"She can start you over at the beginning. She can reshape you and mold you, just like she molds those pieces she makes on her potter's wheel. She did that for me, too, a long time ago, just as her daddy did for her. Your gram can teach you things that I can't."

He thought about this for a minute, his brow furrowed. He loved his grandmother's place—a white house on three thickly wooded acres with plenty of meandering trails to follow—but what would his father say? "When would we go?" he asked.

"Why not in the morning? We could catch the bus down at the grocery store and be there by early afternoon. But we'll go only if you want to."

"What kind of things do I have to learn?"

"Special things," Ramona said. "Things you won't learn anywhere else. Some of it will be easy and fun, and some of it . . . won't be; some of it may even hurt. You're standing on the edge between being a child and being a man, Billy, and maybe there are things you can understand better this summer than you could in the next."

There was a darkly luminous look in Ramona's eyes that both unsettled Billy and sparked his curiosity; it was like seeing something sparkle down along a forest path he'd never dared explore before. He said, "All right. I'll go."

"Then you're going to need to get some clothes together, 'cause we might be staying at Gram's for a while. Why don't you get some of your underwear and socks out of your desk, and while you're doing that I'll get my clothes ready too. Then we'll eat supper. All right?"

In the lamplight, Billy opened one of his desk drawers and laid a few pair of Fruit-of-the-Looms out on his bed. Then he rummaged for some socks, his T-shirts, and—his favorite—his Lone Ranger suspenders. His shirts and jeans were hanging in his mother's closet, so he'd have to get to them later. He leaned down and reached under the cot, pulling out a large paper sack; in it was a Dutch Masters cigar box he'd found on the roadside last summer, and contained within the box—which still smelled vaguely of cheroots—were Billy's earthly treasures.

He could use the paper sack to carry his clothes in, he decided, and now he sat on the cot with the cigar box on his lap and opened the lid.

Inside were several green cat's-eye marbles, smooth brown creek stones, a rock with the faint impression of a skeletal leaf pressed on it, a Duncan yo-yo that whistled, twenty-five Civil War bubble-gum cards with gory battle pictures on them, and . . .

Billy tilted the cigar box toward the light. He stared into the box, his eyes slowly widening; then he turned the lamp's wick up, because suddenly the room had seemed too dark by far.

A small piece of coal, glittering in the orange light, lay half buried under the Civil War cards. I didn't put that in there, Billy thought; or *did* I? He couldn't remember; no, no he was sure he hadn't. At first it looked only like a bulbous black lump, but as he stared at it he found himself recalling Will Booker's face in great detail, and he could remember the good times they'd had together. He picked it up and held it close to his face, studying the dark ridges.

He didn't know how the coal had gotten there, but he knew there was a purpose behind it. Will was dead, yes, Billy knew, but something of the boy lived on in Billy's memories; and if you could remember—*truly* remember, Billy thought—then you could stop time, and nothing ever died. His fist slowly closed around the coal, a sensation of warmth spreading up his arm to his elbow.

His mind went back to the night before. He frowned, recalling the way that young evangelist, Wayne Falconer, had stared at him. He didn't understand what his mother had said about the healing being "akin to murder," but he knew she'd sensed something strange about them as he had, something that he couldn't fully perceive.

Nightsounds pressed in on the house. Billy sat listening for the sound of his father's car pulling up in front, but it didn't come. The image of a beast in a truck's headlights came at him with no warning. He shuddered, then finally replaced the piece of coal in the cigar box and put his clothes down into the paper sack, getting ready for tomorrow's journey.

15

Jimmy Jed Falconer awakened in the soft blue light before dawn, brought out of sleep by Toby's barking in the meadow. He lay awake, his pretty blond wife Camille sleeping at his side, and listened to Toby. Chasin' rabbits, he mused, as the barking faded in the direction of the woods. When he thought of the dog, he naturally thought of the miracle.

It had happened on that day in April. Cammy had been washing dishes in the kitchen when she'd heard Wayne scream, and she'd raced out of the house to see what had happened. Wayne was running toward her with the bloody bag of dogflesh in his arms, and his mouth was open and straining to cry out again. He'd stumbled and fallen to the ground, and when Cammy had reached him she'd seen that Toby was already almost dead, the breath coming in whining hitches from its crushed chest. The big dog's sinewy body was a mess of shattered bones, its head crooked at an awful angle and blood dripping from its floppy ears. Wayne had screamed, "Truck hit him, Momma! I saw it happen! Get somebody to make Toby well!"

But Cammy hadn't known what to do, and all the leaking blood had repulsed her. She'd stepped back, dazed, and her son—the tears streaming down his livid, dusty face—had shrieked at her, "GET SOMEBODY!" in a voice that had shaken her to her soul. She'd started running for the phone to call Jimmy Jed in Birmingham at his advertising meeting, but she knew that Toby wouldn't last more than a few minutes longer. At the front door she'd looked over her shoulder and seen Wayne bent down over the dog, his new jeans filthy with dust and blood.

The long-distance operator had just answered when she'd heard Wayne's voice rise in a blood-curdling shout that stretched on for several seconds: "TOOOOOBBBBBYYYYYY!" She'd dropped the receiver, and was so startled her hair had almost stood on end. She had gone to calm Wayne down, then stopped on the porch, watching Wayne lift Toby, stumble and almost fall again, and then come walking slowly toward her, dust puffing off the driveway around his shoes.

And he was grinning. Ear to ear. His eyes were red and tear-swollen, but they'd burned with an electric power that was like nothing Cammy had ever seen before. She'd actually felt herself shrinking backward, against the white porch railing. He'd said in a hoarse voice, "Toby's all better now. . . ."

Wayne had put Toby down, and Cammy had almost swooned. The dog's bones had been mended as if by a mad scientist . . . or a frantic child. The head was frighteningly crooked, the front legs splayed and the back ones turned inward, the spine twisted and humped like a camel's. It was something that had stepped out of a freak show; but the dog's breathing wasn't labored anymore, and though it staggered for balance and its eyes were dazed, Camille could see that Toby was no longer near death. Then she'd gotten her feet uprooted from the porch floor, and somehow she'd made that call to Birmingham.

Falconer grinned to himself. He'd seen the X rays Dr. Considine had taken; the bones were a mess, jigsawed together haphazardly, but they were firmly cemented and showed only faint signs of having been snapped or crushed. The vet was frankly amazed at Toby's condition, telling Falconer that this was beyond science . . . *way* beyond. Toby's movement was limited, so his legs had to be rebroken and properly set, but now the dog had gotten used to its crimped spine and crooked neck and could run through the meadows of the Falconer estate like blue blazes again. And the question had begun ticking in Falconer's brain: if his son could heal an *animal*, what could he do for human beings?

The answer came in the shape of a beatup blue Ford pickup, carrying a grim-faced man and woman and a little girl with the perfect face of a doll. Their names were Gantt, they lived on the other side of Fayette, and they'd heard talk about J.J. Falconer's son from a friend, who'd heard the story in a direct line from the mouth of a certain veterinarian. The little girl couldn't walk; her father had told Falconer that her legs had "gone to sleep and never woked up."

Falconer had gone upstairs to Wayne's room, where model airplanes hung on thin wires from the ceiling. The boy was at his desk, patiently gluing together the fuselage of a Revell P-38. Falconer had pulled up a chair and watched him work for a minute in silence. The boy was very good with his hands, and was in love with airplanes. "There's somebody downstairs who wants to meet you," the evangelist had said finally.

"Who, Daddy?"

"A man and woman and their little girl. She's seven, and her name's Cheryl. Do you want to know why they're here?"

He nodded, carefully gluing a wing into place.

"Because of how you fixed Toby. Remember what you told me, that when you saw Toby about to die your head started aching so bad you thought it was going to explode, and then you felt that you *had* to lay your hands on Toby, and you wanted Toby to be fixed more than anything in the world?"

Wayne had put down his work and stared at his father, his eyes bright blue and puzzled. "Yes sir."

"And you said that in your mind you thought very hard of Toby's bones coming back together again, that your hands were tingling like they do when they've gone to sleep, and everywhere you touched you could feel the bones move?"

Wayne had nodded.

Falconer had gingerly touched his son's shoulder. "Cheryl and her folks have come here to ask for you help, son. Her legs are asleep, and they need to be fixed."

Wayne looked bewildered. "Did a truck hit her?"

"No. I think this is a sickness in her mind and her nerves. But she needs . . . whatever it is you used before, to fix Toby. Do you think you can do that again?"

"I don't know. It's . . . it's *different*. Maybe I can't ever do it again, maybe I used all of it up the first time because I thought so hard. It made my head hurt so bad, Daddy. . . ."

"Yes, I know. But didn't it make you feel good too? Didn't it set you on fire, couldn't you hear the voice of God and feel His Power at work inside you?"

"I guess, but . . ."

"You're a healer, son. A living, breathing miracle-working *healer!*" He'd placed one of his large rough hands over his son's. "You've got the power in you, and it's been given to you for a very special purpose. Cheryl and her folks are waitin' downstairs, right now. What shall I tell 'em?"

"I . . . I did it because I love Toby so much, Daddy. I don't even know this little girl!"

Falconer had leaned close to him, and lowered his voice. "Do it because you love *me*."

A sheet was draped over the dining-room table, and Cheryl Gantt was laid on her back by her father. The little girl trembled and clutched at her mother's hand as Wayne stood over her, seemingly not knowing what to do. Falconer nodded encouragement to him; Cammy, overwrought by the whole thing, had to leave the house and sit on the porch until it was finished. When Wayne finally touched the little girl's legs, he shut his eyes and rubbed the knobby knees as a vein slowly beat at his temple. Cheryl stared at the ceiling, whimpering softly.

The boy tried for over an hour until his face was shiny with sweat and his hands cramped into claws. The Gantts were as kind as they could be, lifting their daughter off the table and taking her back out to their pickup truck. Wayne stood on the porch until the truck was out of sight, his shoulders slumped in defeat; when he met his father's eyes a sob rattled deep in his chest, and he hurried upstairs to his room.

Falconer went to his book-lined study, closed the double oak-paneled doors, and sat at his desk staring into space. He decided to turn to his Bible for comfort, and wherever it opened would be a message for him. He found himself looking at the thirteenth chapter of Matthew, at Christ's parable of seeds sown on rocky soil, in thorns, and on fertile earth where they yielded fruit; it took three slow readings before he grasped the message. It hit him like a thunderbolt; of course! he thought, newly excited. Just as the word of the Lord was lost on some folks, so were the Lord's miracles! If that little girl wasn't healed, maybe it was because her parents didn't have enough faith, or they were deep sinners who'd strayed far from the light. The problem hadn't been with Wayne, but with either the little girl or her folks! And he was about to go up to talk to Wayne when the telephone rang.

It was Mr. Gantt, calling from a Texaco station on the other side of Fayette. His little girl had started shaking all of a sudden, and she'd said she felt sick so they'd pulled the truck into the station. Mrs. Gantt had held her while the little girl had thrown up in the ladies' room. Suddenly Cheryl had screamed that she felt the blood circulating in her legs, and her startled mother had let her go. Cheryl had collapsed to the floor, but had pulled herself slowly up and staggered out under her own power to the pickup truck, where her father had hugged her in his arms and started shouting about how Little Wayne Falconer had healed his Cheryl.

And three days later an envelope came, addressed to the Falconer Crusade. It was from the Gantts, and inside was a ten-dollar bill wrapped up in tissue paper. The telephone calls and letters began landsliding in, and Falconer had known it was his responsibility to teach Wayne everything he knew about public speaking, getting up in front of a crowd and making them feel the love of God in their hearts. The boy was a natural, and at the last minute Falconer had added Wayne's name to the posters for the summer tent-revival circuit.

Falconer rose up out of bed, careful not to awaken Cammy, and went across the hallway to Wayne's room. He silently opened the door; weak shards of first light glinted off the dozen or so airplane models—a B-52, a pair of navy Hellcats, a British Spad, a Constellation, and others—dangling down from their wires.

Wayne was sitting in a chair drawn up to the window, the curtains luffing in a faint morning breeze. Beyond the window stretched the meadows of Falconer's thirty-six-acre estate.

"Wayne?" The boy's head swiveled around. "You're up awful early, aren't you?" Falconer stepped into the room, ducking his head under a green Spitfire.

"Yes sir. I had something on my mind, is all."

"Is it something so important you couldn't get a good night's sleep? You know, we've got to be in Decatur this evenin'." He yawned and stretched, feeling that long drive already. "What's on your mind?"

"I was thinkin' about what happened in Hawthorne, Daddy. I was thinkin' about that boy and his momma."

"Oh?" Falconer ran a hand through his hair and sat down heavily on the edge of the bed, where he could see his son's face. "You heard what was said about them. They're strange people, and that woman came to the revival just to cause trouble. But you shouldn't concern yourself."

"Is she a witch, like they said? And is the boy a demon?"

"I don't know, but it seems like everybody in Hawthorne thinks so."

The boy stared at him for a few silent seconds. Then he said, "Then why don't we kill them?"

Falconer was startled. "Well . . . Wayne, that would be murder, and murder's against the law. . . ."

"Thought you said that God's laws were above the laws of Man? And if that woman and the boy are Evil, then they shouldn't be allowed to live, should they?"

"Uh . . ." Falconer felt himself slipping in over his head. "The Lord'll take care of them, Wayne. Don't you worry."

"She said what I did was murder," Wayne said.

"Yes, she did. And that goes to show you just how twisted she *is*, doesn't it? She tried to wreck your work, Wayne, and she used that boy to get things stirred up."

"Am I doing *right*, Daddy?"

The question had come like a thunderclap. Falconer blinked. "What do you mean, son?"

"I mean . . . I know I've healed a lot of people this summer, but . . . the first time, with Toby, I felt something happen deep inside me, like my blood was boiling and . . . it was kind of like that time when I was little and I stuck a fork into that electric socket. It hurt, and after it was over I could still feel it in my bones. I don't feel it like I did that first time, Daddy; sometimes I get tingly, or my head aches, but . . . it's not the same. And remember in Sylacauga last week? That blind man who came up to the front? I tried *hard,* Daddy, but I couldn't make him see. And there have been others, too, that I don't think I really touched . . . maybe I pretended to, but . . ." He paused, his face an uneasy mask of deep concerns.

"I think you're lettin' that Creekmore woman make you doubt yourself, is what I think. And that's what she wanted, all along! When you doubt yourself, you make yourself weak. And I've thought about that blind man too, and others like him; it could be you can't heal some people because God has a plan for them just as they *are.* Or it could be there's a sin in their lives that keeps them apart from the Light, and until they confess it they can't receive a healing. But don't you doubt yourself, Wayne; if you do, the demons win. Do you understand?"

"I . . . guess I do."

Falconer patted his shoulder. "Good. You going to be ready for Decatur tonight?"

Wayne nodded.

"Is there something else on your mind?"

"Yes sir. There was . . . something in that boy that made me afraid, Daddy. I don't know what it was, but . . . when I looked in his eyes I felt scared right down in my stomach. . . ."

Falconer grunted softly and gazed out the window. "If you felt fear," he told his son, "it was because you sensed the sin in his heart and mind. Wayne, you're going to have a fine full life, and you're going to meet a lot of good people; but you'll meet people with Satan in their souls too. You'll have to stand up to 'em, and face 'em down. Understand?"

"Yes sir."

"Good. Breakfast is still a couple of hours away. Want to catch some more winks?"

"I'll try." Wayne left the chair and climbed into bed. His father smoothed the sheets and kissed him on the forehead.

"You just rest easy now, big buddy," Falconer said. "I'll come wake you up for breakfast. Okay?" He smiled and then started toward the door.

Wayne's voice stopped him. "I *am* doing right, aren't I, Daddy?"

"Yes. I promise you. Get some sleep now." And Falconer closed the door.

For a long time Wayne lay still, staring at the ceiling. The plastic airplanes stirred in the faint breeze, their wings swaying as if they were soaring amid the clouds. He heard Toby barking way off in the woods, and he squeezed his eyes shut tightly.

16

The sun was rising too on the Creekmore farm. Ramona awakened just after six, when she heard a car pulling up in front of the house. She heard the car door open, but did not hear it close. Then someone was fumbling with keys, trying to get in.

Ramona quickly put on her robe, lit an oil lamp, and walked into the front room just as her husband staggered in. John grinned widely; a shock wave of body odor and the heady smell of moonshine rolled out before him. A red stubble of beard covered his jaw. His clothes were rumpled and a couple of buttons were missing from his shirt. "Hi, hon," he said, and took an unsteady step toward her.

"No."

The word stopped him as if he'd been struck, but his clownish grin stayed hooked in place. His eyes were so bloodshot they looked as if they were about to burst. "Awwww, don't be like that," he said. "Jus' been out howwwwlin', that's all. Saw Mack van Horn and old Wint, too; you'd never believe that damn still they got workin' way back in the woods!" He blinked and ran a grimy hand across his forehead. "Where'd that mule go after he kicked me in the head?" He laughed, his eyes wanting to close on him. "Why don't you go on back there and comb your hair real nice and pretty, huh? Put on some of that sweet-smellin' stuff I like. Then you can welcome me home like a real wife. . . ."

"You're filthy," Ramona said quietly, "and you smell like an outhouse!"

"DAMN RIGHT!" he thundered, his face contorting with anger. "What'd you expect, that I'd come home with roses in my hair? You made me wallow in shit at that tent revival, woman, and I thought I'd jus' bring a little of it home!" He was trembling with rage. "You made a fool out of me," he said. "You disgraced my name, woman! Oh, you planned it *all*, didn't you? That's why you wanted to go all of a sudden, 'cause you figured you could raise some kind of sin at the revival! And I had to stand there while you . . . !" He stumbled over his words and stopped, because Billy had come out of the gray shadows at Ramona's back and stood there watching.

"Billy," John said. "Son. You daddy's back home now. I know I look a mess, but . . . but I had an accident, I guess."

"Go get your clothes on," Ramona told the boy. "Hurry."

Billy stared at his father, his face crumpling, and then went to get ready.

"What's goin' on?"

Ramona said, "I'm taking Billy to his grandmother."

"*Oh.*" It was a soft, stunned exhalation of moonshined breath; John wavered on his feet, the room beginning to spin slowly around him. He felt strangled for a second and couldn't find his voice. Then: "Now I see it. Nowwwwww I see it. Gonna take my son away from me when my back's turned, ain't you?" He advanced a step, and Ramona saw the glint of red in his eyes behind the soft flabby drunkenness.

"No, that's not it." She stood her ground. "You know why I'm doing this. . . ."

"*So you can make him like you are!*" he shrieked. "So you can put all that . . . that *shit* in his head! I won't let you do it, by God! I won't let you have him!"

"Billy saw some part of Will Booker that was left after death, John. Call it a haunt, or a spirit, or maybe even the soul. But he *did* see something in that basement, and he has to understand what's ahead for him. . . ."

"NO!" John staggered backward, almost falling, and splayed himself across the door as if nailed there. "I won't let him be taken over by that *blasphemy!* Maybe I had to stand by and watch you do it, but I won't—I WON'T—let you take my blood into it!"

"Your blood?" she asked him softly. "He's my blood too. He's got both of us in him, but the old Choctaw blood in him is *strong*, John. He's the next link in the chain, don't you see? He has to carry it f—"

He clapped his hands to his ears. "*Evil evil evil evil evil* . . ."

Tears burned around Ramona's eyes at the sight of the pitiful drunken man, pressed frantically against the door of his own house to keep Billy in. "It's not evil, John. It never was."

"You tell me death's not evil? That's been your life, 'mona! Not me or the boy, not really! It's always been death, and ghosts, and demons!" He shook his head, his senses reeling. "Oh God have mercy on your soul! God have mercy on my soul for puttin' up with your lies!"

But then Billy, in his jeans and a striped cotton shirt, stepped into the orange wash of the lamp; he was clutching the paper sack containing his clothes, and his face looked sick and scared.

"Come on, Billy." John stretched out his arms. "Come on, let's show her how men stick together."

"Momma . . . says I should go, Daddy. She says there are things I need to learn."

"No. She's wrong. Know what kind of things she wants you to learn? Stuff about ghosts, and *death*. You're a righteous, God-fearin' boy, and you shouldn't listen to things like that."

"I didn't *want* to see Will Booker, Daddy. But he was there, and he needed my help." He lifted his hand and showed his father the black lump of coal, resting on his palm.

"What's that? Where'd that come from?"

"I don't know, but I . . . I think that Will's trying to help *me* now. I think he's given me this to let me know that . . . I was right to go down in that basement, and just because it was dark and scary didn't mean it was evil. . . ."

A deep groan came from John's throat. "*Poisoned,*" he whispered, staring at the coal. "The poison's in the blood, it's in the blood! Dear God strike me dead if I haven't tried to be the best father—"

"Stop it!" Ramona said sharply.

And suddenly Billy had run across the room, dropping his clothes-filled bag, and was clinging to his father's leg. Through his strangled sobbing the boy moaned, "I'll be good, Daddy, I'll be good, I'll be . . ."

John shivered—whether with emotion or in disgust Ramona couldn't tell—and gripped Billy by the collar, flinging him toward his wife. "TAKE HIM, THEN!" he shouted, and threw the car keys to the floor. "Go on, both of you! Get out of my . . ." His voice cracked, and a terrible sob came up from the depths of his soul. Billy was staring at him, tears streaming down the boy's cheeks, and John raised a hand to ward off Billy's gaze. ". . . house," he whispered. He staggered across the room and fell down into his chair before the cold hearth, his face streaked reddish by the rising sun. "I can't do it, Lord," he said softly, one hand clamped at his temples and his eyes tightly closed. "I can't get the darkness out of them. . . ." Then he was silent but for his rumbled breathing.

"Get your things," Ramona told Billy, and then she went back to slip on socks and shoes and get her traveling bag. She would drive in her robe and change later, but right now she wanted to get herself and Billy out of the house. In the kitchen, Ramona took a few dollars and fifty cents in change from their emergency money, kept in a clay apple-shaped cookie jar that Rebekah had made for them. Then she came back to the front room and picked up the keys. Billy was standing near his father; the boy's eyes were swollen, and now he reached out and gently touched John's arm. John mumbled and groaned in his tortured, drunken sleep.

"Go on to the car," Ramona said. "I'll be there directly."

When Billy had left, Ramona smoothed the tangled, dirty curls of reddish-brown hair away from her husband's forehead. The lines of his face, she thought, were getting deeper. She wiped her eyes with the back of her hand, steadied herself when she began trembling, and got a coverlet for him from the bedroom. She spread it over him, and watched as he gripped at it and curled up into a ball. He moaned softly in his sleep—a sound of sadness and confusion, a lost sound like a night train way off in the distance—and Ramona left the house.

FOUR

Potter's Clay

17

The old woman's hands, wet with clay, moved like brown hummingbirds to give shape to the formless lump that sat on the spinning potter's wheel before her. Vase or jar? she asked herself, her foot rhythmically tapping the horizontal wooden bar that controlled the wheel's speed. Oiled gears meshed with a quiet hissing of friction. She was partial to vases, but jars sold more quickly; Mrs. Blears, owner of the Country Crafts Shoppe twenty miles away in Selma, had told her there was a real market for her small, wide-mouthed jars glazed in dark, earthen colors. They could be used for anything from sugar jars to holding lipsticks, Mrs. Blears said, and people paid a bit more for them if there was the Rebekah Fairmountain signature on the bottom. After all, Rebekah had been written up both in the *Selma Journal* and in *Alabama Craftsman* magazine, and she'd won first prize for most original pottery sculpture four years in a row at the Alabama State Fair. She did the sculpture only once in a while now, to challenge herself, but stuck mainly to the jars, vases, and mugs the crafts shop ordered, because blue ribbons didn't make a very filling meal.

Midmorning sunlight streamed in through two windows before her, slanting across the wood-floored workroom and glinting off the finished pieces arranged on pineboard shelves: there were cups and saucers the color of red autumn leaves, dishes as dark blue as a midnight sky, a series of jars ranging in hue from pink to deep purple, black mugs with a finish as rough as pine bark, unglazed pieces painted with brightly colored Choctaw figures. The workroom was a hodgepodge of colors and shapes, a riot of creativity; at the center of it sat the old woman, smoking a plain clay pipe and regarding the material that lay before her. She had smoothed the sides, wetting her fingers from a can of water to keep the clay soft, and had already worked over several small imperfections that might crack in the kiln's drying heat. Now it was time to decide.

She saw a vase in this one. A tall vase with a fluted rim, glazed deep red like the blood that flows through a woman's heart when she's with the man she loves. Yes, she thought; a beautiful dark red vase to hold white wild flowers. She added more clay from a box at her side, wet her fingers again, and went to work.

Rebekah Fairmountain's strong-boned, deeply furrowed face was spattered with clay; her flesh was the color of oiled mahogany, her eyes pure ebony. Straight silver hair fell to her shoulders from beneath a wide-brimmed straw sunhat, and she wore clay-smeared Sears' overalls over a plaid shirt. As she worked, her eyes narrowed with concentration, and blue whorls of smoke wisped from the right side of her mouth; she was puffing rabbit tobacco that she'd gathered in the forest, and its distinctive burned-leaves aroma filled the workroom. Her house was set far off the main road and surrounded by dense forest; even so, the electric company was running lines out to provide lights to some of her neighbors, but she didn't want that false, cheerless lighting.

A covey of quail burst out of the brush off in the distance, scattering for the sky. Their movement through the window caught Rebekah's attention; she watched them for a moment, wondering what was stalking through the woods after them. Then she saw a faint haze of dust rising in the air, and she knew a car was drawing near. Mailman? she wondered. Too early in the day. Bill collector? Hope not! She reluctantly left the potter's wheel and rose from her chair, stepping to the window.

When she saw it was John Creekmore's car, her heart leapt with joy. It had been Christmas since she'd last seen her daughter and grandson. She opened the screen door and went out to where the Olds was pulling up in front of the white house, built separately from the pottery workshed. Ramona and little Billy were already getting out, but where was John? Something bad had happened, Rebekah told herself as she saw their faces. Then she broke into a hobbled run, and embraced her daughter, feeling the tension that hung around her like a shroud.

Rebekah pretended not to notice Billy's swollen eyes. She tousled his hair and said, "Boy, you're going to be tall enough to snag the clouds pretty soon, aren't you?" Her voice was raspy, and trembled with the excitement of seeing them.

He managed a weak smile. "No, Gram, I won't ever get that tall!"

"You're about five feet there already! Let me just look at the both of you!" She took the pipe out of her mouth and shook her head in awe. "Ramona, you're as lovely as April! You please my eyes, girl!" Then she put her arm around her daughter, sensing that the tears were about to break down Ramona's cheeks. "Could you use a cup of sassafras tea?"

"Yes. I surely could."

They walked to the house—the old woman steadying her daughter, the younger woman clutching to her son. On the porch was a large pile of firewood used for cooking; around behind the house, where the woods had been cleared, was a well, and at the edge of the forest stood a small smokehouse. In the comfortable but sparsely furnished house, Rebekah boiled fragrant sassafras root in a kettle on the kitchen's woodburning stove. She said, "Billy, I've got a piece almost done on the wheel right now. Why don't you run over there and take a look at it, and tell me what color you think it ought to be?"

He scampered out of the kitchen, eager to get to the pottery workroom and its explosion of shapes and colors. Ramona sat down at the kitchen table with her cup of tea, and Rebekah said quietly, "I want to hear it—everything—before the boy comes back."

Ramona couldn't hold back her tears any longer; she'd had to be strong for Billy, but now she felt as weak as water. She trembled, sobbing, and her mother rubbed her neck and shoulders to ease the tension in them. Ramona began with the Booker tragedy, and told her everything. "We came straight here," she said after she was through. "You should've . . . heard what John said today, right in front of Billy. . . ."

The old woman lit her pipe with a long kitchen match and puffed out blue smoke. "What did you expect?" she asked. "For John to send you off with his best wishes? It's not that he sees badness in you or Billy, it's that he's lost all idea of what's bad and what isn't. Anything that makes him afraid—or makes him *think*—is to him as black as a demon's armpit in Hell. Damn it, child! I knew all this was comin'—there I go, rattlin' on like any other old granny, eh?"

"I don't care about myself. It's Billy I worry about."

"Oh, no." Rebekah shook her head. "Don't go sayin' that.

There've been too many martyrs in this family already. So: you went to this Falconer revival, and you think it was *him*, do you?"

"Yes," Ramona said. "I know it was."

"How do you know?"

"If I have to explain that to you, you don't know *me* very well. I wish I'd never gone there! I was a fool to go!"

"But it's done." Rebekah's dark eyes glittered. "Have you told Billy?"

"No, not yet."

"Are you?"

"I . . . don't think the time is right for that. I think it would be too much for him. Last night . . . what he thought was his father came for him, and took him out on the road. He was almost killed by a truck."

Rebekah frowned, then nodded grimly. "It's after him already, then. He may be able to see, child, but he may not be able to know what he sees, or be able to help. Our family's been full of both good and bad fruit. There were the no-'counts, like your great-uncle Nicholas T. Hancock, who was the king of the flimflammin' spirit merchants until he got shot in the head in a crooked poker game. But then there was your great-great-grandmother Ruby Steele, who started that organization in Washington, D.C., to study the afterlife. What I'm tryin' to say to you is: if Billy can't help, there's no use in him bein' able to see. If he can't go forward, he'll go backward. And he's got a lot of tainted white blood in him, Ramona."

"I think he can help. He's helped already."

"And you want him to start the Mystery Walk?"

"I want him to continue it. I think he started when he went down into that basement."

"Maybe so. But you know as well as I do about the Walk—if he's not strong enough, if he doesn't have the inborn sense to understand it, then the ritual could hurt him. I was fifteen when my daddy started mine; you were sixteen. This child is only *ten*. Only one other I ever heard of who started the Walk that early: Thomas X. Cody, back in the 1800s. Interesting man. It was said our old enemy hated Thomas so much, he raised a corpse out of its grave and walked in its skin with a knife in one hand and a hatchet in the other. Thomas and that thing fought on the edge of a cliff for two days straight, until they both went over the side."

"Do you believe that?"

"I believe Thomas was strong. I believe our enemy hasn't begun to show us all his tricks. Changing shapes to deceive is only part of it."

"Then it's important for Billy to start the Walk now," Ramona said. "I want him to know what kind of thing tried to kill him the other night."

"If he's not ready, the ritual could do him damage. You know that, don't you?"

"Yes."

The front door opened and closed. Billy came into the kitchen with wet clay on his hands. He was carrying a particularly large pinecone he thought his gram would like to see.

"That's a mighty hefty pinecone." Rebekah laid it on the table before her. Then she looked into Billy's eyes. "How'd you like to stay here for a few days?"

"I guess so. But we're goin' back to Daddy, aren't we?"

Ramona nodded. "Yes. We are."

"Did you see my new piece?" Rebekah asked. "It's going to be a tall vase."

"I saw it. I think it ought to be . . ." He thought hard. "Red, maybe. Real dark red, like Choctaw blood."

Rebekah paused and nodded. "Why," she said, an expression of pleasure stealing across her face, "I hadn't thought of that!"

18

Billy was awakened by his grandmother who stood over the bed holding a bull's-eye lantern that cast a pale golden glow upon the walls. Through the open window a single cicada sang in an oak tree like a buzz saw's whine, the note rising and falling in the midnight heat. Billy thought he could smell woodsmoke.

"Get dressed," Rebekah said, and motioned with the lantern toward his clothes, laid across the back of a chair. In a pocket of the jeans was the piece of coal, which she'd carefully examined when he showed it to her; earlier in the evening she'd put a coating of shellac on it so the black wouldn't rub off on his clothes or hands.

He rubbed his eyes and sat up. "What time is it?"

"Time starts now," she replied. "Come on, get up."

He rose and dressed, his mind still fogged with sleep. His stomach heaved and roiled, and he feared throwing up again. He didn't know what was wrong with him; after a supper of vegetable soup and chicken wings, Gram had given him a mug of something that was oily and black and tasted like molasses. She'd said it was to keep his system "regular," but within twenty minutes of drinking it he'd been outside, throwing up his supper into the grass. He'd heaved until there was nothing left to come up, and now he felt light-headed and weak. "Can I have some water?" he asked.

"Later. Put your shoes on."

He yawned and struggled with his shoelaces. "What's wrong? Where are we goin'?"

"Just outside, for a little walk. Your mother's going to meet us."

Billy wiped the last ghosts of sleep out of his eyes. Gram was still wearing her overalls and plaid shirt, but she'd taken off her hat and her silver hair gleamed in the lantern's light; there was a brightly colored scarf tied around her forehead like a sweatband. "Follow me," she said when he was ready to go.

They left the house through the kitchen door. The sky was filled with stars, the moon as orange as a bloated pumpkin. Billy followed his grandmother to the small smokehouse, and saw a column of white smoke curling up from the chimney. Suddenly Ramona stepped out of the darkness into the lantern's wash, and she placed a firm hand on his shoulder. His heart began beating harder, because he knew that whatever secret lessons he was supposed to learn were about to begin.

Ramona brushed off his shirt and straightened his collar, as if preparing him for church. She was smiling, but Billy had seen the worry in his mother's eyes. "You're going to do just fine," she said in a small, quiet voice.

"Yes ma'am." He was trying to be brave, though he eyed the smokehouse nervously.

"Are you afraid?"

He nodded.

His grandmother stepped forward and stared down at him. "*Too* afraid?" she asked, watching him carefully.

He paused, knowing they wouldn't teach him if he didn't want to learn; but he wanted to know why he'd seen Will Booker crawl up from the coal pile. "No," he said. "Not too afraid."

"Once it starts, it can't be stopped," Rebekah said, as a last warning to both of them. Then she leaned down in front of Billy, her old back and knees cracking, and held up the lantern so the light splashed across his face. "Are you strong, boy?"

"Sure. I've got muscles, and I can—"

"No. Strong in here." She thumped his chest, over the heart. "Strong enough to go into dark places and come back out again, stronger still. Are you?"

The old woman's gaze defied him. He glanced up at the white column of smoke and touched the outline of the piece of coal in his pocket; then his spine stiffened and he said firmly, "Yes."

"Good. Then we're ready." Rebekah straightened up and threw back the latch of the smokehouse door. A wave of heat slowly rolled out, making the lantern's light shimmer. Ramona took Billy's hand and followed her mother inside, and then the door was shut again and bolted from within.

A pinewood fire, bordered by rough stones, burned on the earthen floor; directly above it, hanging down several feet from the ceiling, was a circular metal flue, through which the smoke ascended to the chimney. The fire, Billy saw, had been burning for some time, and the bed of coals on which it lay seethed red and orange. There were wooden racks and hooks for hanging meat; Rebekah hung the lantern up on one and motioned for Billy to sit down in front of the fire. When he'd situated himself, the hot glow of the flames like a tight mask across his cheeks, his grandmother unfolded a heavy quilt from where it had lain on a storage rack and draped it around Billy's shoulders, working it tightly so only his hands and face were free. Brightly colored blankets had been draped along the smokehouse walls to seal in the heat and smoke. A dark purple clay owl dangled from one of the hooks, its ceramic feathers gleaming; from another hook hung a strange red ceramic mask, from another what looked like a hand gripping a heart, and from a fourth hook a grinning white ceramic skull.

Ramona sat on his right. The old woman reached up to the flue, touched a small lever, and a baffle clanked shut. Smoke began to drift to all sides, slowly and sinuously. Then Rebekah reached into a bag in the corner and came up with a handful of wet leaves; she spread them over the fire, and the smoke instantly thickened, turning bluish gray and curling low to the floor. She took three more objects from the storage rack—a blackened clay pipe, a leather tobacco pouch decorated with blue and yellow beads, and a battered old leather-bound Bible—and then eased herself down to the floor on Billy's left. "My old bones can't take too much more of this," she said quietly, arranging the items in front of her. Flames leapt, scrawling crooked shadows across the walls; burning leaves sparked and crackled. The smoke was getting dense now, and bringing tears to Billy's eyes; sweat dripped down his face and off the point of his chin.

"This is the beginning," Rebekah said, looking at the boy. "From this time on, everything is new and has to be relearned. You should first of all know who you are, and *what* you are. A purpose sings in you, Billy, but to understand it you have to learn the song." The firelight glinted in her dark eyes as her face bent closer to his. Beads of sweat rolled down from her forehead into the sweatband. "The Choctaw song, the song of life sent to us from the Giver of Breath. He's in this Book"—she touched the Bible—"but He's everywhere, too. Inside, outside, in your heart and soul, and in the world. . . ."

"I thought He lived in church," Billy said.

"In the church of the body, yes. But what's brick and wood?" Rebekah opened the pouch and began to fill the pipe with a dark, oily-looking mixture of bark and herbs, plus green shreds from a fernlike plant that grew on the banks of the distant stream. "Hundreds of years ago, all this was Choctaw land," and she motioned with a broad sweep of her hand that stirred the layers of smoke. "Alabama, Mississippi, Georgia . . . our people lived here in peace, as farmers near to the earth. When the whites came, they wanted this land because they saw how good it was; the Giver of Breath decreed to us that we should accept them, and learn to live in the white world while other tribes fought and perished. The Choctaw survived, without fighting, but now we're the people no one remembers. Still, our blood runs strong and proud, and what we've learned in our minds and hearts goes on. The Giver of Breath is God of the Choctaw, but no different from the white man's God—the same God, without favorites, with love for all men and women. He speaks in the breeze, in the rain, and in the

116

smoke. He speaks to the heart, and can move a mountain by using the hand of a man." She finished with the pipe, touched a smoldering twig to the tobacco, and puffed on it to get it going. Then she took it from her mouth, her eyes watering, and gave it to Billy, who looked at her with bewilderment. "Take it," Rebekah said. "It's for you. Ramona, we need more leaves, please."

Billy took the pipe while his mother fed more wet leaves to the fire. He took a tentative puff that almost knocked his head off, and he was convulsed with coughing for a moment. The smoke and heat seemed to be closing in, and he could hardly breathe. Panic streaked through him, but suddenly his grandmother's hand was on his arm and she said, "It's all right. Relax; now try it again."

He did, as acrid gray smoke bellowed from the fire. The pipe smoke seared the back of his throat as he drew it in, and black dots spun before his eyes.

"You'll get used to it," Rebekah said. "Now where was I? Oh, yes. The Giver of Breath. God of the Choctaws. God of the white man. He also gives gifts of talent, Billy, to use for His good. Inhale the smoke, all the way. Yes, that's right. Some people can paint beautiful pictures, some can make sweet music, others work with their hands, and some with their wits; but in all people is the seed of talent, to do *something* of value in this world. And doing that—perfecting that talent, making the seed grow to good fruit—should be the aim of this life."

Billy inhaled again and coughed violently. The quilt was damp with his sweating, and still the heat continued to mount. "Even me, Gram? Is that seed in me?"

"Yes. Especially in you." She took off the kerchief, wiped her eyes with it, and handed it across the boy to Ramona, who mopped at the freely running sweat on her face and neck.

Billy stared into the fire. His head was full of a burning-rope odor, and now the smoke even tasted sweet. The flames seemed to be flaring brighter; they held beautiful glints of rainbow colors, entrancing him. He heard himself speak as if from a distance: "What kind of seed is it?"

"Billy, all three of us share something very special, something that's been passed down to us through the generations. We don't know how it began, or where it will end, but . . . we can see the dead, Billy, and we can speak to them."

He trembled, watching the flames shoot out brilliant green-and-orange lights. Through the thick haze of smoke shadows capered

117

on the walls. "No," he whispered. "That's . . . *evil*, like
. . . like Daddy says!"

"Your father's wrong," Ramona said, "and he's afraid. There's
dignity in death. But sometimes . . . there are those who need
help in passing over from this world to the next, like Will Booker
did. Will couldn't rest until he was lying next to his folks, but his
spirit—his soul—will go on. Call them haunts, or ghosts, or
revenants—but some of them cling to this world after death, out of
confusion, pain, or fear; some of them are stunned and wander
looking for help. But all of them have to find peace—they have to
give up their emotions, and the feelings they had at the instant of
death if those feelings are keeping them here in this world—before
they can pass over. I'm not saying I understand death, and I'm not
saying I know what Heaven and Hell are going to be like, but
death itself isn't evil, Billy; it's the call to rest after a long day's
work."

Billy opened his eyes and put a trembling hand to his forehead.
You're in the darrrrrk place, a voice in his head hissed. It became
Jimmy Jed Falconer's thunderous roar: YOU'RE A GUEST OF
SATAN! "I don't want to go to Hell!" he moaned suddenly, and
tried to fight free of the constricting blanket. "I don't want Satan
to get me!"

Rebekah quickly gripped his shoulders and said, "Shhhhhh. It's
all right now, you're safe right here." She let him lean his head on
her shoulder and rocked him gently while Ramona added wet
leaves to the fire. After another moment he calmed down, though
he was still shaking. The heat was stifling now, but most of the
smoke had risen to the ceiling where it undulated in thick gray
layers. "Maybe Hell's just something a man made up," she said
softly, "to make some other man afraid. I think that if Hell exists,
it must be right here on this earth . . . just like Heaven can be,
too. No, I think death's apart from all that; it's another step in who
and what we are. We leave the clay behind and our spirits take
flight." She tilted his face up and looked into his eyes. "That's not
saying, though, that there isn't such a thing as evil. . . ."

Billy blinked. His grandmother was a shadowy form, surrounded by a halo of reddish white light. He felt weary and struggled to
keep his eyes open. "I'll . . . fight it," he mumbled. "I'll hit
it . . . and kick it, and . . ."

"I wish it was as simple as that," Rebekah said. "But it's
cunning and takes all kinds of shapes. It can even make itself

beautiful. Sometimes you don't see it for what it is until it's too late, and then it scars your spirit and gets a hold on you. The world itself can be an evil place, and make people sick to their guts with greed and hate and envy; but evil's a greedy hog that walks on its own legs, too, and tries to crush out any spark of good it can find."

As if in a dream, Billy lifted the pipe and drew from it again. The smoke tasted as smooth as a licorice stick. He was listening very carefully to his grandmother, and watching the undulating smoke at the ceiling.

The old woman brushed a sweat-damp curl from his forehead. "Are you afraid?" she asked gently.

"No," he replied. "But I'm . . . kinda sleepy."

"Good. I want you to rest now, if you can." She took the pipe from him and knocked the ashes into the fire.

"Can't," he said. "Not yet." And then his eyes closed and he was drifting in the dark, listening to the fire's soft crackling; the dark wasn't frightening, but instead was warm and secure.

Rebekah eased him to the ground, tucking the blanket in around him so he'd continue sweating. Ramona added more leaves to the fire and then they left the smokehouse.

19

Billy came awake with sudden start. He was alone. The fire had burned down to red embers; the heat was still fierce, and thick smoke had settled in a calm, still cloud at the ceiling. His heart was beating very fast, and he struggled to get free of the blanket. The grinning ceramic skull glinted with low red light.

And suddenly something began to happen in the fire. Flames snapped and hissed. As Billy stared, transfixed, a long fiery coil slowly rose from the embers. It rattled, sending off tiny red sparks.

A burning, spade-shaped head with eyes of sizzling cinders rose up. Red coils tangled and writhed, pushing the fiery length of flaming rattlesnake out of the fire and toward Billy. Its eyes fixed upon him, and when its jaws opened drops of burning venom, like shining rubies, drooled out. The snake slithered closer, with a noise like paper charring, across the clay floor; Billy tried to pull away, but he was tangled up in the blanket. He couldn't find his voice. The flame-rattler touched his blanket; the cloth sparked and burned. It reared back, its body a seething red, to strike.

Billy started to kick at it, but before he could, something gray and almost transparent swooped down from the cloud of smoke at the ceiling.

It was a large, fierce-looking eagle, its body and wings wraithlike, flurrying smoke. With a high, angered shriek that echoed within Billy's head, the smoke-eagle dropped through the air toward the flame-rattler, which reared back and spat sparks from between its burning fangs. The eagle swerved and dived again, its smoky claws gripping at the back of the snake's head. The two enemies fought for a few seconds, the eagle's wings beating at the air. Then the fire-snake's tail whipped up, striking into the eagle, and the eagle spun away.

Balancing on tattered wings, the smoke-eagle dropped down again, its claws clamping just behind the snake's head; the flame-rattler buried its burning jaws within the eagle's breast, and Billy could see its dripping fangs at work. But then the eagle slashed downward, and parts of the rattler's body hissed through the air in fragments of fire. Coils of flame wrapped around the eagle's form, and both of them whirled in a mad circle for a few seconds like a burning gray cloth. The eagle's wings drove them both upward, up into the cloud of smoke, and then they were gone except for a few droplets of flame that fell back into the embers.

Sweat blinded Billy, and he frantically rubbed his eyes to clear them, expecting the strange combatants to come hurtling back.

"It's sin, Billy," a quiet voice said from just behind the boy.

Startled, Billy looked around. His father, gaunt and sad-eyed, sat there on the clay floor in overalls and a faded workshirt. "Daddy!" Billy said, astounded. "What're you doing here?"

The man shook his head gravely. "This is all sin. Every last bit of it."

"No, it's not! Gram said . . ."

John leaned forward, his blue eyes blazing with reflected

firelight. "It is rotten, filthy, black evil. That woman is trying to mark your soul, son, so you'll belong to Satan for the rest of your life."

"But she says there are things I have to learn! That I've got a purpose in me, to . . ."

He moaned softly, as if the boy's words had hurt him. "All this . . . this *talk* don't mean a thing, son. You're a smart, upright boy, and you've never given heed to talk about haunts and spirits before, have you? This Mystery Walk thing is wrong, and it's deadly dangerous." He held out his hand. "Take my hand, Billy, and I'll lead you out of this vile place. Come on. Trust your daddy."

Billy almost reached out for him. His father's eyes were bright and pleading, and he could tell how much his father was hurting for him. Still . . . something wasn't right. He said, "How . . . how did you get here? We came in the car, so . . . how did you get here?"

"I came on the bus as fast as I could, to save you from Satan's pitchfork. And he'll stick you, Billy; oh yes, he'll stick you hard and make you scream if you stay in this dark place. . . ."

"No. You're wrong. Gram said . . ."

"I don't care what she said!" the man told him. "Take my hand."

Billy stared at the fingers. The fingernails were black. "You're not . . . my daddy," he whispered, recoiling in terror. "You're *not!*"

And suddenly the man's face began to melt like a wax candle, as Billy saw him clearly for what he was. The nose loosened and oozed down on thick strands of flesh; beneath it was a black, hideous snout. A cheek slid down to the point of the chin like a raw egg, then fell away. The lower jaw collapsed, exposing a thin mouth with two curved yellow tusks. One blue eye rolled out of the head like a marble, and underneath it was a small, terrible red orb that might have belonged to a savage boar. As the face crumbled, that red eye was unblinking. "Boy," the thing whispered in a voice like fingernails drawn down a blackboard, "get out of here! Run! Run and hide, you little peckerhead!"

Billy almost lurched to his feet in panic. The awful face—the same face he'd seen on the road—loomed closer, red in the flickering light. It thundered, "RUN!" But as before, Billy was frozen with fear.

Are you strong? he remembered Gram asking him. *Are you strong in your heart?* "Yes I am strong," he said hoarsely. "Yes I am strong."

The thing paused, and then roared with laughter that hurt Billy's head. The second blue eye rolled out of its face, and the two red orbs glittered. Billy almost leaped up and ran—but then the image of the majestic eagle surfaced in his mind, and he steeled himself. He looked the beast in the face, determined not to show he was afraid. The thing's laughter faded. "All right," it whispered, and seemed to draw away from him. "I have better things to do. Finish this travesty. Learn all you can, and learn it well. But don't turn your back on me, boy." The shape began to melt down into a black, oily puddle on the floor. The misshapen mouth said, "I'll be waiting for you," and then the figure was gone. The shimmering puddle caught blue fire, and in an instant it too had vanished.

Something touched his shoulder, and he spun away with a husky groan of fear.

"Lord God, boy," Rebekah said, her eyes narrowed. "What's got into you?" She eased herself down before the fire again, as Ramona added wood and leaves to the embers. "You're shakin' like a cold leaf! We've just been gone for five minutes!" She stared at him for moment, and tensed. "*What happened?*"

"Nothin'. Nothin' happened. I didn't see a thing!"

Rebekah glanced quickly at her daughter, then back to the boy. "All right," she said. "You can tell me when you like." She helped him to the edge of the fire again, and he stared sightlessly into it as she began to knead his neck and shoulders with her strong brown hands. "Havin' this gift—this talent, I guess you could call it—isn't an easy thing. No kind of real responsibility is ever easy. But sometimes responsibility blocks you off from other people; they can't see into your head, they can't understand your purpose, and they mock you for doin' what you think is right. Some people will be afraid of you, and some may hate you . . ."

As the old woman spoke, Ramona looked at her son, examined his face in the firelight. She knew he'd be a fine-looking young man, handsome enough to knock the girls for a loop when he went to Fayette County High School; but what would his life be like? Shut off from other people? Feared and hated by the community, as both she and her mother had been? She recalled Sheriff Bromley's words, that things would never be the same for Billy again, and she felt an aching in her heart. He was growing up right now, in front of her eyes, though she knew that in following the Mystery Walk it was essential to keep part of childhood always within you as a shelter from the storm of the world, and also because a child's vision and understanding were most times better than a grown-up's hard, rational view of the world.

". . . but usin' that talent right is harder still," Rebekah was saying. "You've got to think of yourself as a gate, Billy, on the edge between this world and the next. You've got to learn to open yourself up, and let those in need pass through. But you'll have to keep their fear and pain inside yourself, like a sponge soaks up water, so they can pass through with an unburdened soul. That's not an easy thing to do, and I can't help you learn it; that'll come from within you, when the time is right. And doing it once doesn't make the next time any simpler, either, but you'll find you can stand it. The first one is the worst, I guess, 'cause you don't know what to expect."

"Does it hurt?"

"Kind of. Oh, not the same hurt like gettin' a shot at the doctor's office, or scrapin' your knee on a rock, but it hurts in here"—she touched the center of her chest—"and in here"—and then her forehead. "It's a hurt you'll inherit from those you're trying to help. And I won't say you'll be able to help all the time, either; some revenants just won't give up this world, maybe because they're too afraid to go on. If they were mean or crazy in life, they may try to do . . . worse things, like hurtin' people." She felt his shoulders tense under her hands. "Or, more rightly, they scare folks into hurtin' themselves, one way or another."

Billy watched the wet leaves curl, blacken, and burn. He sat still trembling from seeing that awful boar-thing, and now he tried to puzzle out what his grandmother was saying. "I thought . . . when you passed on it was like going to sleep, and if you were good you went to Heaven. Isn't that right?"

"But what if you *had* to go to sleep, but didn't want to? Wouldn't you toss and turn for a while, your restless self just makin' you miserable? And what if you were doin' something real important, or plannin' big things, or lookin' forward to a fine tomorrow when all the lights went out? Or what if you tried to sleep with an awful pain in you? Then you'd need help, wouldn't you, to rest easy? I'm not saying all revenants cling to this world; most of them find their own way through. In your lifetime you might only be called on to help two or three, but you *will* be called, and you'll have to do something with it. . . ."

"Like what?" He blew sweat off his upper lip; he was still very dizzy, and heard his grandmother's voice as if listening to crosscurrents of echoes from out of a dark, deep cave.

"I put mine into pottery," Rebekah told him. "Your mother put hers into her needlepoint. Your great-grandfather could sing up a storm in a hot tub on a Saturday night. That's up to you to find, when you have so much hurt inside you that you'll have to get rid of it or . . ." Her voice trailed off.

"Or what, Gram?" Billy prompted.

The old woman said softly, "Or you could lose yourself in other people's pain. Several members of our family . . . lost themselves that way, and took their own lives out of despair. A couple of them tried to escape their purpose in liquor and drugs. One of your uncles, a long way back, lost his mind and spent his life in an asylum. . . ."

That hit him like a fist to the back of his head. Tears welled in his eyes; maybe he was already about to "lose his mind," he thought with numbed horror. After all, hadn't he seen a smoke-eagle and a fire-serpent fighting right in front of him? Hadn't he seen something evil dressed up in his daddy's skin? He sobbed, and haltingly he told his grandmother and Ramona what he'd witnessed. They listened intently, and it seemed to him that his grandmother's eyes were as black as coals in her brown, seamed face.

When he was finished, Rebekah dipped her sweatband in a bucket of cool well-water she'd brought in and wiped his face. The water's chill in the stifling smokehouse heat sent a delicious shock through him, calming his feverish brain. "They're pictures in your head, Billy. There'll be more before you're through. I think everybody has some eagle and some snake in them; they fight to pull your spirit high or drag it to the ground. The question is: which one do you let win, and at what price? The second thing you saw"—a shade seemed to pass before her face, like a thundercloud before the sun—"is what I warned you to watch for. You must've shown it you weren't afraid—but it won't give up so easily. Ramona, will you pass me that jug?" She unscrewed the sealed brown bottle Ramona had brought in with her and poured into the cup a thick dark liquid that smelled of sassafras and cinnamon.

124

"There may come a time, Billy," Rebekah continued softly, "when evil tries to crush you out, like someone snuffing a candle. It'll try to work on your weaknesses, to turn things around in your head so up is down and inside is out. I've seen that thing too, Billy—what looks like a wild boar—and it's so loathsome you can hardly bear to look at it. It used to taunt me in the night, when I was younger than your mother, and one morning not long ago I woke up to find all of my pottery shattered on the floor in the workshed. My house has caught fire before, for no reason at all. You remember that yellow mutt I had, named Chief? I never told you what really happened to him, but I found him scattered in the woods behind the house, like something had just torn him to pieces. That was the last dog I ever had. And what I mean to say is that the thing you saw—what my father used to call the 'shape changer' because it can take on any form it pleases—has been our enemy for a long, long time. Almost everyone in our family's seen it; it's a dangerous, sly beast, Billy, and it tries to hurt us through the people and things we care for. It probes for a weakness, and that's why we have to keep ourselves strong. If we don't, it could work on our mind—or maybe physically hurt us too."

"What is it?" His voice had dropped to a frail whisper. "Is it the Devil, Gram?"

"I don't know. I just know it's very old, because even the first Choctaw spirit healers used to weave stories of the 'beast with skin of smoke.' There are tales of the shape changer going back hundreds of years—and some in our family, those who weren't strong enough to resist it, were either beguiled by its lies or torn to pieces by its hatred. You never know what it's planning, but it must sense a threat in you or it wouldn't have come to take a look at you."

"Why, Gram? Why does it hate us?"

"Because it's a greedy beast that uses fear to make itself stronger. It feeds like a hog at a trough on the human emotions of despair, torment, and confusion; sometimes it traps revenants and won't let them break away from this world. It feeds on their souls, and if there's a Hell, I suppose that must be it. But when *we* work to free those revenants, to take their suffering into ourselves and do something constructive with it, we steal from the shape changer's dinner table. We send those poor souls onward to where the shape changer can't get at them anymore. And that's why the beast wants nothing more than to stop your Mystery Walk."

"I don't know what to do!" he whispered.

"You have to believe in yourself, and in the Giver of Breath. You have to keep pressing forward, no matter what happens, and you can't turn away from your responsibility. If you do, you make a weak hole in yourself that the shape changer might try to reach into. The beast doesn't care about your mother or me anymore, Billy, because most of our work is done; it's you, the new blood, he's watching."

"Can it *hurt* me, Gram?"

"I don't know," she said, and thought of Chief's carcass scattered through the brush, pieces of him hanging from low tree branches as if he'd exploded from within.

"I want you to drink this, Billy. It'll help you sleep. We can talk more about it later." She gave him the cup of liquid from the jug. Its inviting aroma drifted up to him. His head felt like a lead cannonball, his bones aching from the heat. He thought he could easily fall asleep without drinking this stuff, but he sipped at it anyway; it was pleasantly sweet, though just underneath the sugar was a musky taste, like the smell of wild mushrooms growing in a green, damp place.

"All of it," Rebekah said. Billy drank it down. She smiled. "That's very good."

He smiled in return, through a mask of running sweat. The boar-thing was fading now, as all nightmares do in time. He stared into the embers, saw all the hundred variations of color between pale orange and dark violet, and his eyelids began to droop. The last thing he remembered seeing before the darkness closed in was the ceramic owl, watching over him from its smokehouse hook.

They left him lying on his back on the clay floor, the blanket wrapped around him like a heavy shroud. Outside, Rebekah locked the door. "No need for us to look in on him again until morning." She stretched, hearing her backbone creak. "Seems to me he understood everything pretty much, but it's his confidence needs working on. We'll start again tomorrow night."

"Will he be safe?" Ramona asked as they walked to the house, following the track of Rebekah's lantern.

"I hope so. He saw his twin natures, the good and the bad at war inside him, and he looked the shape changer in the face." They reached the back door, and Ramona stopped to peer through the darkness at the smokehouse. Rebekah laid a hand on her shoulder. "Billy's already being poked and prodded, picked at for

126

a weak spot. I didn't know it would start so soon. He resisted this time, but it won't return in that form again. No, the foe will be different and stronger. But so will Billy be, different and stronger."

"Should he know about the black aura yet?"

"No. He'll grow into seeing it, just like you did. I don't want to put that on him just yet." She regarded her daughter, her head cocked to one side. "He'll sleep through the day. If you hear him cry out, you're not to go in there and wake him up. His old life is being shattered so the new one can start. Do you understand?"

"Yes," Ramona said. "It's just that . . . he's alone."

"And that's how it has to be. After these three days are over you might be at his side, but the rest of the way he has to go alone. You knew that before you brought him to me." Rebekah squeezed her daughter's shoulder gently. "I was wrong about him; his blood may be tainted, but his heart and soul are strong. He'll make you proud, girl. Now come on, and I'll make us a pot of tea."

Ramona nodded and followed her mother into the house, shutting the screen door quietly.

Within the smokehouse, the boy had curled up like an infant about to emerge into light.

FIVE

Black Aura

20

"Billy?" Coy Granger called out toward the grocery store's small magazine rack. "Found it for you!" He held up a dusty plastic-wrapped needlepoint kit. "It was buried in a box back in the storeroom. Now you say you need some roofin' nails?"

"Yes sir. Couple of packs will do." The boy looked up from the sports magazine he'd been paging through and then ambled over to the counter while Granger found the nails. It was early May of 1969, and Billy Creekmore was seventeen. He'd already topped six feet, and now stood as tall as his father; though he was big-boned, again like his father, he was on the lean side, just short of being skinny, and his wrists shot out from the old blue workshirt he wore, dappled with grease and oil from his job at the gas station. With the thinning of his face, his cheekbones had angled and risen up from the flesh, and his eyes were dark hazel, flecked with glints of amber when the light hit them just so. The warm spring sunshine had already darkened Billy's flesh to a nut-brown color, and his dark hair was a confusion of curls and unruly cowlicks, jumbling down over his forehead in commas. His hair wasn't cut as severely as it once had been, since Curtis Peel had finally read in a barbershop trade magazine that longer hair was definitely the "in-thing" for his younger customers—much to the chagrin of their parents, who could fly into fits when they happened to hear Beatles music on a radio.

Billy had grown into a handsome young man in the seven years since he'd visited his grandmother and sweated himself into a stupor in her smokehouse. Still, there was a wariness in his eyes, a careful shell to protect himself against the whispers he overheard in the halls of Fayette County High. They could talk about him all they liked; he didn't care, but once he heard his mother's or grandmother's name mentioned, he turned upon the offender with a vengeance. He wasn't mean, though, and was unprepared for the mean tricks used in after-school fights by country boys who were growing up to be the spitting images of their fathers; crotch kicks and eye gouges were common, and many times Billy had found himself ringed by gleefully shouting kids while his face banged into somebody's kneecap. There was no one he could really call a close friend, though he dreamed of being popular and going out on Saturday nights to Fayette with the gregarious bunch of kids who seemed to get along so well with just about everybody. It had taken him a long time to accept the fact that people were afraid of him; he saw it in their eyes when he walked into a room, heard it when conversations were cut off in his presence. He was different—it was difference enough that he was dark-skinned and obviously of Indian heritage—and since entering Fayette County High he'd been effectively isolated. His crust of caution went deep, protecting his self-respect and his still-childlike sense of wonder at the world.

He read a lot—damaged hardbacks and paperback novels he sometimes found at garage sales. He'd come across a real find several weeks ago: a boxful of old *National Geographics* brought up from someone's basement, where they'd been moldering for a while. His treks—through forests, following the disused railroad tracks and old logging roads—were taking him farther and farther away from home; often, when the weather wasn't too chilly, he'd take a bedroll out into the woods and spend the night, content with his own company and listening to the forest noises that punctuated the darkness. Out in the velvet black you could see shooting stars by the hundreds, and sometimes the faint blinking lights of an airplane headed for Birmingham. In the daytime he enjoyed the sun on his face, and could track deer like an expert, sometimes coming up within twenty feet or so of them before they sensed him.

His curiosity always burned within him to take one more step, to just round the next curve or top the next ridge; the world was beckoning him away from Hawthorne, away from the house where his quiet mother and his grim-lipped father waited for him.

"Here you go," Granger said, and laid the packs of nails on the counter along with the other items—bread, bacon, sugar, milk, and flour—that Billy had come for. John owed Granger a good deal of money, and sent Billy in for groceries these days; Granger knew the Creekmores were just getting by on the skin of their teeth, and that those roofing nails would be used to try to hold that shack they called a house together for one more hot summer. The last time that Granger had demanded his money, at the end of winter, Billy had worked for him in the afternoons for free, delivering groceries; now Billy was working out John Creekmore's gasoline and oil tab at the filling station. "Want me to put this on your credit?" he asked the boy, trying to keep a hard edge out of his voice; though he honestly liked Billy, his feelings for John Creekmore's credit were showing through.

"No sir," Billy said, and took out a few dollars from his jeans.

"Well! John go to market early this year?" He started adding up figures on a notepad.

"Mom sold some of her pieces to a dealer in Fayette. I don't think this is enough to take care of what we owe you, but . . ."

Granger took the money and shrugged. "It's all right. I'll still be here." He made change and handed back the few coins. "Too bad John didn't get that job at the sawmill, huh? They pay pretty good up there, I understand."

"Yes sir, but they only hired five new men, and Dad says over fifty showed up to get work." Billy started sacking the groceries. "I guess a lot of folks need the money pretty bad, what with the droughts we've been having."

"Yes," Coy agreed. He couldn't think of any family offhand who needed money any worse than the Creekmores. Perhaps the only business that was really thriving in Hawthorne was the Chatham brothers' sawmill; they had owned the family mill for over forty years, still housed in the same run-down wooden structure with most of the same engines and belts running the saws. "Well, maybe they'll be hirin' more in the fall. Have you given any thought to your own future?"

Billy shrugged. Mr. Dawson, who taught auto mechanics at Fayette County, had told him he was pretty quick at catching on to how machines worked and would probably make a good wrench-jockey after high school; the boy's adviser, Mr. Marbury, had said his grades were very high in English and reading comprehension, but not quite high enough to get him a junior-college scholarship. "I don't know. I guess I'll help out my dad for a while."

Coy grunted. The Creekmore land hadn't produced a good crop in three years. "You ought to get into the construction business, Billy. I hear some of the contractors up around Fayette are going to be hirin' laborers. That's good pay, too. You know, I think

Hawthorne's a losin' proposition for a bright young man like you. I wouldn't say that to just anybody, but there's a real spark in you. You *think*, you reason things out. Nope. Hawthorne's not for you, Billy."

"My folks need me." He grinned. "I'm the only one who can keep the Olds running."

"Well, that's no kind of a future." The bell over the front door clanged, and Billy looked up as Mrs. Pettus and Melissa—her radiant blue-eyed face framed by a bell of hair the color of pale summer straw—came into the grocery store. Billy forgot to breathe for an instant; he saw her every day at Fayette County High, but still there was a quiver of electric tension down in his stomach. The school dance—May Night—was less than two weeks away, and Billy had been trying to muster the courage to ask her before anyone else did, but whenever he thought he was about to approach her he'd remember that he had no money or driver's license, and that his clothes had been worn by someone else before him. Melissa always wore bright dresses, her face scrubbed and shining. Billy picked up his sacked groceries, wanting to get out before Melissa saw his grease-stained hands and shirt.

"My, my!" Coy said. "Don't you two look lovely this afternoon!"

"That's what ladies do best!" Mrs. Pettus said merrily. She put a protective arm around her daughter as the Creekmore boy stepped past.

"Hi," Billy blurted out.

Melissa smiled and nodded her head, and then her mother pulled her on into the store.

He watched her over his shoulder as he neared the door, and saw her look quickly back at him. His heart pounded. And then the cowbell clanged over his head and he ran into someone who was coming through the door.

"Whoa there, Billy!" Link Patterson said, trying to sidestep. "You gatherin' wool, boy?" He grinned good-naturedly; in another instant the grin had frozen on his face, because Billy Creekmore was staring at him as if he'd sprouted horns from the top of his head.

Billy's blood had gone cold. Link Patterson looked healthy and well fed, possibly because he was one of the few men who'd gotten a job at the sawmill and his life had taken a turn for the better; his wife was expecting their second child in October, and he'd just made the first payment on a trailer parked outside the town limits. But Billy saw him enveloped in a purplish black haze of light, a hideous cocoon that slowly writhed around him.

Link laughed nervously. "What's wrong? Looks like you'd seen a . . ." The word *ghost* lay in his mouth like cold lead, and he swallowed it.

Billy slowly reached out; his fingers touched the haze, but felt nothing. Link shrank back a step. "Boy? What the hell's wrong with you?"

Coy Granger, Mrs. Pettus, and Melissa were watching. Billy blinked and shook his head. "Nothing, Mr. Patterson. Sorry. I . . . sorry." And then he was out the door and gone, hurrying along the road with the sack of groceries clamped in the crook of an arm. With a few more steps he began running, feeling scared and sick. *What did I see?* he asked himself, and didn't stop running even when he passed the green, grown-over ruin of the Booker house.

"Pack of Kents, Coy," Link Patterson said. As Granger got his cigarettes, Link stepped to the window and peered out, watching Billy running away. He could hear the high singsong of the saws; in fifteen minutes he'd be on the line, called in to fill the shift for a man who'd gotten sick and had to go home. "That Creekmore boy is . . . really strange, ain't he?" Link said, to no one in particular.

Mrs. Pettus answered. "He's got that wicked seed in him, that's what. My Melissa sees him at school every day and he's always picking fights, isn't he?"

"No, Momma," she replied, and pulled away from her mother's arm. "That's not how it is."

"Always picking fights. And he's such a nice-lookin' boy, too, to have such bad blood in him."

"Billy's all right," Coy said. "He's a smart boy. He'll go far if he can cut himself loose from that farm. Link, here're your cigarettes. How's work at the mill?"

"In bits and pieces," Link joked, trying to summon up a grin. The way Billy had stared at him had made him jittery. He paid for the cigarettes, went out to his pickup truck, and drove on toward the mill.

Link parked his truck in the gravel lot, took a few pulls from a cigarette to calm his jittery nerves, then crushed it out and put on his heavy canvas safety gloves. Then he walked the few dozen yards to the main building, past bunks of yellow pine logs sitting alongside the railroad tracks; they were newly arrived, oozing sap, and ready to be hauled into the small pond behind the mill before the hot weather made them harden and swell. He went up a flight of rickety stairs to the main hall.

Before he opened the door, the noise of the saws was simply irritating; when he stepped inside, into a golden haze of sawdust and friction heat thrown off by the whirring circular saws, band saws, and ponies, the shrill scream of machinery pounded into his forehead like a sledgehammer. He fished earplugs from his pocket and screwed them in place, but they helped hardly at all. The smell of raw lumber and sawdust in the air scratched the back of Link's throat. He clocked in next to the glassed-in office where Lamar Chatham sat at his desk, the telephone to one ear and an index finger plugging the other.

The mill was working at full speed. Link saw where he was needed—the master sawyer, Durkee, was operating the headrig and aligning the logs, a two-man job that was slowing down the flow of timber—and hurried toward the far end of the line. He took his place next to the whining headrig and began operating the long lever that sped up or braked the circular saw, while grizzled old Durkee judged the raw logs and maneuvered them so they'd go into the headrig at the proper angle and speed. Link worked the lever, adjusting the saw's speed to Durkee's shouted orders.

The logs kept coming, faster and faster. Link settled down to the routine, watching the oil-smeared gauge set into the machinery next to him, reading the saw's speed.

Bare light bulbs hung from the ceiling, illuminating the mill with a harsh and sometimes unreliable light: many men who'd worked the mill were missing fingers because they couldn't judge exactly where a fast-spinning sawrim was, due to poor lighting. Link let himself relax, became part of the trembling headrig. His mind drifted to his new trailer. It had been a good buy, and now that his second child was on the way it was good that he, Susie, and his son Jeff were out of that shack they'd lived in for years. It seemed that finally things were working out his way.

Durkee shouted, "This one's as punky as a rotten tooth!" and jabbed at the wood with a logger's hook. "Damn, what sorta shit they tryin' to pass through here!" He reached out, pushed the log's far end a few inches to line it up correctly, and made a motion with his forefinger to give the saw more speed. Link pushed the lever forward. The log started coming through, sawdust whirling out of the deepening groove as the teeth sank in. The headrig vibrated suddenly, and Link thought: This sonofabitch is gonna come a—

And then there was a loud *crack!* that vibrated through the mill. Link saw the log split raggedly as the saw slipped out of line. Durkee roared, "*SHUT HER DOWN!*" and Link wrenched the lever back, thinking *I've screwed up, I've screwed up, I've* . . .

Something flew up like a yellow dagger. The three-inch-long shard of wood pierced Link's left eye with a force that snapped his head back. He screamed in agony, clutched at his face, and stumbled forward, off-balance; instinctively he reached out to keep himself from going down . . . and the saw's scream turned into a hungry gobbling.

"*Help!*" Durkee shouted. "*Somebody cut the master switch!*"

Link staggered, blood streaming down his face. He lifted his right hand to clear his eyes, and saw in his hazed half-vision the wet nub of white bone that jutted from the mangled meat of his forearm. His hand, the fingers still twitching, was already moving down the conveyor belt wrapped in its bloody canvas glove.

And then the stump of his ruined arm shot blood like a firehose.

Someone hit the master switch. The machinery stopped, the saws whining down like angered wasps. Link's knees buckled. He was trying to scream, but he couldn't find his voice; instead, he could still hear the noise of the circular saw in his head— screaming, screaming in a hideous metallic voice. He couldn't get a breath, he was lying in sawdust, he was going to get dirty and he didn't want Susie to see him like this. ". . . Not like this," he moaned, clutching his arm close to his body, like an infant. "Oh God . . . oh God, not like this. . . ."

Voices cut through the haze above him. ". . . call the doc, hurry . . ."

". . . bandage it . . . tourniquet in the. . . !"

". . . somebody call his wife!"

"My hand," Link whispered. "Find . . . my hand. . . ." He couldn't remember now which hand was hurt, but he knew it had to be found so the doctor could stitch it back on. The sawdust around him was wet, his clothes were wet, everything was wet. A black wave roared through his head. "No!" he whispered. ". . . Not fair, not this way!" Tears streamed down his cheeks, mingling with the blood. He was aware of someone knotting a shirt around his forearm; everything was moving in slow motion, everything was crazy and wrong. . . .

". . . too much blood, the damned thing's not gonna . . ." a disembodied voice said, off in the distance. A shout, full of sharp echoes: ". . . *ambulance!*" and then fading away.

The black wave came back again, seemingly lifting him up from where he sat. It scared him, and he fought against it with his teeth gritted. "NO!" he cried out. "I WON'T LET IT . . . be . . . like this. . . ." The voices above him had merged into an indistinct mumbling. His eye hurt, that was the worst of it, and he couldn't see. "Clean my eye off," he said, but no one seemed to hear. A surge of anger swelled in him, searing and indignant. There was still so much to do, he realized. His wife to take care of! The new baby! The trailer he was so proud of and had put so much work into! I won't let it be like this! he screamed inwardly.

The light was fading. Link said, "I don't want it to get dark."

Above him, an ashen-faced and blood-spattered Durkee looked at the ring of stunned men and said, "What'd he say? Anybody hear him? Jesus, what a mess!" Durkee went down on his knees, cradling the younger man's head. Now that all the saws were quiet, they could hear an ambulance coming, but it was still on the other side of Hawthorne.

There were droplets of blood across the front of Lamar Chatham's white shirt. He was trembling, his hands curled into helpless fists at his sides. His brain was working furiously on two tracks: how to make up the work that was being lost and how to smooth this thing over with the safety inspectors. He saw Link Patterson's gloved hand lying on a conveyor belt like a large squashed spider; the air was rank with blood and icy with shock.

Durkee rose to his feet. He let out a long sigh and shook his head. "Somebody else'll have to close his eyes. I've had enough." He walked past Chatham without looking back.

21

John Creekmore stood stiffly in an ill-fitting black suit, the sun hot on his neck through a break in the pines. As Reverend Laken spoke, John looked back over his shoulder at the figure sitting up the hill perhaps fifty yards away, watching the funeral through the rows of small granite tombstones. Billy had been up there since John had arrived, before the funeral had started. The boy hadn't moved a muscle, and John knew the others had seen him up there too. John looked away, trying to concentrate on what Hawthorne's new minister was saying, but he could *feel* Billy sitting back amid the pines; he shifted his weight uneasily from one foot to the other, not knowing what to do with his hands.

"Amen," Reverend Laken finally said. The coffin was cranked down into the ground, and Susie sobbed so terribly John had to walk away from her. He stood and stared up at his son for a moment. Billy was motionless. John thrust his hands into his pockets and walked carefully toward him between the mounds of earth, his shoes slipping on the carpet of fresh pine needles. The boy's face was a tight mask of secrets; John knew that Ramona and Billy kept a world of secrets from him—dark things that had to do with the time Billy had spent at his grandmother's house. John didn't want to know what they were, fearing contamination, but for one thing he could be happy: Rebekah Fairmountain had gone to her hellish reward two years ago. Ramona and Billy had found her on the day after Christmas, sitting with her eyes closed in her easy chair, a yellowed picture of her late husband and a red vase full of wild flowers on a table at her side.

John reached his son. "What're you doin' here?"

"I wanted to come."

"People saw you sittin' up here. Why didn't you come down?"

He shook his head, amber lights glinting in his eyes; he was unable to explain his feelings, but when he'd seen that strange black haze clinging to Link Patterson he'd known something terrible was about to happen. He hadn't told his mother about it until later, after Mr. Patterson was lying dead up at the sawmill and the whole town knew there'd been an awful accident. As he'd watched the coffin being lowered, he'd wondered if he had had the power to change the man's destiny, perhaps with a single word of warning, or if the accident was already waiting for Link Patterson to step into it and nothing Billy could've said or done would've mattered.

"What did you come for?" John asked. "I thought you were supposed to be workin' at the gas station this afternoon."

"I asked for the afternoon off. It doesn't matter anyway."

"The hell it don't!" John felt a flush of unreasoned anger heat his face. "People see you sittin' up here among the graves, what are they gonna *think?* Damn it, boy! Don't you have a lick of sense anymore?" He almost reached down and hauled Billy to his feet, but restrained himself; lately his nerves had been on edge all the time, and he lost his temper like a shatterpated fool. A pang of shame stabbed him. *This is my son!* he thought. *Not a stranger I don't even know!* He abruptly cleared his throat. "You ready to go home now?"

They walked down the hill together, past the new grave with its bright bouquets of flowers, and to the Olds. The car was held together with more wire and odd junkyard pieces than Frankenstein's monster. The engine, when it finally caught, sounded as if it were gargling nuts and bolts. They drove out of the cemetery and toward home.

John saw it first: a white pickup truck with CHATHAM BROTHERS stenciled on its side in red was parked in front of the house. "Now what?" he said, and then thought: could be it's a job! His hands tightened around the steering wheel. Sure! They needed a new man on the line, since Link was . . . He was sickened at what he was thinking, but—sickened or not—his heart was beating harder in anticipation.

Lamar Chatham himself was sitting on the front porch with Ramona. He rose to his feet, a short heavy man in a seersucker suit, as the Olds approached.

John stopped the car, then stepped out. He was sweating profusely in the dark suit. "Howdy, Mr. Chatham," he called.

The man nodded, chewing on a toothpick. "Hello, Creek-more."

"My son and I went to pay our respects to Link Patterson. That was a terrible thing, but I guess a man can't be too careful around those saws. I mean, when you're workin' fast you've got to know what you're doin'." He caught Ramona's dark gaze on him, and again he felt a hot surge of anger. "I hear the mill's gonna be shut down for a while."

"That's right. I've been waitin' to speak to you."

"Oh? Well . . . what can I do for you, then?"

Chatham's fleshy face looked loose and slack, and there were gray patches beneath his blue eyes. He said, "Not you, Creek-more. I've been waitin' to speak to your boy."

"My boy? What for?"

Chatham took the toothpick from his mouth. "I meant to go to the funeral," he said, "but I had business. I sent some flowers, you probably saw 'em there. Orchids. One thing about funerals: they're supposed to be final, ain't they?"

"I guess so," John agreed.

"Yeah." He gazed off at the field for a moment, where a new crop of corn and pole beans were struggling out of the dusty earth. "I came to see your wife, and we had a good long talk about . . . things. But she says I should speak to Billy." He looked at John again. "Your wife says that Billy can do what has to be done."

"What? What has to be done?"

"Billy," the other man said quietly, "I need to talk to you, boy. . . ."

"Talk to *me*, damn it!" John's face flamed.

Ramona's voice was as soft as a cool breeze, but carried strength as well. "Tell him," she said.

"All right." Chatham inserted his toothpick again, looking from Billy to John and back again. "Yes ma'am, I will. First off, I want you all to know I don't believe in . . . in *haunts*." He gave a little lopsided grin that slipped off his uneasy face like thin grease. "Nosir! Lamar Chatham never believed in anything he couldn't see! But, you know, the world's just full of superstitious folks who believe in rabbit's feet and demons and . . . and especially *haunts*. Now you take rugged men who work hard for a livin', and who work in a place that maybe—*maybe*—is danger-ous. Sometimes they can be more superstitious than a gaggle of old farm women." He let out a nervous burp of a laugh, his cheeks swelling like a bullfrog's. "Link Patterson's been dead three days, and now he's buried. But . . . sometimes superstitions can get hold of a man's mind and just gnaw at him. They can chew a man down to nothin'."

"Like that damned saw did to Link," John said bitterly, all hopes of a job dashed to the winds. And worse, this bastard Chatham wanted *Billy!*

"Yeah. Maybe so. Sawmill's closed now. Shut down."

"About time some work was done to make that place safe. Those belts and drive gears ain't been changed for *years*, I hear tell."

"Maybe. Well, that ain't the reason the mill's shut down, Creekmore." He poked the toothpick at an offending bit of barbecue. "The mill's shut down," he said, "because the men won't work. I hired new ones. They walked out on me in less than an hour, yesterday. Production's fallin' behind. We turn a pretty fair profit, but too many days like these last few and"—he whistled and drew the stump of his index finger across his thick neck in a slashing gesture—"the whole town suffers for it. Hell, the sawmill *is* Hawthorne!"

"So what's that to us?"

"I came to see your wife because of who she is, and what her reputation says she can do. . . ."

"Get off my land."

"Now just a min—"

"GET OFF, I SAID!" he roared, and rushed the porch. Chatham stayed planted like a slab of wood, his thickset body tensed for a fight. He'd been a logging man since he was old enough to swing an ax, and he'd never run from a tangle yet in any of the rough camps where muscle was king. His posture and steady glare flared a warning, and John stopped halfway up the porch steps, his fists knotted and the cords in his neck as tense as piano wires. "Maybe you've got money," John snarled, "and maybe you wear fancy suits and fancy rings and you can work men like dogs, but this is *my* land, mister! And I'm tellin' you to move off of it, right *now!*"

"Creekmore," Chatham said with a hiss of breath between his teeth, "I own half this town. My brother owns the other half. Paper can be torn up, do you understand me? It can be misplaced. Listen, I don't want no trouble. Hell, I'm tryin' to offer your boy a job and pay him for it, too! Now back off, man!"

In the porch swing, Ramona saw the trapped-animal look in her husband's eyes, and her heart ached. She sat with her hands clasped in her lap as John said, "I don't . . . I don't . . . want you here. . . ."

And then Billy was coming up the steps, passing his father. He walked right up to Lamar Chatham and looked him directly in the eyes. "Are you threatening my father, Mr. Chatham?"

"No. 'Course not. Hell, there's a lot of steam needs to be blowed off around here! Ain't that right, John?"

The other man whispered, "Damn you . . . damn you. . . ."

"What is it you want with me?" Billy asked him.

"Like I say, I had a long talk with your mother. We came to an understandin', and she's asked me to talk to you. . . ."

John made a strangling sound; then he stepped back down the stairs and stood facing the pond. He clamped his hands to his ears.

Chatham paid him no attention. "I don't believe in haunts, Billy. No such thing in my book. But a lot of the men do. They won't work and I had to close the mill because . . . because of the saw Link Patterson stuck his hand into."

"The saw? What about it?"

Chatham glanced uneasily at Ramona Creekmore, then looked back into the boy's face. There were amber glints in Billy's eyes, and his gaze seemed so deeply penetrating Chatham thought he felt the short hairs at the back of his neck stir. Chatham said, "The saw screams. Like a man."

22

Twilight framed the sawmill against a sky of blue and gold. Shards of sunlight lay across the gravel parking lot like pieces of broken glass, and bunked piles of timber threw dark blue shadows.

"You drink yet, boy?" Lamar Chatham asked as he switched off the pickup's ignition and took the keys out.

"No sir."

"Time you started. Open that glove compartment there and fetch the bottle."

It was a flask of moonshine that Billy could smell even before Chatham uncapped it. The man took a swig and closed his eyes; Billy could almost see the veins in his bulbous nose lighting up. "You believe me when I say I don't think there's such a thing as a haunt?"

"Yes sir."

"Well, I'm a goddamned liar, boy. Sheeeit! My old daddy used to tell me ghost stories that made the hair on my ass curl! You won't catch me closer than a mile to a cemetery, that's for truth!" He passed the flask to Billy. "Mind you now, I don't care what you or your momma can or can't do. I've heard the stories about your mother, and I was there that night at the Falconer tent revival. That was one hell of an uproar. Once you go in my mill and . . . do whatever it is that has to be done, then I figure my men will come on back to work. And I'll make sure every last one of them knows what you did . . . even if you don't do a damned thing. Get my drift?"

Billy nodded. His insides were quaking. When he'd said he would help Mr. Chatham, his father had looked at him as if he were a leper. But Mr. Chantham had said he'd pay fifty dollars and so wasn't it right, Billy reasoned, that he help out the family as much as he could? Still, he didn't know exactly *what* he was supposed to do; he'd brought his good-luck piece of coal, but he knew that whatever had to be done would have to come from inside him, and he was on his own. Before he'd left the house, his mother had taken him inside and talked to him quietly, telling him that *his* time had come now, and he would have to do the best he could. Oh, she'd said, she could go with him this time to give him confidence, but it would all be his work anyway; there might not even be anything in the sawmill, she'd told him, but if there was it could be part of Link Patterson, in agony and unable to find its way across. Draw it to you with trust, and remember the lessons your grandmother taught you. Most importantly: blank the fear out of your mind, if you can, and let the revenant find *you*. It'll be searching for help, and it'll be drawn to you as if you were a candle in the dark.

As Billy had climbed into the white pickup truck, Ramona had stood on the porch and said to him, "Remember, son: *no fear.* I love you."

The light was slowly fading. Billy sniffed at the moonshine and then took a drink. It felt like lava at the back of his throat, and bubbled down his gullet searing tissues all the way to his stomach; it reminded him of the stuff Gram had made him drink to clean his stomach out before he'd gone into the smokehouse.

Sometimes at night, on the edge of sleep, he seemed to relive that entire strange experience. He'd stayed inside that sweltering smokehouse for three days, wrapped in the heavy blanket, with nothing to eat and only home-brewed "medicines" to drink. Lulled by the fierce heat, he'd drifted in the dark, losing all sense of time and space; his body had seemed cumbersome, like a suit of armor, trapping his real self within it. He was aware, though locked into sleep, of his mother and Gram looking in on him, and sitting with him for a while: he could tell the difference in their heartbeat, in their rhythms of breathing, in the aromas of their bodies and the sound of air parting around them as they moved. The crackling of the burning wood and leaves had become a kind of music alternating between soft harmony and rough pandemonium; smoke at the ceiling rustled like a silk shirt as it brushed the boards.

When he'd finally awakened and had been allowed out of the smokehouse, the morning sunlight had pierced his skin like needles, and the quiet forests had seemed a riot of cacophonous noise. It was several more days yet before his senses had settled down enough for him to feel comfortable again, yet even so he was and had remained fantastically aware of colors, aromas, and sounds; thus the pain was terrible when they'd returned home from Gram's, and his father had hit Ramona a backhanded blow across the face and then stropped Billy with a belt. Then the house was filled with his father's voice, torn between begging their forgiveness and loudly reading Bible verses.

Billy looked at the golden streamers of cloud across the sky and thought of how the papier-mâché decorations would look in the Fayette County High gym on May Night. He wanted very much to go to that dance, to fit in with all the others; he knew it might be his last chance. If he said no to Mr. Chatham now, if he let everybody know he was just a scared kid who didn't know anything about haunts or spirits, then maybe he could ask Melissa Pettus, and maybe she'd go with him to May Night and he'd get a job as a mechanic in Fayette and everything would be just fine for the rest of his life. Anyway, he'd hardly known Link Patterson, so what was he doing here?

Chatham said nervously, "I want to get through with this before it gets dark. Okay?"

Billy's shoulders slowly sagged forward. He got out of the truck.

They walked in silence up the wooden steps to the sawmill's entrance. Chatham fumbled with a ring of keys and then unlocked the door; before he stepped inside he reached in and switched on several banks of dimly glowing blubs that studded the raftered ceiling.

Greased machinery gleamed in the mixture of electric light and the last orange sunlight that filtered through a series of high, narrow windows. The smells of dust, woodsap, and machine oil thickened the air, and the place seemed hazed with a residue of sawdust. Chatham closed the door and motioned to the far end of the building. "It happened up there, right at the headrig. I'll show you." His voice sounded hollow in the silence.

Chatham stopped ten feet away from the headrig and pointed at it. Billy approached the saw, his shoes stirring up whorls of dust, and gingerly touched the large, jagged teeth. "He should've been wearin' safety glasses," Chatham said. "It wasn't my fault. Punky timber comes in all the time, it's a fact of life. He . . . he died about where you're standin'."

Billy looked at the floor. Sawdust had been spread over a huge brown stain; his mind went back to the stained floor in the Booker house, the hideous mark of death hidden with newspapers. The saw's teeth were cold against his hand; if he was supposed to *feel* anything here, he didn't: no electric shock, no sudden sure realization, nothing.

"I'm gonna turn it on now," Chatham said quietly. "You'd best stand back."

Billy retreated a few paces and put his hands in his pockets, gripping in his right hand the lump of coal. Chatham unlocked a small red box mounted to the wall; there was a series of red buttons and a red lever. He slowly pulled the lever down and Billy herd a generator come to life. The lights brightened.

A chain rattled, and an engine moaned as it gained power. The headrig's circular saw began spinning, slowly at first, then rapidly picking up speed until it was a silver-blue blur. It hummed—a machine sound, Billy thought; not a human sound at all. He could feel Mr. Chatham watching him. He thought of faking it, of pretending to hear something because Chatham seemed to expect it. But no, no, that wouldn't be right. He looked over his shoulder and raised his voice to be heard above the saw's metallic noise. "I don't hear any . . ."

The saw's voice abruptly changed; it made a shrill sound like a startled cry of pain, then what might have been a harsh grunt of surprise. The noise rippled and faded, and then the machine-humming had returned again.

Billy stared at it, his jaw slack. He wasn't certain what he'd heard; now the saw was quiet, running almost silently but for the clatter of chains. He stepped away from it a few paces, and heard Chatham's harsh breathing behind him.

And then there was a high, terrible scream—an eerie union of a human voice and the sound of the spinning saw—that reverberated through the mill.

The scream faded and died; then came back, stronger than before, more frantic and anguished. With the third scream the windows rattled in their loose casements. Billy had broken out in a cold sweat, the urge to flee from this place gnawing at the back of his neck; he put his hands to his ears to block out the next scream, but he heard it in his bones. He twisted around, saw Chatham's bleached face and terror-stricken eyes; the man was reaching for the lever, to cut power to the headrig.

The scream carried a high note of desperate pleading; and it was the same scream over and over, rising in the same pattern of notes to an abrupt end. Billy's decision was made: whatever this was, he wouldn't run from it. "No!" he shouted. Chatham froze. "Don't turn it off!" Each scream was seemingly louder than the one before, each one freezing his spine a little harder. He had to get outside to think, he had to figure out what to do, he couldn't stand this sound anymore and his whole brain was about to burst open. . . .

Billy turned and started for the door, his hands clamped over his ears. Just a machine noise, he told himself. *That's all . . . that's all . . . that's . . .*

The sound suddenly changed pitch. Through the screaming there was a hushed metallic whisper that stopped the boy in his tracks.

Billlleeeee. . . .

"Jesus Christ!" Chatham croaked. He was plastered against the wall, his face shiny with sweat. "It . . . *knows* you're here! It knows you!"

Billy turned and shouted, "It's just a noise, that's all! It's just a . . . just a . . ." The words choked in his throat; when his voice bubbled up again it was in a frantic yell: "You're dead! You're dead! You're . . . !"

Above the headrig a light bulb popped and exploded, raining hot fragments of glass. Then another, in the next row of bulbs; blue sparks of electricity leaped from the sockets.

"It's a demon! It's the goddamned Devil himself!" Chatham grasped the red lever and started to throw it. Above his head a bulb exploded and glass hornets stung the man's scalp; he yelped in pain and huddled to the floor, his arms up to protect his head. Two more blubs blew at the same time, zigzagging arcs of electricity. The air was full of ozone, and Billy could feel his hair dancing on his head.

Billlleeeee . . . Billlleeeee . . . Billlleeeee. . . .

"STOP IT!" Bulbs were popping all across the mill now, glass tinkling down into the machinery like off-key piano notes. An instant of sheer panic shook through Billy, but he stood firm until it had passed. *No fear,* he remembered his mother saying. And then he tasted blood in his mouth and realized he'd bitten into his lower lip. He concentrated on rooting himself to the floor, on clinging to what his mother had told him before he'd left the house. The mill's air had turned tumultuous, thick and hazed; most of the bulbs had exploded, the rest throwing harsh shadows. "STOP IT!" Billy shouted again. "STOP IT, MR. PATTERSON!"

Down at the other end of the mill, another bulb popped. The saw's scream faltered, fading to a low moan, a rumbling that seemed to shake the floor. He'd called the thing by name, Billy realized, and that had made a difference. It was, in its own way responding. He stepped past the cowering man on the floor. "You don't have to stay here anymore!" Billy shouted. "You can . . . you can go on to where you're supposed to be! Don't you understand?"

Softer: *Billlleeeee . . . Billlleeeee. . . .*

"You don't belong here anymore! You've got to go on!"

Billlleeeee. . . .

"LISTEN TO ME! You . . . you can't go home anymore, not

to your wife and kids. You've just got to . . . stop *trying* so hard to stay here. There's no sense in . . ." And then something seemed to crash into him, staggering him back; he moaned, feeling panic bloom in his head like a dark flower. He went to his knees in the sawdust, and his head was jarred as a savage pain sliced into his left eye. There was a burning fever of rage and agony in him, bubbling up to the top of his throat; and then his mouth opened as if it had been forced by rough, spectral hands, and he heard himself cry out, *"No no it's not my time yet! I want to be back again, I'm lost, I'm lost and I can't find my way back! . . ."*

Chatham whined like a dog, watching the boy writhe and jerk.

Billy shook his head to clear it. He shouted, "You can't come back! I saw Link Patterson buried today! You can't come back, you have to let everything go! *No no I'm lost, I've got to find my way back!* You have to rest and forget the pain! You have to *help me I'm lost oh God help me!*" And then he howled in torment, because he'd had the quick and clear vision of his right hand being chewed away to bloody bone; he cradled the phantom injury to his chest, and rocked back and forth with tears streaming down his cheeks. "I feel it!" he moaned. "I feel how it was for you! Oh God . . . please . . . just let the pain go, let everything go . . . just rest and let go. No fear . . . no fear . . . no . . ."

The headrig vibrated, about to tear its cleats from the floor. Billy looked up, saw something like a thin blue haze between him and the machine. It undulated and began to take on the shape of a man. "You don't have to be afraid," Billy whispered. His arm was on fire, and he gritted his teeth to hold back a scream. "I've got the pain now. Just . . ."

And then the blue haze moved toward him, thickening and roiling; when it touched him he was enveloped with cold and sheer dread, and he recoiled from it, trying to crawl away through the dust. Terror of the unknown swept through him, and he clenched his hands against the floor as if resisting a huge frigid wave. He heard himself shrieking, ". . . *let gooooooooo! . . .*"

The windows shattered with the noise of shotguns going off, all exploding outward as if from a terrible, awesome pressure.

And then the saw was humming again, the headrig slowing its rocking motions, slowing, slowing . . .

A last light bulb flickered, flickered, and went out. The

remaining few buzzed and blinked, and raw sparks jumped from the open sockets. The saw's sound pitched softer, until there was only the noise of the humming generator.

Lying on his side in the dust, Billy heard the mill's door slam shut. Then, in another moment, an engine started. Tires threw gravel. He raised his head with an effort, one side of his face pasted with sawdust, and saw that Mr. Chatham had fled. He lay back down again, totally exhausted; within him flowed the currents of desperate emotions, of fear and confusion and loss. He was sure that he now held within himself the emotions that had bound Link Patterson to this sawmill, to this world, perhaps even to the moment of physical death. He wasn't certain if he'd done it right or not, but he didn't think there was anything left of Mr. Patterson; the revenant had passed on, leaving its pain behind.

Billy forced himself to his feet. The saw was spinning silently, and he turned off the power. Billy clutched his right wrist and worked his hand. There was a needles-and-pins sensation in it, as if the blood flow had been cut off. A soft, warm breeze was blowing in through the shattered windows; in the last blue light a fine mist of golden dust was stirred up and floated through the air to coat the silent sawmill machinery.

When he was strong enough to move, Billy started home. His legs were leaden, and a dull pressure throbbed at his temples; for one thing he was grateful though—the feeling was slowly seeping back into his right hand. He took a shortcut through the dark and quiet forest, with the man in the moon grinning down, and prayed he'd never have to do anything like what happened tonight again. *I'm not strong enough,* he told himself. *I never was.*

Nearer Hawthorne, he was startled by something moving at the crest of a rise, there amid pines and boulders. It looked like a large man in the moonlight, but there was something animalish and disturbing about it. Billy stood still for a moment, his senses questing, but the figure was gone. As he skirted the rise, he thought he'd seen moonlight glinting wetly off what might have been curved, sharp tusks.

And he remembered the beast's warning and promise.

I'll be waiting for you.

23

"Feed the fire, brothers and sisters!" Jimmy Jed Falconer roared, his face licked with firelight above the bright yellow suit. "Feed the fire and starve the Devil!"

He stood on a wooden platform out in the middle of a dusty dumping ground near Birmingham. A backdrop had been constructed to hold the huge FALCONER CRUSADE banner.

Falconer grinned. Before him was a huge crackling circle of fire, feeding on hundreds of pounds of paper and several hundred black vinyl discs. There was a line of teen-agers waiting to throw their record albums into the flames, and people with boxes of books obtained from school and public libraries. The service had been going on for almost three hours, starting with psalm singing, then one of J.J. Falconer's most searing sermons on the Devil trying to consume America's youth, followed by an hour-long healing session that had left people dancing and talking in tongues.

Burning pages wafted into the air like fiery bats. Embers puffed out and drifted down. Records cracked and melted. "Here, gimme those, son." Falconer carefully leaned over the platform's edge and took several records from a heavyset young man with newly cropped black hair and acne scars. He looked at the jacket art, all psychedelic drawings and pictures, and held up one of them, by a group called Cream. "Yeah, this'll 'blow your mind,' won't it? It'll send you to Hell, that's what it'll do!" He sailed the record into the fire, to shouts and applause. The Jefferson Airplane flew into the flames next, followed by Paul Revere and the Raiders. "Is this what the Lord wants you to hear?" he asked, baiting the crowd. "Does He want you to grow your hair to your knees and take drugs and 'blow your mind'?" He tossed Sam the Sham and the Pharaohs into the flames.

There were resounding cheers as Falconer broke a Beatles record over his knee, then held it at the jacket's edge, with his other hand clamping shut his nostrils. He threw it in to burn. "Folks, if somebody tells you that everybody's growin' long hair and fillin' themselves full of LSD and runnin' away from the Commies like yellow cowards, then you tell them this: *I'm* the American majority, and I'm proud to . . ."

Suddenly he couldn't draw a breath. A sharp, cold pain ripped across his chest, and he felt as if he might pass out. He held the microphone at his side, afraid that it might pick up his whimper of agony; then he was sinking down to his knees, his head bent over, and he heard people clapping and hollering, thinking that this was all part of his message. He squeezed his eyes shut. *Oh God*, he thought. *Not again . . . please . . . take this pain away.* He struggled to draw in air, his chest heaving, but he stayed crouched on his knees so no one could see his graying face.

"Burn it!" he heard a high, merry voice shout.

A hand gripped his fleshy shoulder. "Dad?"

Falconer looked up into his son's face. The boy was growing into a handsome young man, with a lean strong body that looked trim in the tan suit he wore. He had a long, sharp-chinned face topped with a mass of thickly curled red hair, and now his deep-set, electric-blue eyes glinted with concern. "You all right, Dad?"

"Lost my breath," Falconer said, and tried to struggle to his feet. "Let me rest for just a minute."

Wayne glanced out at the congregation, and realized they were waiting for someone to lead them. He grasped the microphone his father held.

"No, Wayne," Falconer said, grinning, with the sweat running down his face. "I'm fine. Just lost my breath is all. It's the heat."

"The TV cameras are on us, Dad," Wayne said, and pulled the microphone away from his father. As Wayne straightened up and turned toward the congregation, his face abruptly pulled tight, the blue eyes widening and the perfect white teeth showing in a wide smile that hung on the edge of a grimace. His body tensed, as if gripping the microphone had sent a charge of power through him.

"The glory of the Lord is with us *tonight!*" Wayne crowed. "It's cracklin' in the air, it's fillin' our hearts and souls, it's put my daddy on his knees because it's not a weak thing, no it's not a frail thing, no it's not a feeble thing! If you want to listen to sex- and drug-music and you want to read sex- and drug-books, you'll be real happy in Hell, neighbors! Lord says WHAT?"

"BURN IT!"

Wayne balanced on the edge, seemingly about to leap into the fire himself. "Lord says WHAT?"

"Burn it! Burn it! Burn . . ."

Falconer knew the boy had them now. The local TV station cameras were aimed at the young healer. Falconer rose unsteadily to his feet. The pain was gone and he knew he'd be all right. But he wanted to get back to the Airstream trailer to rest, then he'd return and give the benediction. He made his way across the platform to the steps. All eyes were on Wayne. Falconer stopped for a moment to turn back and watch his son. Wayne's entire body seemed to glow with energy, with wonderful strength and youth. It was Wayne who'd come up with the idea of holding a "sin-burning," sure that there would be local media coverage. The ideas and plans just seemed to pop out of the boy's head fully formed; Wayne had suggested they move the Crusade into Louisiana, Mississippi, and Georgia, and into Florida where they could work year-round. The schedules had been drawn up, and for the past seven years the Crusade had expanded like a tick on a bloodhound. Now Wayne was talking about pushing the Crusade into Texas, where there were so many little towns and so far apart, and he wanted Falconer to buy a Fayette radio station that was about to lose its license. Wayne was taking flying lessons, and had already piloted the Crusade's Beechraft on short business trips.

The boy was strong and had God in his heart, Falconer knew, but still . . . something ate at Wayne, day and night. Something drove him, and tried to control him. He had fits of moods and temper, and sometimes he locked himself in the prayer chapel at home for hours on end. And Wayne had been complaining of a strange recurring nightmare lately, some nonsense about a snake and an eagle. Falconer couldn't make heads or tails of it.

Falconer was tired. He felt a sudden and awful pang of jealousy, and of anger at growing older and heavier and weaker.

He walked toward the trailer. His heart was deteriorating, the doctors had told him. Why, as he'd asked himself many times, was he afraid to ask Wayne to heal his heart, to patch up the leaks and make him strong again?

His answer was always the same as well: Because he was deeply afraid that Wayne's healing Toby had been a strange—and

153

terrible—fluke. And if Wayne tried to heal him and nothing happened, then . . . What had stayed with him for seven years was the voice of that Creekmore woman, the Hawthorne Valley witch, raised to tell everybody that he and his young son were murderers of the worst kind. Down deep inside, far from the light, in a dark place that knew neither God nor Satan but was instead wholly frightened animal, a nerve of truth had been trembling for seven long years. *What if? What . . . if . . . ?*

What if Wayne already knew? And had known since he'd touched the legs of a little girl whose frightened mind had kept her from *wanting* to walk.

"No," Falconer said. "No. The Lord's workin' through my son. He healed a dumb animal, didn't he? He's healed more than a thousand people." He shook his head. He had to shut off his thinking before it was harmful. He reached the shining silver trailer, unlocked it, and stepped inside. There was a plaque on the wall that said BELIEVE, and that was good enough for him.

SIX

May Night

24

They had driven in silence since leaving the house. John Creekmore watched the road unwinding before him in the yellow glare of the headlights; he was purposely keeping their speed ten miles per hour below the limit. "You sure you want to do this?" he asked, finally, without looking at his son. "I can turn the car around on the next dirt road."

"I want to go," Billy said. He was wearing a spotless but tightly fitting dark suit, a starched white shirt, and a bright paisley tie.

"Your choice. I've said all I can, I guess." His face was set and grim; he looked much the same as he had when he'd stepped out of the house one morning last week and had seen the scarecrow dummy hanging by its neck from an oak-tree limb. It was wrapped with used toilet paper. Ever since that evening Billy had gone up to the sawmill with Lamar Chatham the air had been ugly; Chatham had gone around telling everybody with ears what had happened, and the story soon became embellished and distorted to the point that it was said Billy was in command of the demons that infested the mill. John knew all of that was ridiculous, but he wasn't given the chance to explain; when he'd last gone over to Curtis Peel's to play checkers, the other men had frozen him out, talking and looking right through him as if he were invisible. Less than ten minutes after he'd gotten there, they'd all decided they'd had enough and left, but John had seen them later, sitting on the benches in front of Lee Sayre's hardware store; Sayre was with them, the center of attention, and Ralph Leighton was grinning like a hyena. "Did your mother put you up to this?" John asked suddenly.

"No sir."

"Don't you know who's gonna *be* there, son? Just about

157

everybody in the junior and senior classes, and a lot of their folks too! And everybody *knows!*" He tried to concentrate on his driving as the road snaked to the left. Fayette County High wasn't far now, just a mile or so ahead. "You ever ask anybody to go with you?"

Billy shook his head. He'd gathered the courage to call out Melissa's name in the hallway one day; when she'd turned toward him, Billy had seen her pretty face blanch. She'd hurried away as if he were offering her poison.

"Then I don't see why you want to go."

"It's May Night. It's the school dance. That's why."

John grunted. "No, that's not all of it, is it? I think you want to go because you want to prove something." He flicked a glance at the boy.

"I want to go to May Night, that's all."

He's stubborn as a deaf mule, John thought, and he's got a hell of a lot of guts, I'll say that for him. Billy was different, stronger-willed, somehow, and much more intense. Looking into his eyes was like seeing a thunderstorm on the horizon, and you didn't know which way the storm would turn or how fast it was moving.

"You may think you're not different," John said quietly, "but you're wrong. Lord knows I've prayed over you, Billy, and over your mother too. I've prayed until my head aches. But the Lord isn't gonna change you, son, not until you turn away from this . . . this black belief."

Billy was silent for a moment. The lights of Fayette brightened the sky before them. "I don't understand it," he said. "Maybe I never will, and maybe I'm not supposed to. But I think that part of Mr. Patterson *was* in that mill, Dad; it was a scared and hurt part, and too confused to know what to—"

"You don't know what you're talkin' about!" John snapped.

"Yes I do, Dad." The strength of his voice frightened John. "I helped Mr. Patterson. I *know* I did."

John felt the quick, hot urge to strike his son across the face. Seventeen or not, the boy had no right to dispute his father's word. In John's way of thinking the boy was like a corrupting tarbaby, and John was afraid some of that evil tar might fix itself to him, too.

The county high school stood just outside the Fayette city limits. It was a large, two-storied red brick building that had gone up in the early forties and had survived, like a defiant dinosaur, the

158

ravages of weather, vandalism, and county-education budget cuts. A gymnasium had been built off to the side in the mid-fifties, a square brick structure with a band of louvered windows beneath the slate roof. Outside the gym was a fenced-in football field, home to the Fayette County High Bulldogs. The parking lot held a varied assortment of vehicles, from rusted-out pickups to spit-shined sports cars. The school building itself was dark, but a few bright streamers of light shot out through the gym's open windows, and in the air there was the growl of a bass guitar and the high notes of laughter.

John slowed the car to a halt. "I guess this is the place. You sure you want to go through with it?"

"Yes sir."

"You don't have to, you know."

"I do have to."

"Ask me, you're lettin' yourself in for misery." But then Billy was opening the door, and John knew his mind was set. "What time do you want me to come for you?"

"Ten o'clock?"

"Nine-thirty," John said. He fixed his son with a hard gaze. "When you go through them doors, you're on your own. Anything happens to you in there, I can't help. You got your money?"

Billy felt in his pocket for the couple of dollars he'd brought along. "Yes sir. Don't worry, there are chaperones inside."

"Well," John said, "I guess I'll go on, then. Anybody says something to you that don't set well, you just remember . . . you're a Creekmore, and you can be proud of that." Billy shut the door and started to walk away, but John leaned toward the open window and said, "You look real good, son." And then, before the boy could respond, he was driving away across the lot.

Billy walked to the gym. His nerves were jangling, his muscles knotted up; he was ready for the unexpected. The gates to the football field were open, and Billy could see the huge mound of bits and pieces of wood—probably waste from the sawmill, he realized—that would be ignited later in the evening for the traditional May Night bonfire; then the ashes would be spread over the field before summer tilling and the replanting of grass for next season. From the gym's open doors came the tinny sounds of electric guitars playing "Alley Cat"; a large blue-and-gold poster hung across the front of the gym, and read MAY NIGHT! JUNIOR-

SENIOR SOCKHOP! 25¢ ADMISSION! with the drawing of a stocky bulldog dressed in football gear.

He paid his admission to a pretty dark-haired girl who sat at a desk just inside the gym. Golden and blue streamers crisscrossed the exposed metal rafters, and at the ceiling's center hung a large mirrored globe that cast reflected shards of light over the dancing mob. Papier-mâché planets painted in Day-Glo colors dangled on wires, high enough not to be yanked down but low enough to be stirred by the crowd's motion. On the brick wall behind the bandstand, where a group with the legend PURPLE TREE stenciled across the bass drumhead began to hammer out "Pipeline," was a large banner proclaiming SENIORS '69 WELCOME THE AGE OF AQUARIUS!

A chaperone, a thin geometry teacher named Edwards, materialized out of the crowd and pointed at Billy's feet. "Shoes off if you're going to stay on the floor. Otherwise, you go up into the bleachers." He motioned toward a sea of shoes scattered in a corner, and Billy took off his dusty loafers. How all those shoes would ever get back to their owners was a mystery, he thought as he placed his shoes with the others. He stood against the wall, underneath a stretched-tight American flag, and watched as the dancers Boog-a-looed and Ponied and Monkeyed to strident electric chords. Almost everyone had a date, he saw; the few boys who'd come stag—fat, or with terminal acne—sat up in the green-painted bleachers. Chaperones paced the dance floor. A glued-together couple passed Billy in search of their shoes, and he could smell the distinct aroma of moonshine.

"Well, well," someone said. "Is that Billy Creekmore standing over there by his lonesome?"

Billy looked to one side and saw Mr. Leighton leaning against the wall several feet away, wearing a checked coat and a shirt open at the collar; his crew cut looked as sharp as a bed of nails. "Where's your date, Billy?"

"I came stag."

"Oh? Didn't you ask anybody? Well, I guess that's your own business. How's your momma doin'? Ain't seen her in a month of Sundays."

"She's fine."

"Lots of pretty girls here tonight," Leighton said in a silk-smooth voice. His grin stopped south of his eyes, and in them Billy saw a cunning kind of anger. " 'Course, all of them have dates. Sure a shame you don't have a pretty girl to dance with, maybe cuddle up to after the dance is over. My boy's out there with his girl. You know Duke, don't you?"

"Yes sir." Everyone knew Duke Leighton, the senior-class cutup; Duke was a year older than Billy, but he'd failed the eighth grade. He'd been an All-American linebacker for the Bulldogs two seasons in a row, and had won a football scholarship to Auburn.

"He's goin' with Cindy Lewis," Leighton said. "She's head cheerleader at Indian Hills High."

The rich kids' school, Billy knew.

"You ought to know a lot of people here, Billy. Lot of people know *you*."

Leighton's voice was getting louder, as if he were pretending to shout over the music, but the shout was exaggerated. Billy noticed uneasily that he was being watched by some of the kids who hung around the edge of the dance floor; and he saw some of them whispering to each other.

"Yep!" Leighton said, very loudly. "Everybody knows Billy Creekmore! Heard you had a job up at the sawmill for a while, ain't that right? Huh?"

He didn't reply; he could feel people watching, and he shifted his position uneasily. To his horror, he realized there was a small hole in his left sock.

"What'd you do up there for the Chathams, Billy? Kinda sweep the place up? Did you do an Indian dance, or . . ." Billy turned away and started walking, but Leighton hurried after him and grasped his sleeve. "Why don't you show everybody your Indian dance, Billy? Hey! Who wants to see an Indian dance?"

Billy said, in a quiet and dangerous voice, "Let go of my arm, Mr. Leighton."

"What're you gonna do?" the man sneered. "Put a *curse* on me?"

Billy looked into his fierce, unreasoning glare and decided to play this game his way. He leaned closer to Leighton, until their faces were only a few inches apart, and he whispered, "Yes. I'll make your legs rot off to stumps. I'll make your hair catch fire. I'll make frogs grow in your fat belly."

Leighton's hand fell away, and he wiped his fingers on his trousers. "Sure you will. Yeah, sure. You listen to me, boy. Nobody wants you here. Nobody wants you in this school, or in

161

this town. One damned witch is e—" He stopped suddenly, because Billy's eyes had flared. He stepped back a few paces, mashing down shoes. "Why don't you just get the hell out of here?"

"Leave me alone," Billy said, and walked away. His heart was pounding. The Purple Tree was playing "Double Shot," and the crowd was going wild.

Billy walked around the gym to a booth that sold Cokes and corndogs. He bought a Coke, drank it down, and was about to throw the crumpled cup into a trashcan when fingers grazed his cheek. He turned around; there was a short, shrill scream and four figures backed away from him. A girl said, her voice brimming with delicious terror, "I touched him, Terry! I really touched him!" There was a chorus of braying laughter, and someone off to the side asked, "Talked to any ghosts lately, Creekmore?"

He ducked his head down and pushed past a boy in a Bulldog letter jacket; his face flamed, and he knew that coming to this dance, that trying to pretend he was just like the others and could fit in after all, had been an awful mistake. There was nothing to do now but to try to get out of here, to withdraw from people yet again. Suddenly someone shoved him from the rear, and he almost went down; when he turned he saw perhaps eight or nine grinning faces, and a couple of boys with clenched fists. He knew they wanted to fight so they could show off in front of their girls, so he backed away from them and then started across the packed dance floor, twisting through a human maze of gyrating bodies. A heavyset boy with a mop of dark hair pushed his girl friend into Billy; she let out a mouselike squeak when she looked up into his face, and then the boy pulled her away to let her cower in his arms.

They're using me to scare their girl friends, Billy thought, like I was a horror movie at the drive-in! Rather than angering him, that realization struck him as being funny. He grinned and said, "Boo!" at the next girl whose boyfriend thrust her forward; she almost went gray with shock, and then the people who recognized him—people he saw every day in the high-school halls—were moving out of his way, making a path for him to get through. He laughed and bent over like a hunchback, letting his arms dangle, and moved along the human corridor like a lurching ape. Give 'em a show! he thought. That's what they want! Girls screamed, and even their protective boyfriends edged away. Now he was getting more attention than the Purple Tree, and he knew he was making a damned fool of himself but he wanted to turn around on them the fearful image they had of him; he wanted to rub it in and let them see how stupid it was to be afraid. He grimaced like a ghoul, reaching out toward a girl whose boyfriend slapped his hands away and then backed into the crowd; he danced and jerked his head as if he'd been struck by the palsy, and now he heard people laughing and he knew he was about to break through . . . just about to break through—

And then he abruptly stopped, a cold chill running through him. He was facing Melissa Pettus, radiant in a pink dress and with pink ribbons in her long flowing hair; she was pressed close to a boy named Hank Orr, and she was cowering away from Billy.

Billy stared at her, and slowly straightened up. "You don't have to be afraid," he said, but his voice was lost in the bass-boom as the Purple Tree started to play "Down in the Boondocks."

Something wet hit him in the face and streamed into his eyes. He couldn't see for a few seconds, and from off to one side he heard a snort of laughter. When Billy had cleared his eyes, he saw Duke Leighton grinning several feet away; the boy was bulky, already getting fat. A slim red-haired girl clung to one arm, and his other hand held a plastic watergun.

And then Billy could smell the reek of beer rising off of himself, and he realized that Leighton had filled that gun with beer instead of water; it was one of his many practical and sometimes cruel jokes. Now if a chaperone happened to get a whiff of Billy's clothes, Billy would be immediately thrown out. He reeked like a shithouse on a hot summer night.

"Want some more, Spookie?" Leighton called out, to a chorus of laughter. He grinned slickly, as his father had.

Anger surged within Billy. At once he propelled himself forward, shoving through several couples to get at Leighton. The other boy laughed and sprayed him in the eyes again, and then someone edged out a foot and Billy tripped over it, sprawling on the gym floor. He struggled to his feet, half blinded with beer, and a hand caught roughly at his shoulder; he spun to strike at his attacker.

It was a chaperone, a short and stocky history teacher named Kitchens; the man grabbed his shoulder again and shook him. "No fighting, mister!" he said.

"I'm not! Leighton's trying to start trouble!"

Kitchens stood at least two inches shorter than Billy, but he was a large-shouldered man with a deep chest and a crew cut that was a holdover from his Marine days. His small dark eyes glanced toward Duke Leighton, who was standing in a protective circle of football buddies. "What about it, Duke?"

The other boy raised empty hands in a gesture of innocence, and Billy knew the watergun had been passed to safety. "I was just mindin' my own business, and old Spookie wanted to fight."

"That's a damned lie! He's got—"

Kitchens leaned toward him. "I smell *liquor* on you, mister! Where you keepin' it, in your car?"

"No, I'm not drinking! I was . . ."

"I saw him with a flask, Mr. Kitchens!" someone said through the crowd, and Billy was almost certain it was Hank Orr's voice. "Throw him out!"

Kitchens said, "Come on, mister," and started pulling Billy toward the door. "You rule-breakers got to learn some respect!"

Billy knew it was pointless to struggle, and maybe it was for the best that he get kicked out of the May Night dance.

"I ought to take you to the boys' adviser, that's what I ought to do," Kitchens was saying. "Drinking and fighting is a bad combination."

Billy looked back and caught the reflection of light off Melissa Pettus's hair; Hank Orr had his arm around her waist, and was pulling her toward the dance floor.

"Come on, pick out your shoes and get out of here!"

Billy stopped, resisting the man's tugging. He had seen—or *thought* he'd seen—something that had driven a freezing nail of dread into his stomach. He blinked, wishing he wouldn't see it, but yet, there it was, right there, right there. . . .

A shimmering black haze hung around Hank Orr and Melissa Pettus. It undulated, throwing off ugly pinpoints of purplish light. He heard himself moan, and Kitchens stopped speaking to stare at him. Billy had seen the black aura glittering around another couple who were walking on the edge of the dance floor; he saw it again, from the corner of his eye: it was enveloping a senior girl named Sandra Falkner, who was doing the Jerk with her boyfriend. Panic roiled in Billy's stomach; he wildly looked around, sure of impending disaster. The black aura glittered around a biology teacher named Mrs. Carson. A very weak aura, more purple than black, undulated around a senior football player

164

named Gus Tompkins. He saw it yet again, clinging to a fat boy who was sitting up in the bleachers eating a corndog.

"Oh God," Billy breathed. "No . . . no . . ."

"Come on," Kitchens said, more uncertainly. He let go of the boy and stepped back, because the boy suddenly looked as if he might throw up. "Find your shoes and get out."

"They're going to die," Billy whispered hoarsely. "I can see . . . Death in this place. . . ."

"Are you drunk, mister? What's wrong with you?"

"Can't you see it?" Billy took a faltering few steps toward the crowd. "Can't *anybody* else see it?"

"Shoes or not, you're getting your ass out of here!" Kitchens grasped his arm to shove him toward the door, but the boy broke free with an amazing strength and then he ran toward the dance floor, sliding in his socks. He pushed through the throng hanging around the floor, almost slipping on a spilled Coke, then he was through them and reaching for Melissa Pettus, reaching through the black haze to touch and warn her that Death was very near. She jerked away from him and screamed. Hank Orr stepped in his way, purplish black tendrils glittering around his body, and brought his fist up in a quick arc that snapped Billy's head back. Billy staggered and fell, hearing the shout "FIGHT! FIGHT!" ringing in his ears. A forest of legs crowded around, but Purple Tree kept on playing "Rolling on the River."

"Get up!" Hank Orr said, standing over him. "Come on, you . . . freak! I'll stomp your ass!"

"Wait . . . wait," Billy said. His head was filled with stars, exploding novas and planets. "The black aura . . . I see it . . . you've got to get—"

"FIGHT! FIGHT!" someone yelled gleefully. The Purple Tree stopped in midchord. Shouts and laughter echoed through the gym.

"You're going to die!" Billy wailed, and the blood drained out of Orr's face. He raised his fists as if to protect himself, but he didn't dare touch Billy Creekmore again. "You . . . and Melissa . . . and Sandra Falkner . . . and . . ." There was a sudden stunned silence except for kids whooping and laughing on the other side of the gym. Billy started to rise to his feet, his lower lip swelling like a balloon, but then the crowd parted and the boys' adviser, Mr. Marbury, came through like a steam engine, smoke swirling from the bowl of the pipe clenched between his teeth.

Close in his wake was Mr. Kitchens. Marbury hauled Billy up with a hand clamped at the back of his neck, and bellowed "OUT!" He shoved Billy so fast the boy was sliding across the floor, through the throng, and past the scattered shoes toward the door.

"He's drunk as a skunk!" Kitchens was saying. "Picking fights all over the place!"

"I know this boy. He's a troublemaker. Drinkin', huh? Where'd you get the booze?"

Billy tried his best to shake free, but then he was propelled through the door and Marbury spun him around. "I asked you a question, Creekmore!"

"No! I'm not . . . drunk. . . ." He could hardly talk because his lip was swelling so fast. Bells still pealed in his head. "Not drunk! Something's gonna happen! I saw it . . . saw the black aura! . . ."

"Saw *what?* I've had a gutful of you, boy! You smell like you've been swimmin' in booze! I ought to suspend you on the spot!"

"No . . . please . . . listen to me! I don't know what's going to happen, but . . ."

"I do!" Marbury said. "You're gonna stay *out* of that gym! And come Monday mornin' I'm gonna have a long talk with your parents! Go on, now! If you want to drink and fight, it'll be somewhere else!" He shoved Billy backward. Faces peered out, watching and smirking; one of them belonged to Ralph Leighton. Marbury turned and stalked to the door, then faced Billy again. "I said get out of here!"

"How about my shoes?"

"We'll mail 'em to you!" Marbury said, and then he vanished within the gym.

Billy looked at Mr. Kitchens, who stood a few feet away from him and who now began edging toward the door. "They're going to die," he told the man. "I tried to warn them. They won't listen."

"You come back in the gym again, mister, and I might help the boys clean your clock." Kitchens glared at him for a few seconds, then went into the gym.

Billy stood in the darkness, weaving on his feet. He shouted, "THEY'RE GOING TO DIE!" and in another few seconds someone closed the gym door. He staggered to it and hammered on the metal; he could feel the bass-drum vibrations of Purple Tree knocking back, and he knew everybody was dancing and having a good time again. I can't stop it, he told himself; whatever it is, I can't stop it! But I *have* to keep trying! If he couldn't get back inside, he'd stop them when they came out; he walked away from the gym on weak, rubbery legs and sat down on a curb facing the parking lot. He could see the vague shapes of people huddled in their cars, and moonlight glanced off an upturned bottle in the backseat of a spiffy red Chevy. He wanted to sob and scream, but he gritted his teeth together and held everything inside.

Within fifteen minutes he heard shouting and laughter from the football field, and he stood up to see what was happening. Kids were leaving the gym to congregate around the mound of timber; a couple of the chaperones were dousing the wood with gasoline, and the bonfire was about to be lighted. People chased each other around the field like wild stallions, and some of the girls started doing impromptu Bulldogs cheers. Billy stood at the fence, his hands gripped into the metal mesh. A lighter sparked, and the flame touched the gasoline-soaked wood at several places around the base; the wood, most of it rough kindling, caught quickly. Fire gnawed toward the top of the pile. More students were coming out to ring the bonfire as the flames grew brighter; the heap was about twelve or thirteen feet tall, Billy saw, and some practical joker had set a chair on top of it. Sparks danced into the sky. As Billy watched, some of the kids linked hands and started to sing Fayette County High's alma mater:

> Nestled in the quiet valley
> Home we love and always will;
> Stands our revered alma mater
> Below the woodland and the hills . . .

The bonfire was growing into a huge finger of flame. Billy leaned against the fence, rubbing his swollen lip. In the quick orange spray of sparks from a wet piece of wood Billy saw Melissa Pettus and Hank Orr, holding hands and standing near the bonfire's base. The aura around them had turned blacker still, and seemed to be spreading out its dark, twisting tentacles. He saw Sandra Falkner's face, brushed with orange light, as she stood looking up toward the bonfire's crest. She was almost cocooned in the black aura. Gus Tompkins was standing to her left, and back about ten feet.

Billy's fingers clenched the fence as the cold realization struck him: they were all out here now, all the kids who were enveloped by the ugly aura, and most of them were standing closest to the fire. The blackness seemed to be reaching toward itself, connecting, drawing all the victims together.

A red glow pulsated at the bonfire's center. The chair collapsed, to a scattering of applause and whoops.

> . . . *We give thanks for all God's blessings,*
> *Underneath his crowning sky;*
> *Home of learning and of friendship,*
> *Our alma mater, Fayette County* . . .

"GET AWAY FROM THE FIRE!" Billy screamed.

The bonfire heaved, as if something were growing within it. Suddenly there were several ear-cracking pops that stopped all laughter. From the fire's center exploded three multicolored streaks of light that shot in different directions over the field.

Roman candles, Billy thought. How did Roman candles get inside the. . . ?

But then there was an earth-shuddering *whummmmmp!* and the entire mound of flaming timbers exploded from within. Billy had time to see jagged shards of wood flying like knives before a hot shock wave hit him like a brick wall, flinging him to the ground so hard the breath burst from his lungs. The earth shook again, and again; the air was filling with whistlings and shrieks, human and fireworks noises.

Billy sat up, his head ringing, his face scorched with heat; he numbly realized his hands were bleeding, and he'd left most of their skin in the fence's mesh. Caught all along the fence were shards of wood that could've sliced through him like butcher knives. Roman candles shot across the field, a golden flower of sparks opened up high in the air, M-80s hammered at the sky, purple and blue and green fireworks zigzagged from the center of the bonfire's rubble. People were running, screaming, rolling on the ground in agony. Kids with their hair and clothes on fire were dancing now to a new and hideous rhythm, others were staggering around like sleepwalkers. Billy stood up; a rain of cinders was falling, and the air stank of black powder. He saw a boy crawling away from the still-exploding bonfire, and then Billy was running toward the center of the field to help. He grasped the boy's blackened shirt and hauled him away several yards as Roman candles rocketed overhead. A girl was screaming for her mother, over and over again, and when Billy grabbed her hand to pull her away from the mound of fire her skin came off like a glove; she moaned and passed out.

A green pinwheel whistled toward Billy's face; as he ducked it he smelled his hair burn. A red star exploded in the sky, washing the field with bloody light. The chilling shriek of the Civil Defense air-raid siren began whooping from atop the high school, cutting through the night like a clarion of disaster.

Billy grasped the collar of a boy whose shirt had been all but blown off his back, and he screamed, "I TOLD YOU! I TRIED TO WARN YOU!" The boy's face was as pale as marble, and he walked on as if Billy were invisible. Billy looked wildly around, saw June Clark lying on the ground in a fetal curl, Mike Blaylock lying on his back with a shard of wood through his right hand, Annie Ogden on her knees as if praying to the bonfire. Above the screaming, he heard the sound of sirens approaching from Fayette; suddenly his knees gave way and he sat on the black ground as fireworks kept whistling all around him.

Someone staggered out of the haze before him and stood looking down. It was Mr. Kitchens, blood leaking from both his ears. A white spray of sparks exploded behind him, and his face worked as if he were trying very hard to open his mouth. Finally, he said in a hoarse, chilling whisper, *"You. . . !"*

25

The Creekmores found their son sitting on the floor in a corner of the tense, crowded Fayette County Hospital waiting room. They had heard the Civil Defense siren, and Ramona had sensed tragedy.

Billy's face was heat-swollen, his eyebrows all but singed away. There was a thin blanket draped across his shoulders, and resting in his lap were his bandaged hands. The stark overhead lighting made the Vaseline smeared on his face shine, and his eyes were closed as if he were asleep, removing himself from the noise and tension by sheer willpower alone.

John stood behind his wife, his spine crawling from being stared at by all the other parents. Someone at the high school, where they'd stopped first, had told him that Billy was dead and the boy's body had already been carried away in an ambulance, but Ramona had said no, she'd have known if her son was dead.

"Billy?" Ramona said, in a trembling voice.

The boy's eyes opened painfully. He could hardly see through the swollen slits, and the doctors had told him there were maybe forty wood slivers in his cheeks and forehead but he'd have to wait until the burned kids were treated.

She bent down beside him and hugged him gently, her head leaning against his shoulder. "I'm all right, Mom," Billy said through blistered lips. "Oh God . . . it was so *terrible*. . . ."

John's face had been gray ever since they'd left the school and had seen those bodies lying under the blankets, the gurneys being pushed along the hallway with burned teenagers on them, parents shrieking and sobbing and clinging to each other for support. The night was filled with ambulance sirens, and the burned-flesh stink floated in the hospital like a brown haze. "Your hands," he said. "What happened?"

"I lost some skin, that's all."

"Dear God, boy!" John's face crumpled like old sandpaper, and he put his hand against the tiled wall to support himself. "Lord God, Lord God I never saw anything like what I saw at that school!"

"How'd it happen, Dad? One minute it was just a bonfire, like every year. Then it all changed."

"I don't know. But all those pieces of wood . . . they cut those kids up, just cut them to ribbons!"

"A man there said I did it," Billy said tonelessly. "He said I was drunk, and I did something to the fire to make it explode."

"That's a damned lie!" John's eyes blazed. "You didn't have a thing to do with it!"

"He said I have Death inside me. Is that right?"

"NO! Who said that to you? Show him to me!"

Billy shook his head. "It doesn't matter now, anyway. It's all over. I just . . . wanted to have fun, Dad. Everybody wanted to have a good time. . . ."

John gripped his son's shoulder, and felt something like deep ice crack inside him. Billy's gaze was strangely dark and blank, as if what had happened had blown all the mysterious fuses in his head. "It's all right," John said. "Thank God you're alive."

"Dad? Was I wrong to go?"

"No. A man goes where he wants to, and he has to go some places he don't want to, as well. I expect you've done a little of both tonight." Farther along the corridor, someone wailed in either pain or sorrow, and John flinched from the sound.

Ramona wiped her eyes on her sleeve and looked at the tiny slivers embedded in Billy's face, some of them dangerously close to having blinded him. She had to ask, though she already suspected the answer. "Did you *know?*"

He nodded. "I tried to tell them, I tried to warn them something was going to happen, but I . . . I didn't know what it was going to be. Mom, why did it happen? Could I have changed it if I'd done anything different?" Tears slipped down his Vaseline-smeared cheeks.

"I don't know," Ramona replied; an honest answer to a mystery that had plagued her all her life.

There was a sudden commotion over at the far side of the waiting room, where a corridor led to the main doors. Ramona and John both looked up, and saw people thronging around a large, thick-bellied man with gray curly hair and a boy about Billy's age, lean and red-haired. A shock of recognition pierced Ramona. That bitter night at the tent revival replayed itself in her mind—it had never been very far beneath the surface, not in all of seven years. A woman grasped Falconer's hand and kissed it, begging him to pray for her injured daughter; a man in overalls pushed her aside to get to Wayne. For a few seconds there was a shoving melee of shoulders and arms as the parents of hurt and dying kids tried to reach Falconer and his son, to get their attention, to touch them as if they were walking good-luck charms. Falconer let them converge on him, but the boy stepped back in confusion.

Ramona stood up. A state trooper had come in, trying to settle everybody back down again. Through the mass of people, Ramona's hard gaze met the evangelist's, and Falconer's soft, fleshy face seemed to darken. He came toward her, ignoring the appeals for prayer and for healing. He looked down at Billy, his eyes narrowing, then back into Ramona's face. Wayne stood behind him, wearing jeans and a blue knit shirt with an alligator on the breast pocket. He glanced at Billy and for an instant their eyes held; then the boy's gaze locked upon Ramona, and she thought she could actually feel the heat of hatred.

"I know you," Falconer said softly. "I remember you, from a long time ago. Creekmore."

"That's right. And I remember you, as well."

"There's been an accident," John told the evangelist. "My boy was there when it happened. His hands are all cut up, and he . . . he saw terrible things. Will you pray for him?"

Falconer's eyes were locked with Ramona's. He and Wayne had heard about the bonfire explosion on the radio, and had come to the hospital to offer consolation; running into this witch-woman again was the last thing he'd expected, and he feared the influence her presence might have on Wayne. His bulk dwarfed her, but somehow, under her hard and appraising stare, he felt very vulnerable and small.

"Have you brought your boy here to heal?" she asked him.

"No. Only to minister, alongside me."

Ramona turned her attention to the boy, and stepped a pace closer to him. Billy saw her eyes narrow, as if she'd seen something that scared her about Wayne Falconer, something he wasn't able yet to see, perhaps. Wayne said, "What're you looking at?"

"Don't mind her. She's crazy." Falconer took the boy's arm and started to herd him away; suddenly a hollow-eyed man in blue jeans and a T-shirt stood up from his seat and grasped Wayne's hand. "Please," the man said, his voice sad and raspy, "I know who you are and what you can do. I've seen you do it before. Please . . . my son's hurt bad, they brought him in a little while ago and they don't know if he's gonna . . ." The man clung to Wayne's hand as if he were about to collapse, and his bathrobed wife rose to support him. "I *know* what you can do," he whispered. "Please . . . save my son's life!"

Billy saw Wayne glance quickly at his father. The man said, "I'll give you money. I've got money, is that what you want? I'll turn to the Lord, I'll go to church every Sunday and I won't drink or gamble no more. But you've got to save him, you can't let those . . . those doctors *kill* him!"

"We'll pray for him," Falconer said. "What's his name?"

"No! You've got to touch him, to heal him like I've seen you do on television! My son's all burned up, his eyes are all burned!" The man gripped at Falconer's sleeve as other people thronged around. "Please let your boy heal him, I'm begging you!"

"Well just lok who's here, everybody!" Falconer suddenly boomed, and pointed toward Ramona. "The Creekmores! Wayne, you know all about them, don't you? The mother's a Godless witch, and the boy calls up demons like he did at a certain sawmill around here! And now here they stand, on the eve of the worst disaster in Fayette history, turning up like bad pennies!"

"Wait," John said. "No, you're wrong, Reverend Falconer. Billy was at the high school, and he got hurt—"

"Hurt? You call that hurt? Look at him, everybody! Why isn't he all burned up, like the son of this poor soul here?" He gripped the man's shoulder. "Why isn't *he* dyin', like some of your sons and daughters are right this minute? He was out there with the other young people! Why isn't he burned up?"

All eyes turned toward Ramona. She was silent, unprepared for Falconer's attack. But she understood that he was trying to use her and Billy as scapegoats, to avoid explaining why Wayne couldn't go from room to room in this hospital and heal everyone in them.

"I'll tell you why," Falconer said. "Maybe there are forces working behind this woman and boy that are better left alone by Christian folk! Maybe these forces, and God only knows what they are, protected this boy. Maybe they're *inside* him, and he carries Death and destruction with him like a plague—"

"Stop it!" Ramona said sharply. "Stop trying to hide behind smoke! *Boy!*" She'd addressed Wayne, and now she moved past the evangelist to face his son. Billy rose painfully to his feet and held onto his father's arm. "Do you know what you're doing, son?" she asked softly, and Billy saw him wince. "If you do have a healing gift, it's not to be used for wealth or power. It can't be part of a show. Don't you understand that by now? If you're pretending to heal folks, you've got to stop giving them false hope. You've got to urge them to see a doctor, and to take their medicines." Her hand came up, and gently touched Wayne's cheekbone.

He suddenly thrust his jaw forward and spat in her face.

"Witch!" he shouted, in a strident and frightened voice. "Get away from me!"

John leaped forward, his fists clenched. Instantly two men blocked his way, one of them shoving him back against the wall, the other pinning him there with an arm across his throat. Billy didn't have a chance to fight, for he was facing a knot of desperate and fearful people who wanted to stomp him under their shoes.

Falconer's voice raised above the din of shouting. "Hold on now, folks! We don't want any trouble on our hands, do we? We've got enough to concern ourselves with tonight! Leave 'em be!"

Ramona wiped her face with the back of her hand. Her gaze was gentle but full of deep sadness. "I'm sorry for you," she told Wayne, and then turned to Falconer. "And for you. How many bodies and souls have you killed in the name of God? How many more will you destroy?"

"You're Godless trash," the evangelist said. "My son carries Life inside him, but yours spreads Death. If I were you, I'd take my trash with me and get out of this county." His eyes glinted like cold diamonds.

"I've said my piece." She took a few steps, stopped, and stared at a man and woman who blocked her path. "Move," she said, and they did. John was shaking, rubbing his throat and glaring at Falconer. "Let's go home," Ramona told her men; she was close to tears, but damned if she'd let any of these people see her cry!

"We gonna just let this filth walk out of here?" someone shouted from the other side of the waiting room.

"Let them go," Falconer said, and the crowd quietened down. "Vengeance is mine, sayeth the Lord! You'd better pray, witch! You'd better pray real hard!"

Ramona stumbled on her way across the room, and Billy took her weight on his shoulder to lead her out. John kept looking back, afraid of being jumped. Shouts and catcalls followed them all the way. They got in the Olds and drove away, passing ambulances that were bringing dead teen-agers wrapped in black rubber bags.

J.J. Falconer hurried Wayne out of the waiting room before anyone else could stop them. His face was flushed, his breathing rapid, and he motioned Wayne toward a utility room. Amid brooms and mops and cans of detergent, Falconer leaned against a wall and dabbed his face with a handkerchief.

"Are you all right?" Wayne's face was shadowed and grim; a single light bulb hung on a cord just above his head.

"Yeah. It's just . . . the excitement. Let me get my breath." He sat down on a detergent can. "You handled yourself pretty good out there."

"She scared me, and I didn't want her touching me."

He nodded. "You did real fine. That woman's pure trouble. Well, we'll see what we can do about her. I've got friends in Hawthorne. Yeah, we'll see. . . ."

"I didn't like what she said to me, Dad. It . . . made me hurt to hear her."

"She speaks in Satan's language, trying to trick and confuse you, and make you *doubt* yourself. Somethin's got to be done about her and that . . . that *mongrel* of hers. Vic Chatham told me the whole story, about what his brother Lamar saw up at the mill. That boy spoke to the Devil up there, and went wild and almost tore the place apart. Somethin's got to be done about both of them, and soon."

"Dad?" Wayne said after another moment. "Could I . . . could I heal a dying person, if I . . . tried hard enough?"

Falconer carefully folded his damp handkerchief and put it away before answering. "Yes, Wayne. If you tried hard enough, and prayed strong enough, you could. But this hospital is not the proper place to heal."

Wayne frowned. "Why not?"

"Because it's . . . not a house of God, that's why. Healing is only right in a sanctified place, where people have gathered to hear the Lord's Word."

"But . . . people have a need right *here*."

Falconer smiled darkly and shook his head. "You've got that witch's voice in your head, Wayne. She's confused you, hasn't she? Oh sure, she'd like to see you go from room to room in this hospital, and heal *everybody*. But that wouldn't be right, because it's God's Will that some of these young people die here tonight. So we let the doctors work on 'em, and do all they can, but *we* know the mysterious ways of the Lord, don't we?"

"Yes sir."

"That's right." When he stood up, he winced and gingerly touched his chest. The pain was almost gone now, but it had felt like an electric shock. "Now I'm feelin' a bit better. Wayne, I want you to do me a favor. Will you go outside and wait in the car?"

"Wait in the car? Why?"

"These poor folks will expect you to heal if you stay here, so I think it's best if you wait while I pray with them."

"Oh." Wayne was puzzled, and still disturbed by what the witch had said to him. Her dark eyes had seemed to look straight to his soul, and she'd scared the daylights out of him. "Yes sir, I guess that would be best."

"Good. And will you slip around to the side door? If you go back out through that waitin' room, there might be another commotion."

Wayne nodded. The woman's voice echoed in his head: *Do you know what you're doing, son?* Something within him suddenly seemed to be tottering over a cliff's edge, and he jerked himself back with the savage thought: She's as evil as sin itself, her and the demon boy, and they should both be cast into the Lord's fire! Lord says what? BURN THEM! "We'll get them, won't we, Dad?"

"We'll get 'em," Falconer replied. "Just leave it to me. Come on, I'd best get out there. Remember: out the side way, okay?"

"Yes sir." A low flame of rage was burning inside Wayne. How dare that woman *touch* him like that! He wished now that he'd struck her across the face, knocked her to her knees for everyone to see. He was still shaking from being so close to them. Their darkness, he knew, was pulling at him, trying to lure him. There would be a next time, he told himself; oh yes, and then . . .

He had the vague beginnings of a headache. He said, "I'm ready now," and followed his father out of the utility room.

26

John was awake in the dark, thinking.

Ramona shifted softly in the crook of his arm; they'd slept closer in the last three nights, since what had happened at Fayette County Hospital, than they had in many years. His throat was still bruised from where a man's forearm had pressed against it, and he'd been hoarse the next day until he'd accepted a tea of sassafras root and dandelion that Ramona had brewed for him.

The kids who'd died in the accident had been buried the previous day. John's trips into town during the last few days had been brief; at Lee Sayre's hardware store no one would come to wait on him, and when he went to get a haircut Curtis Peel suddenly announced he'd close up for the afternoon. So he drove into Fayette for a bucket of roofing pitch, and decided to let his hair grow longer. While he was in Fayette, he heard from a clerk that somebody had hidden two crates of assorted fireworks down inside the bonfire, and the intense heat had made them all go off at once. The troopers had said that the amount of black powder had been equal to a couple of short sticks of dynamite; it had looked like a kid's prank, done by somebody who'd thought the fireworks going off would take the others by surprise, but all that explosive powder in such a small space, the heat of the gasoline-fed fire, and the small, sharp shards of wood had added up to seven deaths and a score of terrible injuries. One boy, a senior football player named Gus Tompkins, was still lingering at the Burn Center Hospital in Birmingham, blinded and shocked dumb.

By the light of the anger he'd felt toward Jimmy Jed Falconer, John had seen amazing things, both true and unsettling, about his own life and beliefs. He hadn't been able to understand why Falconer had deliberately tried to hurt Ramona and Billy, tried to stir up the crowd against them like that; the man had spouted one lie after another about them, had even tried to make it out that Billy had been to blame for the accident! Thinking about these things had started rusted wheels turning in his head; there was pain, yes, but it seemed that for the first time in a very long while he was being powered from his own dynamo, not from the cast-off sparks of someone else's.

Now it seemed to him that Falconer was a man of God, but yet he was still *only* a man, too. And that boy of his could heal, but not all the time and not everybody. It was too simple to say that a man belonged either to God or to Satan; no, even the best of men had bad days—or bad thoughts—and every once in a while might slip off the righteous path. Did that necessarily damn you to Hell for eternity? Falconer himself had slipped off, by his lies, and so had the boy, by his actions; did that make them more human, or did it mean that Satan was at work in their lives?

And what about Ramona and Billy? What *was* this power they had, to lay the dead to rest? Where did it come from: God? Satan? Neither one, or a combination of both? And what if he'd been wrong, all these years, about Ramona and her mother?

He started to roll over on his side, but then he realized how quiet it was; usually the crickets in the grass were fiddling fit to bust on a warm summer night like . . .

The house was suddenly filled with a white glare. John sat up abruptly, half blinded, and heard a loud metallic clanging and crashing outside, seemingly all around the house. He grabbed his pants off a chair and struggled into them as Ramona sat up in bed. "What is it?" she asked frantically. "What's that sound?" He drew aside the curtains to look out the small window; bright beams of light cut into his eyes, and he couldn't see a thing out there. He said, "Stay here!" and ran for the front door. He stepped out onto the porch, shielding his eyes from the light. White orbs ringed the house, and now he could make out human shapes, banging together pots and pans and iron pipes. The raucous rough music rang in John's head, and dull terror throbbed within him as he realized the shapes were sheeted in Klan garb. Cars had been pulled up close to the house, their headlights all switched on at the same time. "What do you want?" John shouted, pacing from one side of the porch to the other, like a trapped animal. "Get off my land!"

The clanging went on, in rhythmic cadence. Then the screen door opened and Billy came out on the porch, his face peeling as if from sunburn; there were still thick bandages on his hands, but the doctor had said they'd be fine after the raw places scabbed over. Ramona was behind him, wrapped in her gray robe; she was carrying a long carving knife.

"Stop it! You damned dogs, what do you want?" John thought of the old pistol he had, wrapped in oily rags in a drawer, and he started to go get it when the clanging suddenly died.

One of the hooded shapes stepped forward, silhouetted in bright light, and pointed toward John. "Creekmore," the man said, and John knew it was Lee Sayre's voice even muffled through the mask, "this town's suffered enough misery from that woman and her boy! Surely *you* know by now they're not gonna renounce their ways! So we've come to set forth our terms. . . ."

"*Terms?*" John said. "Lee, what're you talkin' about?"

"No names, Creekmore! You took an oath!"

"That was when I was on the other side of that mask! What are y'all supposed to be? A vigilante squad? A hangin' party? Did you bring your tar and feathers? What right do you have runnin' your cars up on my land and raisin' hell like—"

"Every right!" Sayre bellowed. "Because of the uniform we wear, and because we live in this town!"

"We've got the right to beat your ass too, Creekmore!" someone called out—Ralph Leighton's voice. "You'd best watch your mouth!"

Sayre said firmly, "We want the woman and the boy out of Hawthorne. We want 'em out tonight. John, you and your parents were all born and raised here, and you've always been a good, God-fearin' man. For years you were able to keep that woman in her place, but now that the boy's got the demon in him too the both of them are too strong for you. But we've decided you can stay here if you want to, John. It's not your fault you've been saddled with this corruption. . . ."

"NO!" John shouted. "This is our *home*, damnn it! This is my wife and son you're talkin' about!"

"It's been decided," Sayre said. "We want them gone before something else happens around here."

"We want that accursed boy out of this town!" Ralph Leighton stepped forward, jabbing a finger at Billy. "First the crops went bad after he was born, and the land ain't been too good ever since! Then Dave Booker killed his whole family, and guess who was the Booker boy's friend? Then Link Patterson got sliced up at the sawmill, and we *all* know about that! Now there are fine kids lying in the ground and in the hospital, and just guess who was there to see it happen? My son got a faceful of splinters and broke his arm, but thank God he'll be all right, or I'd be carryin' a gun right now! He told me he heard that boy shout that everybody was going to die, that the boy was cursin' everybody and puttin' some kind of spell on 'em! Even J.J. Falconer himself said the boy's just like the mother! That boy spreads Death with him wherever he goes!"

"You lyin' sonofabitch!" John shouted, trembling with rage.

"Who's stirred you up?" Ramona's voice carried over the angered yelling, and she stepped forward to the edge of the porch. She stared down at the sheeted shapes. "You're like dumb cattle, stampeded this way and that by the sound of thunder! You don't understand a *thing* about me or my son! Did that evangelist put you up to this?"

"Come on," Leighton shouted. "Time's wastin'!" He moved toward the house, and the ring of Klansmen closed in. "Put that knife down, you squaw-cat, 'fore I have to take it and cut off your tits. . . ." And then he grunted with pain and surprise, because John had leaped upon him, driving him to the ground. They cursed and rolled, grappling at each other as the Klansmen cheered Leighton on.

A rock crashed through the window behind Ramona. Then another stone was flung, hitting her on the shoulder. She gasped and went down on her knees, and then a white hooded shape leaped up onto the porch and kicked the knife from her hand. The Klansman looked up as Billy came at him like a whirlwind; the boy couldn't clench his hands yet to make fists, so he hit him with a shoulder block that lifted the man up and carried him off the porch and onto the ground on his back, sounding like a potato sack as he hit.

John had ripped the hood from Leighton's head and was hammering blows to the man's face. Leighton staggered and fell to his knees, his robes grimed with dirt; he yelled through purple, pulped lips, "Somebody get the bastard!"

Ramona screamed. Billy saw light glint off a length of iron pipe as one of the figures lifted it high. He shouted, "Look out!" John started to turn, but the pipe came down with terrible force upon the back of his head, staggering him forward. Leighton hit him in the stomach, and even as John fell the pipe came down again, its arc ending with an awful crunching sound.

There was a sudden silence. John lay on his stomach, his legs twitching, his fingers clawed into the dirt.

And then Billy, with a scream of rage that ripped through the night, leaped from the porch and flung himself onto the man who'd struck his father; they careened backward, slamming over the hood of a red Chevy. Billy forced his stiff fingers around the iron pipe, and he held onto it as someone gripped his hair and yanked him off. He rammed an elbow back into a set of teeth and pulled free, turning upon the Klansmen. With his first blow he broke a man's nose; he dodged a cast-iron skillet that had been used to make the raucous noise, came up under it, and slammed his weapon into an unprotected shoulder.

An arm caught him around the throat from behind; he kicked back into a shinbone, wrenching free as an aluminum pot swung for his head. He drove the pipe deep into someone's stomach and heard an agonized retching from inside the hood. He spun and struck again, blindly swinging the pipe with all his strength; the man in front of him backed away, but a skillet caught him a glancing blow on the shoulder and drove him to the ground.

"Kill him!" Leighton shrieked. "Go on, finish him off!"

Billy reared up and struck into a blue-jeaned kneecap. The Klansman howled with pain and hopped away like an injured toadfrog. Then someone landed on his back, pushing his face into the dirt. He struggled wildly, expecting the back of his head to be caved in.

Then there was a *crack!* like a car backfiring and the weight was off him. Around him a forest of legs scurried for the safety of their cars; Billy looked up, saw his mother on the porch holding his father's pistol in a shaky, two-handed grip. Sparks leaped with her next shot, and Billy heard a windshield crack. Engines caught, and now the vehicles were racing away from the house, their tires throwing up tails of mud.

Two cars banged into each other on the narrow drive leading down to the highway. Ramona fired two more shots that went wild before the old pistol jammed up. Then the night was filled with red taillights, and tires shrieked on the highway. As Billy rose to his feet, he saw the last of the red lights disappear. He was breathing hard, his head spinning, and his agonized hand let the iron pipe drop to the ground.

"COWARDS!" Billy shouted. "YOU DAMNED DIRTY COWARDS!" And then he heard his mother sob, and he turned to see her leaning over his father's body. He saw how white his father's face was, and how red the blood was that spilled from his mouth and nostrils. "*Dad? . . .*" Billy whispered.

Ramona looked up at her son with terror in her eyes. "Go get help, Billy! *Run!*"

27

Almost every afternoon in June, and now through July, the man and woman had sat together on the front porch. Crickets sang in the high grass, and a single cicada whined in the top branches of the big oak tree, mimicking the sawmill's distant noise. A soft breeze went by, cooling the sweat on Billy's face and back as he worked atop the roof, tearing up the rows of rotten shingles. His hair was a tangle of reddish black curls, commas of it sticking damply to his forehead; the summer sun had tanned him to a rich dark coppery color, and the physical work he'd been doing—the work of two men done by one, since his father had been hurt—had tightened the muscles in his shoulders and back so they were sharply defined under the flesh. The roof had leaked all through June, but this was the first chance he'd had to strip off the shingles and look for holes that he'd later plug with roofing pitch.

Billy had tried to get a job as a mechanic in every gas station for fifteen miles around, but when the owners learned his name their eyes went blank, like shutters being closed over windows. He'd been offered a job sweeping up in a broomcorn warehouse on the far side of Rossland City, but the place stank and was hot as hell and they expected him to be so grateful he'd work almost for free; he'd decided he would do better putting all his time and energy into the farm. All the houses and even the trailers in Hawthorne had electricity now, except for the Creekmore place, which sat so far off the highway no one from Alabama Power ever came to inquire.

Still, Billy felt the stirring of wanderlust in his soul. Yesterday, while tilling the ground for a sprinkling of tomato seeds, he'd looked up into the clear blue sky and seen a hawk, riding the breezes that carried to the east, and he'd wanted to see the land through the hawk's eyes. Beyond the valley's forested crown, he knew, were more towns and people, and roads and woods and cities and seas and deserts; beyond the valley were things both wondrous and fearful. They were calling to him, using such messengers as hawks and high, fast-moving clouds and a distant road seen from the top of a hill.

He ripped up another few shingles and dropped them over the roof's edge to the ground. He could hear his mother's voice, reading the Twenty-seventh Psalm to his father; it was one of his favorites, and hardly a day went by that he didn't ask to hear it. She finished, and he heard his father say, in his slurred unsteady voice, " 'Mona? Where's Billy?"

"He's gone up on the roof to tear off the old shingles."

"Oh. Yeah. That needs to be done. I meant to do that myself. Think he needs any help?"

"No, I believe he can do it by himself. Do you want another sip of tea?"

There was a slurping sound. Billy ripped off three shingles and tossed them over his shoulder.

"That's mighty good, 'Mona. Think you could read the Twenty-seventh Psalm to me today? Sure is a strong, hot sun up there ain't it? Cornfield'll need a dose of well-water pretty soon, I reckon. . . ."

Billy concentrated on his work while his father's mind skipped tracks like a scratched-up record. Then John lapsed into silence, and Ramona began to read the psalm again.

The doctor in Fayette had said the first lead pipe blow had fractured John Creekmore's skull; the second had driven bone splinters into the brain. John had lain in a coma for two weeks, in a charity-ward bed. What was left when he came out of the hospital was more child than man; in his eyes there was a look of painful bewilderment, but he seemed to remember nothing at all of what had happened. He recognized Ramona and Billy as his wife and son, but he made no demands on them and the day was just fine if he could sit out on the porch in the shade, or down at the pond listening to the bullfrogs. He slept a lot, and often he would ask the strangest questions, as if things were at a low boil inside his head and there was no telling what might pop up from the soup of memory.

Sometimes the gnaw of guilt got too bad inside Billy, and he'd have to get away by himself into the woods for a day or so. He knew that what had happened to his father would have been averted had he not gone to the May Night dance; no, he'd wanted to show the other kids that he was just like them and he could fit in . . . but he'd been wrong. He wasn't like them; he wasn't like anybody else. And now his father had been made to pay for it. The police had never found out who'd buried those fireworks within the bonfire, just as Sheriff Bromley had never found out who'd struck those blows to the back of John Creekmore's head; everybody had airtight alibis, the sheriff had told Ramona. It was true that Ralph Leighton's face looked as if a mule had kicked it, but his wife and son and three hunting buddies said they'd all been together playing cards the night John was hurt. They'd all sworn that Ralph had tripped down some steps and fallen right on his face.

Billy sensed movement, and looked toward the highway to see dust rising into the air. A black, battered old Volkswagen van had turned off and was coming up the road to the house. The ruts must've been too much for the suspension though, because in another moment the van stopped and a man wearing a straw hat climbed out of the driver's seat. Billy called down, "Mom! Somebody's coming!"

Ramona glanced up from the Bible and saw the figure walking slowly up the road. "Hon? We're gonna have some company."

"Company," John repeated. One half of his face was drawn tight, the other was loose and immobile. He could only speak from one side of his mouth, and on the dead half of his face the eye was a cold blue stone.

Ramona stood up. There was something written across the black van's side, but she couldn't quite make out what it said. The man was short and rounded, and now he paused to shrug off the jacket of his seersucker suit; he pegged the jacket on a finger, let it rest across his shoulder, and then continued up the slight incline, visibly huffing and puffing.

He stopped underneath the spreading oak to catch his breath. "Ma'am, I certainly hope this is the Creekmore property. If it isn't, I'm afraid I'm going to have to sit in this shade and rest."

"It is. Who might you be?"

"Ah!" The man's round, cherubic face brightened. There were spots of color on his cheeks, and he had a gray, neatly clipped mustache above a wildly sprouting goatee. "I stopped at a residence just down the way, but when I asked directions, they were quite rude. These roads around here do twist and turn, don't they? So: are you Ramona Creekmore?"

"I might be, or I might not be. I haven't heard your name yet."

The little man, who reminded Ramona of a short, fat goat, smiled and took out his wallet. The smile faltered a fraction when Billy walked out from around the house to see what was going on. "And you must be Billy," the man said.

"Yes sir."

There was a stony silence from Ramona. She stepped down off the porch as the man produced a dog-eared white business card; she took it, looked at it briefly, and then handed the card to Billy. Written across the card in an ornate script was *Dr. Reginald Mirakle, Performer Extraordinaire.*

"We don't need any doctors; we've seen enough to last us for a long time."

The man's canny gray eyes darted toward John Creekmore, sitting motionless in his chair with the Bible on his lap. "Oh. No, ma'am, you misunderstand. I'm not a medical doctor. I'm a . . . a performer."

"You mean a charlatan?"

He raised gray eyebrows as thick as caterpillars. "Some have said so in the past, I'm afraid. But that's neither here nor there. If I may? . . ." He took the card back from Billy and replaced it in his wallet. "Mrs. Creekmore, might I trouble you for a glass of water? I've driven from Haleyville this morning, and it sure is warm on the road."

Ramona paused for a few seconds, mistrustful of the man. But then she said, "All right. Billy, keep the man company, will you?" And then she went back onto the porch and inside the house. John called out to the man, "Howdy!" and then he was silent again.

Dr. Mirakle eyed the house, then looked out toward the cornfield where the scraggly stalks and scarecrow stood. "Billy," he said quietly. "Does anyone ever call you William?"

"No sir."

"How old are you?"

"Seventeen. I'll be eighteen in November."

185

"Ah, yes. Eighteen usually follows seventeen. Then you're twenty, and thirty; and pretty soon you're fifty-eight." He folded his jacket carefully and laid it on the porch floor, then took off his hat. Sweat gleamed on his balding pate, and two horns of gray hair stood up from each side of his head.

"Billy," Mirakle said, "have you ever been to a carnival?"

"No sir."

"*Never?*" Mirakle asked incredulously. "Why, when I was your age I could smell candied apples and popcorn in the air two days before the carnival got to town! And you've never been? Why, you've missed out on one of the best things life has to offer: fantasy."

Ramona came out with the man's glass of water. He drank half of it at a gulp. She said, "Now just what can we do for you?"

"Fine house you've got here," Mirakle said. He finished the water at his leisure, pretending not to notice the woman's hard stare. Then he said quietly, "I've searched for this house since the first of June. I had no idea if it was real or not. But here it is, and here are both of you. I've covered most of the northern half of Alabama looking for you."

"Why?" Ramona asked.

"In my line of work," the man said, "I travel a great deal. I meet a lot of people, and I hear a great many stories. Most of them untruths, or at best half-truths, like the tale of the giant ghost boy who walks the forest near Moundville. Or the rebel who still haunts his ruined plantation and fires at hunters who stray too near. Or the black dog that runs the road between Collinsville and Sand Rock. Maybe there was a grain of truth there once, but who knows? A gnarled oak on a moonlit night could become a giant boy. A plantation house creaks and groans with age, and someone hears a ghost walking. A wild dog runs from a car's headlights. Who knows?" He shrugged and ran a hand through his unruly hair to smooth it. "But . . . when one hears a tale about living people; well, that makes a difference. An old man in Montgomery told me that what I did was pretty fair, but had I ever heard of the Indian woman in north Alabama who could lay the dead to rest!"

Ramona's spine stiffened.

"I disregarded that story at first. But my profession draws the type of person who might be interested in the spirit world, and in four months on the road I might hit a hundred small towns. Soon I heard the story again, and this time I heard a name as well:

Creekmore. In the next town, I began asking some questions. It wasn't until much later that I heard about the boy. But by then I had to know if you were real or simply a half-truth. I began searching, and asking questions along the way." He smiled again, lines crinkling around his eyes. "It wasn't until several days ago that I heard of Hawthorne, from a man who lives in Chapin. It seems there was an accident involving a pickup truck and a large oak tree. . . ."

"Yes," the woman said.

"Ah. Then I believe my search is over." He turned his gaze toward Billy. "Are the stories about you true, young man? Can you see and talk to the dead?"

The way that question came out caught Billy off-guard. He glanced at his mother; she nodded, and he said, "Yes sir, I can."

"Then is it also true that you exorcised a demon from a house where a murder took place? That you have a power over Death itself? That you called up Satan in a deserted sawmill?"

"No. All those are made-up stories."

"That's usually the way tales are spread. A grain of truth is taken and a luster is spun around it, like an oyster with a pearl. But there is the grain of truth in those stories, isn't there?"

"Sort of, I guess."

"People talk to hear their damned lips flap!" Ramona told him. "I know full well what's said about us. Now I'd like to hear why you searched us out so long and hard."

"No need to get upset," Mirakle said. "Folks are afraid of you, but they respect you, too. As I said, I'm a performer. I have my own show, and I travel with carnivals. . . ."

"What kind of show?"

"I'm pleased you ask. It's a show that goes back to the rich vaudeville heritage of England. As a matter of fact, I learned it from an aged magician who'd performed the very same show in his heyday, in London before the Second World War."

"Mister," Ramona said, "your tongue takes more turns than a snake on wet grass."

Mirakle smiled. "What I perform, Mrs. Creekmore, is a ghost show."

An alarm bell went off in Ramona's head. She said, "Good day, Mr. Doctor Mirakle. I don't think we're interested in—"

But Billy asked, "What's a ghost show?" and the sound of curiosity in his voice made his mother uneasy. She thought of ghost-chasing charlatans, false seers, seances in dark rooms where painted skeletons danced on wires and "dire warnings" were spoken through voice-distorting trumpets: all the nasty tricks her grandmother had seen and told her to be wary of.

"Well, I'll just tell you. What I'd like to do, though, is sit down underneath that oak tree there and rest my legs, if that's okay." Billy followed him, and Ramona came down off the porch as Mirakle eased himself to the ground at the tree's base. He looked up at Billy, his gray eyes sparkling with crafty good humor. "The ghost show," he said reverently. "Billy, imagine a theater in one of the great cities of the world—New York, London, Paris perhaps. Onstage is a man—perhaps me, or even *you*—in a black tuxedo. He asks for volunteers from the audience. They tie him securely into a chair. Then a black cloth is draped around his body, and the cloth tied to the chair's legs. He is carried into a large black cabinet. The cabinet's doors are padlocked, and the volunteers go to their seats as the houselights dim. The lights go *out*. The audience waits, as a minute passes. Then another. They shift nervously in their seats." Mirakle's gaze danced from Billy to Ramona and back to the boy again.

"And then . . . a muted noise of wind. The audience *feels* it across their faces; it seems to come from all directions, yet from no direction in particular. There is the scent of flowers on the edge of decay and then . . . the distant, echoing sound of a funeral bell, tolling to twelve midnight. Above the audience there is a scattering of bright lights that slowly take on the shape of human faces, hovering in midair: the spirit guides have arrived. Music sounds; the blare of trumpets and rattle of drums. Then . . . *boom!*" He clapped his hands together for emphasis, startling both of his listeners. "A burst of red flame and smoke at center stage! BOOM! Another, stage right, and BOOM! on the left as well! The air is filled with smoke and the odor of brimstone, and the audience knows they are on a perilous voyage, into the very domain of Death itself! A wailing dark shape darts across the stage, leaps high, and soars to the ceiling; strange blue and purple lights dance in the air; moans and clanking noises fill the theater. A chorus of skeletons take center stage, link arms and kick their bony legs, accompanied by the dissonant music of a spectral orchestra. Sheeted spirits fly through the air, calling out the names of some members of the audience, and predicting events that only the all-seeing dead could know! And when the audience is driven to a peak of excitement and wonder, Old Scratch himself appears in a grand burst of red sparks! He clutches his pitchfork and prowls the stage, casting fireballs from the palms of his hands. He glares at the audience, and he says in a terrible, growling voice: 'Tell your friends to see Dr. Mirakle's Ghost Show . . . or *I'll* be seeing you!' And Satan vanishes in a grand display of pyrotechnic artistry that leaves the eyes dazzled. The lights abruptly come up; the volunteers return, unlocking the black cabinet. The form within is still securely covered with the shroud, and underneath that he is still tied exactly as before! He rises, to the applause of a stunned and pleased audience.''

Mirakle paused for a few seconds, as if regaining his breath. He smiled at Billy. "And *that*, young man, is a ghost show. Mystery. Magic. Delicious terror. Kids love it."

Ramona grunted. "If you can find a way to put all that in a sack, you could go into the fertilizer business."

Mirakle laughed heartily; as his face reddened, Billy saw the broken blue threads of veins in his nose and across his cheeks. "Ha! Yes, that's a possibility I hadn't thought of! Ha!" He shook his head, genuine mirth giving his face a rich glow. "Well, well. I'll have to consider it."

"You're a faker," Ramona said. "That's what it boils down to."

Mirakle stopped laughing and stared at her. "I'm a *performer*. I'm a supernatural artiste. I admit the ghost show isn't for everyone's taste, and I suppose that with movies and television the effect of a ghost show has taken a beating, but rural people still like them."

"You haven't answered my question yet. What are you doing here?"

"In a few days I'm going to be joining Ryder Shows, Incorporated. I'll be touring with them on the carnival circuit for the rest of the summer; then, in the fall, Ryder Shows becomes part of the state fair, in Birmingham. I need to upgrade my ghost show, to give it style and dazzle; there's a lot of work to be done, maintaining the machinery—which is in a Tuscaloosa warehouse right now—and getting the show in shape for Birmingham. I need an assistant." He looked at Billy. "Have you finished high school yet?"

"Yes sir."

"*No*," Ramona snapped. "My son workin' with a . . . a

189

fake thing like *that?* No, I won't hear of it! Now if you'd please get your caboose on down the road, I'd be grateful!" She angrily motioned for him to get up and leave.

"The pay would be quite equitable," Mirakle said, looking up at the boy. "Forty dollars a week."

"*No!*"

Billy dug his hands into his pockets. Forty dollars was a lot of money, he thought. It would buy tar and shingles for the roof, caulking for the windows, white paint for the weathered walls; it would buy new brake shoes for the Olds, and good tires too; it would buy gasoline and kerosene for the lamps, milk and sugar and flour and everything his folks would ever need. Forty dollars was a world of money. "How many weeks?" he heard himself ask.

Mirakle smiled. "The state fair ends on the thirteenth of October. Then I'll need you to help get my equipment back to Mobile, for winter storage. You'll be home by the sixteenth, at the latest."

Ramona grasped his arm and squeezed it. "I forbid it," she said. "Do you hear me? This 'ghost show' stuff is blasphemy! It mocks everything we stand for!"

"You sound like Dad used to," Billy said quietly.

"I know what you're thinkin'! Sure, forty dollars a week is a lot of money and it could be put to good use, but there's better ways of makin' an honest dollar than . . . than puttin' on a *side-show!*"

"How?" he asked her.

She was silent, the wheels turning fiercely in her brain for an answer. How, indeed?

"You'd be my assistant," Mirakle said. "You'd get a real taste of show business. You'd learn how to work in front of an audience, how to hold their attention and make them want more. You'd learn . . . what the world is like."

"The world," Billy said in a soft, faraway voice. His eyes were dark and troubled as he looked back at his father again, then at his mother. She shook her head. "It's a lot of money, Mom."

"It's nothing!" she said harshly, and turned a baleful gaze on Mirakle. "I didn't bring my son up for this, mister! Not for some sham show that tricks people!"

"Fifty dollars a week," Billy said. Mirakle's smile disappeared. "I'll do it for fifty, but not a red cent less."

"*What?* Listen, do you know how many kids I can get to work for *thirty* a week? A few thousand, that's all!"

"If you looked so long and hard to find my mother and me, I figured you must think I could add something to that show of yours that nobody else could. I figure I'm worth the fifty dollars to you, and I think you'll pay me. Because if you don't, I won't go, and all that looking you did will be wasted time. I also want a week's pay in advance, and I want three days to fix the roof and put brake shoes on the car."

Mirakle shot up from the ground, sputtering as if he'd been dashed with cold water. His head barely came up to Billy's shoulder. "Nope! Won't have it, not at all!" He strode to the porch, got his seersucker jacket, and put his hat on; the seat of his trousers was dusty, and he brushed it off with red-faced irritation. "Try to take advantage of *me*, huh?" He marched past Ramona and Billy, dust stirring up around his shoes. After ten steps his stride slowed; he stopped and let out a long sigh. "Forty-five dollars a week and two days," he said, looking over his shoulder.

Billy kicked at a pebble and considered the offer. He said, "Okay. Deal."

Mirakle clapped his hands together. Ramona clutched her son's arm and said, "So *fast?* Just like that, without talkin' it over? . . ."

"I'm sorry, Mom, but I already know what you'd say. It won't be so bad; it'll just be . . . pretending, that's all."

Mirakle walked back to them and thrust out his hand. Billy shook it. "There's no business like show business!" the man crowed, his face split by a grin. "Now did you say you wanted thirty dollars in advance?" He brought out his wallet again, opening it with a flourish. Billy saw, sealed in a plastic window, a yellowing picture of a smiling young man in a service uniform.

"Forty-five," Billy said, evenly and firmly.

Mirakle chuckled. "Yes, yes of course. I like you, William. You drive a hard bargain. And speaking of driving, do you have your license? No? You *can* drive a car, can't you?"

"I've driven the Olds a few times."

"Good. I'll need you at the wheel some." He counted out the bills. "There you are. It just about breaks me, too, but . . . I suppose you'll put it to good use. Is there a motel around here that might take a personal check?"

"The Bama Inn might. It's in Fayette. There's a Travel-Lodge,

191

too." Behind him Ramona abruptly turned and walked back toward the house.

"Ah, that's fine. I'll see you, then, in two days. Shall we say at four in the afternoon? We'll be meeting Ryder Shows in Tuscaloosa, and I'd like to get on the road before dark." He put his wallet away and shrugged into his jacket, all the time staring at Billy as if afraid the boy might change his mind. "We're set then? It's a deal?"

Billy nodded. He'd made his decision, and he wouldn't back down from it.

"You'll have to work hard," Mirakle said. "It won't be easy. But you'll learn. In two days, then. A pleasure meeting you, Mrs. Creekmore!" he called out, but she stood with her back to him. He walked off down the road, his stubby legs moving carefully as he avoided sliding on loose stones; he turned around to wave, and from the porch John suddenly called out, "Come back soon!"

28

"It's finished," Billy said, and stood on the ladder to appraise his work. It was a good job; chinks and holes in the roof had been filled in with pitch, and new shingles laid down smoothly and evenly. Midafternoon sunlight burned down upon Billy's back as he descended the ladder with his jar of roofing nails and his hammer. The gloves he wore were matted with pitch, and black streaks of it painted his chest and face. He scrubbed his face and hair with strong soap, then put away the ladder and the pitch bucket.

He let the sun dry his hair as he stood and looked in all directions. I'll be back, he told himself. Sure I will be, in mid-October. But something within him told him that when he did come back, he wouldn't be the same Billy Creekmore who'd left. He walked past the Olds—new brake shoes installed, the tires put back on but one of them already dangerously flat—and around the house to the front porch. John was in his favorite chair, a glass of lemonade at his side, the Bible in his lap. John smiled at him. "Sun's sure hot today."

Something clenched hard in Billy's stomach and throat; he managed to return the smile and say, "Yes sir, sure is."

Inside, Ramona was sitting in the front room, in the old gray easy chair. Her hands were gripping the armrests; beside her, on the floor, was a battered brown suitcase packed with her son's clothes.

"I'll be fine," Billy said.

"Tuscaloosa isn't so far away, y'know. If you don't like what you've gotten yourself into, you can just catch the bus and come home."

"I won't give it up at the first sign of trouble, though," he reminded her. "I'll stick with it as long as I can."

"A *carnival*." Ramona frowned and shook her head. Her eyes were red and puffy, but all of her crying was done. Her son was going out into the world, following the winding road of his Mystery Walk, and that was what the Giver of Breath had decreed. "I went to one of those once, when I was a little girl. The lights cut your eyes, and the noise sounds like a tea party in Hell. They show freaks at those things, poor people who can't help the way they were born. And folks stand around and laugh." She was silent for a moment. "Don't let them make a freak out of you, son. Oh, they'll try, just like the folks in Hawthorne have tried; but don't let them. You'll be tested, mark my words."

"I know."

"Do you understand"—she turned her face toward him—"that the Mystery Walk is more than the ritual your grandmother took you through? The ritual was to get your head opened up, to expand your senses; it was to make you *ready* for what's ahead. You began your Mystery Walk when you were ten years old and saw the Booker boy's revenant, but your whole life will be a Mystery Walk, just like mine has been. Events will hinge on events, like a series of opening doors; people will touch and be touched by you, and you must never belittle the power of the human touch. It can work wonders."

She leaned slightly toward him, her eyes shining. "You'll have to go into places that are *dark*, son, and you'll have to find your way out alone. What you saw in the smokehouse—the shape changer—isn't the only kind of darkness in this world. There's human darkness, too, misery and pain and torment that comes right from the soul. You'll see that kind, too.

"But the shape changer will be back, Billy. I'm sure of that. It's still picking at you, maybe even without you knowing it. Your grandmother was never certain of what the shape changer's limits were, or what it was capable of doing. I'm not, either . . . but expect the unexpected, always."

He thought of the boar-thing, and its whispered promise: *I'll be waiting for you.*

"How did you feel," she asked, "after . . . what you did at the sawmill?"

"I was afraid. And I was mad, too." For a couple of weeks afterward he'd had nightmares of a spinning saw blade grinding his arm down to bloody pulp. Sometimes he felt a fierce, jagged pain stabbing his left eye. Worse then the pain, though, was a hot center of anger that had raged in him until he'd attacked the Klansmen in the front yard; afterward both the phantom pain and the rage had steadily faded.

"Those were the emotions that kept Link Patterson chained to this world," Ramona said. "When you persuaded the revenant to give them up, he was able to pass on. You'll have those feelings inside you again; what will you do with them? The next time might be worse. You'll have two choices: you can turn the emotions into something creative, or into something mean and violent. I don't know, that's up to you."

"I'll handle it."

"And then there's the other thing." She gazed out the window for a moment, dreading to see dust rise off the road. That man would be here soon. "The black aura."

Billy's heart gave a cold kick.

"You'll see it again. That's why I stopped goin' out, stopped goin' to church or to town; I just don't want to know who'll be the next to die. That night at the tent revival, I saw it around a couple of people who that Falconer boy said was healed; well, those people were near death, and so they stopped takin' their medicine and went home and died. I believe that the human mind can work miracles, Billy: mighty, earth-movin' miracles. The human mind can heal the body; but sometimes the mind can make the body sick, too, with imagined ailments. What do you think went on in the minds of those families whose loved ones went to the Crusade and were told to throw away their medicines and not to go to the doctor anymore? Well, they probably cursed the name of God after their loved ones died, because they'd been filled with false hope and then death struck. They were made to turn their backs on the idea of death, to close their eyes to it; and that made it so much more terrible when they lost their loved ones. Oh, I'm not sayin' give up hope, but everybody gets sick, Christians and sinners alike, and medicines are to be used to help . . . plus a good old-fashioned dollop of sunshine, laughter, and faith. The human touch spreads; when Wayne Falconer played God, he turned good people with brains into stupid sheep ripe for the shearing."

"Are you sure those people died afterwards?" Billy asked. "Maybe the black aura got weaker, and they regained their health. . . ."

She shook her head. "No. I saw what I saw, and I wish to God I hadn't because now I *know*. I know and I have to be silent, because what can one aging old witch do?" She paused for a moment, and Billy saw in her eyes a deep concern that he couldn't fully understand. "The worst evil—the very worst—wears the robes of a shepherd, and then it strikes down those who've trusted in it. Oh, Lord. . . ." She gave a deep sigh, and then was silent.

Billy put his hand on her shoulder, and she covered it with her own. "I'll make you proud of me, Mom. You'll see."

"I know. Billy, you're goin' a long ways. . . ."

"Just to Tuscaloosa. . . ."

"No," she said quietly. "*First* to Tuscaloosa. Then . . . your Mystery Walk will be different from mine, just as mine was different from my mother's. You'll walk a further path, and you'll see things I never dreamed of. In a way, I envy you; and in a way, I fear for you. Well . . ." She rose up from her chair, and in the afternoon light Billy saw all the strands of silver in her hair. "I'll make you some sandwiches while you get dressed. Lord only knows when you'll have a chance to eat."

He went to his chest of drawers and got out the clothes he'd planned to wear on the trip—clean blue jeans and a green-and-blue madras shirt. He dressed hurriedly, wanting to have time to talk to his father before he had to go. Then he took the gleaming piece of good-luck coal from the dirty jeans he'd worn atop the roof, and put it in his pocket. His heart was beating like a drum corps. He took his suitcase out to the porch, where his father was squinting toward the road, his head cocked to one side as if listening.

"Hot day," John said. "Listen to that corn rustle."

"Dad?" Billy said. "I don't know if you can understand me or not, but . . . I'm going away for a while. See? My suitcase is all packed, and . . ." There was a lump in his throat, and he had to wait until it subsided. "I'll be gone until October." A sudden thought speared him: *Your Dad won't be here, come October.* He forced it away, looking at the good side of his father's face.

John nodded. "Crickets sure like to sing on a hot day, don't they?"

"Oh, Dad . . ." Billy said. His throat constricted and he grasped one of his father's leathery hands, dangling over the chair arm. "I'm sorry, it was because of me this happened to you, I'm sorry, I'm sorry. . . ." Tears burned his eyes.

"Splash!" John said, and grinned. "Did you see that? Old bullfrog jumped down at the pond!" He squinted and leaned forward, visoring his eyes with his free hand. "Looky there. Company's comin'."

Dust was rising off the road. *Not now!* Billy said mentally. *It's too soon!* Birds scattered up out of the lumbering van's path; the vehicle didn't stop this time, but braved the rocks and ruts all the way up to the front yard. On the van's sides, written in spooky-looking white letters, was DR. MIRAKLE'S GHOST SHOW.

"Who's our company today?" John asked, the grin stuck lopsided on his face.

"The man I told you about, hon," Ramona said from behind the screen door; she came on out carrying a paper sack with a peanut-butter-and-jelly sandwich, a bologna sandwich, and two red apples in it. Her eyes glazed over as the van's door opened and Dr. Mirakle, looking as if he'd slept in his seersucker suit and straw hat, stepped out.

"Fine afternoon, isn't it!" he called and approached the house on his stubby legs; his wide smile lost wattage with every step he took, as he felt Ramona Creekmore's icy glare on him. He cleared his throat and craned his neck to see the roof. "All finished?"

"He's finished," Ramona said.

"Good. Mr. Creekmore, how are you today?"

John just stared at him.

Mirakle stepped up to the edge of the porch. "Billy? It's time to go now."

As Billy bent to pick up his suitcase, Ramona caught at his arm. "Just a minute! You promise me one thing! You take good care of my boy! You treat him like you'd treat a son of your own! He's a hard worker, but he's nobody's mule. You treat my boy fair. Will you promise me that?"

"Yes, ma'am," Mirakle said, and bowed his head slightly. "I do so promise. Well . . . I'll take this on to the van for you, then." He reached up and took the suitcase, then carried it to the van to give them a moment alone.

"Billy." John's voice was slow and sluggish; his blue eyes were dull, hazed with half-remembered days when the young man standing before him was a little boy. A smile worked around the good edge of his mouth, but wouldn't take hold.

"I'm going away, Dad. I'll work hard, and I'll mail you money. Everything'll be fine. . . ."

"Billy," John said, "I . . . I want . . . to read you something." Emotion had thickened his speech, made it more difficult for him to say the right words. He was trying very hard to concentrate; he turned in the Bible to the Book of Matthew, and searched for a particular passage. Then he began to read, with difficulty: "Matthew seven, verses thirteen and fourteen. 'Enter ye in . . . at the strait gate; for wide is the gate, and broad is the way that . . . leadeth to destruction, and . . . many there be which . . . go in thereat. Because strait is the gate and . . . narrow is the way which leadeth unto life, and few there be . . . that find it.' " He closed the Bible and lifted his gaze to his son. "I'm readin' better," he said.

Billy leaned down, hugged him and kissed his cheek; he smelled of Vitalis, and Billy was reminded of the times they used to get their hair cut together at Curtis Peel's. When he raised up, his father's eyes were shining. "Good-bye, Dad," Billy said.

Ramona put her arm around her son, and they started walking toward Dr. Mirakle's van. "Be careful," she said, her voice husky with emotion. "Be strong and proud. Brush your teeth twice a day, and hang your clothes up at night. Just remember who you are: you're Billy Creekmore, there's Choctaw blood in your veins, and you can walk with the likes of *anybody!*"

"Yes ma'am. I'll send the money every week, and I'll . . ." He glanced up at the van, and a shadow of true fear passed over him; he felt like a shipwrecked sailor, slowly drifting away from land. "I'll be fine," he said, as the feeling began to fade. "You should take the car down to the gas station and put air in the tires. I meant to do it myself, but . . . time just got away. . . ."

"You write now, you hear? Mind your manners, and say your prayers. . . ."

Mirakle had leaned over and opened the passenger door. Billy climbed up into the slightly greasy interior; when he closed the door, his mother said, "Remember who you are! You've got Choctaw blood in your veins, and . . ."

Mirakle started the engine. "Are you ready, Billy?"

"Yes sir." He looked toward the house, waved at his father, and then said to Ramona, "I love you." The van started moving.

"I love you!" she called back, and walked alongside the van as it eased over the ruts. "Get your sleep, and don't stay out until all hours of the night." She had to walk faster, because the van was picking up speed. Dust blossomed from beneath the tires. "Do right!" she called out.

"I will!" Billy promised, and then his mother was left behind as the van moved away. Ramona stood shielding her face from the dust as the black van reached the highway. It turned left and disappeared behind the curtain of full green trees, but Ramona stood where she was until the sound of its engine had faded, leaving faint echoes in the hills.

29

Ramona turned away and walked back to the house through the hanging layers of dust. She sat on the porch with John for a few minutes more, and told him she was going to take the car down to the gas station, then drive in to Fayette for a little while, and she'd be gone for maybe two hours. He nodded and said that was fine. In the house, she took two dollars from the kitchen cookie jar, made sure John would have everything he needed while she was gone, then took the car keys from where they lay on the mantel. It was four-twenty when she got on the road, and she wanted to reach a particular shop in Fayette before it closed at five.

In Fayette, Ramona parked the Olds near a rather run-down pawnshop and loan service. Arranged in the window were displays of cheap rhinestone rings, radios, a couple of electric guitars, a trombone, and a few cheap wristwatches. Above the doorway a sign read HAP'S PAWNS AND LOANS and YOU'RE ALWAYS HAPPY WHEN YOU TRADE WITH HAP. She stepped into the shop, where a single ceiling fan stirred the heavy, dusty air. "Is Mr. Tillman in today?" she asked a sallow-faced woman behind one of the counters.

"Hap?" The woman had flame-red dyed hair and one glass eye that looked off into empty space; with her good eye she quickly appraised Ramona. "Yeah, he's back in his office. What do you want to see him a—" But Ramona was already moving, heading back along an aisle toward the shop's rear. "Hey! Lady! You can't go back there!"

Ramona stepped through a green curtain into a narrow, dank corridor. She rapped on a door and entered the office without being asked in.

"Hap" Tillman's thick body was reclining in his chair, his legs up on the desktop, as he smoked a Swisher Sweet cigar and paged through a *Stag* magazine. Now he sat up, outraged that someone had dared to invade his inner sanctum, and was about to curse a blue streak when he saw it was Ramona Creekmore. The red-haired woman stuck her head in. "Hap, I told her not to come back here."

"It's okay, Doris." He had a fleshy, square-jawed face and wore a stark-black toupee that was entirely at odds with his gray eyebrows. "I know Mizz Creekmore. You can leave us be."

"I *told* her not to come back," Doris said; she shot Ramona a black look and closed the door.

"Well! Mizz Creekmore, what a surprise to see you of all people!" Tillman tapped ash off his Swisher Sweet and plugged the cigar into his mouth. Around his desk was a sea of stacked boxes; over in one corner were black filing cabinets, and on the wall hung a calendar that showed a well-endowed woman in a bikini straddling a watermelon. "Whatever can I do for you today?"

She said, "I want to know."

"What?" he asked. "Did I hear you right?"

"Yes, I want to know. *Now*."

"Shit you say!" Tillman leaped up, belching out smoke like a furnace, and stepped past Ramona to throw open the door. He peered out into the empty corridor, then closed the door again and locked it. "That bitch Doris listens outside my office," he told her. "I've caught her at it twice. Damn it, lady, you've got an awful short memory! We did *business*. Know what that means? *Business* means we got a binding contract!"

"I think I already know, Mr. Tillman. But I . . . I have to make sure. It's important. . . ."

"My *ass* is important, too! We may have done business, but a lot of it was out of the kindness of my heart. I pulled a lot of strings!" He tried to stare her down and failed. Shaking his head, he puffed on his cigar and retreated behind the fortress of his boxes and desk. His eyes glinted. "Oh, I see. Sure. It's blackmail, is that it?"

"No. It's not that at—"

Tillman's head darted forward. "It better not be! I may be in deep, but *you're* in *deeper!* You just remember that, if you try to get me in trouble!"

"Mr. Tillman," Ramona said patiently, and stepped closer to his desk. "I wouldn't be here asking you about this if I didn't think it was very, very important. I'm not going to blackmail anybody. I'm not going to cause any trouble. But I'm not leaving here until I know."

"Lady, you signed a goddamned contract. . . ."

"I don't care if I signed ten contracts!" Ramona shouted, and instantly the man winced and put a finger to his lips to shush her.

"Please . . . please," Tillman said, "keep your voice down! Sit down and calm yourself, will you?" He motioned toward a chair, and reluctantly Ramona sat down. He puffed on his cigar for a moment, trying to think what to do.

"Shitfire, lady!" Tillman crushed the cigar in an ashtray, and sparks jumped like tiny red grasshoppers. "It's just . . . it's just not ethical! I mean, there's a lot to think about, and I wish you'd—"

"I've thought about it," Ramona said. "Now do you tell me or do I have to go see a policeman?"

"You *wouldn't*," he sneered. Tillman sat down, and faced Ramona in silence for a moment. Then he sighed deeply and said, "I'm a born fool for doin' business with a crazy woman!" He slid the top drawer out of his desk and reached into the slot, his fingers searching for the strip of masking tape; he found it, peeled it off, and brought it out. Stuck to the tape was a small key. He looked up at Ramona. "Don't you *ever* show your face in my shop again," he said gravely. "Do you understand me, lady?" He stood up, went to one wall, and lifted a framed paint-by-numbers picture of a harbor scene. There was a combination safe behind it. Tillman dialed it open, careful to stand in front of it so Ramona couldn't see the numbers.

"You may fool everybody else," he said, "but not me, lady. Nosir! You and that boy of yours are natural-born con artists! Pretendin' to talk to ghosts! That's the biggest fool thing I ever heard tell of!" He brought a small metal strongbox out of the safe, laid it on his desk. "Everybody else might be afraid of you, but *I'm* not! Nosir!" He opened the strongbox with the little key, and flipped through index cards. "*Creekmore*," he read, and brought the card out. It was slightly yellowed with age; Tillman couldn't suppress a wicked grin as he read it. Then he handed it to the woman. "Here!"

Ramona looked at it, her mouth set in a tight, grim line.

"Ha!" Tillman laughed. "Bet *that* galls your Indian ass, doesn't it?"

She handed the card back and rose from her chair. "It's as I thought. Thank you."

"Yeah, that's a real hoot, ain't it!" Tillman returned the card to the strongbox, closed the lid, and locked it. "But you know my motto: You're always happy when you trade with Hap!"

She looked into his ugly, grinning face and felt the urge to slap it crooked. But what good would that do? Would it change things, or make them right?

"Yeah, that's a real dipsy-doodle!" Tillman chuckled, put the box away in the safe, and closed it, spinning the combination lock. "Forgive me if I don't see you to the door," he said sarcastically, "but I've got a business to—" He turned toward Ramona, but she was already gone. He opened the door and yelled out, "AND DON'T COME BACK!"

SEVEN

Ghost Show

30

Satan came shambling out into the red spotlight. There was a chorus of screams and jeers. Behind the foul-smelling mask, Billy said, "Don't forget to tell your friends to see Dr. Mirakle's Ghost Show . . . or I'll be seeing you!" He shook his plastic pitchfork at the dozen or so people who sat before the stage, and heard the muffled *thump!* as Dr. Mirakle sneaked back inside the black cabinet and closed the lid. Haze drifted in the air from the smoke bombs Mirakle had exploded. At the tent's ceiling bobbed papier-mâché ghosts and skeletons as eerie tape-recorded organ music played.

Billy was glad to get backstage and take off the mask of his Satan suit. Last night someone had pelted him with a tomato. He switched the laboring engine to reverse, which drew all the wires and dangling figures backward behind the stage curtain. Then Billy turned on the tent's lights. Dr. Mirakle was "freed" from the black cabinet—though the lock was a fake and had never been locked at all—and the night's last show was over.

Billy checked all the chains and wires that operated the Ghost Show figures, then went out to pick up the litter of cigarette butts and empty popcorn boxes. Dr. Mirakle went backstage, as he did every night, to place the prop figures in their little individual boxes, like small white coffins. They had one more day in a shopping-center parking lot south of Andalusia; about this time tomorrow night the carnival would be on its way to another small town.

When he was finished, Billy went backstage and washed his hands in a bucket of soapy water, then changed into a fresh shirt.

"And where are *you* going?" Mirakle asked, carefully placing a ghost into a styrofoam box.

Billy shrugged. "I thought I'd just walk up the midway, see what's going on."

"Of course, even though you know every game on the midway is as crooked as a pig's tail. Let's see: clean hands, fresh shirt, combed hair—if I recall my ancient history, 'spiffing up' is what I used to do when I was about to meet a member of the opposite sex. Do you have a certain young lady in mind?"

"No sir."

"Walking up the midway, eh? You wouldn't be planning to visit a certain sideshow that's got all the roustabouts in such agitation, would you?"

Billy grinned. "I thought I might look in on it." The Jungle Love show, down at the far end of the midway, had joined the carnival at the first of the week. There were pictures of the girls out front, and a red-painted legend read SEE TIGRA! SANTHA THE PANTHA! BARBIE BALBOA! LEONA THE LIONESS! Not all of the girls were so attractive, but one picture had caught Billy's eye when he'd strolled over there a few days before. The girl in it had short, curly blond hair, and it looked as if all she wore was a black velvet robe. Her legs were bare and shapely, and her pretty gamine face sent out a direct sexual challenge. Billy felt his stomach do slow flipflops every time he looked at that picture, but he hadn't had the time yet to go inside.

Mirakle shook his head. "I did tell your mother I'd look after you, you know, and I hear some rough customers hang around that 'exhibition.'"

"I'll be all right."

"I doubt that. Once a young man sees a nude woman gyrating on stage a few feet from his face, he's never quite the same again. Well, go ahead if your hormones are in such a galloping fit. I'll just finish putting the kiddies to bed."

Billy left the tent, walking into the humid August night. Around him the air glowed with lights. Some of the sideshows were closing down, but most of the rides still jerked and swung their passengers through the night, their engines growling like wild beasts. The carousel, topped with white and blue bulbs, was spinning merrily as recorded calliope music rang out. The Ferris wheel was a jeweled pendant set against the darkness.

Billy had received a letter from home today. The letters sometimes caught up with him late, though he tried to let his mother know in advance where the carnival would be stopping. There was a message in his father's scrawl: *Hope you are fine. I went to the doctor yesterday. I feel good. Love, Dad*. He'd written back that he was doing fine, and business was good; he left out the fact that he had to dress up as Satan. He also didn't mention that he'd seen the black aura several times in the throng of customers.

He'd found out that Dr. Mirakle's real name was Reginald Merkle, and that he had a real affinity to J.W. Dant bourbon. Several times the man had gone through his Ghost Show routine barely able to stand. Dr. Mirakle had started out to be a dentist, he'd told Billy, until he realized he couldn't stomach the idea of peering into people's mouths all day long. Billy at one point had inquired about Mirakle's family, but the man quickly said he had no family except for the little figures of ghosts and skeletons. He had names for all of them, and he treated them like children. Billy was puzzled about the picture of the young man Dr. Mirakle carried in his wallet, but it was obvious Dr. Mirakle didn't want to discuss his personal life.

Billy saw the blinking red neon sign ahead: JUNGLE LOVE . . . JUNGLE LOVE. He could hear the faint booming of bass drums.

Another new sideshow had been added to the midway as well. It stood between the Ghost Show and the Tiltawhirl on the other side of the midway, its white clapboard structure festooned with garish paintings of snakes with venom-dripping fangs. The entrance was through the open mouth of a huge snake, and above the entrance the sign read ALIVE! SEE KILLER SNAKES OF THE WORLD! ALIVE!

It was a strange thing, Billy thought, but after four days he still hadn't seen the man who ran the snake show. The only sign of life over there, besides the paying customers, was that the entrance was open at three in the afternoon and closed at eleven. Right now he saw that the door was slightly ajar. The huge red-painted snake eyes seemed to watch Billy as he hurried past.

"Stop it!" he heard someone wail.

"Please . . . going too fast . . . !"

Between Billy and the Jungle Love sideshow loomed another new ride that was shaped like the skeleton of a huge umbrella. Four gondolas—yellow, red, purple, and one still wrapped up in a protective green tarpaulin—whirled on the end of thick metal spokes connected to a central piston mechanism. Hydraulics hissed, and the gondolas wildly pitched up and down. Screams erupted as the ride went faster and faster, the gondolas dipping to within three feet of the ground and then quickly pitching upward to almost thirty feet. The entire mechanism groaned, swinging in a fierce circle. Two people were riding in each of the three gondolas, which had safety canopies of wire mesh that closed down over their heads. At the control lever, his foot poised above a metal brake pad, was a thin man with lank, shoulder-length brown hair. A sign with mostly burnt-out bulbs said OCTOPUS.

". . . please stop it!" a voice wailed from one of the gondolas.

Billy saw the man give it more speed. The Octopus was vibrating, the noise of pounding pistons was almost shaking the ground. The man was grinning, but Billy saw that his eyes were dead. The machine seemed barely in control.

Billy stepped closer to him and touched his shoulder. "Mister—"

The man's head whipped around. For an instant Billy saw a red gleam in his eyes, and he started, remembering the way the beast had grinned at him out on that highway in the dead of night. Then the man blinked. "Shitfire!" he shouted, and stomped down on the brake as he disengaged the gears. With a high metallic shriek, the Octopus began to slow. "Damn it, boy!" the man said. "Don't you sneak up on people like that!" A jagged scar ran through the man's right eyebrow, and in a breath of wind from the Octopus his hair lifted to show he was missing an ear. One hand had only three fingers.

The Octopus was slowing. The whine of brakes had faded. But in the absence of noise Billy imagined he heard another sound: a high-pitched, eerie screaming—like a dozen voices at once. The sound faded in and out, and Billy felt his flesh crawl.

The man went to each gondola and unlocked the mesh canopies, letting out angry and tearful kids. "So sue me!" he shouted at one of them.

Billy stared at the Octopus. He saw scaly, rust-eaten metal behind a hanging flap of tarpaulin. The faint screaming went on and on, drifting in and out. "Why's that gondola covered up?" he asked the man.

"Needs work. Gonna repaint it. Don't you have nothin' better to do?" He glared up at a couple of approaching teen-agers and snapped, "We're closed!"

Abruptly, the eerie voices stopped, as if they'd been silenced by a stronger force. Billy felt himself stepping closer to the hidden gondola. He had the sudden urge to climb into it, to close the canopy over his head, to let the Octopus whirl him high into the air. It would be the best ride in the world, he thought. The most thrilling ever. *But for the most excitement, the very most, you have to ride in the covered gondola.* . . .

He stopped in his tracks, and he knew.

There was something deadly in that scabrous gondola.

"What're you lookin' at?" the man said uneasily. When Billy turned toward him, he saw a heavyset woman with a sad face and coarse blond hair coming out of the shadows.

"Buck?" she said tentatively. "Buck, it's time to close down now."

"Don't bother me, woman!" he shouted, and then he paused, frowning. "I'm sorry, hon," he said wearily, and then he looked again at the Octopus. Billy saw a strange combination of fear and love on his face. "You're right. It's time to shut it down for tonight." Buck started walking to the generator that powered the ride.

The woman came toward Billy. "Get away from that machine, boy. Get away from it right now!" she warned him. And then the Octopus sign went out.

"What's wrong with it?" he asked her, quietly so the man wouldn't hear.

She shook her head, obviously afraid to say any more.

"Go on about your business!" Buck shouted at him. "This is a good ride, boy!" Something was about to break behind the man's eyes. "I was in control all the time!"

Billy saw the torment in both their faces, and he hurried away. Lights were flickering off all over the midway. He saw the Jungle Love sign go out, and knew he'd missed the last show.

The Octopus had just gone up this morning. He remembered that one of the roustabouts had split his hand open on a bolt, but then he'd thought nothing of it because accidents were common. The roustabout had bled a great deal. He decided to stay away from that machine, because he remembered his mother telling him that evil could grow in the most unexpected places—like an oak tree.

Or a machine.

The screams were silenced, Billy thought, as if the machine had offered them up to whet his curiosity. When he looked over his shoulder, the man and woman were gone. The midway was clearing out.

Billy glanced over at the Jungle Love sideshow. There was a figure standing near the entrance, where the sexy photographs were tacked to a display board. He decided to walk over, to find out if the man worked with the sideshow. But before Billy could reach him, the man stepped into the darkness between the Jungle Love trailer and the Mad Mouse maze.

When Billy reached the display board, he saw that the photograph of the blond girl—the one who troubled his dreams so much—had been ripped away.

31

"You'd better slow down," Helen Betts said. "Wayne won't like it."

At the wheel of his fire-engine-red Camaro, Terry Dozier was watching the speedometer climb to sixty-five. Before the headlights, the highway—ten miles north of Fayette—was a yellow tunnel cut through the mountain of night. Terry smiled, his eyes full of devilment. No one, not even his steady girl friend, Helen, knew that one of Terry's favorite hobbies was beating out the brains of stray cats with a Louisville Slugger.

Wayne was stretched out in the backseat, his legs sprawled on a half-empty box of Falconer Crusade Bibles, the last of a dozen boxes that Terry and Helen had helped Wayne hand-deliver. Fayette County residents who'd donated upward of one hundred dollars during the highly publicized "Bible Bounty Week" got a Bible and a visit from Little Wayne Falconer. It had been a long, tiring day, and Wayne had healed whole families today of everything from inner-ear trouble to nicotine addiction. His restless sleep was haunted by two recurring dreams: one of a snake of fire fighting an eagle of smoke; and one in which the Creekmores were standing in that hospital waiting room, the woman's eyes fixed on him as if she could see right through his skin to the soul, her mouth opening to say *Do you know what you're doing, son?*

He feared he was falling under some kind of spell, because he couldn't get his mind off the woman and boy. They were using strong power on him, he thought, to draw his mind from the straight-and-narrow path. He'd been reading a lot lately about demon possession, about demons that were so strong they could inhabit both the living and the dead, and nothing scared him any worse. Praying in the chapel at home seemed to ease his brain for a while.

Wayne came up out of a light sleep and saw Helen's autumn hair blowing in the breeze from the open window. Both she and Terry were going to college in a few weeks on Falconer Crusade scholarships. Helen was a pretty girl, he mused. Her hair smelled nice, like peppermints. He was horrified when he realized he was getting an erection, and he tried to blank out the thought of sinful sex. Nude girls sometimes cavorted in his mind, begging him to take off his clothes and join them. Stop it! he told himself, squeezing his eyes shut. But as he drifted off again he thought: *I'll bet Helen and Terry do it do it do it.* . . . .

"Where are you going?" she asked Terry in a nervous whisper. "You missed the turnoff!"

"On purpose, babe. Don't worry, it's cool."

"Tell me *where*, Terry!"

"Steve Dickerson's having a party, isn't he? We were invited, weren't we?"

"Well . . . sure, but . . . that's not exactly Wayne's type of crowd. I mean . . . with everybody going off to college and all, it might be kinda wild."

"So what? It'll do old Wayne good." He squeezed her thigh and she gave his hand a little love-slap. "And if somebody gets drunk, Wayne can just touch his hand and draw out the deeeemon of al-ke-hall!" He giggled as Helen looked at him, horrified. "Oh come on, Betts! You don't take that healing crap seriously, do you?"

Helen blanched, turning quickly to make sure Wayne was still sleeping. She was sure glad it was such a clear August night, no thunderstorms around—struck by lightning would be a bad way to go.

The Dickerson house was a two-story colonial on the edge of a six-acre lake. There was a long expanse of emerald green lawn, dew glittering in the squares of light cast from the windows. Terry whistled softly when he saw the tough specimens of high-horsepower cars parked along the curb.

He parked the Camaro and winked at Helen. "Wayne? We're here."

"Huh? We're home?"

"Well . . . no, not just yet. We're at Steve Dickerson's house."

Wayne sat up, bleary-eyed.

"Now, before you say anything," Terry told him, "there's a party goin' on. Steve's folks are out of town this weekend, so he invited everybody. I thought we could all . . . you know, unwind."

"But"—Wayne stared at the house—"Steve Dickerson isn't *saved*."

"Helen and I worked hard today, didn't we? By the time we take you home and come back, it'll be pretty late. So why don't we go in for a while, just to be social?"

"I don't know. My . . . my father's expecting me home by . . ."

"Don't worry about it!" Terry was getting out. Helen was irritated at him for dragging Wayne to this party, because she knew the hell-raisers of Indian Hills High would be here, the kind of people Terry associated with before he'd been Saved. Sometimes she thought that Being Saved was rubbing off Terry like old paint.

Uneasily, Wayne followed them up the flagstone walkway. They could hear the muffled thump of loud music from inside. Helen said nervously, "Wayne, it'll be fun. I bet there are a lot of girls who'd like to meet you."

Wayne's heart skipped a beat. "Girls?"

"Yeah." Terry rang the doorbell. "Girls. You know what they are, don't you?"

The door opened, and the riotous noise of a party in full swing came crashing out. Hal Baker stood on the threshold, his arm around a skinny blond girl who looked drunk. "How's it hangin', Terry!" Hal said. "Come on in! Old Steve's around here some—" His blurry gaze fell upon Wayne Falconer, and his face went into shock. "Is that . . . Little Wayne?"

"Yep," Terry chortled, "sure is. Thought we'd stop by to check out the action!" Terry and Helen stepped into the house, but Wayne paused. Laughter and music were thunderous inside there.

The blond girl's nipples were showing through the purple halter-top she wore. She smiled at him.

"Comin' in?" Terry asked.

"No . . . I think I'd better . . ."

"What's wrong, man?" the girl asked him, a foxy grin on her face. "You afraid of big bad parties?"

"No. I'm not afraid." And before he'd realized it, Wayne had taken a step forward. Hal closed the door behind him. The Amboy Dukes singing "Journey to the Center of the Mind" blasted from the rear of the house. Sinful drug music, Wayne thought, as he followed Terry and Helen through a mass of people he didn't know. They were drinking and smoking and running as wild as bucks through the entire house. Wayne's spine was as stiff as pineboard. He felt as if he'd stepped onto another planet. An aroma of burning rope scorched his nostrils, and a boy stumbled past him stinking drunk.

Terry pressed a paper cup into Wayne's hand. "There you go. Oh, don't worry. It's just Seven-Up."

Wayne sipped at it. It was Seven-Up, all right, but it had gone flat and tasted like the inside of an old shoe. It was as hot and smoky as Hades inside this house, and Wayne sucked on the ice in his cup.

"Mingle, Wayne," Terry told him, and pulled Helen away into the crowd. He didn't dare tell her that he'd laced Wayne's drink with gin.

Wayne had never been to an unchaperoned party before. He wandered through the house, repelled and yet fascinated. He saw many pretty girls, some wearing tight hotpants, and one of them even smiled at him across the room. He blushed and hurried away, trying to hide the stirring in his pants. On the patio that overlooked the dark, still lake, people were dancing to the roar of a stereo. *Dancing!* Wayne thought. *It was inviting sin!* But he watched the bodies rub, transfixed. It was like watching a pagan frenzy. That burned-rope smell followed him everywhere, and he saw people smoking hand-rolled cigarettes. His eyes began to water. Across the patio he saw Terry talking to a girl with long black hair. He tried to catch Terry's attention, because he was feeling a little light-headed and needed to get home; but then Terry and Helen had started dancing to Steppenwolf music, so Wayne went off toward the lakeshore to get away from the noise.

The party, to him, was like the inside of a nervous breakdown.

213

He almost stumbled over a pair of bodies entwined on the ground. Catching a glimpse of exposed breasts, he apologized and continued on as a boy cursed at him. Walking far away from the house, Wayne sat down on the shore near a couple of beached canoes and sucked on his ice. He was trembling inside, and wished he'd never stepped across that doorway.

"You all alone?" someone asked. A girl's voice, with a thick backhills accent.

Wayne looked up. He couldn't see her face, but she had thick waves of black hair and he thought she was the same girl Terry had been talking to. She was wearing a low-cut peasant blouse and bell-bottoms, rolled up as if she'd been wading in the water. "Want some company?"

"No, thank you."

She swigged from a can of beer. "This party's fucked up. I hear Dickerson put acid in the punch. That would really fuck everybody's mind, huh?"

He winced at the first use of that awful four-letter sex word; the second gave him a funny feeling in the pit of his stomach. She was the kind of girl who did it, he realized.

"Pretend I'm blind," the girl said, and crouched down in front of Wayne. She ran her hand all over Wayne's face. He flinched because she smelled so strongly of beer. "See, I'm blind and I've got to feel what you look like. You go to Indian Hills?"

"I graduated." Beneath the beer odor was another aroma: the rich, musky, forbidden scent of a woman. He told himself to get up and go back to the car. But he didn't move.

"My name's Lonnie. What's yours?"

"Wayne." He almost said Falconer, but the name hung on his lips. He shifted his position, hoping she wouldn't notice his swelling penis. Tell her who you are, he told himself, so she'll get up and leave you alone!

"You know Randy Leach? Well me and him broke up tonight. Sonofabitch is going to Samford University in Birmingham, says he's got to date other girls. Shit!" She drank from the beer and offered it to him, but he shook his head. "I wasted a whole summer on that bastard!"

"I'm sorry to hear that."

"Well, that's how it goes I guess." She looked at him and laughed. "Hey, what's wrong? You look like a whore in church, you're so tense!"

Blasphemy and sacrilege! Wayne thought. He looked at her in the darkness, but could only make out the pale oval of her face. He couldn't tell if she was pretty or not, but he knew she was a lost sinner. "Are you saved, girl?" he asked.

There was a moment of shocked silence. Then the girl laughed uproariously. "Oh, wow! I thought you really meant that! You sounded just like my damn momma, always after me to go to churchy-wurchy! Are you rich?"

"Rich?" Wayne echoed. "I . . . guess I am," he said truthfully.

"I knew it. Know how I knew? 'Cause there's somethin' so squeaky-clean about you. And you don't even drink beer, do you, 'cause it's too low-class for you. Where you going to college?"

"Up in Tennessee." Tell her it's the Southeastern Bible College!

He could sense the girl staring at him. "You're sweet," she said softly. "Who'd you come here with?"

"Terry Dozier and Helen Betts."

"Don't know them." She sat close to him and looked out toward the lake. Wayne could feel her body heat, and again he shifted uncomfortably. The images tumbling through his mind were nasty and sinful, and he knew he was walking close to the Pit. "I've went with a lot of boys," Lonnie said after a while. "How come every boy I ever go with just wants to have sex?"

Jezebel! Wayne thought.

"I mean, I know I've got a good body and all. I was in the Miss Fayette Junior High contest last year, and I got the most points in the swimsuit competition. But seems like everybody tries to take advantage of me. Wonder why that is?"

"I don't know," Wayne said in a husky voice. From a black part of his mind a sibilant voice said, *She wants to do it and she uses the four-letter sex word.*

Then, before Wayne could shift away again, Lonnie leaned toward him and whispered in his ear, "Why don't we go out in one of them canoes?"

"I can't. I've . . . I've got my good clothes on."

She giggled and tugged at his shirt. "Then take your good clothes *off.*"

"You'd better get back to the party. Somebody'll miss you."

"Miss me? Naw! Randy left with somebody else! Come on, sweet thing, let's got out in a canoe. Okay? You're so tense, what's wrong? Little Lonnie make you nervous?" She took his hand and tugged at him until he stood up, and then she pulled him with her to the nearest canoe.

Wayne's head was dizzy, throbbing from the echo of the rock music from way up on the patio. Lake water lapped softly at the shore. "I don't see any paddles in there."

She climbed in carefully and rummaged around, then held up a paddle. "Here you go. Just one, though, so you'll have to drive the boat." She sat down. "What're you waitin' for, sweet thing?"

"I . . . don't think we should go out on the lake in the dark."

She said softly and invitingly, "I trust you."

Wayne looked over his shoulder at the house, where kids were dancing on the patio. He had a strange sense of isolation, a feeling that all wasn't right and he should know what was wrong, but it evaded him. Wasn't it right, he thought, that he should be a human being too?

"Let's do it, sweet thing," the girl whispered.

Wayne had to step through the water to shove the canoe off. He slipped into it, almost capsizing them and bringing a squeal of laughter from her; then they were gliding through the dark water, leaving the party noise behind.

"See?" Lonnie said. "Ain't this nice?"

Wayne heard water rolling in the bottom of the canoe. His expensive loafers were getting ruined. The moon was rising, an amber scythe that looked so close and sharp you could cut your throat on it. Bullfrogs croaked from the shore, and the night closed around the drifting canoe.

Lonnie sighed deeply, a sexy, needful sigh, and Wayne thought his head might crack open like an eggshell. "There's somethin' awful familiar about you," she said. "It's your voice, I guess. Do I know you from somewhere?"

"No."

The music faded to a low murmur. The Dickerson house was a distant glow on the shore.

A dark object lay ahead. Wayne said, "What's that?" and then the canoe grazed a square wooden diving platform. He took the paddle out of the water and held it over his knees. His heart was beating harder, and when Lonnie's voice came, it was like balm on a fever blister. "We could rest here for a little while."

He almost laughed. Rest? Oh, she was a sinful Jezebel! She wanted him, he knew. She wanted to be naked for him, and to do it. "If you want to," he heard himself say, as if from a stranger's mouth.

Wayne found a rope trailing from the platform and tied up the canoe. Then he was helping Lonnie out onto the platform, and she was pressing herself against him and he could feel her breasts, her nipples jutting against his chest. His heart was pounding, his head was filled with heat and he couldn't think.

"I'm cold," she whispered. "Please hold me, I'm cold."

He put his arms around her, and realized it was he who was trembling.

Lonnie pulled him down onto the platform, as lake water chuckled around them and the smell of moss drifted up. A dam of pent-up passions cracked inside Wayne—she wants to do it and there's nobody to see, nobody to know!—and he fumbled at her clothes, his breathing harsh. His hands roamed over her body, as she held him close and whispered urgings in his ear. Her blouse came open. Wayne worked at her bra and then her breasts were free and warm against his hands. Her body pressed against his as his penis throbbed with heat. She rubbed at his crotch and then began pulling his belt loose, her teeth nipping at his neck. His pants started coming down. "Hurry," she whispered. "Hurry hurry, please . . ."

His penis was exposed as his underwear came down, and the girl put her hand on it.

And Wayne heard in his head the crack of his father's voice like a lash across his back: *Sinner! Would you lie down with Jezebel?*

He was excited and dizzy, his eyes squeezed shut, his mind tormented between what he wanted and what he knew he shouldn't do. She gripped his penis, and he opened his eyes.

He was no longer in the embrace of a girl.

It was something that looked like a beast, a wild boar, red-eyed and grinning.

Wayne tried to pull away, but then the vision passed and it was Lonnie again, dark-haired Lonnie, faceless Lonnie.

Sinner! Would you lie with Jezebel?

"No!" Lonnie said. "Make it big again! Make it big!"

"I . . . can't . . . I . . ." He was concentrating, trying as hard as he could. His father's voice rang in his brain, a bass rumble of Doom: *Sinner!* He'd go to Hell for lying with a harlot, he'd been tricked by Satan into coming out here!

"Make it big!" Lonnie was saying, a note of anger and

frustration in her voice. She handled his penis like a small twig. "Come on, can't you get it up?" After another minute or two, she released him and sat over on the platform's edge, putting her bra and blouse back on.

"I'm sorry," he said, hurriedly getting his pants on. He felt slimed by the Jezebel's touch, but wicked needs and desires still coursed through him. "Next time," he said. "It's just . . . I don't feel right about this. Okay?"

"Forget it. I need a man, not a little boy who can't even get it up! Come on, take me back to shore!"

Her voice was ugly. The sound of it scared Wayne. "I just . . . you won't tell anybody about this, will you?"

"What's wrong with you? Are you queer?"

"No! Please . . . you won't tell anybody, will you?"

Lonnie buttoned her blouse. He saw her head tilted to one side, as if in concentration. Then, slowly, she turned toward him. "Why not? It'd be somethin' for a laugh, wouldn't it?"

"Satan's in you," he whispered. "That's it, isn't it?"

"*What?*" He thought she smiled in the darkness.

"You're a Jezebel, a dirty sinner and oh God I shouldn't have come out here!"

"*Now* I know where I've heard your voice!" the girl said and Wayne cringed. "My momma made me listen to that Crusade crap on the radio! You're—oh, wow! You're the little healer himself, ain't you?" She whooped with laughter. "Yeah! You're Little Wayne Falconer! Oh, wow, everybody's gonna laugh their—"

"*No,*" he said forcefully, and she was silent. "You're not going to tell *anybody.*"

"Who says? Take me back or I'll start screamin'!"

He had to make her understand! He had to make her see he was a righteous boy! He took a step toward her.

And then Lonnie abruptly turned toward shore and yelled, "HELP!"

"Shut up!" he hissed, and pushed her. She staggered across the platform.

"HELP!" she shouted again, her voice echoing across the water.

Wayne exploded. He pushed her as hard as he could, and suddenly Lonnie's feet slipped out from under her on the moss-slick boards. She fell backward, her arms windmilling. There was a violent, sickening *crunch!* as the side of her head hit a corner of the platform.

She fell into the lake, and the black water covered her.

At once Wayne reached down to grasp her, but she was gone. Bubbles burst upward, smelling of lake mud. He leaned down, whining with panic, and thrust his arms underwater to find her. He got up, ran across the platform to the canoe to retrieve the paddle, and used that to probe the depths. He looked up toward the house, and started to scream for help. No! he thought. She's not hurt, she's all right! She only bumped her head a little bit, she'll come up in just a few seconds!

"Lonnie!" he whispered. "Come on up, now! Come on!"

Black water sighed around the platform. He reached underwater again—and felt her hair. He gripped it and wrenched upward. It was a rotten tree limb with a green mane of algae.

He started to ease himself into the water to look for her, but realized that if he got wet everyone would know at the party. She was probably swimming to shore.

"Lonnie?" he called out, a little louder. Only crickets and bullfrogs answered.

After a while he began to cry, and he prayed as he'd never prayed before. The dark voice in his mind whispered, *She was a Jezebel a dirty sinner and she deserved what she got!* He sat on the platform for a long time, shaking, his head bowed.

Wayne was sitting in the Camaro's backseat when Terry and Helen found him about an hour later. His face was very pale. The gin got to him, Terry thought.

"Where've you been, Wayne?" Terry asked as he slipped behind the wheel. "We were lookin' for you."

Wayne's smile made his face look like a skull. "Just around. I went for a long walk. The music was too loud."

"You meet any of those pretty girls?" Helen asked.

"No. Not a one."

"Great party, huh?" Terry started the engine. "Listen, Wayne. Since I'm on a scholarship, you . . . uh . . . won't tell your dad about this, will you? I mean, I didn't smoke or drink."

"No, I won't tell."

"Good." Terry winked at Helen. "It'll be our secret, right?"

"Right," Wayne said. "Our secret."

32

It was after eleven o'clock, and Wayne was way late getting home. Jimmy Jed Falconer, in his robe and slippers, stood on the front porch in the cool night air and looked out toward the highway.

He'd slipped out of bed without waking Cammy, because he didn't want her to be worried. His belly bulged the knot at the front of his robe, but still his stomach growled for food. Where could the boy be at this time of night? he wondered. He stood on the porch for a few minutes longer, then went back through the large, rambling house to the kitchen.

He switched on the lights, opened the refrigerator, and brought out a piece of blueberry pie Esther the cook had baked just that afternoon. Pouring himself a cold glass of milk, he sat down for a late-night snack.

The summer was almost over. And what a glorious summer it had been, too! The Crusade had held tent revivals throughout Alabama, Mississippi, and Louisiana—hitting the larger towns and the cities—and next year would be ready for expansion into Texas and Arkansas. An ailing Fayette radio station had been purchased, as well as a South Carolina publishing company, and the first issue of *Forward*, the Crusade's magazine, would be out in October. Wayne had touched and healed a few thousand people over the course of the summer: the boy was a masterful orator, and could hold that stage like he'd been born on it. When Wayne had finished the healing segment of the program, the offering plates came back filled to the brim. Wayne was a good boy, and he was as smart as a whip; but he had a stubborn streak in him, too, and he persisted in going out in the airfield where his Beechcraft Bonanza was hangared and flying without a co-pilot, getting up in the sky and doing all kinds of crazy loops and rolls. That sort of

·thing scared Falconer to death: what if the plane should crash? Wayne was a good pilot, but he took a lot of risks, and he seemed to enjoy the danger.

Falconer gulped down the milk and chewed on a bite of pie. Yessir! It had been a glorious summer!

Suddenly he realized his left arm was tingling. He shook the hand, thinking it had somehow fallen asleep. It was very hot here in the kitchen, he noticed; he'd begun sweating.

Do you know what you're doing, son?

Falconer stopped with another piece of pie right at his mouth. He'd thought about the night in May many times, and the question the Hawthorne witch-woman had posed to Wayne. That question had surfaced in his mind as he'd watched the pale and hopeful faces of the sick and infirm passing by in the Healing Line, reaching up with trembling hands toward Wayne. Suddenly, the blueberry pie tasted like ashes. He put the fork down on his plate, and touched his chest where a quick needle-jab of pain had pierced. Now it had passed. The pain was gone. Good.

But his mind was wandering in dangerous territory. What if— what *if*—the witch-woman was right? And he'd known it all along, that Wayne's internal battery was getting weaker and weaker, and that was why he never dared ask Wayne to heal his diseased heart. And what if *Wayne* knew it, too, and was continuing to play the part because . . . because it was all he'd ever been taught to do.

No! Falconer thought. Wayne healed Toby, didn't he? And thousands of letters came in from people who said they were healed by Wayne's touch and presence!

He recalled a letter from long ago, sent to the Crusade office a week or so after the tent revival in Hawthorne. It had been from a woman named Posey, and Falconer had thrown it away as soon as he'd read it:

Dear Rev. Falconer, we just want to tell you that our son Jimmie has been took by Jesus. Your boy healed him at the revival in Hawthorne, but Jesus must have a purpose for our Jimmie in Heaven. I have paid my sin for selling my baby to Mr. Tillman. May the Lord be with you, and all of your teachings. Sincerely, Laura Posey.

Falconer had made sure Wayne would never see that letter, nor the few dozen letters similar to it that the Crusade had gotten. No, it was better that the boy never, *never* doubt himself.

Rising unsteadily from the kitchen table, Falconer went to the den and sat down in his easy chair. The framed Falconer Crusade poster, with him looking much younger and braver and stronger, was spotlit by a ceiling light.

Pain speared his chest. He wanted to get up now, and go upstairs to bed, but he couldn't make his body respond. Maybe he needed to take some Tums, that was all. His mind was tormented with the thought of Ramona Creekmore looking at his son and *knowing* it was all a lie; she had the eyes of Satan, and that boy of hers was walking Death, and it wasn't until he'd met them that his heart had begun to get worse.

Do you know what you're doing, son?

YES HE KNOWS! Falconer raged. HE KNOWS, YOU SATAN-SPAWN BITCH! When Wayne got home, Falconer would tell the boy how they would run the Creekmores out of Hawthorne, drive them off like dogs, far away to where their wicked influence couldn't seep back into the Falconer Crusade. Pain ran up and down his body, lancing across his ribs. "Cammy!" he moaned. "*Cammy!*"

Pluck them out! he thought. PLUCK THEM OUT!

"CAMMY!"

His hands curled around the armrests, the knuckles whitening. And then the pain struck him full-force, and his heart began to twist and writhe in his chest. His head rocked back, his face turning a deep reddish blue.

From the doorway, Cammy screamed. She was shocked, couldn't move.

"Heart . . ." Falconer said in a hoarse, agonized voice. "Call . . . somebody. . . ."

She forced her legs to move, and raced for the telephone; she heard her husband moan for Wayne, and then as if from an awful fever dream he cried—or Cammy thought she heard—"Creekmore . . . pluck them out . . . oh, God, pluck them out. . . ."

33

Dear Mom and Dad,

Hello, I hope everything is all right and you're doing fine. I'm writing this letter from Dothan, where the carnival is set up at the fairgrounds. We'll be here until the first of September, and then we go to Montgomery for a week. So far business has been good, Dr. Mirakle says, and he thinks we'll do real good when we get to Birmingham the first week in October. I hope all is well with both of you.

Dad, how are you feeling? I hope your reading is still getting better. I had a dream about you a couple of nights ago. We were walking to town on the highway, just like we used to do, and everybody waved and said hello to us. It must have been springtime in my dream, because there were new buds in the trees and the sky was the soft blue of April, before the heat sets in. Anyways, we were walking just to get out and see the sights, and you were as fit as a new fiddle. It was good to hear you laugh so much, even if it was just in a dream. Maybe that means you'll get better soon, do you think?

Mom, if you're reading this letter aloud to Dad you should skip this next part. Just keep it to yourself. About two weeks ago a new ride called the Octopus joined the carnival. I found out the man who runs the Octopus is named Buck Edgers, and he's been traveling around with it for the better part of four years. A couple of the roustabouts told me there've been accidents on the Octopus. A little girl and her father died when one of the gondolas—that's the part you ride in—broke loose. Mr. Edgers took the Octopus down to Florida for a while, and a teen-age boy fell out of that same gondola when the ride was moving. I don't know if he died or not, but another roustabout told me a man had a heart attack on the Octopus two years ago, in Huntsville. Mr. Edgers changes his name when he applies for a permit from the safety inspectors, I hear, but it seems the inspectors always pass the Octopus because they can never find anything wrong with it. Mr. Edgers is always working on something or another, and I hear his hammer banging late at night when everyone else is asleep. It seems he can hardly stand to leave it alone, not even for a whole night. And when you ask him what he's working on, or how he got the Octopus in the first place, his eyes just cut you dead.

Mom, something's wrong with that ride. If I said that to anybody around here, they'd laugh in my face, but I get the feeling that a lot of other people stay their distance from the Octopus too. Just last night, when we were setting up, a roustabout helping Mr. Edgers got his foot crushed when a piece of machinery fell on it, like he did it on purpose. There have been a lot of fights lately, too, and there weren't before the Octopus joined us. People are irritable, and spoiling for trouble. A roustabout named Chalky disappeared just before we left Andalusia, and a couple of days ago Mr. Ryder got a call from the police because they found Chalky's body in a field behind the shopping center where we were set up. His neck had been crushed, but the police couldn't figure out how, I heard tell. Anyway, there's a bad feeling in the air. I'm afraid of the Octopus too, probably more than anybody else, because I think it likes the taste of blood. I don't know what to do.

Dr. Mirakle and I have been talking after the Ghost Show closes up for the night. Did I tell you he wanted to be a dentist? Did I tell you the story he told me about the machine Thomas Edison invented to try to communicate with spirits? Well, Edison drew up the blueprints for it, but he died before he could build it. Dr. Mirakle says nobody knows what happened to the blueprints. Dr. Mirakle drinks a lot and he loves to talk while he drinks. One thing he told me that is interesting: he says there are institutes where scientists are studying something called parapsychology. That has to do with your mind, and spirits and stuff. I've never told Dr. Mirakle about Will Booker, or the sawmill, or the black aura. I've never told him about Gram or the Mystery Walk. He seems to want to know about me, but he never comes right out and asks.

Well, I'd better get to sleep now. Dr. Mirakle is a good man, and he's been right about one thing: the carnival does get into your blood.

I know you can put this thirty-five dollars to good use. I'll write when I have time. I love you both.

Billy

34

Wayne Falconer sat with his mother in the backseat of the chauffeured Cadillac limo. They were on their way to the Cutcliffe Funeral Home in downtown Fayette. Jimmy Jed Falconer had been dead for two days, and was going to be buried in the morning. The monument was already picked out, ready to be put in place.

Cammy had been sobbing all morning. She wouldn't stop. Her eyes were red, her nose was running, her face was bloated and blotchy. It disgusted Wayne. He knew his daddy would've wanted her to carry herself with dignity, just like Wayne was trying to do. He wore a somber black suit and a black tie with small red checks on it. Last night, while his mother was drugged and sleeping, he'd taken a pair of scissors and cut his silk shirt and trousers, both of them stained with grass and lake mud, into long strips of cloth that he could easily burn in a trash barrel behind the barn. The stains had gone up in smoke.

Wayne winced as his mother cried. She reached out and grasped his hand, and he gently but firmly pulled away. He despised her for not getting the ambulance to the house soon enough, despised her for not having told him about his father's weak heart condition. He had seen his daddy's dead face in the hospital: blue as frost on a grave.

The last word J.J. Falconer had spoken in the hospital, before he went into a deep sleep that he never came out of, was a name.

Cammy was puzzled over it, had racked her brains trying to remember what message it might carry—but Wayne *knew*. Demons had been afoot in the darkness that terrible night; they had been grinning and chuckling and drawing a net around Wayne and his daddy. One of them had appeared to him as a faceless girl on a lake's diving platform whose body—if indeed she had existed as flesh and blood at all—hadn't yet emerged from the depths. Wayne had checked the newspaper, but there was no account of the drowning. Terry Dozier had called yesterday to give his sympathy, but again there was no mention of a girl named Lonnie found floating in the lake. And Wayne had found himself feverishly wondering if she had existed at all . . . or if her body was caught in a submerged tree limb down on the muddy bottom . . . or if his daddy's death had simply eclipsed that of a poor white-trash girl.

The second demon had come creeping in the darkness to steal his father's life away; it had been sent by the Hawthorne witch-woman in revenge for his father's urging a few Hawthorne men, in a secret meeting, to put a scare into the Creekmores and get them out of the county. It was for the best of the community, Wayne remembered his daddy telling the men, their faces washed by candlelight. If you rid Hawthorne of this corruption, Falconer had said, then God will see fit to favor you. In the darkened, shadowy room Wayne had imagined he'd seen movement over in the far corner, beyond the ring of listening men; he'd had the impression—just for an instant—of something standing there in a place where the candlelight couldn't reach, something that looked almost like a wild boar that had learned to walk upright, seven feet tall or more. But when Wayne had stared into that corner the thing wasn't there at all. Now, he thought it might've been Satan himself, spying for the witch-woman and her son.

There were scores to settle. Wayne's hands were curled into fists in his lap.

The Crusade, the Falconer Foundation, the radio station, the magazine, the real-estate holdings in Georgia and Florida, the stocks and bonds, the Airstream trailer, and all the road equipment had become his, Henry Bragg and George Hodges had told him yesterday. He'd spent the morning signing papers—but not before he'd read them over several times and knew exactly what was happening. Cammy was to receive a monthly allowance from

J.J.'s personal account, but the remainder of the estate, and the responsibilities that went with it, had fallen to Wayne.

An evil voice hissed through his mind like the noise of wind through lake reeds: *You can't get it up.* . . .

Reporters and photographers were waiting in front of the funeral home when the limousine pulled to the curb. Cameras clicked as Wayne helped his mother out of the car, and she still had enough presence of mind to lower the black veil of her hat across her face. He waved the questions aside as George Hodges came out of the funeral home to meet them.

The interior was cool and quiet and smelled like a florist's shop. Their heels clicked on a marble floor. Many people were waiting for Wayne and Cammy outside the memorial room where Jimmy Jed Falconer lay; Wayne knew most of them, and began shaking their hands and thanking them for coming. Women from the Baptist Ladies' League came over to comfort Cammy. A tall, gray-haired man in a dark blue suit shook Wayne's hand; he was, Wayne knew, the minister of a nearby Episcopal church.

Wayne forced a smile and a nod. This man was one of his father's enemies, he knew—one of the coalition of ministers who had questioned J.J. Falconer's passionate approach to the gospel. Falconer had kept files on the ministers who opposed the tone of his Crusade, and Wayne planned to keep the files in good shape.

Wayne went to his mother's side. "Are you ready to go in, Momma?"

She gave a barely perceptible nod, and Wayne led her through a pair of large oak doors into the room where the casket was displayed. Most of the people followed them in at a respectable distance. The room was filled with bouquets of flowers; the walls were painted with a pale mural, in soothing blues and greens, of grassy hills where flocks of sheep were watched over by lyre-playing shepherds. From concealed speakers "The Old Rugged Cross" was played on a mellow-sounding church organ—it was J.J. Falconer's favorite hymn. The gleaming oak casket was back-dropped by white curtains.

Wayne couldn't stand being at his mother's side for another second. *I didn't know he was sick!* he screamed mentally. You didn't tell me! I could've healed him and then he wouldn't be dead right now! Suddenly he felt terribly alone.

And the whispering, leering voice said, *You can't get it up.* . . .

Wayne stepped toward the casket. Three more steps, and he'd be looking in at the face of Death. A tremor of fear shot through him, and again he was a little boy on a stage, not knowing what to do, as everyone stared at him. He closed his eyes, put his hands on the casket's edge, and looked in.

He almost laughed. That's not my daddy! he thought. Somebody's made a mistake! The corpse, dressed in a bright yellow suit, white shirt, and black tie, was so perfectly made up it looked like a department-store mannequin. The hair was combed just so, every curl in place; the flesh of the face filled with lifelike color. The lips were tightly compressed, as if the corpse were trying to hold back a secret. The fingernails, on the hands crossed over the body, were spotless and manicured. J.J. Falconer, Wayne realized, was going to Heaven like a dime-story dummy.

The full realization of what he'd done—lying in sin with a scarlet Jezebel while his father lay with Death pressed close to his chest—hit him like a shriek. His daddy was gone, and he was just a little boy playacting on a stage, mouthing his healing rites, waiting for the same bolt of lightning he'd felt when he had placed his hands on Toby. He wasn't ready to be alone, not yet, oh Lord not yet. . . .

Tears filled his eyes—not tears of sadness, but of livid rage. He was shaking and couldn't stop.

"Wayne?" someone said behind him.

He whirled upon the strangers in the memorial room, his face a bright, strangled red. He roared, "GET OUT OF HERE!"

There was a shocked stillness. His mother cowered, as if afraid of being struck.

He advanced upon them, "I SAID GET OUT OF HERE!" he shrieked, and they retreated, stumbling into each other like cattle. "GET OUT!" Wayne was sobbing, and he pushed George Hodges away when the man reached for him. Then they were all gone, and he was alone in the room with his father's corpse.

Wayne put his hands to his face and moaned, the tears leaking out between his fingers. After another moment he walked forward and locked the oak doors.

Then he turned to face the casket.

It could be done, he knew. Yes. If he wanted to hard enough, he could do it. It wasn't too late, because his daddy wasn't in the ground yet! He could lift up J.J. Falconer, the South's Greatest Evangelist, and all the doubts and torments that had ever plagued him about his healing powers would fly like chaff in a strong wind. Then he and his daddy would march upon the Creekmores, and send them to burn in Hell forever.

Yes. It could be done.

Someone jiggled the doorknob. "Wayne?" a voice asked meekly. Then: "I think he's locked himself in!"

"Lord, let me do it," Wayne whispered, as tears ran down his face. "I know I sinned, and that's why you let the demons take my daddy away. But I'm not ready to be alone! Please . . . if you let me do this one thing, I'll never ask you for anything else again." He trembled, waiting for electricity to charge through him, for God's Voice to speak through his mind, for a sign or an omen or anything. "PLEASE!" he shouted.

Then he reached into the coffin and was grasping his father's thin hard shoulders. Wayne said, "Get up, Daddy. Let's show them what my healing power is really like, and how strong it is. Get up, now. I need you here with me, come on and get up. . . ."

His hands clamped harder; he closed his eyes and tried to summon up the raw healing power—where was it? Had it been all used up, a long time ago? No lightning struck him, no blue burn of power surged from his hands. "Get up, Daddy," Wayne whispered, and then he threw his head back and shouted, "I COMMAND YOU TO GET UP AND WALK!"

"Waynnnne!" Cammy screamed from beyond the locked door. "Don't, for God's sake . . . !"

"I COMMAND YOU TO THROW OFF THE CHAINS OF DEATH! DO IT NOW! DO IT NOW!" He shook like a lightning rod in a high wind, his fingers gripped tightly into yellow cloth, sweat and tears dripping from his face. The flesh-toned makeup on the corpse's cheeks were running, revealing an undercolor of whitish gray. Wayne concentrated on bringing up the power from deep within himself, from a place where volcanoes raged in his soul, where wild flames leapt. He thought of nothing but pumping Life into this casket-caged body, of *willing* Life back into it.

Something ripped in his brain, with a sudden sharp pain and a distinct tearing sound. A startling image whirled through his mind—the eagle and serpent in deadly combat. Black pain beat at Wayne's head, and drops of blood began leaking from his left nostril to spot the casket's white satin lining. His hands were tingling, now itching, now burning. . . .

Falconer's corpse twitched.

Wayne's eyes flew open. "YES!" he said "GET UP!"

And suddenly the corpse shook as if plugged into a high-voltage socket; it contorted and stretched, the facial muscles rippling. The hands with their perfect fingernails began rhythmically clenching and unclenching.

And then the eyelids, sewn shut with flesh-colored thread by the mortician, ripped themselves open. The eyes were sunken deep into the head, the color of hard gray marbles. With a violent twitch the lips stretched, stretched . . . and the mouth tore open, white sutures dangling; the inside of the mouth was an awful oyster gray, and cotton had been stuffed in to fill out the cheeks. The head jerked as if in agony, the body writhing beneath Wayne's hand.

Someone hammered wildly at the door. "WAYNE!" George Hodges shouted. "STOP IT!"

But Wayne was filled with righteous healing power, and he would atone for his sins by bringing J. J. Falconer back from the dark place. All he had to do was concentrate a little harder, sweat and hurt a little more. "Come back, Daddy," Wayne whispered to the writhing corpse. "Please come back. . . ."

In Wayne's tortured mind there was the image of a dead frog, stiff and smelling of formaldehyde, lying on a table in biology class. Its leg muscles had been sliced open, and connected up with little electrodes; when the current was switched on, the frog jumped. And jumped. And jumped. *Jump frog,* Wayne thought as crazed laughter rang through his head. Falconer's corpse writhed and shook, the hands clawing at the air. *Jump frog, jump.* . . .

"Wayne!" his mother screamed, her voice on the raw edge of hysteria. "He's dead, he's dead, leave him alone!"

And he realized, with a sickening certainty, that he had failed. All he was doing was making a dead frog jump. His daddy was dead and gone. "No," he whispered. Falconer's head twisted to one side, the mouth yawning wide.

Wayne unclenched his fingers and stepped back. Instantly the corpse lay still, the teeth clicking together as the mouth shut.

"Wayne?"

"Unlock the door!"

"Let us in, son, let us talk to you!"

He stared down at the drops of blood on the marble floor. Numbly, he wiped his nose on his sleeve. It was all over, and he had failed. The one thing he'd asked for, the most important thing, had been denied him. And why? Because he had plummeted from the Lord's grace. Somewhere, he knew, the Creekmores must be celebrating. He touched his pounding forehead with his bloody hand, and stared at the opposite wall with its mural of sheep and shepherds.

Outside the memorial room, Cammy Falconer and the assembled mourners heard the terrible crashing noises begin. It was, as a Methodist minister would later tell his wife, as if "a hundred demons had gotten in that room and gone mad." Only when the noises stopped did George Hodges and a couple of men dare to force the doors open. They found Wayne huddled in a corner. Vases of flowers had been thrown against the walls, scarring the beautiful mural and slopping water all over the floor. The corpse looked as if Wayne had tried to drag it out of the coffin. Cammy saw her son's bloody face and fainted.

Wayne was rushed to the hospital and checked in for nervous exhaustion. He was given a private room, pumped full of tranquilizers, and left alone to sleep. During the long night he was visited by two dreams: in the first, a hideous shape stood over his bed, its mouth grinning in the darkness. In the second, an eagle and a snake were locked in mortal combat—the eagle's wings sought the open sky, but the snake's darting fangs struck again and again, its poison weakening the eagle and dragging it to the earth. He awakened in a cold sweat, before the dream combat was finished, but this time he knew the snake was winning.

He chewed on tranquilizers and wore dark glasses as he watched the South's Greatest Evangelist enter the earth at ten o'clock in the morning.

His duty was crystal-clear.

EIGHT

Serpent
and
Octopus

35

Dr. Mirakle was slightly drunk and exuded the aroma of Dant bourbon like a cheap cologne. A flask full of the stuff sat on the table near his elbow. On a plate before him was a soggy hot dog and baked beans. It was lunchtime, and the air was filled with dust as the trucks and cranes set up the sideshows at the Gadsden fairgrounds; in another week the carnival would be heading into Birmingham, and the season would be over.

Billy sat across from Dr. Mirakle beneath the wooden roof of the open-air café. The Ghost Show tent was already up, ready for tonight's business. Dr. Mirakle looked distastefully at his food and swigged from the flask, then offered it to Billy. "Go ahead, it won't kill you. God, to eat this food you need a little antibiotic protection! You know, if you expect to stay with the carnival you'd better get used to the taste of alcohol."

"Stay?" Billy was silent for a moment, watching as the trucks rumbled along the midway with various parts of rides and sideshows. The Octopus was being put together out there, somewhere in the haze of dust. "I wasn't planning on staying after we leave Birmingham."

"Don't you like the carnival?"

"Well . . . I guess I do, but . . . there's work to be done at home."

"Ah yes." Mirakle nodded. He was unshaven and bleary-eyed from a long night of driving and then raising the Ghost Show tent. "Your home. I'd forgotten: people have homes. I had thought you might be interested in seeing my workshop, where I put together all the Ghost Show figures. It's in that house I own in Mobile—a *house*, mind you, not a home. My home is this." He motioned toward the midway. "Dust and all, I love it. Next year the Ghost Show will be bigger than ever! It'll have twice as many ghosts and goblins, twice as many optical effects! I thought . . . perhaps you'd like to help me with it."

Billy sipped at a cup of hot black coffee. "Something I've been meaning to ask you for a long time. Maybe I thought you'd get around to telling me, but you haven't. Just exactly why did you want me to be your assistant this summer?"

"I told you. I had heard about you and your mother, and I . . ."

"No sir. That's not all of it, is it? You could've hired anybody to help you with the Ghost Show. So why did you search so long and hard for my mother and me?"

The man looked out at the billowing yellow dust and swigged from his flask. His nose was laced with bright red and blue veins, and the whites of his eyes were a sad yellowish color. "Can you really do what . . . people have said?" he asked finally. "Do you and your mother have the ability to communicate with the dead?"

Billy nodded.

"Many people before you have said they could, too. I've never seen anything remotely resembling a ghost. I've seen pictures, of course, but those are easily faked. Oh, what I'd give to be able to see . . . *something* that would hint of life in the beyond—wherever that might be. You know, there are institutes devoting their whole resources to exploring the question of life after death . . . did I tell you that already? One is in Chicago, another in New York—I wrote the Chicago people once, and they sent me back a questionnaire, but by then it was too late."

"What was too late?" Billy asked.

"Things," Mirakle replied. He looked at Billy for a moment and then nodded. "If you *can* see apparitions, doesn't that fill you with a hope that there is an afterlife?"

"I never thought there wasn't."

"Ah. Blind faith, eh? And how do you arrive at that conclusion? Your religious beliefs? Your crutch?" Something angry and bitter flared behind Dr. Mirakle's rheumy eyes for an instant, then subsided. "Damn," he said softly. "What is Death? The ending of the first act, or the final curtain? Can you tell me?"

Billy said, "No sir."

"All right, I'll tell you why I sought you out. Because I wanted desperately to believe in what I heard about you and your mother; I wanted to find *someone* who might . . . help me make sense of

236

this preposterous joke we refer to as Life. What's beyond all this?" He made a wide gesture—the café, the other workers and carny people sitting around talking and eating, the dusty midway.

"I don't know."

Dr. Mirakle's gaze fell to the table. "Well. How would you? But you have a chance to know, Billy, if what you say about yourself is true. My wife, Ellen, had a chance to know, as well."

"Your wife?" It was the first time the man had mentioned his wife's name. "Is she in Mobile?"

"No. No, not in Mobile. I visited her one day before I found my way to Hawthorne. Ellen is a permanent resident of the state insane asylum in Tuscaloosa." He glanced at Billy, his lined face tight and tired. "She . . . saw something, in that house in Mobile. Or did she? Well, she likes to fingerpaint and comb her hair all day long now, and what she saw that pushed her over the edge is a moot point, isn't it?"

"What *did* she see?"

Mirakle took out his wallet and opened it to the photograph of the young man in the service uniform. He slid it across the table to Billy. "Kenneth was his name. Korea. He was killed by mortar fire on . . . oh, what's the date? I carried the exact day in my head for so long! Well, it was in August of 1951. I seem to remember that it happened on a Wednesday. I was always told that he favored me. Do you think so?"

"In the eyes, yes."

Mirakle took the wallet back and put it away. "Wednesday in August. How hot and final that sounds! Our only child. I watched Ellen slowly fall into the bourbon bottle, a tradition I have since clung to wholeheartedly. Is there such a think as ever really letting a dead child go? Over a year after the burial, Ellen was taking a basket of clothes up the stairs in our house, and right at the top of the stairs stood Kenneth. She said she could smell the pomade in his hair, and he looked at her and said, 'You worry too much, Ma.' It was something he used to say to her all the time, to tease her. Then she blinked and he wasn't there. When I got home, I found she'd been walking up and down those stairs all day hoping she could trigger whatever it had been that had made her see him. But, of course . . ." He looked up at Billy, who'd been listening intently, and then shifted uneasily in his chair. "I stay in that house for most of the winter, in between seasons. Sometimes I think I'm being watched; sometimes I can imagine Ken calling me, his voice echoing through the hallway. I would sell that house and move away, but . . . what if Ken *is* still there, trying to reach me, but I can't see him?"

"Is that why you want me to go to Mobile with you? To find out if your son is still in that house?"

"Yes. I have to know, one way or the other."

Billy was pondering the request when three women, laughing and talking, came in out of the dust. One of them was a lean black girl, the second was a coarse-looking redhead—but the third young woman was a walking vision. One glance and he was riveted; it was the girl whose picture he'd admired outside the Jungle Love sideshow!

She had a smooth, sensual stride, and she wore a pair of blue jeans that looked spray-painted on. Her green T-shirt read *I'm a Virgin (This Is a Very Old T-Shirt)* and she wore an orange CAT cap over loose blond curls. Billy looked up into her face as she passed the table, and saw greenish gold eyes under blond brows; her aroma lingered like the smell of wheatstraw on a July morning. She carried herself with proud sexuality, and seemed to know that every man in the place was drooling. She was obviously used to being watched. Several roustabouts whistled as the three women went to the counter to order their food.

"Ah, youth!" Even Dr. Mirakle had tried to suck in his gut. "I presume those ladies are dancers in that exhibition down the midway?"

"Yes sir." Billy hadn't been inside yet. Usually after a day's work it was all he could do to fall onto his cot at the back of the Ghost Show tent.

The three women got their food and sat at a nearby table. Billy couldn't keep his eyes off the one in the CAT cap. He watched as she ate her hot dog with a rather sloppy abandon, talking and laughing with her friends. Her beautiful eyes, he noticed, kept sliding toward two guys at another table. They were staring at her with a silent hunger, just as Billy was.

"She's got ten years on you, if a day," Dr. Mirakle said quietly. "If your tongue hangs down any farther you could sweep the floor with it."

There was something about her that set a fire burning in Billy. He didn't even hear Dr. Mirakle. She suddenly glanced over in his direction, her eyes almost luminous, and Billy felt a shiver of excitement. She held his gaze for only a second, but it was long enough for wild fantasies to start germinating in his brain.

"I would guess that your . . . uh . . . love life has been rather limited," Dr. Mirakle said. "You're almost eighteen and I have no right throwing in my two cents, but I did promise your mother I'd look after you. So here's my advice, and take it or leave it: Some women are Wedgwood, and some are Tupperware. *That* is the latter variety. Billy? Are you listening to me?"

"I'm going to get some more coffee." He took his cup to the counter for a refill, passing right by her table.

"Live and learn, son," Dr. Mirakle said grimly.

Billy got his fresh cup of coffee and came back by the table again. He was so nervous he was about to shake it out of the cup, but he was determined to say something to the girl. Something witty, something that would break the ice. He stood a few feet away from them for a moment, trying to conjure up words that would impress her; then he stepped toward her, and she looked up quizzically at him, her gaze sharpening.

"Hi there," he said. "Haven't we met somewhere before?"

"Take a hike," she said, as the other two giggled.

And suddenly a flask was thrust under her nose. "Drink?" Dr. Mirakle asked. "J.W. Dant, finest bourbon in the land."

She looked at them both suspiciously, then sniffed at the flask. "Why not?" She took a drink and passed it around the table.

"Allow me to introduce myself. I'm Dr. Reginald Mirakle, and this is my right-hand man, Mr. Billy Creekmore. What Mr. Creekmore meant to offer you lovely ladies is an open invitation to visit the Ghost Show at your convenience."

"The Ghost Show?" the redhead asked. "What kind of crap is *that?*"

"You mean that funky little tent on the midway? Yeah, I've seen it." The blonde stretched, her unfettered breasts swelling against her shirt. "What do you do, tell fortunes?"

"Better than that, fair lady. We probe into the world of spirits and speak to the dead."

She laughed. There were more lines in her face than Billy had thought, but he found her beautiful and sexually magnetic. "Forget it! I've got enough hassles with the living to screw around with the dead!"

"I . . . I've seen your picture," Billy said, finally finding his voice. "Out in front of the show."

Again, she seemed to pull away from him. "Are you the bastard who's been stealin' my pictures?"

"No."

"Better not be. They cost a lot of money."

"Well . . . it's not me, but I can understand why. I . . . think you're really pretty."

She gave him the faintest hint of a smile. "Why, thank you."

"I mean it. I really think you're pretty." He might have gone on like that, had Dr. Mirakle not nudged him in the ribs.

"Are you an Indian, kid?" she asked.

"Part Indian. Choctaw."

"Choctaw," she repeated, and her smile was a little brighter. "You look like an Indian. I'm part French"—the other women hooted—"and part Irish. My name's Santha Tully. Those two bitches across the table don't have names, 'cause they were hatched from buzzard eggs."

"Are you all dancers?"

"We're *entertainers*," the redhead told him.

"I've been wanting to see the show, but the sign says you have to be twenty-one to get in."

"How old are you?"

"Almost eighteen. Practically."

She gave him a quick appraisal. He was a nice-looking boy, she thought. Really nice, with those strange dark hazel eyes and curly hair. He reminded her, in a way, of Chalky Davis. Chalky's eyes had been dark brown, but this boy was taller than Chalky had been. The news of Chalky's death—*murder*, she'd heard—still disturbed her, though they hadn't slept together but two or three times. Santha wondered if this boy was involved in any of the creepy things that had been happening to her in the last few weeks; somebody had put a half-dozen dead roses on the steps of her trailer, and she had heard strange noises late at night as if someone were prowling around. That's why she didn't like to sleep alone. One night last week, she could've sworn that somebody had been inside her trailer and gone through her costumes.

But this boy's eyes were friendly. She saw in them the unmistakable sheen of desire. "Come see the show, both of you. Tell the old bat out front that Santha sent you. Okay?"

Dr. Mirakle took the empty flask back. "We'll look forward to it."

Santha looked up into Billy's eyes. She decided she wouldn't kick him out of bed for eating crackers. He seemed nervous and shy and . . . *virgin?* she wondered. "Come by the show, Choctaw," she said, and winked. "Real soon."

Dr. Mirakle almost had to drag him out.

Santha laughed. The two cute roustabouts were still eyeing her. "Virgin," she said. "Bet you twenty bucks."

"No takers," the black girl told her.

And in the swirl of dust spun up by the heavy trucks Dr. Mirakle shook his head and muttered, "Entertainers *indeed*."

36

"Last show of the night!" the platinum-blond female barker was bellowing through a microphone. "Hey you in the hat! How about a thrill, huh? Well come on in! It's all right here, five lovely sensually young girls who just looooove to do their thang! Hey mister, why don't you leave your wife out here and come on in? I guarantee he'll be a better man for it, honey! Last show of the night! Hear those drums beat? The natives are restless tonight, and you never can tell *who* they're gonna do . . . I mean *what* they're gonna do, ha ha!"

Billy stood with the rest of the interested males grouped around the Jungle Love show. He wanted to go in there, but he was as nervous as a cat in a roomful of rockers. A man wearing a straw hat and a flashy printed shirt drawled, "Hey, lady! They dance *nude* in there?"

"Does a big bear shit in the woods?"

"*You* don't dance nude do you, big mamma?"

She let out a husky laugh that shook her rouged cheeks. "Don't you *wish*, little boy? Last show of the night! Fifty cents, fifty cents! Half a dollar'll get you in, you provide your own sin! Come on, step in line!"

Billy paused. Dr. Mirakle had told him that if he absolutely insisted in coming to the "strip show," then he should put his wallet in a place where light fingers couldn't get to it, and he shouldn't sit next to anybody who put a hat in his lap.

When Billy had passed the Octopus he felt a rush of dread through him, and thought he heard awful distant shrieks emanating from the covered gondola. But no one else seemed to hear them. Buck had given him a baleful glare, warning him to stay away. In motion, the Octopus chittered and groaned, the tired engine snorting steam; the green tarpaulin covering the scabrous gondola cracked in the wind. As far as Billy knew, Buck never took the tarpaulin off; the gondola itself had to be attached to the machine, otherwise the Octopus would be off-balance and would go pinwheeling across the midway like a huge, deadly top. Buck was trying to keep riders out of that gondola, Billy knew, because the man must be fearful of what might happen should anyone get inside it. Maybe Buck was trying his best to keep it muzzled, Billy thought. What if, for lack of steady victims, it was feeding on Buck's soul and body—taking an arm, slicing a finger or an ear—while the dark ripples of its power strengthened and spread?

"Fifty cents, fifty cents! Don't be shy boys, come on in!"

At least in there he could lose himself, Billy thought. He moved forward, and the barker motioned toward a cigar box. "Fifty cents, hon. If you're twenty-one I'm little Orphan Annie, but what the hell! . . ."

Inside, in a smoky haze of green light, a dozen long benches faced a stage with a garishly painted backdrop of twisted jungle foliage. The drumbeats bellowed from a speaker hidden off to the left. He sat in a center row as the place filled up with hooting, shouting men. They started clapping in time with the drumbeats, and there were hoarse yells for the show to begin. Suddenly the blond barker was up on the stage, and the drumbeats ceased. She said through a microphone that buzzed and warbled with feedback, "Okay, hold it down! We're gonna start in a minute! Right now I want you to take a look at these playing cards I hold in my hand, but don't look too close unless you want your eyebrows burned off! Yessir, straight from Paris, France, showing the kind of pictures that make a man want to get up and crow! You can't buy these in the local Woolworth's! But you can buy 'em right here, for only two dollars and seventy-five cents! Yessir, they know how to play cards in Paris! . . ."

Billy shifted uneasily in his seat. Cigar smoke drifted in front of his face. Somebody shouted, "Get off the stage or strip nekkid, baby!" He had the vague and unsettling sensation of being watched, yet when he looked around toward the back he saw only a mass of leering faces daubed in green light.

The show began. To a blare of rock music, a fleshy redhead in a black bikini—one of the women who'd been with Santha that afternoon, Billy realized—came strutting out on stage with a large stuffed chimpanzee doll. Her thighs quivered as she rolled her hips, letting the chimp sniff around her barely covered breasts and moving it slowly all over her body. The men were suddenly very quiet, as if mesmerized. After a minute or two of gyrating, the woman rolled around on the floor with the chimp and pretended dismay when her breasts popped free. She lay on her back, thrusting as the chimp sat astride her crotch. She began to moan and writhe, scissoring her legs into the air; her hips bucked faster and faster, her bare breasts trembling. Billy was sure that his eyes were about to pop from their sockets. Then the green lights went out and when they came back on again the barker was there, offering for sale something called Tijuana comic books.

The next dancer was the thin black girl, who contorted herself into positions that would've snapped any ordinary backbone. Most of the time her crotch, clad in flimsy panties with a cat's-eye strategically placed, was aimed toward the audience while her head was resting on the floor. The music hammered and roared, but the girl moved very slowly, as if to her own inner rhythm. Billy caught a glimpse of her eyes once, and saw they were blank of all emotion.

After the barker had tried to sell a Pecker Stretcher, a tall, big-boned girl wearing a bright yellow gown came out to dance; she had a huge mane of yellow hair that flowed down her back, and halfway into her act, when her huge breasts were peeking out from the material and it was obvious she was totally nude underneath, she suddenly whipped off the mane to show she was bald-headed. There was a collective stunned gasp, and then she made sure everybody could see that something else was bald, too.

The lion-girl was followed by a harsh-looking, slightly over-weight brunette in a tiger-skin bikini; she mostly stood in one place, making her breasts bounce, flicking the nipples with her fingers, or clenching her buttocks. Then she did a few deep-knee bends that were obviously torturous for her and left her face sheened with sweat. After she'd gone offstage, the barker hawked a set of "French ticklers," and then she said, "Okay, are you ready to fry? You ready to have your eggs scrambled, boiled, and turned sunny-side up?"

There was a roar of assent.

"Meet Santha . . . the Panther Girl. . . ."

The lights went out for a few seconds. When they came back on, there was a black shape curled up at center stage. The drums started beating again. Slowly, a shaft of red light strengthened across the stage, like the red dawn on an African veld. Billy found himself leaning forward, utterly entranced.

From the black curl a single bare leg lifted up, then sank down again. An arm reached up, stretching. The figure stirred and slowly began to rise. She was wearing a long robe made of sleek black fur, and she kept it tightly around her as she surveyed the audience, her blond curls a shining red halo. Billy saw the dark in her hair where the real color had grown out, and she seemed to have on an inch of make up, but there was a challenge and a defiance in her glowing eyes that made the Pecker Stretcher obsolete. She smiled—faintly, with a touch of dangerous promise—and then, though it hadn't appeared she'd even moved at all, the black robe dropped slowly lower and lower until it was resting on the full rise of her bosom. She clasped the robe with one hand, and now as she began to move slowly and sinuously to the drumbeats the robe would part to show a brief glimpse of stomach, thigh, or the dark and inviting V between them. She kept her eyes on the audience, and Billy knew she loved to be looked at, loved to be *wanted*.

And Billy, though he knew lust was a terrible sin, wanted her so badly he thought he would burst apart at the seams.

The black robe continued to drop, but slowly—at Santha's pace, not the audience's. There was a heavy silence but for the drumbeats, and smoke swirled in layers like a jungle mist. Then the robe was off and kicked aside, and Santha was naked but for a brief black G-string.

Her hips moved faster. Santha's face radiated hot need, the muscles of her smooth thighs tensing; she reached out, her fingers rippling through the currents of smoke. Then she was down on her knees, reaching for the audience, on her side, writhing with lust and desire. She stretched like a beautiful cat, then lay on her back and lifted her legs, slowly scissoring them. The drumbeats hammered at Billy's head, and he knew he couldn't stand much

244

more of this. She curled her knees up toward her chin, and suddenly the G-string fell away and there was a liquid wink between her thighs.

And then the lights went out.

Breath burst from several sets of lungs. A harsh white light came on, showing all the rips and seams in the painted backdrop, and the barker said, "That's all, gentlemen! Y'all come back now, hear?"

There were a few shouts of "More!" and assorted catcalls, but the show was over. Billy couldn't move for a few minutes, because he was as big as a railroad spike and he knew he'd either split his pants or burst his balls if he tried to stagger out. When he finally did stand up, the place was empty. He could just imagine what his folks would say if they knew where he was right now. He limped toward the exit.

"I *thought* that you was out there. Hey, Choctaw!"

Billy turned. Santha was onstage again, wrapped up in her black robe. His heart almost stuttered to a stop.

"How'd you like it?"

"It was . . . okay, I guess."

"*Okay?* Jeez, we worked our asses off for you boys! And all you have to say is 'okay'? I saw you out there, but sometimes it's hard to make out faces in that damned light. How'd you like Leona? You know, the lion-girl."

"Uh . . . she was fine."

"She just joined the show at the first of June. She had a disease when she was a little girl that made her hair fall out." She smiled when she saw the bewildered look in his eyes. "Not *all* her hair, dope! She shaves that part."

"Oh."

The bulky platinum-blond barker came out, coiling up the microphone cord. She was smoking a cheroot and scowling with an expression that might've shattered a mirror. "Christ! Did you ever *see* such a bunch of losers? Cheap bastards, too! Fuckers wouldn't even buy one set of ticklers! You goin' to Barbie's birthday party!"

"I don't know," Santha said. "Maybe." She glanced over at Billy. "Want to go to a party, Choctaw?"

"I . . . guess I'd better be getting back to—"

"Oh, come on! Besides, I need somebody to help me carry my

makeup case and my wardrobe to my trailer. And I feel bad about jumping your case this afternoon."

"Better take it while you can," the barker said, not looking at Billy but rather examining something up in the lights. "Santha's never fucked an Indian before."

"Just a party," Santha told him. She laughed softly. "Come on, I won't bite."

"Are you . . . gonna get dressed?"

"Sure. I'll put on my chastity belt and my suit of armor. How about that?"

Billy smiled. "Okay, I'll go."

"You mean you don't have to sign out for that old ghost nut you work for?"

"Nope."

"Good. You can be my date, and get me past all the local horny old men who'll be waiting outside. Come on back to the dressing room."

Billy paused just for a few seconds, then followed her back behind the stage. His head was reeling with possibilities, and he thought how wonderful love felt.

The barker muttered, "Another one bites the dust . . ." and then she switched off the lights.

------------------------------ **37** ------------------------------

Being drunk, Billy thought as he staggered down the midway, was a lot like being in love. Your head spun like a top, your stomach lurched, and you knew you'd done crazy things but you couldn't quite remember what they were. The last couple of hours were all blurred in his mind; he recalled leaving with Santha, carrying her makeup case to her trailer for her, and then going with her to somebody else's trailer where there were a lot of people laughing loud and drinking. Santha had introduced him as Choctaw, somebody had put a beer in his hand, and an hour after that he was seriously contemplating Leona's bald pate while she told him her life story. The trailer had overflowed with people, music blared into the night, and after his sixth beer Billy had found himself on the wrong end of a stubby cigarette that had set fire to his lungs and, strangely, reminded him of the pipe he'd smoked with his old grandmother. Only this time, instead of seeing visions, he'd giggled like an ape and told ghost stories that he invented off the top of his ripped-open head. He remembered feeling a green burn of jealousy as he saw Santha being embraced by another man; he thought that the man and Santha had left the party together, but now it didn't matter. In the morning, it might. When he'd finally left, Barbie the black contortionist had hugged him and thanked him for coming, and now he was trying to keep from walking in circles and right angles.

He was not so drunk that he didn't take a long detour around the Octopus. A pale mist lay close to the earth along the midway. He wondered vaguely if he was a fool for being in love with a woman like Santha, older than he was and more experienced by a country mile. Was she playing with him, laughing behind his back? Hell, he thought, I hardly even *know* her! But she sure is pretty, even with all that glop on her face. Tomorrow he might just wander by her trailer to see what she looked like palefaced. *Never fucked an Indian.* He had to stop thinking like this now, or even the beers wouldn't help him sleep.

"Boy?" someone said quietly.

Billy stopped and looked around; he thought he'd heard a voice, but . . .

"I'm over here."

Billy still couldn't see anyone. The Ghost Show tent was just a few yards away. If he could make his legs cross the midway without folding on him, he'd be okay. "Huh? Where?"

"Right here." And the entrance to the Killer Snakes sideshow slowly opened, as if the painted reptile had yawned its jaws wide for him.

"I can't see you. Turn on a light."

There was a pause. Then, "You're afraid, aren't you?"

"Hell, no! I'm Billy Creekmore and I'm a Choctaw Indian and know what? I can see *ghosts!*"

"That's very good. You must be like me. I enjoy the night."

"Uh-huh." Billy looked across the midway at the Ghost Show tent. "Gotta get to sleep. . . ."

"Where have you been?"

"Party. Somebody's birthday."

"Well, isn't that nice. Why don't you step inside, and we'll talk."

He stared at the dark entrance, his vision going in and out of focus. "No. I don't like snakes. They give me the creeps."

There was a soft little laugh. "Oh, snakes are wonderful creatures. They're very good at catching rats."

"Yeah. Well"—he ran a hand through his tousled hair and started to walk away—"been nice talkin' to you."

"Wait! Please. We can talk about . . . about *Santha,* if you like."

"Santha? What about her?"

"Oh, about how lovely she is. And innocent really, deep in her heart. She and I are very close; she tells me all her secrets."

"She does?"

"Yes." The voice was a silken whisper. "Come in, and we'll talk."

"What kind of secrets?"

"She's told me things about you, Billy. Step in, and then I'll turn on the lights and we'll have a nice long talk."

"I . . . can only stay a minute." He was afraid of crossing that threshold, but he wanted to know who this man was and what Santha might've told him. "Are any of those snakes loose?"

"Oh, no. Not a one. Do you think I'm crazy?"

Billy grinned. "Naw." He took the first step, and found the second one easier. Then he was moving into the clammy darkness and he thrust out his arms to touch whoever was standing there. "Hey, where are . . ."

Behind him, the door slammed shut. A bolt was thrown. Billy spun around, his beer-fogged brain reacting with agonized slowness. And then a thick rope was coiled around his throat, almost choking him; the weight of it drove him to his knees, where he gripped at the rope to pull it loose. To his horror, it undulated beneath his fingers—and grew tighter. His head was pounding.

"Boy," the figure whispered, bending close, "there's a boa constrictor around your neck. If you struggle it's going to strangle you."

Billy moaned, tears of terror springing to his eyes. He grabbed at the thing, desperately trying to loosen it.

"I'll let it kill you," the man warned solemnly. "You're drunk, you stumbled in here not knowing where you were—how can I be at fault for that? Don't struggle, boy. Just listen."

Billy sat very still, a scream locked behind his teeth. The snakeman knelt down beside him so he could whisper in Billy's ear. "You're going to leave that girl alone. You know the one I mean. Santha. I saw you tonight at the show, and I saw you later, at the party. Oh, you couldn't see *me*—but I was there." The snake-man gripped his hair. "You're a very smart young man, aren't you? Smarter than Chalky was. Say yes, Mr. Fitts."

"Yes, Mr. Fitts," Billy croaked.

"That's good. Santha is such a beautiful girl, isn't she? *Beauty*." He spoke that word as if it were exotic poison. "But I can't keep all the men away from her, can I? She doesn't understand how I feel about her yet, but she will . . . she will. And when she does she won't need scum like you. You're going to leave her alone, and if you don't I'll find out about it. Understand?"

Red motes spun before Billy's eyes. When he tried to nod, the boa tightened.

"Good. That machine whispers to me at night, boy. You know the one: the Octopus. Oh, it tells me everything I need to know. And guess what? It's watching you. So whatever you do, I'm going to know about it. I can pick any kind of lock, boy—and my snakes can get in *anywhere*." He released Billy's hair, and sat back on his haunches for a moment. Over the ringing of blood in his ears, Billy heard small hissings and slitherings from elsewhere in the tent.

"Don't move, now," Fitts said. He slowly worked the boa free from Billy's neck. Billy pitched forward onto his face in the sawdust. Fitts stood up and prodded him in the ribs with his shoe. "If you're going to puke, do it on the midway. Go on, get out of here."

"Help me up. Please. . . ."

"No," the snake-man whispered. "*Crawl*."

The bolt was thrown back, the door opened. Billy, shaking and sick, crawled past the man, who remained a vague outline in the darkness. The door closed quietly behind him.

249

38

Wayne Falconer was awakened when something began slowly dragging the sheet off his body.

He sat up abruptly, sleep still fogging his brain, and saw an indistinct form sitting at the foot of his bed. At first he cowered, because for an instant he thought it was that dark and hideous shape he'd seen in his dreams, and now it had come to consume him; but then he blinked and realized it was his father, wearing his bright yellow funeral suit, sitting there with a faint smile on his ruddy, healthy-looking face.

"Hello, son," J.J. said quietly.

Wayne's eyes widened, the breath slowly rasping from his lungs. "No," he said. "No, you're in the ground. . . . I saw you go into the . . ."

"Did you? Maybe I *am* in the ground." He grinned, showing even white teeth. "But . . . maybe you *did* bring part of me back to life, Wayne. Maybe you're a lot stronger than you thought you were."

Wayne shook his head. "You're . . ."

"Dead? I'll never be dead to you, son. Because you loved me more than anybody else did. And now you realize how much you needed me, don't you? Keeping the Crusade going is a hard job, isn't it? Working with the businessmen and the lawyers, keeping all the accounts straight, pushing the Crusade forward . . . you've hardly begun, and already you know there's more to it than you thought. Isn't that right?"

Wayne's headache had come back again, crushing his temples. Since the funeral a month ago, the headaches had gotten much worse. He ate aspirin by the handful. "I can't . . . I can't do it alone," he whispered.

"*Alone.* Now isn't that an awful word? It's kind of like the word *dead*. But you don't have to be alone, just like I don't have to be dead . . . unless you want it that way."

"No!" Wayne said, "But I don't . . ."

"Shhhhh," Falconer cautioned, with a finger to his lips. "Your mother's right down the hall, and we wouldn't want her to hear." The shaft of silver moonlight that filtered through the window winked off the buttons on his father's coat; the shadow that was thrown from his father was huge and shapeless. "I can help you, son, if you let me. I can be with you, and I can guide you."

"My . . . head hurts. I . . . can't think. . . ."

"You're only confused. There's so much responsibility on you, so much work and healing to be done. And you're still a boy, just going on eighteen. No wonder your head aches, with all that thinking and worrying you have to do. But there are things we have to talk about, Wayne; things you can't tell anybody else, not in the whole world."

"What kind of . . . things?"

Falconer leaned closer to him. Wayne thought there was a red spark in his eyes, down under the pale blue-green. "The girl, Wayne. The girl at the lake."

"I don't want to . . . think about that. No, please. . . ."

"But you *have* to! Oh, you have to take the consequences of your actions."

"She didn't drown!" Wayne said, tears glittering in his eyes. "There was never anything in the paper about it! Nobody ever found her! Nobody ever found her! She must've . . . just run away or something!"

Falconer said quietly, "She's under the platform, Wayne. She's caught up underneath there. She's already swelled up like a balloon, and pretty soon she'll pop wide open and what's left will sink down into the mud. The fish and the turtles will pick her clean. She was a wild, sinful girl, Wayne, and her folks probably think she's just run away from home. Nobody would ever connect you with her, even if they find her bones. And they *won't*. There was a demon in her, Wayne, and she was waiting there for you."

"Waiting for me?" he whispered. "Why?"

"To keep you from getting home, where I needed you. Don't you think you could have saved me, if you'd known?"

"Yes."

Falconer nodded. "Yes. You see, there are demons at work everywhere. This country is rotten with sin, and it all festers from a little run-down shack in Hawthorne. *She* calls dark powers to do her bidding. You know who I mean. You've known for a long time. She and her boy are strong, Wayne; they've got the forces of Death and Hell behind them, and they want to destroy you just like they destroyed me. They weakened my faith in you, and I reached out for you too late. Now they'll work on your faith in yourself, make you doubt that you could ever heal at all. Oh, they're strong and wicked and they should go down in flames."

"Flames," Wayne repeated.

"Yes. You'll have the chance to send them into Hellfire, Wayne, if you let me guide you. I can be with you whenever you need me. I can help you with the Crusade. So you see? I'm not really dead, unless you want me to be."

"No! I . . . need your help, Dad. Sometimes I just . . . I just don't know what to do! Sometimes I . . . don't know if the things I've done are good or bad. . . ."

"You don't have to worry," Falconer said, with a gentle smile. "Everything'll be fine, if you'll trust me. You need to take a drug called Percodan for your headaches. Tell George Hodges, and make him get it for you."

Puzzled, Wayne frowned. "Dad . . . I thought you said medicines were sinful, and those people who took medicines were doing the Devil's bidding."

"*Some* medicines are sinful. But if you're in pain, and you're confused, then you need something to take the burden off you for a little while. Isn't that right?"

"I guess so," Wayne agreed, though he could never remember his father talking about drugs like this before. Percodan, had he said?

"I'll be here when you need me," Falconer said. "But if you tell anyone, even your mother, then I can't come back and help you anymore. Do you understand?"

"Yes sir." He paused for a moment, then whispered, "Dad? What's being dead like?"

"It's . . . like being in a black hole, son, on the blackest night you can imagine, and you try to crawl out but you don't know which is the top and which is the bottom."

"But . . . haven't you heard the angels sing?"

"Angels?" He grinned again, but his eyes were still gelid. "Oh, yes. They do sing." And then he put his fingers to his lips, glancing quickly toward the door.

An instant afterward, there was a soft knocking. "Wayne?" Cammy's voice carried a tremble.

"What is it?"

The door opened a few inches. "Wayne, are you all right?"

"Why shouldn't I be?" He realized he was alone now; the yellow-suited figure was gone, and the room was empty. *My dad is alive!* he shrieked inwardly, his heart pounding with joy.

"I . . . thought I heard you talking. You're sure you're all right?"

"I said I was, didn't I? Now leave me alone, I've got a long day tomorrow!"

She looked nervously around the room, opening the door a little wider so the hallway light could stream in. The mounted airplane models and large wall posters of military aircraft took up a lion's share of the room. Waynes clothes were strewn on a chair. Cammy said, "I'm sorry I bothered you. Good-night."

Wayne lay back down as the door closed. He waited for a long time, but his father didn't come back. You bitch! he seethed at his mother. You killed him a second time! But no, no . . . his father would return to the world of the living when he was needed; Wayne was sure of it. Before he drifted to sleep, Wayne repeated the word *Percodan* ten times to burn it into his mind.

And in her room down the hallway, Cammy Falconer lay in bed with all the lights blazing. She was staring at the ceiling. Every so often a shiver passed through her. It was not Wayne's voice, in the middle of the night, that had been so bad.

It had been the guttural, harsh mumbling that Cammy had heard faintly through the wall.

Answering her son.

39

The game booths, rides, and sideshows had sprung up from the mud covering Birmingham's fairgrounds. The rain fell in drizzles and sheets for three days, blasting the state fair business to hell. Still, people continued to slog through the sawdusty mud; drenched to the bone, they sought refuge in the arcades and enclosed shows, but they left the rides alone as light bulbs and wires sputtered under the rain.

That was for the best, Billy knew. Because people wouldn't be riding the Octopus in the rain, and it would be deprived of what it needed. This was the last stop of the season. If whatever presence that controlled the Octopus was going to strike, it would have to be in the next four days. At night, even while the rain pattered on the Ghost Show tent's roof, Billy could hear Buck Edgers working on his machine, the hammer's noise echoing down the long ghostly corridor of the midway. While setting up the Octopus on the slippery field, a roustabout's shoulder was broken by a piece of metal that toppled from above. Word had gone out about the machine, and now everyone avoided it.

Billy stood outside Santha Tully's trailer, in a light drizzle that had washed away the last of the night's customers. He had been here twice since the carnival had reached Birmingham: the first time, he'd heard Santha laughing with a man inside there, and the second time he'd come out through the rows of trailers to find a short, balding figure standing in the shadows not ten feet from him. The man had instantly whirled toward him, and Billy had gotten a quick glimpse of his startled face, wearing dark-tinted glasses, before the man had run away. Billy had followed him for a short distance, but lost him in the maze of trailers. He'd told no one about the incident at the Killer Snakes tent, fearing that the man would find out and put his snakes to work, perhaps on Santha or Dr. Mirakle. But he still desired her, and still needed to see her.

He screwed up his courage, looked around to make sure no one had followed him, and then walked up a couple of cinder-block steps to the trailer's door. A curtain was closed in a single oval window, but light leaked out around it; he could hear the scratchy whine of a country singer. He knocked at the door and waited. The music stopped. He knocked again, less hesitantly, and heard Santha say, "Yeah? Who is it?"

"Me. Billy Creekmore."

"Choctaw?" A bolt slid back, and the thin door opened. She stood there in the dim golden light, wearing a black silk robe that clung to the curves of her body. Her hair was a dusky halo, and Billy saw that she wore practically no makeup. There were a lot of lines around her eyes, and her lips looked sad and thin. In her right hand there was a small chrome-plated pistol. "Anybody else out there?" she asked.

"No."

She opened the door wider to let him in, then bolted it again. The room was a cramped half living area and half kitchen. The bed, an unsteady-looking cot with a bright blue spread, was right out in the open, next to a rack of clothes on their hangers. A dressing table was cluttered with a dozen different kinds of creams, lipsticks, and various cosmetics. On a tiny kitchen table was a battered record player, next to a small stack of unwashed dishes. Posters of Clint Eastwood, Paul Newman, and Steve McQueen decorated the walls, along with a rebel flag and a Day-Glo Love poster. A door led into a tiny bathroom and shower stall.

Billy stared at the pistol. Santha flicked the safety on and put it away in a dresser drawer. "Sorry," she said. "Sometimes I get jumpy late at night." Santha stepped past him and peered out the window for a moment. "I was expecting a friend of mine. He was supposed to be here about thirty minutes ago."

"Anybody special?"

Santha looked at him, then gave him a little crooked smile. "No. Just a friend. Somebody to pass the time with, I guess."

Billy nodded. "I'd better go, then. I don't want to—"

"No!" She reached out and grasped his arm. "No, don't go. Stay here and talk to me until Buddy gets here, okay? Really, I don't like to be here alone."

"What'll he think if he finds me with you?"

"I don't know." She didn't release her grip. "What *would* he think?"

Her eyes were luminous in the weak light from a single table lamp, her fingers cool against his rain-dampened skin. Billy said, "Maybe he'd think . . . something was going on between us."

"Do you want something to go on between us?"

"I . . . I hardly know you."

"You didn't answer my question, Choctaw. Is it you who's been sneaking around my trailer at night?"

"No." Tell her about the man, he told himself; but what good would it do? It would only scare her more, and the police couldn't prove the snake-man had had anything to do with Chalky's death. No. In four days, the fair would be over and she'd be leaving, and then that man couldn't bother her anymore.

"Well, I think it *has* been you. I think you've been sneakin' around and spyin' on me! Naughty, naughty!" She grinned and let go of him. "Sit down. Do you want a beer?"

"No, thanks." He sat down on a faded blue sofa while Santha rummaged through her small refrigerator and popped open a Miller's.

"Excuse the mess in here. Sometimes I'm as lazy as a leaf." She sipped from the can, walked to the window, and looked out again. "Damn! Rainin' harder." The drops sounded leaden on the trailer's roof. "I've been meanin' to come by that Ghost Show of yours." She let the curtain fall and stood over him. "Do you believe in ghosts?"

He nodded.

"Yeah, I do too. I was born in New Orleans, see, and that's supposed to be the most haunted city in the whole country, did you know that? Spooks just come out of the woodwork. 'Course, I've never seen one, but . . ." She sat down beside him and stretched out her long bare legs. Her thighs showed through a slit in the robe, and Billy saw a fine light down like flecks of copper on them. "Jeez. I don't think Buddy's coming, do you? Bastard lies like a rug. Told me he'd get me a job here in Birmingham after the fair closes up."

"What will you do?"

"I don't know, maybe go home. My kids live with my mother. Yeah, don't look so surprised! I've got two little girls. I don't look like I've had two kids, do I?" She patted her flat belly. "Sit-ups. How old do you think I look?"

He shrugged. "Maybe . . . . twenty-two." He was being kind.

Her eyes glittered with pure pleasure. The drumming of the rain on the roof was hypnotic and soothing. "Do you think I have a good body?"

He shifted and cleared his throat. "Well . . . sure I do. It's nice."

"I'm proud of how I look. That's why I like to dance. Oh, maybe someday I'll open up my own dance studio and give lessons, but right now I love being on that stage. You feel important, and you know that people enjoy watching you." She sipped at her beer and watched him mischievously. "*You* enjoyed watching, didn't you?"

"Yeah, I did."

She laughed. "Ha! Choctaw, you beat all I've ever seen! You're sittin' there like a priest in a whorehouse!" Her smile faded a fraction, her eyes darkening. "That's not what you think, is it? That I'm a whore?"

"No!" he said, though he wasn't exactly certain she was or wasn't.

"I'm not. I just . . . live my own life, that's all. I do what I please when I please. Is that so bad?"

Billy shook his head.

"Your shirt's wet." She leaned toward him and began unbuttoning it. "You'll catch a cold if you keep it on."

He shrugged out of it and she tossed it aside. "That's better," she said. "You have a nice chest. I thought Indians didn't have any hair on their bodies."

"I'm just part Indian."

"You're a nice-lookin' kid. How old are you, eighteen? No, seventeen, didn't you say? Well, I don't guess that bastard Buddy is coming tonight, do you?"

"I don't guess he is."

Santha finished her beer and set it on the table before her, then returned her gaze to his. She stared at him, a smile working around her lips, until Billy felt his face flaming. She said in a soft voice, "Have you ever been with a woman before?"

"Huh? Well . . . sure."

"How many?"

"A few."

"Yeah. And the moon is made of green cheese." She leaned closer, looking deeply into his eyes. He was such a handsome boy, she thought, but there were secrets in his eyes; secrets, perhaps, that it was best not to know. Buddy wasn't coming, that was for sure. It was raining and she was lonely and she didn't like the idea of sleeping alone when somebody who'd sent her a bunch of rose stems was out there somewhere, maybe lurking around the trailer. She traced a finger down the center of his chest and watched the flesh tighten. "You've wanted me all along, haven't you? You don't have to be shy about it." Her finger stopped at his belt buckle. "I like you. Jeez, listen to me. Usually I have to fight the guys off! So why are you different?"

"I'm not different," Billy said, trying to keep his voice steady. "I just . . . respect you, I guess."

"Respect me? I've learned a long time ago that respect doesn't keep your bed warm on a cold night. And, Choctaw, I've lived through some *very* wintry ones. And will again." She paused, running her finger along his belt line; then she grasped his hand and drew it closer to herself. She licked his fingers, very slowly.

He squeezed her hand and said, "I . . . don't know what to do. I'm probably not any good."

"I'm going to turn off that light," Santha told him, "and get into bed. I'd like for you to get undressed and come to bed with me. Will you?"

He wanted to say yes, but he was too nervous to speak. Santha recognized the glassy gleam in his eyes. She stood up, let the robe fall, and walked naked to the lamp. The light went out. Billy heard the sheets go back. The rain drummed down, punctuated now by the boom of distant thunder. Billy stood up, as if in a dream, and unbuckled his belt.

When he was ready, he approached the bed and saw Santha's golden hair on the pillow, her body a long S-shape beneath the pale blue sheet. She reached out for him, softly whispering his name, and when he touched her electricity seemed to jump between them. Trembling with excitement and shyness, he got under the sheet; Santha folded her arms around him, her warm mouth finding his, her tongue darting between his lips. He was correct in that he didn't know what to do, but when Santha scissored her legs around his hips he very quickly learned. Then there was heat, dampness, the sound of hurried breathing, and thunder getting closer. Santha summoned him deeper, deeper, and when he was about to explode she made him lie motionless, both of them locked together, until he could continue for a while longer.

Carnival lights filled Billy's head. She eased him onto his back, and sat astride him with her head thrown back, her mouth open as if to receive the rain that pounded on the roof. She impressed upon him the varying sensations of rhythms, from a hard pulse that ground them together to a long, slow, and lingering movement that had the strength of a tickling feather. He lay stunned while Santha's tongue played over his body, like a soft damp brush tracing the outlines of his muscles; then she told him what she liked and gave him encouragement as he first circled her nipples with his tongue, then her navel, then her soft belly and down into the valley between her legs, where her thighs pressed against the sides of his head and she gripped his hair as her hips churned. She moaned softly, her musky aroma perfuming the air.

Outside in a driving rain, Fitts stood with a raincoat pulled up around his neck. He'd seen the boy go in, and he'd seen the light go out. His blue-tinted eyeglasses streamed with water, but he didn't have to see anything else. He knew the rest of it. His heart throbbed with rage and agony. A *boy?* he thought. She would even take a stupid boy into her bed? His fists clenched in his coat pockets. Was there no hope for her? Lightning streaked, followed by a bass rumble of thunder that seemed to shake the world. He'd tried everything he could think of, and now he felt defeated. But there was one thing left.

He would go to the Octopus, stand before it in the gray downpour, and wait for the voice that came out of it to reveal to him what he should do. He stood a while longer, staring at the darkened trailer, and then trudged through the mud toward the midway. Long before he reached the Octopus, he could hear its sibilant whisper in his tormented brain:

Murder.

40

It was the twelfth of October, and tomorrow night the State Fair would be closing down, the carnival season over until spring. The rain had passed, and for the last two nights business had been booming. Billy helped Dr. Mirakle clean up after the final Ghost Show of the night, simply grinning when Mirakle pointedly asked him why he'd look so happy lately.

Billy left the tent and walked down the midway as the lights started flickering out. He shut the noises out of his head as he passed the Octopus, and he waited around back of the Jungle Love show, where Santha had said she'd meet him. When she did come out, fifteen minutes or so late, he saw she'd scrubbed off most of the garish makeup for him.

In her trailer, Santha continued Billy's education. An hour later, he was as weak as water, and she was pressed as close to him as a second skin. Through the dim haze of sleep, Billy could hear Buck Edger's hammer, striking metal again and again out on the darkened midway. He lay awake, listening, until Santha stirred and kissed him deeply and sweetly.

"I wish things could stay like this," Billy said after a moment.

Santha sat up. A match flared as she lit a cigarette; in its glow she looked beautiful and childlike. "What are you going to do after the fair's over?"

"I'm going down to Mobile with Dr. Mirakle, driving his equipment truck for him. Then . . . I guess I'll go back to Hawthorne. It's been a good summer. I don't think I'll ever forget it. Or *you*."

She ran her fingers through his hair and then said, "Hey! I know what would be real nice! A hot shower! We can just about both fit into the stall, and we can get real soapy and slippery and . . . ooh, I'm tinglin' just thinkin' about it! Okay?"

"Sure," he said, thrilled.

"One hot shower, comin' up!" Santha rose up from the bed and, still naked, went to the tiny bathroom. She reached in and flipped on the light. "I'll call you when I'm ready," she said, and giggled like a schoolgirl. Then she went inside and shut the door.

Billy was sitting up. His heartbeat had quickened, and there was a sick sensation in the pit of his stomach. He wasn't sure, wasn't sure at all, but just for an instant—as Santha had been silhouetted in the bathroom light—he though he'd seen a pale gray haze around her. An alarm went off in the back of his head, and he climbed out of the bed to approach the bathroom.

Santha, her body rosy, reached in through the green-plastic shower curtain and turned on the hot water. It sprayed downward into the tub, but instead of the sound of water against porcelain there was a different sound—a wet, thickened noise. Santha drew aside the curtain and looked into the tub.

The water was hitting a large burlap bag, drawn closed at the top. She reached for it even as Billy said, "Santha?" from just outside the door.

She pulled at the bag. It came open. It was very heavy, and wouldn't slide.

"Santha?"

And then a triangular head with blazing eyes shot out of the burlap bag, the nightmarish thing stretching high through the hot-water fog. Santha threw her arms up instinctively, but the cobra struck her on the cheek and she slammed backward against the wall, striking her head on the tiles. Her scream gurgled away as she pitched forward, her legs dangling over the tub, the scalding water beating down on her exposed back.

Billy burst through the door, barely able to see because of the rising fog. The cobra came flashing out of it toward him. He jerked his head back, and the fangs missed him by bare inches. It was uncoiling out of the tub. Billy saw that Santha was being burned, and he reached forward to grasp her ankles. The cobra hissed, its hood spreading wide, and struck at him again. He backed away. The cobra reared up over four feet, watching him with its terrible baleful gaze as steam filled the bathroom.

Billy was still naked, but he didn't think about his clothes. He ran to the door, threw aside the bolt, and tried to push it open . . . but it wouldn't budge. He slammed his shoulder against it, and heard the rattle of a lock in the clasp. But Santha had taken off the lock when they'd come in! He realized, then, what must've happened: the snakeman had gotten in here and put that cobra in the bathroom hours ago, to kill them both, and then while they were sleeping he'd put one of his own locks through the clasp. He hammered against the door, and shouted for help.

Steam was rolling out into the room. He fumbled with the lamp, knocked it to the floor, bent and found the switch. The low, harsh light spread out in irregular rays, and Billy saw the cobra winding out through the bathroom door in what looked like foot after foot. It reared up again, its gaze fixed on him, and now Billy could hear Santha's low, terrified moaning. The cobra hissed and slithered forward, trying to defend its newfound territory.

Billy backed up against the dresser. He opened the drawer, threw aside lipsticks and makeup until his hand closed on the chrome-plated pistol. When he turned, the cobra was only a few feet away from him, its head weaving back and forth. Billy picked up a pillow from the bed, and suddenly the cobra darted forward; its head hit the pillow with the force of a man's fist. He aimed the pistol and squeezed the trigger, but nothing happened. The safety was on! The snake was motionless, its tongue flickering out as it watched him. Billy would have to drop the pillow and push back the safety with his free hand. The cobra was still within striking range, and Billy had backed up as far as he could.

Someone hammered at the door. The cobra's head whipped to one side, toward the vibrations, and Billy threw the pillow at it with a guttural shout. He flicked off the safety, and the pistol was ready as the cobra's head started to wiggle free from beneath the pillow. Billy fired at it—one, two, three, four, five. The air stank of powder, and now the cobra was twisting madly, its head almost severed from the thick body. It started to rise, but the mangled head was out of control and the body snapped and writhed, the tail clenching around one leg of the dresser. Billy stood over the thing, and stretched his arm down. He had a glimpse of one single terrible eye, burning to his soul, and then the head exploded with the force of the sixth bullet. The body continued to jerk.

The door burst open, and two men who came in recoiled from the sight of the writhing snake. Billy was already in the steamy bathroom, pulling Santha out of the hot water; her back was a mass of blisters, and she was sobbing hysterically. He saw the snakebite, and saw the gray aura darkening. "Call an ambulance!" he shrieked to the men. "Hurry! The snake bit her!"

262

They wrapped her up in a sheet, and Billy struggled into his pants. A knot of people had gathered outside the trailer, trying to find out what had happened. When the ambulance came, Billy told the attendants that Santha had been bitten by a cobra, and if they didn't hurry she was going to die. He watched them roar away, and he heard someone say that the police were on their way.

He realized he still held the pistol. He went back into the trailer, avoiding the blood and mess, and found another box of bullets in the dresser drawer. He loaded the pistol, and then walked out through the gawking carnival people toward the midway. He could hear approaching sirens, but their noise neither increased his pace nor slowed him. As he passed the Octopus, he imagined he heard a high shriek of laughter. Buck Edgers, hammer still in his hand, looked up from his work through dark-circled, disturbed eyes. Billy paid him no attention. His heart was pounding, a fever of revenge burning in his brain as he reached the Killer Snakes sideshow and flicked the safety off his pistol. He pushed at the entranceway and was not surprised when the door—the reptile's mouth—noiselessly opened.

"Come out of there, you bastard!" Billy shouted.

Darkness lay thickly within. Nothing moved, but Billy thought he could hear the soft slidings of the man's pets. "I said come out, or I'll drag you out!" He aimed the gun into the darkness. "I've got a gun, you bastard!"

He steeled himself and stepped into the darkness, his hand almost melded to the pistol. "I've got a gun!" he warned, tensing for an expected attack. Nothing moved, and now he could see the vague shapes of the cages, set in orderly rows. A few feet away and above, a light bulb caught a speck of reflected light; Billy reached up, found the switch and turned it on. The bulb flickered, slightly swinging back and forth to throw huge and distorted shadows.

A short, balding man in a brown suit was lying on his back, on a mattress at the rear of the place. His hands were clamped around the grayish green boa constrictor that had strangled him to death. His glasses were off, and his face was bluish white. There was a note safety-pinned to the man's checked shirt. Billy approached the body, and ripped the note away. It said MURDER MURDER MURDER MURDER MURDER. And then, at the bottom: SUICIDE. Billy stared at it, wondering what madness had prompted this man to wrap the boa around his own throat and lie down to die. He returned the note to the body, where the police could find it, and then a wave of anguish crashed over him. He'd seen a gray aura enveloping Santha, not a black one: what did it mean? Tears searing his eyes, he left the sideshow and looked out to where he could see red and blue police lights spinning amid the trailers.

A cool breeze had kicked up, breaking his flesh into goosebumps. Bits of paper wheeled along the midway, spinning in miniature tornadoes. Billy's cold gaze fell upon the Octopus. Buck Edgers was working like a machine.

"Billy? My God, what's going on!" Dr. Mirakle, in an old undershirt and his pajama bottoms, had staggered out of the truck parked behind the Ghost Show, next to the Volkswagen van. His eyes were swollen with heavy sleep, and he exuded the aroma of bourbon. He looked down at the pistol and stopped. "*Billy?*"

"It's all right. They took Santha to the hospital. The cobra bit her, it was there in the bathtub when she . . ." His voice cracked.

Mirakle eased forward and took the pistol from his hand. "You look like death warmed over, boy. Come on, I'll pour you a drink and you can tell me—"

"No. Not yet." Oblivious to the commotion, Edgers was driving his hammer up and down on a bolt that had probably never been loose in the first place. It dawned on Billy that the Octopus was wearing Edgers down, commanding all of his time and attention, using him as its puppet. There were revenants caught within the Octopus, crying out in their confusion and terror. Perhaps now, Billy thought, it possesses some part of the snakeman as well. He could hear the faint screaming, and he knew the Octopus wanted him too. It wanted to consume him, to draw his spirit and power into its black, greedy gears and pistons.

Are you strong? Are you strong in your heart, where strength counts?

Billy's hand had gone into his pocket. Now he brought the hand out and looked at the nugget of coal in his palm. He didn't remember putting it in these pants; he'd thought it was still with his belongings, in his suitcase under the cot at the rear of the Ghost Show tent. It reminded him of the strength he possessed, the risks he must take if he was to continue his Mystery Walk. If he backed down, if he failed to trust his own inner will, then whatever inhabited the Octopus would win, and in some terrible way it might even grow stronger still. He clenched the coal in his fist and returned it to his pocket.

"Billy?" Dr. Mirakle said. "Where are you going?"

"You can come with me, if you like. But don't try to stop me. I have to do this right now. Right *now*."

"Do . . . *what?* My God, have you lost your mind?" But he was following along, holding the pistol out to his side as if it were a dead fish.

Before Billy reached the Octopus, Edgers stopped hammering. He straightened up from his work, and turned to face the boy. Across his features was a hideous grin that stretched his mouth wide in eager anticipation. The Octopus had him, Billy knew. It was not Buck Edgers grinning.

When Dr. Mirakle saw that grin, he was shocked motionless for a moment. He said in a nervous voice, "Billy, I don't . . . think you should . . ."

"Step right up, pard!" Edgers boomed, shuffling forward. "Thought you'd *never* come!"

"I'm here. Start it up."

"Come on, then! Yessir! Oh, you're a special guest, you don't even need a fuckin' ticket! Been savin' a ride just for *you*." He moved to the shrouded gondola and tugged at the tarpaulin until it tore away. There were holes in the rusted metal, and faint streaks of bright orange paint. He pulled the warped metal-mesh canopy open, exposing the rust-riddled interior. "Perfect fit, I'd say."

"I wouldn't get in that rust-bucket if I were you," Dr. Mirakle said, tugging at Billy's arm. "No, I forbid it! I told your mother I'd take care of you, and I forbid you to do it! Now listen, come on back to the tent and we'll—"

"Shut your mouth, you old cocksucker," Edgers said softly, his eyes blazing into Billy's. "The boy's grown up now. He's a *man*. He's got a mind, and he knows what he wants to do. Show's about to start!" He gestured toward the open gondola.

Billy pulled free of Dr. Mirakle. He had to do this now, while there was still a rage burning in him. He moved forward, but suddenly Edgers's wife stepped out of the shadows, her round-cheeked face pasty with dread. She said, "No, please . . . don't do it, boy. You don't *understand* it. You don't see—"

"SHUT UP YOU GODDAMNED BITCH!" the man howled, brandishing the hammer at her. She flinched but did not step back.

"That machine," she said, staring at Billy, "is Satan's

265

handiwork. Buck bought it out of a junkyard in Georgia, and from the first day he couldn't do anything but work on it, trying to put it back together. It slashed his face, and broke both his legs, and—"

"SHUT UP SHUT UP SHUT UP!" He hobbled toward her, raising the hammer, and she screamed, "Please Buck, don't!" and dodged a vicious blow that might've broken her shoulder. She slipped and fell to her hands and knees; her husband stood over her, panting like an animal. She looked up at him, an awful pleading expression in her eyes, and said, "I love you, Buck. . . ."

Billy saw the man's face change; he blinked uncertainly, and his terrible grimace slipped a few notches. For an instant, he resembled nothing more than a tormented man who'd been down on his luck for most of his life; then the savage grin came back, and his eyes flared. He put his booted foot against his wife's side and pushed her down into the sawdust. He said, "Now you stay right there, like a good little girl."

"Come on!" Billy said. "I'm waiting for you!"

"Oh, yes. Of course. The master speaks, the servant obeys. Of course, of course!" He giggled and watched as Billy climbed into the gondola. The seat was a hard mass of cracked vinyl and Billy could see the ground through a few quarter-sized holes in the metal. He stretched his legs out into the gondola's nose, his back straight against the seat. There was a seatbelt, and Billy drew it tightly across his lap. Edgers rushed forward and clanged the mesh canopy down, drawing a small metal bar through a safety clasp. He grinned in through the mesh. "All comfy-cozy? Good. Then we're ready to begin, aren't we?"

Edgers scuttled to the generator that powered the Octopus and switched it on; it hummed, sending electricity through cables as thick as a man's wrist. The ride's lights flickered, flickered again, and then blazed brightly. The remaining bulbs that spelled out OCTOPUS buzzed like angry hornets. Edgers stood over a small control board and turned on the ride's engine; it hooted and moaned, gears and wheels spinning. "I've got you!" he shouted. His face was ruddy and demonic as he let off the brake's foot pedal and slowly pushed forward the lever that engaged the drive-train.

"Billy!" Dr. Mirakle shouted, stepping back as the Octopus began to move.

The gondolas slowly gained momentum. Billy's head was forced back by centrifugal motion. Edgers bore down on the lever;

266

Billy's cheeks rippled with the rising g-forces. The gondolas began rising—five feet, ten feet, fifteen feet.

And then a garble of screams, moans, and sobbings—agonized sounds, some high-pitched and others so low Billy felt them in his bones rather then heard them—began to rise up around him, faintly at first, then with increasing intensity. He could hear a cacophony of voices, cries for help, sudden shrieks that seemed to pierce him. This gondola was the evil heart of the Octopus, Billy knew, and within it were the disembodied revenants of its victims—God only knew how many.

The gondola pitched upward suddenly, then fell with a frightening speed. It stopped with a squeal of cables and pistons, then jerked upward again. The Octopus was spinning faster, the world beyond the gondola a dizzying blur. Billy, his face twisted into a rictus, tried to force his concentration on the voices, tried to focus his energy on drawing the revenants to him.

No fear, he thought. *No fear. I can help you. I can . . .*

A roar filled his head: *No you can't! You can't reach them I won't let you reach them!*

The gondola was rising and falling, faster and faster, Billy's head brushing the mesh canopy with its upward sweep. He shut his eyes, his hands gripping the cracked vinyl armrests. There was a coldness in the air, gradually creeping up his body; he let it overtake him, and suddenly his brain was crackling with the last thoughts and images of perhaps a dozen people the Octopus had destroyed.

"No fear," Billy breathed. "Just touch me . . . no fear. . . ."

And suddenly electricity seemed to sear through him, and there was something else in the gondola with him, something laughing and shrieking.

The voice came in a triumphant cackle: *"You're mine now, boy!"*

Billy shouted, "NO!" The voice rippled and faded, and he knew he'd touched the pulse of wickedness in this machine. "I know you! I know what you are now!"

Do you, boy? Then come join me.

Billy heard something grind and rip. He opened his eyes, and saw with horror that the long bolts securing the mesh canopy in place were slowly unscrewing. Smaller screws that held the safety bar were being ripped out. The canopy assemblage tore away and

267

flew into the air. Wind screamed into Billy's face, forcing his chin backward. Another bolt clattered loose down around Billy's knees. The quarter-sized holes tore open still wider, like rotten cloth. The gondola was coming to pieces around him, and when it pitched him out to his death the entire machine would break loose, off-balance, and go spinning down the midway trailing live electric cables.

"STOP IT!" Billy yelled to Buck. He caught a quick glimpse of the man, bent over the control board like a hunchback, his hand pressed down on the lever. Above him more bolts unscrewed, in the central mechanism that held the gondolas to the Octopus, and a cable tore loose to spit orange sparks.

He could feel presences all around him, trying to cling to him. He forced himself to concentrate on their anguished voices again, and now he saw a faint mist taking form and shape, a figure with many heads and arms and legs, the faces indistinct, the whole thing reaching for him, clinging to him like a frightened animal. "Oh God," he whispered, "help me do it, please help me. . . ."

Bolts sheared off. A section of the flooring fell away under Billy's legs, and on the ground Dr. Mirakle ducked as the sharp metal sailed over his head.

Billy sank his arms into the mass of apparitions before him, like plunging into an ice-veined pond. His teeth chattered. "You can get away from here . . . through me!" he shouted into the wind. "I'll take your pain, if you give it up!"

No! I've got you now I've got all of you!

"Please! I'll take it for you, I'll keep it so you can go on! Please *let* me! . . ."

The gondola shuddred and swayed, loosened from its supporting arm. Currents of terror ripped through Billy.

The misty shape undulated, a dozen hands reaching for him. A dozen terror-stricken faces writhed like smoke. A section of the gondola's side fell away with a shriek of torn metal.

I'm their master their keeper you can't win.

"No! You feed on them, you use their hurting to make yourself stronger!" The gondola fell and jarred, rose again with a force that clicked Billy's teeth together. He gripped at the revenants, his arms inside a deep-freeze. "Let me help you get away! Please!"

And then the mass began to spread over him, to cover him up, icy threads of white matter racing over his face, into his hair around his shoulders. Many people, events, and emotions filled him up, almost to bursting, and he cried out at the force of a dozen life-experiences entering his mind. Spectral hands gripped at him, clutching at his face and body, as the cold mass began to move into him.

You can't! I won't . . .

". . . let you!" Buck shouted, his eyes bright with rage. He pressed the lever down as far as it would go, then threw his body against it. The wood cracked off, and Edgers flung it aside with a delightful grin. The machine was locked now, and would continue to spin until the gondola, hanging by only two bolts, was torn free. "I'll win! Look at the boy fly, watch him fall!"

Mirakle placed the pistol barrel against the back of his head. "Stop that damned machine or I'll put a bullet through your brain!"

Edgers turned his head; his eyes had rolled backward, just the whites exposed. He grinned like a death's-head, and whispered in a singsong, "Here we go 'round the mulberry bush, the mulberry bush, the mulberry—"

"STOP IT NOW, I SAID!"

"You won't shoot me, old man! You won't *dare* shoot me!"

Mirakle swallowed, and stepped back a pace. He saw that the gondola was about to break free. Snapped cables popped through the air. Mirakle said, "Damn you to Hell!" and swung the barrel against Edger's face. The man's nose splintered, blood streaming from the nostrils. The demonic face with its fish-belly eyes began to laugh. Mirakle struck again, opening a jagged cut over one eye. Edgers howled with laughter and spat blood out of his mouth. "Here we go 'round the mulberry bush, the mul—"

Suddenly there was a sharp cracking noise, and sparks flew. The woman had picked up the length of wood, and was hammering madly at the generator, tearing the cables loose.

The thing that was inside Buck Edgers shouted, "NO! GET AWAY FROM THAT!" He started forward, pushing Dr. Mirakle aside, but then the last of the cables tore free with a blast of sparks, the wooden lever rippling with flames in the woman's hands. The rest of the live bulbs that said OCTOPUS blew out, and the lights that decorated the machine flickered and went dark. Mirakle put his foot to the brake pad and pressed down hard. Gears shrieked as the machine began to slow.

"NO!" Edgers whirled around, his face as yellow as old parchment. He took a staggering step toward Mirakle, as the

269

gondolas slowly settled toward the ground and the machine's rotations weakened. Edgers whined, "It's not fair! Not fair!" His voice began to deepen like a record played at too slow a speed, as the Octopus continued to slow down. "Nootttt fairrrrr. Noooottttt fairrrrrrrr . . ." And then he fell to his face in the sawdust, drawing up like a fetus, and began sobbing.

The Octopus stopped. At once Mirakle was dragging Billy out. The boy was cold to the touch, was shaking and moaning. He put his hands under Billy's shoulders and pulled him away as the dead cables whipped and writhed all around. Something cracked in the guts of the machine; bolts sheared off, the huge central cylinder of the machine swayed, swayed as the four gondolas came free and fell to the ground. Then the entire machine was coming apart, collapsing in a haze of spark-smoke and sawdust. Its steel arms thudded down, as if the cement that had held the Octopus together had suddenly dissolved. Dust welled up, rolling across the midway in a yellow wave.

"No fear," Billy was saying, "please let me take it oh God I don't want to die let me out no fear no pain . . ."

Mirakle bent over him. "It's all right. It's over now . . . my God!" The boy contorted in some imagined pain, trembling, freezing cold. He moaned and whimpered, his head thrashing back and forth. Mirakle looked up, and saw the woman kneeling down beside her sobbing husband.

She clung to him, rocking him like a baby. "It's done," she said, tears streaming down her face. "Oh dear Lord, we're rid of that monster. We're finally rid of it!"

Mirakle saw that there was very little left of the Octopus that wasn't fit for a junkyard. He shivered, because now he had an idea of what kind of power Billy had; he didn't understand it, but it made his blood run cold.

Suddenly Billy gasped for breath and opened his eyes, as if emerging from a nightmare. His eyes were bloodshot, ruby-red. "Are they gone?" he whispered. "Did I do it?"

Mirakle said, "I . . . think so." He was aware of figures emerging through the dust. Mirakle gripped Billy's hand; it was as cold as what he'd always imagined death to be.

For both him and Billy Creekmore, the fair was over.

41

They reached Mobile at twilight the following day, traveling in the equipment truck. Because Billy was in no shape to drive, the Volkswagen van had been left in Birmingham. Mirakle would hire someone to bring it down.

The boy's sick, Mirakle had repeatedly thought during the long drive. Billy had been racked alternately with chills and fever; he'd slept for most of the trip, but the shudderings and moanings he'd made spoke of nightmares beyond Mirakle's experience. It had been Dr. Mirakle's intention to put Billy on a bus and send him back to Hawthorne, but Billy had said no, that he'd promised to come to Mobile and he'd be all right if he could just rest.

Billy's pallor had faded to a grayish brown, his face covered with sweat as he huddled on the seat under a green army blanket. Emotions sizzled within him, and terror had a grip on his bones.

They were driving along the flat expanse of Mobile Bay, where small waves topped with dirty green foam rolled in to a bare brown shore. Mirakle glanced over and saw that Billy was awake. "Are you feeling better?"

"Yeah. Better."

"You should've eaten when we stopped. You need to keep up your strength."

He shook his head. "I probably couldn't keep food down."

"I don't expect you to help me now. Not after what happened. You're just too sick and weak."

"I'll be okay." Billy shivered and drew the coarse blanket closer around him, though the Gulf air was thick and sultry. He stared out the window at the rolling waves, amazed at the vista of so much water; the sun was setting behind gray clouds, casting a pearly sheen over the bay.

"I should put you on a bus and send you home," Dr. Mirakle

said. "You know, I . . . don't understand what happened last night and maybe I don't *want* to, but . . . it seems to me you're a very special young man. And possibly you have a very special responsibility, too."

"What do you mean?"

"I mean . . . taking this power, or gift, or ability—whatever you choose to call it—and helping those parapsychologists I was telling you about. If you can communicate with the dead—'lay the dead to rest,' I suppose you might call it—then you should be working with scientists, not traveling with a two-bit carnival or spending your life in a town the size of a postage stamp. Billy, you have much to offer; perhaps the answer to a great many mysteries . . . or perhaps the beginning of new ones. Does it . . . affect you like this, every time?"

"It's only happened like this once before. That was bad too, but this is . . . agony. It's like having a long scream bottled up inside you, but you can't find your voice to let it out. I feel like I'm burning up, but I'm cold too. There's too much going on in my head, and I . . . I can't think straight." He sighed, more of a breathy moan, and let his head fall back against the seat, his eyes closed. He had to open them again, quickly, because strange blurred visions—the last things those people had seen before they died in the gondola: spinning sky and blinking lights, fingers curled in the mesh of the canopy, the world turning at frightening speed in a blaze of colors—whirled in his brain.

Dr. Mirakle drove the truck over a long bridge, and then turned off the road into an area of older clapboard houses; most of them were two-storied structures that spoke of the harsh hand of time and salt-air abrasion. Mirakle stopped the truck before a large house with a front porch and boarded-over windows. The white paint was peeling in long strips, showing the bleached gray wood underneath. They sat in the truck for a moment more, as the gray light darkened. "You don't have to do this," Mirakle said.

"I know. The way I feel, I don't even know if I *can*."

"Was what you did worth the pain?"

Billy considered the question, then nodded. "Yes. It was."

"And you'd do the same thing again?"

"I don't know. I try to . . . think I'm strong enough, but I'm afraid. And I know that when I'm afraid, I get weaker." He turned his weary gaze onto Mirakle. "I don't want to be like I am. I never asked for it. Oh God, if I just could forget about revenants and the

272

black aura and Death for a *little* while! . . . . I want to be like everybody else."

"Everybody else is afraid, too," the man said quietly. "But don't *you* understand that you of all people shouldn't be afraid, because you can see past Death to another kind of life? *You* know that going into the ground isn't the end of it; and if you can help other people see that, then . . . your life can make a difference in the whole scheme of things! My God, what an opportunity you have! If I were in my right mind, I'd try to talk you into touring the country with me, and giving some sort of demonstration of the spirit world! We'd wind up as either millionaires or skid-row bums!"

Billy smiled grimly.

"But," Mirakle continued, "your future lies far beyond the carnival circuit, Billy. Think about that parapsychology institute I told you about in Chicago. Will you?"

"Okay," Billy said. "I will."

"Good. Well. Are you ready? We'll leave the equipment in the truck for now." They got out, Billy following Dr. Mirakle up a weeded-over sidewalk. It was all he could do to climb the porch steps.

The interior was filmed with dust and sparsely furnished, though the rooms were large and once might have been quite beautiful. In the front room crates and boxes were stacked everywhere; a rug had been rolled up and stood in a corner with the cobwebs, there was a battered old pale green sofa with sagging springs and a coffee table littered with newspapers and magazines. On either side of an ash-filled fireplace were shelves packed with books. A calendar frozen on April 1968 hung from a nail.

"Forgive the place," Mirakle said. He left the door open so air could circulate. "I had to board up the windows after the glass was broken out one summer. It wouldn't be worth putting new glass in. Thank God the electricity still works."

"Do you have a telephone?" Billy wanted to call the hospital in Birmingham again, to check on Santha Tully. Early this afternoon, when he'd called for the second time, a nurse had told him that Santha was still on the critical list and that the antivenom flown up from Florida had been administered soon after Santha had been brought in.

"No, I'm afraid not. I don't have any callers. Please, sit down." He scooped newspapers out of the sofa and dumped them

273

on the floor. "I know you're concerned about your friend, but I'm sure they're doing everything they can for her. We'll find a phone booth later, if you like."

Billy nodded, wandering over to the bookshelves. He'd seen a pale gray aura around her, not a black one—did that mean there was a chance she might survive?

Mirakle said, "Why don't you sit down and rest. I'll look in the kitchen, perhaps I can find something to eat. All right?" Billy nodded, and the man went back through a corridor to the rear of the house. "Chicken noodle okay with you?" he called out in another moment. "It's canned, so I presume it's safe to eat."

"That's fine, thanks." Billy stepped into another large room, his shoes stirring up clouds of dust. The room held a cluttered desk and an upright piano with yellow keys. He punched his finger at a few of them, hearing off-key notes ring like a stabbed cat. Then he went through another door into the hallway, and there was the staircase that Dr. Mirakle had told him about. A single bulb studded the ceiling at the top of the stairs, casting a murky gray glow.

Billy touched the banister. He could hear Mirakle wrestling with pots and pans in the kitchen, at the hallway's end. He climbed the steps slowly, his hand clenching the banister, and when he reached the top he sat down. Water was running in the kitchen. Billy said softly, "Kenneth?" He waited for a few minutes, trying to concentrate through a wall of leftover terrors. "Kenneth?" he whispered.

There was a figure at the bottom of the stairs. It stood motionlessly for a moment, then placed a foot on the first step.

Billy sighed and shook his head. "I don't think there's anyone here. There might not have ever been."

"I know," Mirakle replied softly. "I . . . had once hoped that Kenneth *was* here, but . . . that's a selfish hope, isn't it? If some part of him remained, that would mean he was troubled, wouldn't it?"

Billy nodded.

"I don't know what Ellen saw, if indeed she saw anything at all, but we both had to shoulder a lot of pain. I think . . . seeing Kenneth's ghost was a way for Ellen to deal with his death, but instead of laying him to rest she tried to resurrect him. He was a very good boy. You would've liked him. Is there . . . is there *nothing* of him left?"

"Oh yes." Billy rose to his feet. "You bring him back to life when you remember him. Remembering doesn't have to be sad; it's a good thing, because you can keep your son with you all the time, in your heart and your memory. I think he's resting easy now, and he's gone on to whatever's waiting, but he's still alive inside *you*."

Dr. Mirakle smiled wistfully. "Yes. And I guess that's good enough, isn't it? Kenneth always remains a young man in my memories; he's always handsome in his uniform, and he's always the best son any man could ask for." He lowered his head and Billy heard him sigh deeply. Then he said, "I'd better check the soup. I've been known to burn it," and returned to the kitchen.

Billy stood at the top of the stairs for a while longer, his hand on the railing. But there was nothing there. Nothing stirred the air around him, nothing tried to make desperate contact, nothing yearned to shrug off its earthly pains and pass on. The house was silent and at peace. Billy descended the stairs and returned to the piano room. He ran his hands over the heat-cracked wood of the piano, tracing fingers over the battered and worn keyboard. He sat down on the bench and hit a single note that reverberated sharply in the air. Then another note, down in the bass register, that moaned like a low wind on a winter's night. He hit three notes at the same time, and winced at their discordant wail. The next try, though, the sound was sweet and harmonious, like a cooling balm against the fever that churned within him. Looking at the keyboard, trying to figure it out, was a mystery in itself: why were some keys black and others white? How could anybody make music out of it? What did those pedals down there do?

And suddenly he brought both fists crashing down onto the keyboard. Notes shrieked and shrilled, and Billy could feel the vibration thrumming up his wrists, up his forearms, his shoulders, his neck, and right to the top of his skull. The sound was awful, but somehow the energy he'd expended had cracked the hot cauldron of emotions in him, a tiny crack allowing a trickle to escape. Billy hammered again, with his left fist. Then with his right. Then both fists were coming down like pistons, and the house was pounding with a rough, jarring noise that perhaps harmonized with the music of terror and confusion. The old piano seemed about to burst with explosive noise; under Billy's relentless pounding several pieces of ivory flew off like rotten teeth. But when he stopped and he listened to the last echoes dying away there did seem to be a music in them: an eerie harmony of ignorantly struck chords, fading away now, fading into the very walls of the house. And Billy felt as if that cauldron had split down the middle, all the terrors and pains streaming out and flooding through him into this instrument that stood before him. He felt lightened, cleansed, and exhilarated.

And he remembered his grandmother saying, a long time ago, that it would be up to him to find a way to release the emotions he absorbed through contact with the revenants. She had her pottery, just as his mother had her needlepoint, and now . . . what was closer to human emotion than music? But how to bring out real music from this assembly of wood and metal wires? How to caress it instead of beating it half to death? How to let it soothe away the pain instead of ripping it out?

"Well," Dr. Mirakle said from behind him, holding a tray with two bowls of soup, "I'm glad to see my house is still standing. I'm sure the police are on their way by now, but we'll ask them to join in the jamboree."

"Is this yours? Do you know how to play it?"

"Me? No, I couldn't play a kazoo. My wife is . . . was a piano teacher for a while. Can I venture to say that you're no Liberace?"

"Who?"

"Never mind. Then again, neither is Liberace a Billy Creekmore. Come on, we'll eat in the front room, it's too dark in here." He paused, because Billy wasn't rising from the bench. Instead, the boy was fingering the keyboard again, picking at various notes as if he'd stumbled upon Captain Kidd's treasure. "It's probably not too hard to learn," Mirakle said. "I never had the inclination, but there are a stack of old instruction books down in the basement. Are you interested?"

He struck a high note and listened to it sing. "Yes sir."

"I'll get them for you, then. They're probably so mildewed you can't read them, but . . ." Mirakle came over and set the tray down atop the piano. He saw the look of excitement in Billy's eyes, and noticed also that his coloring had improved. It had been a great relief, in a way, to hear that Kenneth was resting far from the confines of this house. "You've been a great help to me," Dr. Mirakle said. "I appreciate all the work you've done. I . . . don't know what's ahead for you, but I think I'll be hearing from you again. At the very least, I hope you'll write to let me know how you're doing."

"Yes sir, I will."

"I have an idea you're the kind of young man who means what he says. That's rare enough in itself, in this day and age. In the morning I'll take you to the bus station; I would offer you a sizeable increase in pay to join me on the carnival circuit next season, but . . . you've got better things to do, I think." He smiled. The thought streaked through him that somehow he was losing a second son, and he touched Billy's shoulder. "The soup's getting cold. Come on, let's eat."

Mirakle took the tray into the front room; Billy paused at the keyboard a moment longer, then joined him. Young man, Mirakle thought, I wish you much luck. That is the very least of what you'll need on your journey.

And it was possible—no, probable, Mirakle told himself—that sometime before winter's cold set in he might drive the truck back up to Hawthorne, back to that little shack off from the road, and deliver a piano that might yet learn to sing again.

NINE

Revelations

42

Billy had asked to see his father. The simple granite gravestone read JOHN BLAINE CREEKMORE, 1925–1969. It stood up the hill from Link Patterson's grave, and was sheltered by pine trees that would filter the sun and rain. The earth was still rough from the work of shovels, but soon the pine needles would fall and it would all be covered.

"He went to sleep," Ramona said, long gray strands of her hair blowing from around her scarf. There were deep lines under her eyes and on each side of her nose, yet she refused to bend to the will of the years; she carried herself strong and straight, her chin uplifted. "I read the Bible to him that night, and we ate a good dinner of vegetables. He talked a lot about you, as he had for the few days before that, and he said he was trying very hard to understand . . . what we're like. He said he knew you were going to be a great man, and he'd be proud of you. Then he said he was going to take a nap, and I washed the dishes. When I went in later to see about him, he . . . was as peaceful as a child. I pulled the covers over him, and then I went to get the doctor."

Billy touched the granite marker. A chill breeze was sweeping down into their faces from the hills, and already winter was knocking at the door though it was hardly the middle of October. He'd come walking up the road yesterday, lugging his suitcase from the Greyhound bus stop at Coy Granger's, and had seen his mother out in the field, gathering pecans in a bowl. His father wasn't sitting on the front porch. The Oldsmobile was gone—sold for scrap, he'd later learned, to pay for his father's casket. The house was the same, fixed up and painted with the money he'd sent home; but things had changed. He could see the passage of time in his mother's face, and from what she'd told him his father had died near the time Billy had dreamed of him and his dad walking along the road to Hawthorne. Billy said, "You had to know. The aura. Didn't you *see* it?"

"Yes, I did," Ramona replied quietly. "I knew, and so did he. Your father had made his peace with the world . . . and especially with himself. He raised you with a good, strong hand and he worked very hard for us. He didn't always agree with us or understand us, but that was never the point: at the end, he loved us just as much as he always had. He was ready."

"*Ready?*" Billy shook his head disbelievingly. "Do you mean he just . . . wanted to die? No, I don't believe that!"

She looked at him with a cool, level gaze. "He didn't fight it. He didn't want to. At the end he had the mind of a child, and as all children have faith, so did he."

"But . . . I . . . should've been here! You should've written me! I . . . didn't . . . get to say good-bye! . . ."

"What would that have changed?" She shook her head and put a hand on his arm. A tear streaked down his cheek, and he let it fall. "You're here now," she said. "And though *he* is not, you'll always be John Creekmore's son, and he'll be in your child's blood as well. So is he really gone?"

Billy felt the restless wind pulling at him, heard it whispering around the pungent pines. It was true that his father lived within him, he knew, but still . . . separation was so hard to take. It was so hard not to miss someone, not to cry for him and mourn him; easy to look at death from a distance, more difficult to stare into its face. He already felt a world away from the carnival with its riotous noises and flashing lights; here on this bluff, framed by hills covered with woodland and overshadowed by gray sky, he seemed to stand at the center of a great silence. He ran his hands over the rough gravestone and remembered how his father's unshaven jaw had felt against his cheek. The world was spinning too fast! he thought; there were too many changes in the wind, and the summer of his childhood seemed lost in the past. For one thing he could be happy: before leaving Mobile yesterday morning, he'd called the hospital in Birmingham and had been told that Santha Tully was going to be all right.

"Winter's on the way," Ramona said. "It's going to be a cold one, too, from the way these pines have grown thick."

"I know." He looked at his mother. "I don't want to be like I am, Mom. I never asked for this. I don't want to see ghosts and

282

the black aura, I want to be like everybody else. It's too hard this way; it's too . . . *strange*."

"Just as your father's in your blood," she replied, "so am I. No one ever said it would be easy. . . ."

"But no one ever gave me a choice, either."

"That's true. Because there can *be* no choice. Oh, you can live as a hermit and shut out the world, as I tried to do after you were born, but sooner or later there comes a knock at your door."

He thrust his hands into the pockets of his jacket, and hunched over as a cold wind blew around him. Ramona put her arm around him. Her crying was done, but it almost broke her heart to see so much pain in her son. Still, she knew that pain sculpts the soul, molds the will, and would leave him standing stronger when he'd finally straightened up.

After another moment he wiped his eyes on his sleeve and said, "I'm all right. I didn't mean to . . . act like a baby."

"Let's walk," she told him, and together they went down the hill among the tombstones, heading toward the road. It was over two miles back to the house, but they were in no hurry.

"What do I do now?" Billy asked.

"I don't know. We'll see." She was silent for a few minutes as they walked, and Billy knew that something important was on her mind. They came to a place where a stream spoke over flat stones, and Ramona suddenly motioned for him to stop. She said, "My legs aren't what they used to be, I'll tell you. When I was a girl I could run this distance without breathing hard, and now already I'm hiccuping like a frog." She sat down on a rock that had people's initials scraped on it. He lay on his stomach in the grass, watching the pattern of water as it swirled over the stones. "There are things you need to know now," Ramona said. "I couldn't have told you while your father was living, though he was well aware of them too. I'm going to tell you, and then you'll have to make up your own mind about what to do."

"What things?"

She looked up, watching a squadron of crows fly across her field of vision. Off in the distance there was the faint reflection of sunlight off an airplane, climbing toward the clouds. "The world's changing so fast," she said, almost to herself. "People fighting in the streets, killing and hating each other; children trying to escape through God knows what kind of drugs; a war going on and on and on without clarity or point . . . these things are making me afraid, because evil's walking without fear, and it changes its shape and voice to gain its own greedy end. It's reaching out, wanting more and more. You saw it once before, a long time ago, in the smokehouse."

"The shape changer," Billy said.

"That's right. It was testing you, probing at you. It tested you again, at the carnival, but you were stronger than it took you to be."

"Have *you* ever seen it?"

"Oh yes. Several times." She looked at him through narrowed eyes. "It always taunted me and tried to trick me, but I saw through its tricks. I wouldn't let it get into my mind; I wouldn't let it make me doubt myself, or my abilities. But now my work's almost done, Billy. Now the shape changer sees no threat in me; it wants *you,* and it'll do everything it can to destroy you."

"But I'll be all right, won't I? As long as I don't let it into my mind?"

She paused, listening to the sound of wind through the trees. "The shape changer never gives up, Billy," she said quietly. "Never. It's as old as time, and it knows the meaning of patience. It means to catch you unawares, in a weak moment. And I think it's most dangerous when it's feeding off the dead, like a beast gnawing on bones. It draws in a revenant's energy to make itself stronger. I wish I could tell you that I know the limits of the shape changer's powers, but I don't. Oh, there's so *much* you need to know, Billy!" She gazed at him for a moment. "But I can't teach you. Life will."

"Then I'll learn," he replied.

"You'll have to." Ramona sighed deeply. "This is what I have to tell you: you were not born into this world alone."

Billy frowned. "What?"

"You were one of two," she said, staring off at the trees. "You were born first, but behind you there was a second child. You were so close inside me that the doctor could only hear one heartbeat, and in those days the medical facilities weren't very good. So: there were two children, born in a pickup truck on the way to the hospital on a cold night in November. Both of you were born with cauls, a sure sign of spiritual powers. Yours covered your face. His . . . had torn loose, and he was gripping it in his hands. Even so young, something within your brother made him want to escape his Mystery Walk. You weren't identical twins, though; you had my coloring, while he looked more like his father."

Her eyes were dark pools as she gazed solemnly at Billy. "You see, your father and I were very poor. We could hardly feed ourselves, much less two more mouths. We were expecting one, and we had to choose. That was the most terrible decision of my life, son. There's . . . a man named Tillman, who buys and sells babies. He bought your brother from us, and he promised to find him a good home." Her hands clenched into fists, and strain showed on her lined face. "It was . . . the only thing we could do, and we both agonized over it so long. Your father was never the same after we went through with it. We had to choose, and we chose you. Do you understand?"

"I . . . think so." Billy recalled the woman at the tent revival, a long time ago, confessing the sin of selling her baby. God, how that moment must've pained his mother!

"For years I thought nothing would come of it," she said. "Your father and I often wondered what had happened to him, but you were our son and we wanted to give you our full love and attention. But then . . . I saw him, and I knew from the first minute who he was. I knew that he might have a special power too, but that it might be different from yours . . . and I saw in his eyes that he was being used without knowing it. I saw him that summer night at the Falconer Crusade. He looks just like your father, but enough like Jimmy Jed Falconer to pass as his son."

Billy sat frozen for a moment, shocked numb. "No," he whispered. "No, not *him*. . . ."

"You know it's true. I've seen the way you look at each other. You've felt the same thing, probably, as him—maybe a kind of curiosity or attraction. I think . . . both of you need the other, without knowing it. You understand the meaning of your Mystery Walk, but Wayne is afraid and floundering in the dark."

"*Why?*" he asked, rising to his feet. He was angry and confused and dazed, and he realized he had always felt a pull toward the young evangelist, but he'd fought against it. "If it was a secret for so long, why tell me now?"

"Because J. J. Falconer passed on this summer. He was all that stood between Wayne and the grinding gears of that Crusade machine he built. Wayne is a young businessman now, and his mind is sealed with Jimmy Jed Falconer's thumbprint. He'll follow his father's path, but he doesn't know what's waiting for him at the end of it. He was taught at an early age how to use the power of fear and hatred and call it religion. His spirit is weak,

285

Billy. The shape changer looks for weakness, and if it can use Wayne Falconer against you, it will—in a *minute*."

Billy bent and picked up a rock, flinging it into the stream. A bird wheeled for the sky from its cover of brush. "Why does he hate us?"

"He may feel the same pull we do. He may mistake it for our trying to lure him away from what he thinks is the righteous path. He doesn't understand us, and neither did his father."

"Do you think he could . . . ever *really* heal?" Billy asked her.

"I don't know. He's charismatic, there's no doubt. He can make a person believe they've been healed, even if maybe nothing's wrong with them. Falconer had a hand in teaching him that. But if Wayne *can* heal, he has to find that power deep inside himself, just like you do when you take on the revenants. He has to hurt, just like you do. The Crusade demands that he heal time after time, with no stopping. I think he pretends to heal so he won't have to feel that pain, if indeed he ever really felt it. Oh, he may be able to throw those people a spark or two—but if you throw off enough sparks, you don't have enough left to start a fire when you really need it."

"What's going to happen to him?"

"He may crack under the weight of the Crusade, or he might find the strength to stand on his own two feet. For him, that might be turning away from the greed that's all around him, and finding out he can learn more about his healing power and he doesn't have to sell it every day on a stage." She shook her head. "I don't think he'll leave the Crusade, though. It would be too much of a leap into the dark for him."

Billy's shoulders sagged. Ramona stood up, unsteadily. "We'd better be getting home before it gets dark," she said wearily.

"No, not yet. I need to . . . be alone for a while, to think. All right?"

She nodded. "Take all the time you need." She touched his cheek with a lingering hand, then started to walk away.

He asked, "Are you afraid of him?"

"Yes," she said. "There's something in him that wants to come home, but he doesn't know the way." She walked on, alongside the littered road, toward Hawthorne.

Billy watched her go, then crossed the stream to lose himself in the forest.

43

Beneath the same forbidding October sky, a group of men in business suits were slowly walking the length of the county's huge public swimming pool just outside Fayette. The pool was drained and in need of painting.

"I want it rebuilt," Wayne Falconer was saying to O'Brien, the architect from Birmingham, "in the shape of a Cross. I want the church there." He pointed to the concessions building. "I want it to be the biggest church this state has ever seen. And I want a fountain in the middle of the pool. One with colored lights. Can you do that?"

O'Brien chewed on a toothpick and nodded thoughtfully. "I think so. Have to be careful with wiring. Don't want to electrocute anybody. It would be some visual effect though, wouldn't it?" He grinned. "Not electrocution . . . I mean the colors."

Henry Bragg and George Hodges laughed. Bragg was still lean and boyish-looking, only a touch of gray in his stylishly cut sandy-brown hair; as a rule he wore blue blazers and gray slacks with razor-sharp creases. He'd moved his growing family to Fayette four years ago and had taken over the job of chief attorney for the Falconer Crusade, Inc.

George Hodges, by contrast, had not aged so gracefully. He was bald except for a fringe of brown hair, and his face had slowly collapsed into folds under the pull of gravity. He wore a rumpled brown suit, his breast pocket lined with pens.

"I want this to be the biggest baptismal pool in the world," Wayne said. The Crusade had recently purchased the pool for a million and a half. "People will come here from everywhere, wanting to be baptized. Of course, there'll be regular swimming here too—for Christian youth only—but the baptisms will be the big thing. It'll be . . . like a Christian swim club, but there won't be membership fees. There'll be donations to the Falconer Memorial. . . ." His voice trailed off. He was staring at the high-diving platform, the Tower. He remembered when he was almost ten, and he'd finally gotten the nerve to climb up there and try to jump. Poised on the edge, he felt his knees shaking—and then the older kids down in the pool had started yelling for him to jump, jump, Wayne, jump. It was just too high, and from way up there it looked like a sheet of blue glass that would cut him to pieces. Coming carefully down, he'd tripped and fallen and busted his lip and, crying, had run out to where the church bus was parked to get away from the laughter.

"I want that down," Wayne said quietly. "The Tower. I want it down, first thing."

"That's been here for over twenty-five years, Wayne," George Hodges said. "It's sort of a symbol for the whole—"

"*Down*," Wayne told him, and Hodges was silent.

At the far end of the pool, Wayne suddenly dismissed Bragg and O'Brien. As the two men walked away, Hodges waited uneasily for Wayne to speak. The young man stared at the pool, took a small bottle from his coat, and popped a pill into his mouth. His eyes were almost the same shade as the pool's faded paint. "I know I can trust you, George. You've always been there when I needed you." Hodges had done such a good job in his years as the Crusade's business manager that he could now afford a colonial-style house a few miles from the Falconer estate.

"That's right, Wayne," Hodges replied.

Wayne looked at him. "My daddy came again last night. He sat on the foot of my bed, and we had a long talk."

Hodges's face pulled tight. Oh God! he thought. Not again!

"He told me that the Creekmore witch and her boy want *me* now, George. They want to destroy me, like they destroyed my daddy."

"Wayne," Hodges said quietly, "please don't do this. That woman lives in Hawthorne. She's no threat to you. Why don't you just forget about her, and let's go on like—"

"I can *feel* her wanting me to come to her!" Wayne said. "I can feel her eyes on me, and I can hear her filthy voice, calling to me at night! And that boy's just as bad as she is! He puts himself in my head sometimes, and I can't get him out!"

Hodges nodded. Cammy was calling him at all hours of the night now, and driving him crazy with her complaints about

288

Wayne's fits of black temper. One night last week Wayne had left the house and gone to the airport, flying up in the company Beechcraft and doing loops and circles like a maniac. Wayne wasn't yet eighteen, yet already he was faced with decisions that would stagger a seasoned business executive. Maybe it was understandable, Hodges thought, that Wayne should pretend to be counseled by his father's ghost as a way of shouldering the burden.

"My daddy says the Creekmores should burn in Hell," Wayne was saying. "He says, 'Thou shalt not suffer a witch to live.'"

"Wayne, we sent some people over to Hawthorne to ask around about her, just as you wanted. She stays to herself and never goes out, her son went and joined the circus or something, and her husband died not too long ago. She's strange, but so what? She's nothing but a faker. If she could really see ghosts and all that junk, then why isn't she out doing seances or stuff like that for rich people? And your daddy is dead, Wayne. He doesn't come to you at night. He doesn't advise you about business deals. Please, Wayne. Let him *go*."

Wayne blinked and touched his forehead gingerly. "I'm tired," he said. "All these meetings make me so tired. I wish I could sleep at night. I need more sleeping pills. The ones you got me before aren't strong enough."

"They'd knock out a horse!" Hodges grasped Wayne's arm. "Now listen to me. You've got to stop taking so many pills! I swear to God I could cut my throat for getting you that damned Percodan! Now you take stuff to put you to sleep and stuff to get you up in the morning."

"Daddy says for me to," Wayne said, his face expressionless.

"No. No more pills." Hodges shook his head and started to walk away.

"George?" Wayne's voice was soft and silken. Hodges stopped in his tracks and clenched his fists at his sides. "George, you forget. If I can't sleep, I can't address all those civic groups I'm supposed to meet with. I can't do the radio and the television shows. I can't go over the magazine material. I can't plan for next year's revival circuit. Can I?"

Hodges turned, his face reddening. "You don't need any more damned pills, Wayne!"

"Get them. Or I'll find someone who *will*."

Oh, that would be just dandy! Hodges thought. If someone

outside the organization found out that Little Wayne Falconer was turning into a junkie, and having strange delusions as well, the press would tear the Crusade to pieces! "You need help. And not the kind you get from pills."

Wayne's eyes flashed. "I said get them for me, George! I want to be able to sleep without hearing that witch and her boy calling my name!"

Hodges knew he should say no. He knew he should tell Henry about the delusions. Wayne was coming apart at the seams. The entire Crusade was in danger. But his mouth opened and he said in a harsh rasp, "This is the last time, damn it! Do you hear me? If you ask me again, I walk. I swear it!"

Wayne smiled. "Fine. Now, I want this done too: I want an electric fence put up around the house by the time I get back from Nashville. And I want a new watchman hired. A younger man. I don't feel safe in the house anymore."

Hodges nodded grimly.

Wayne patted his back. "I know I can depend on you. Daddy says so." And then Wayne walked away to rejoin Bragg and O'Brien, new confidence in his stride.

George Hodges was in agony. The boy was killing himself with those pills! He'd promised J.J. he'd do his best to help Wayne with the business, but very often now he thought that they were all in danger of being consumed by a monstrous machine that had very little to do with personal worship. The Christian rock bands, the prayer cloths and the Clowns for Jesus at those revival meetings were just too much!

"George?" Bragg called to him. "What're you dreamin' about?"

I could walk away from it, he told himself. Yes. Anytime I want to. But he switched a ragged smile on his face and said, "Nothing. You boys want to get some lunch? I know a place that serves fine barbecue."

TEN

Krepsin

44

The lights were lowered in the projection room. Mr. Niles picked up the telephone receiver set into the arm of his chair. "Mr. Krepsin's ready," he said.

A thin beam of light hit the screen. Luxuriating on a deserted beach was a beautiful brunette in a black skintight bikini. Palms stirred indolently behind her as she combed her long, shining black hair. She glanced at the camera, smiling as she spread suntan oil across her stomach. She undid her bikini top and tossed it aside.

Lovely young woman, Niles thought. Coarse-looking, but certainly attractive. The projector was silent, but the room itself seemed to breathe: there was a muted noise of machinery at work, and the hiss of manufactured air. Niles was a lean man of indeterminate age; though his close-cropped hair was gray, his face was as smooth as a teenager's. His deep-set eyes were such a pale tint of gray that they seemed almost white. He wore a lightweight dark blue suit, comfortable for the Palm Springs climate. Around him the room throbbed quietly; the air was being cleaned over and over again, drawn in and out of a maze of hidden ducts in the thick, windowless walls. There was a faint aroma of pine-scented disinfectant.

On the screen, the young woman smiled nervously and took off her bikini bottom. There was a small dark birthmark on her lower stomach. A man, heavyset and wearing only khaki slacks, stepped into the frame, his back to the camera. Without ceremony he took off his pants.

"This time the photography's very clear, isn't it?" A large, indistinct shape sitting in a special double-width seat a few chairs away from Niles stirred slightly. Heavy-duty springs moaned. A football-shaped bald head was tilted to one side, and tiny black eyes glinted in thick folds of flesh. "Yes, very good. You see all the details in this film." His breathing was like the harsh noise of a bellows, and he had to gulp for air between words. "I didn't like the last two films. Too grainy."

"Yes sir." Niles watched the sexual acrobatics on the screen with only mild interest.

"Popcorn?" the obese man asked, offering a box to Niles.

"No thank you."

He grunted and dug one hand into the buttered popcorn, then filled his mouth. A second man, thin and with the tattoo of a skull on his shoulder, had joined in the action.

Niles never knew what films they'd be viewing. Sometimes they were simply parodies of Roadrunner or Tom and Jerry cartoons, other times old and rare silent films. Usually, though, they were like these—sent up from Mexico by Señor Alvarado. They didn't bother Niles, but he thought they were a waste of good film.

The girl lay on her stomach in the sand, her eyes closed. She was obviously exhausted. The first man came back onscreen. He was carrying a ball peen hammer.

The bulk of bone and fat had leaned forward. He tilted the popcorn to his mouth and then put the empty box on the floor. He wore a royal-blue caftan that seemed the size of a tent. "She doesn't know, does she?" Augustus Krepsin said quietly. "She thinks she's going to take her money and go buy herself a new dress, doesn't she?"

"Yes sir."

The hammer rose and fell. Krepsin's hands clenched in his lap. The second man, now wearing a black mask, stepped back onto the screen. He pulled the cord on a chain saw he was holding, and his skinny arms vibrated.

Krepsin's breathing was audible; his eyes darted from one figure to the next as the true action and intent of the film unfolded. When the screen finally went black, Niles could hear Krepsin's soft moan of pleasure. The projectionist was smart enough not to turn the lights up yet. Then Krepsin said, in a childlike voice, "I want light now, Mr. Niles."

He relayed the order through the telephone. As the lights slowly came up, Krepsin was leaning back in his chair with an oxygen mask pressed to his face, his eyes closed.

Niles watched him for a few silent moments. He'd worked for

Augustus Krepsin for almost six years, first as a liaison between Krepsin and the overlords of organized crime in Mexico, now as a companion and righthand man here in Palm Springs. Still, he knew very little about the man. Krepsin was the king of his own hard-won empire. He had originally come to this country from Greece before World War II, and somewhere along the line Krepsin had become entranced with two subjects: death and disease. He talked about each with a clinical interest, and he watched the snuff films as if he could see the center of the universe in a dismembered corpse. Krepsin had built his Palm Springs fortress with strict cleanliness in mind, and rarely ventured out of it.

The telephone in the arm of Niles's chair buzzed softly. He picked up the receiver. "Yes?"

The operator said, "Mr. Niles? Jack Braddock's on the line again from Nashville."

"Mr. Krepsin doesn't want to be disturbed. Tell Braddock—"

"Just a moment," Krepsin said. "Jack Braddock?" He breathed deeply and then took off his oxygen mask. "I'll talk to him." Krepsin's organization had taken over Braddock's Essex Records Company in Nashville several years ago. Essex was continuing to lose money, and there had been a record-pirating scandal two years ago that Essex had barely squeaked out of. Krepsin was beginning to regret letting such a poor manager as Braddock stay on, though Essex had been purchased primarily as an avenue to launder dirty money.

Niles told the operator to put the call through, and Krepsin answered the phone. "What do you want?"

There was a startled intake of air almost fifteen hundred miles away. "Uh . . . sorry to bother you, Mr. Krepsin. But somethin's come up that I need to—"

"Why don't you take speech lessons, Braddock? Everyone down there sounds as if they haven't had a good bowel movement in years. I can send you some herbal pills that will clean you out."

Braddock laughed nervously.

"I hope your line is green," Krepsin said. A bugged line would be "red." After the pirating mess, Krepsin suspected the FBI tapped Essex's phones.

"I'm calling from a pay phone."

"All right. What is it?"

"Well, I got a visit from a lawyer named Henry Bragg

yesterday afternoon. He represents the Falconer Crusade, and they want to start making records. They're looking for an independent company to buy, and—"

"Falconer Crusade? What is that?"

"Religious bunch. They're into publishing, radio, lots of stuff. I don't suppose you get the 'Wayne Falconer Power Hour' on TV out there, do you?"

"I don't watch television. It sends out radiation, and radiation causes bone cancer."

"Oh. Yes sir. Well, this Mr. Bragg is backed by a lot of money. They want to make an offer for Essex."

Krepsin was silent for a moment. Then he said, "Essex is not for sale. Not to anyone. We worked too hard getting through our troubles with the authorities to give it up just yet. Is this the important reason you've called me?"

On the other end, Braddock coughed. Krepsin knew the man was addicted to cigars, and he thought: Throat cancer. Malignant cells, running rampant through Braddock's body. Disease breeding disease. "There is one other thing I thought you might be interested in," Braddock said. "Wayne Falconer. He runs the whole Crusade from a little town in Alabama. He's only about twenty years old, but he's a hell of a preacher. And he's a healer, too."

Krepsin paused. His face folded in thought. "Healer?"

"Yes sir. Cures people of all kinds of diseases. I saw him straighten a man's back on television last week, saw him heal a pair of crippled legs, too. Bragg says they want to make self-healing records for people to listen to. He says the boy wants to tour Essex, if it's on the market.

"A healer?" Krepsin asked. "Or is he simply a good actor?"

"An awful lot of people believe in him. And like I say, that Crusade's just rollin' in the money."

"Oh?" Krepsin grunted softly, his small black eyes glittered. "A healer? Mr. Braddock, I may have been hasty. I want you to contact those people. Let them tour Essex. Talk it up. I'm going to send Mr. Niles to represent the corporation. You and he will work together, and I want to know *everything* about this Falconer boy. Understand?"

"Yes sir."

"Good. And one more thing: I don't want Mr. Niles returning to Palm Springs with his suits fouled by cigar smoke. Now get in contact with those people at once." He hung up and turned toward Niles. "You're leaving for Nashville today. I want something called the Falconer Crusade thoroughly investigated. I want to know everything about a boy named Wayne Falconer."

"Yes sir," Niles said. "May I ask why?"

"Because he's either a cunning charlatan—or he's a genuine healer. And if that's so, I want him here. With me. It's time for my massage now."

Niles helped Krepsin rise from the chair. The man's huge bulk—over four hundred pounds on a large-boned frame five-feet six-inches tall—left its shape impressed in the leather. As they neared the door, an electric eye triggered the mechanism that both unlocked the door and started a new flow of charcoal-filtered air in the outside corridor.

After they'd gone, a Mexican maid in a long white smock entered the empty projection room and began vacuuming the carpet. She wore spotless white gloves and white cotton slippers, and across the lower half of her face was a surgical mask.

45

There was a letter from Dr. Mirakle in the mailbox today. Billy read it as he walked up the hill to the house in the clear golden light of late October.

Dr. Mirakle said he had his eye on a cottage in Florida. He asked if Billy had read the last batch of books on spiritualism he'd sent, and how his piano lessons were coming along. He asked also if Billy had given any more thought to visiting that institute in Chicago.

Billy slipped the letter back into its envelope. Since that strange autumn three years ago, Dr. Mirakle had written frequently, and often sent him books on a variety of subjects. He'd visited once, about three months after Billy had come home to find his father buried, and had brought the old piano, tuned and repaired, that now stood in the front room.

Six months after that, a letter had come from Chicago, marked special delivery and addressed to Mr. Billy Creekmore. Its return address was The Hillburn Institute, 1212 Cresta Street in Chicago. In the crisp white envelope was a typewritten letter from a Dr. Mary Nivens Hillburn, who said she was writing because of some correspondence the institute had had with a Mr. Reginald Merkle of Mobile. Merkle, the doctor wrote, had impressed upon her and the institute's staff that Billy might be of interest to them. Were there other witnesses who could verify Billy's "allegedly paranormal abilities?" He'd let his mother read it, then had put it away in a drawer. He'd heard nothing further from them.

The house was painted white, its windows glinting with sunlight. A wisp of smoke curled from the chimney. Around the house the trees had burst into color, and in the breeze there was a faint chill of approaching winter. An old brown pickup truck, ugly and unreliable beast bought over a year before with money from a sizable corn crop, rested in front of the house. The Creekmore place was now one of the last houses that didn't have electricity, but Billy didn't mind. The dark wasn't threatening, and late at night the kerosene lanterns cast a soft golden glow that was much better, to his way of thinking, than harsh white electricity.

He was less than a month shy of turning twenty-one. In the last three years he'd grown another two inches and had gained twenty pounds, all of it firm muscle that came from hard outdoor work. His face had sharpened and matured, and thick dark curls tumbled over his forehead; his dark eyes glittered with an earthy intelligence, and could shine with good humor as well. He walked up onto the front porch and went into the house, past the upright piano in the front room; he'd been taking lessons for two years from a retired music teacher at two dollars a week, and had progressed from pounding hell out of the instrument to letting it draw the moods from him as his fingers rippled across the keyboard. Many evenings his mother sat with her needlepoint, listening to the slightly warped chords but appreciating the feeling behind the music.

"Any mail?" she called from the kitchen.

"One letter, from Dr. Mirakle. He says hello." He sat down in a chair before the hearth and read Dr. Mirakle's letter again. When he looked up, Ramona was standing over him, drying her hands on a dishrag. "Did he mention that place again?" she asked quietly.

He nodded and handed her the letter, but she didn't read it.

"Chicago. I wonder what kind of city that is?"

"Probably dirty," Billy replied. "They've got gangsters up there, too."

Ramona smiled. "I believe that was a long time ago you're thinking of. But I suppose there are gangsters just about everywhere." She rubbed her callused fingers; they were stiff and unresponsive. The lines in her face were many and deep. "I wonder what that institute would be like. Don't you wonder sometimes?"

"No."

"We could afford a bus ticket, if you wanted to go. From what I recall, they were eager to hear from you."

Billy grunted, watching the small tongues of flame in the hearth. "They'd probably treat me like a freak."

"Are you afraid to go?"

"I don't want to go."

"That's not what I asked." She stood over him for a moment more, then she went to a window and looked out. The breeze stirred reddening leaves. "You'll be twenty-one in November," she said. "I know . . . things happened to you when you joined that Ghost Show. I know that you came back home bearing scars. That's all right. Only tough folks carry scars. Maybe I shouldn't stick my nose in where it doesn't belong, but . . . I think you should go to that institute, I think you should see what they have to say."

"I don't belong up there. . . ."

"No." Ramona turned toward him. "You don't belong *here*. Not anymore. The land and the house are in fine shape, and now you're just filling up your days trying to stay busy. What kind of life is ahead for you in Hawthorne? Answer me that."

"A good life. I'll work hard, and I'll read, and I'll keep up my music . . ."

". . . and there goes another year, doesn't it? Boy, have you forgotten everything your grandmother and I tried to teach you about the Mystery Walk? That you have to be strong enough to follow it wherever it leads, and that it's up to you break new ground? I've taught you all I know about the ceremony, about the use of the jimsonweed and hemp, and how to recognize the mushrooms that must be dried and crushed into powder to be smoked. I've taught you what I know of the shape changer, and how it can use other souls against yours; I've taught you to be proud of your heritage, and I *thought* you'd learned how to see by now."

"See? See what?"

"Your future," she said. "The Choctaw doesn't choose who's to make the Walk; only the Giver of Breath can make that choice. Oh, many before you lost their faith or their courage, or had their minds swept away by evil forces. But when evil can break the chain of the Mystery Walk, then all that's gone before is disrupted, all the learning and experience and pain might just as well be for nothing. I know that it left a scar on you that summer and autumn; but you can't let it win. The ceremony is important, but most important is what's out there." Ramona motioned toward the window. "The world."

"It's not *my* world," Billy said.

"It can be. Are you afraid? Are you giving up?"

Billy was silent. His experience on the Octopus was still burned into him, and there had been many nightmares of it to keep the wounds raw. Sometimes a cobra reared up in the darkness, and sometimes he had a gun that wouldn't fire as the thing coiled closer toward him. Soon after arriving home that autumn, he'd taken the bus to Birmingham and had gone to the hospital to see Santha Tully. The nurse there had told him that Santha Tully had left the day before, and had gone back to New Orleans; he'd stood in the empty room she'd occupied, knowing he'd never see her again. He silently wished her good luck.

"I'm not afraid," he said. "I just don't want to be . . . treated like a freak."

"And you think they will, at this institute in Chicago? You understand who and what you are; what else matters? But if the institute works with people like us, then they can teach you . . . and learn from you as well. I think that's where you belong."

"No."

Ramona sighed and shook her head. "Then I've failed, haven't I? You're not strong enough. Your work isn't done—it hasn't really started—and already you think you deserve rest. You don't, not yet."

"Damn it!" Billy said sharply, and abruptly stood up. "Leave

300

me alone!" He snatched Dr. Mirakle's letter from her and angrily ripped it up, throwing the pieces into the fireplace. "You don't understand what it was like on the Octopus! You didn't hear it! You didn't feel it! *Leave me alone!*" He started past her, toward the front door.

"Billy," Ramona said softly. When he turned, she held out the piece of coal in the palm of her hand. "I found this on the top of your dresser this morning. Why did you take it out of the drawer?"

He couldn't remember if he had or not. Ramona tossed it to him. There seemed to be heat in it, and it gleamed like a black, mysterious amulet.

"Your home is here," she said. "It'll always be here. I can take care of myself, the house, and the land; I've done it before. But you've got to go into the world and use what you know, and learn more about yourself. If you don't you've wasted everything that's gone before you."

"I need to think," he told her. "I'm not sure what to do."

"You're sure. You're just taking your time coming around to it."

Billy clenched the piece of coal in his fist. He said, "I want to sleep out tonight, out in the forest. I want to be by myself for as long as it takes."

Ramona nodded. "I'll get some food ready for you, if you . . ."

"No. If I can't catch my food or dig it up, I won't eat. I'll just need a sleeping bag."

She left the room to get what he wanted. Billy put the coal into his pocket and stepped out onto the porch; he wanted to lie on Southern earth tonight, to watch the stars move and let his mind drift. It was true that he'd felt the Hillburn Institute in Chicago pulling at him. He was curious as to what kind of place it might be and what might lie ahead of him in a city that size. Chicago seemed as far away as China, and just as foreign. It was true also that he was afraid.

He faced the horizon, ablaze with the colors of late autumn. The musky scent of dead summer wafted in the air like old wine. He didn't want to leave all the work to his mother, but he knew she was right; the Mystery Walk was beckoning him onward, and he had to follow.

Ready or not, he thought, recalling the games of hide-and-seek he used to play with Will Booker, whose symbol of faith in Billy's potential rested in his jeans pocket, *here I come.* . . .

Hodges saw a few seats behind Wayne, close to the high whine of the twin jet engines at the rear of the fuselage. Niles, Hodges

46

The blue-and-silver Canadair Challenger had been in the air for less than an hour, and was now streaking over central Arkansas at twenty-three thousand feet. The late October sky was a dazzling blue, while beneath the jet a rainstorm whipped Little Rock.

Wayne Falconer, sitting in the plane's "quiet pocket"—the area just behind the flight deck—was stunned and delighted. This silent eagle made his Beechcraft seem like a clumsy moth. Leaving the ground at Fayette's airport had been one of the most sublime feelings he'd experienced. Up here the sky was so clear and blue, and he felt as if he'd left his worldly responsibilities very far behind. He wanted a jet like this, he *had* to have one and that was all there was to it.

The business jet's interior was done in dark blue and black, with a lot of shining chrome and waxed wood surface. The motorized swivel-and-reclining seats were upholstered in black Angus steerhide, and there was a long comfortable-looking sofa next to a fruit and vegetable juice bar. Danish teakwood tables were bolted to the carpeted floor in case of rough weather; on one of the tables were neatly arranged copies of the Falconer Crusade's magazine. Everything in the long, spacious cabin sparkled with cleanliness, as if someone had polished every fixture and surface with a strong disinfectant cleanser. The oval Plexiglass windows, George Hodges had noticed, didn't have one streak or fingerprint on them. He'd decided that this Mr. Augustus Krepsin must be a very fastidious man, though something about the display of Crusade magazines bothered him; it was maybe too clever, and was trying to win Wayne over too fast. Krepsin's assistant, Mr. Niles, bothered Hodges too. The man was polite, intelligent, and well informed about the Crusade's business policies, but there was something about his eyes that disturbed Hodges; they looked soulless, and they lingered on Wayne far too often.

Hodges sat a few seats behind Wayne, closer to the high whine of the twin jet engines at the rear of the fuselage. Niles, Hodges had noticed, was quick to take the seat across the aisle from Wayne. Henry Bragg was paging through a *Field and Stream* a couple of seats behind him. Bragg was pleased to be away from his wife and three stairstep children; he sipped ginger ale through a straw and watched the clouds move far below, a dreamy and contented smile on his face.

Beth, their attractive young flight attendant, came down the aisle with a cup of orange juice for Wayne. The cabin was more than eight feet wide and six feet high, so she had no trouble making her way to the young man. "Here you go," she said with a sunny smile. "Can I get you a magazine?"

"No, thank you. What's our airspeed now, ma'am?"

"*Beth.* Oh, I think we're flying around five hundred miles per hour by now. I understand you're a pilot."

"Yes, ma'am. Beth, I mean. I've got a Beechcraft Bonanza, but it's nothing like this. I've always loved planes and flying. I . . . always feel so free when I'm up in the air."

"Have you ever been to California?"

He shook his head, sipped at the orange juice, and put the cup down on his service tray.

"Sun and fun!" Beth said. "That's the life-style there."

Wayne smiled, though uneasily. For some reason, Beth reminded him of a half-forgotten nightmare: a dark-haired girl slipping on a slick platform, the awful noise of her head hitting the sharp edge, the sound of painfully exhaled breath and water closing over her like a black shroud. In the past three years his face and body had thickened, and the texture of his red hair had become dense and wiry. His eyes were deep-set and glowed as blue as the sky beyond the jet's windows. But they were haunted eyes, holding back secrets, and there were purplish hollows beneath them. He was very pale except for a few rashes of late-blooming acne across his cheeks. "Beth?" he said. "Do you go to church?"

Mr. Niles had given her a thorough briefing on Wayne Falconer before they'd left Palm Springs. "Yes I do," she said, still smiling. "As a matter of fact, my father was a minister just like yours was."

Across the aisle, Niles's eyes were closed. He smiled very slightly. Beth was a resourceful person who could think on her feet.

"An evangelist," Wayne corrected her. "My daddy was the greatest evangelist that ever lived."

"I've never seen you on television, but I'll get it's a good show."

"I hope it does good for people. That's what I'm trying to do." He smiled wanly at her, and was pleased when she returned his smile with sunny wattage. She left him to his thoughts, and he drank his orange juice. He had just finished a three-day-long healing revival in Atlanta. It was estimated that he'd touched five thousand in the Healing Line, and he'd preached three scorching hellfire-and-brimstone messages. He was bone-tired, and in two weeks the Falconer Crusade was booked into the Houston Astrodome for yet another revival. If only he could find a record of a jet engine in flight, Wayne thought, maybe he could sleep better; the sound would soothe him, and he could pretend he was very far away from the Crusade, flying across a night sky sparkled with stars.

His daddy had told him buying this record company was a smart move to make. He should listen to this Mr. Krepsin, and trust in what the man said, his daddy had told him. It would all work out for the best.

"Wayne?" Mr. Niles was standing over him, smiling. "Come on up to the flight deck with me, will you?"

Niles led the way forward and pulled aside a green curtain. Wayne was breathless at the sight of the cockpit, with its magnificent control panel, its gleaming toggles and gauges and dials. The pilot, a husky man with a broad sunburned face, grinned below his smoke-tinted sunglasses and said, "Hi there, Wayne. Take the co-pilot's seat."

Wayne slipped into glove-soft leather. The engine noise was barely audible way up here; there was only the quiet hissing of air around the Challenger's nose. The windshield gave an unobstructed, wide-angle view of brilliant blue sky dotted with high, fleecy cirrus clouds. Wayne noticed the movements of the control yoke before him, and knew the jet was flying under autopilot command. The instruments he faced—altimeter, airspeed indicator, horizontal situation indicator, attitude director, and a few more he didn't recognize—were set in a Basic T formation, similar to the Beechcraft panel but of course much more complex. Between the pilot and co-pilot was a console holding the engine thrust throttles, the weather radar controls, the speed brake lever, and other toggle switches Wayne knew nothing about. He stared at the panel with rapt fascination.

"Everything's right there," the pilot said, "if you know where to look for it. My name's Jim Coombs. Glad to have you aboard." He shook Wayne's hand with a hard, firm grip. "Mr. Niles tells me you're a flyer. That right?"

"Yes sir."

"Okay." Coombs reached up to an overhead console and switched off the autopilot. The control yokes stopped their slight correction of ailerons and elevators; the Challenger slowly began to nose upward. "Take her and see how she feels."

Wayne's palms were sweating as he gripped the guidance wheel and placed his feet against the hard rubber pedals that controlled the rudder.

"Scan your instruments," Coombs said. "Airspeed's still on autopi, so don't worry about that. Bring your nose down a few degrees. Let's level her off."

Wayne pushed the yoke forward, and the Challenger instantly responded, the silver nose dropping back to level flight. He had overestimated, though, and had to pull slightly up from a six-degree downward pitch. The plane began to roll just a bit to the right, and Coombs let Wayne work with the yoke and pedals until he'd gotten the jet trimmed again. The controls needed a feather-light but decisive touch, and compared to this he'd had to fight the Beechcraft across the sky. He grinned and said in a shaky voice, "How was that?"

Coombs laughed. "Fine. Of course, we're about a hundred miles off our flight path, but you're okay for a prop-jockey. Want to co-pilot me into Palm Springs?"

Wayne beamed.

Less than two hours later the Challenger was landing at Palm Springs Municipal Airport. In the co-pilot's seat, Wayne watched intently as Coombs went through the landing procedure.

Two Lincoln Continental limousines awaited the Challenger. Wayne was escorted by Niles into the first one, and Hodges and Bragg climbed into the other. They started off together, but after ten minutes the Mexican driver of the second limo announced he felt "something funny" and pulled off the expressway. He got out to check, and reported that the left rear tire was going flat. Hodges watched the car carrying Niles and Wayne driving away out of sight, and he said tersely, "Fix it!"

The driver had already pocketed a small icepick-like blade as he unlocked the trunk to get the spare.

Wayne was driven along the edge of a huge golf course. A purple line of mountains undulated in the distance. Everywhere there was green grass being saturated with water from sprinklers, and palm trees sprouted bright green fans. The limo turned into a residential area where only roofs and palm trees showed high above stone walls. A uniformed watchman waved to them and opened a pair of wide wrought-iron gates. The limo continued up a long driveway bordered with bursts of red and yellow flowers, carefully trimmed hedges, and a few large species of cactus. Gardeners were at work, pruning and spraying. Wayne caught a glimpse of a red-slate roof capped with turrets, and then there was a huge structure before him that was perhaps the strangest house he'd ever seen.

It was made of pale brownish stone, and was a riot of angles and protuberances, blocks upon blocks, high towers, mansard roofs and gables and Gothic arches and masonry carved in geometric shapes and statuelike figures. It looked like the work of ten insane architects who'd all decided to build a structure on the same property and connect them with domes, parapets, and sheltered walkways. Work was still going on, Wayne saw; more stones were being placed one atop the other by workmen on a scaffolding. There was no telling how many floors the place had, because one level seemed to stop in midair and another shot up at a different place. But, oddly, only the ground floor had windows.

The limo pulled under a porte cochere, and Mr. Niles escorted Wayne up a few stone stairs to a massive front door. It was opened for them by a white-jacketed Mexican butler with a brown, seamed face. "Mr. Krepsin's expecting you, Mr. Falconer," the butler said. "You can go up immediately."

"This way," Niles said. He led Wayne across a gleaming hardwood floor to an elevator; when the elevator doors opened, a rush of cool dry air came out. As they ascended, Wayne could hear the quiet throbbing of machinery somewhere in the house, growing louder as they rose.

"Shouldn't we wait for the others?" he asked.

"They'll be along." The doors slid open.

They stood in a featureless white room. A pair of glass doors stood just opposite them, and beyond that was a dimly lit corridor. Machinery hissed and hummed from the walls, and Wayne could smell the distinct odor of disinfectant.

"If you'll be so kind," Niles said, "as to take off your shoes? You can put these on." He stepped across to a chrome-topped desk and picked up one of the several pairs of cotton slippers. A box of surgical gloves sat atop the desk as well. "Also, if you'll take any change you might have in your pockets and put it in one of these plastic bags? Currency, too."

Wayne took his shoes off and slipped into the cotton ones. "What's this all about?"

Niles did the same, taking the change out of his pockets and putting it in a bag. "Shoes and money carry bacteria. Will you put on a pair of gloves, please? Ready? Follow me, then." He pressed a button on the wall next to the doors and they slid quickly open, like a pair of automatic supermarket doors. When Wayne followed him through, into an atmosphere that was cooler and noticeably drier than the rest of the house, the doors thunked shut like the closing of a bear trap. The corridor, illuminated by recessed lighting, was totally bare and uncarpeted; the thick stone walls radiated a chill, and somewhere in them an air-purifying system hissed faintly.

Wayne was taken almost to the end of the corridor, to a pair of large oak doors. Niles pressed a buzzer set into the wall, and a few seconds later Wayne heard the sound of the doors unlocking electronically. "Go right in," Niles said. Wayne, his stomach twisted into nervous knots and his head aching again, stepped through the doors.

There were skeletons in the room. Skeletons of fish, birds, animals, and one of a human being, laced together with wire and standing in a corner beneath a track light's beam. Smaller skeletons, of lizards and rodents, were placed under glass display cases. The doors closed automatically behind Wayne, and a lock softly clicked.

"Welcome."

Wayne looked toward the sound of that voice. In front of glass-enclosed bookcases there was a teakwood desk topped with a green blotter. A man sat in a wide, high-backed black leather chair, a track light shining down upon a white, bald head. The room was wood-paneled, and on the floor was a dark blue Persian rug with gold figures. Wayne stepped closer to him, and saw that the head sat atop a mountain of caftan-dressed flesh; his face was made up of folds within folds, and small black eyes glittered. He smiled, showing tiny white teeth. "I'm so glad you could come," the man said. "May I call you Wayne?"

Wayne glanced uneasily around at the mounted skeletons. There was an entire skeleton of a horse, caught in midstride.

Augustus Krepsin waited until Wayne had almost reached the desk, then extended a hand. Only after Wayne had shaken it did he realize Krepsin was also wearing flesh-colored surgical gloves. "Please, sit down." Krepsin motioned toward a chair. "Can I offer you something? Fruit juice? Vitamins to perk you up?"

"No, thanks." Wayne took the seat. "I had a sandwich on the plane."

"Ah, the Challenger! How'd you like it?"

"It was . . . fine. Mr. Coombs is a good pilot. I . . . don't know what happened to the others. They were in the car right behind us. . . ."

"They'll be along soon, I'm sure. I see you're intrigued by my collection, aren't you?"

"Well, I . . . I've never seen anything quite like it."

Krepsin grinned. "Bones. The very framework of the body. Strong, durable, highly resistant to disease, yet . . . sadly, often the first thing to weaken in a body. I'm fascinated by the mysteries of the human body, Wayne: its flaws and faults as well as its strengths." He motioned toward the human skeleton. "What a grand design, isn't it? Yet . . . doomed to return to dust. Unless, of course, you treat it and varnish it and wire it together so it won't dissolve for a few hundred years."

Wayne nodded, his hands clasped together in his lap.

"You're a handsome young man," Krepsin said. "Twenty-one next month, am I right? Lived in Fayette all your life? You know, there's something about a Southern accent that's so . . . earthy. I've become quite a fan of yours, Wayne. I had Mr. Niles obtain video tapes of some of your shows when he visited Nashville, and I've watched them all several times. You have quite a commanding presence for such a young man."

"Thank you."

Krepsin's large head dipped in respect. "You've come a long

way, I understand. Now you have an influential television show, a radio station that's turning at least a hundred thousand in profits every year, and a publishing company that will break even sometime in 1974. You speak before approximately a half-million people per year, and your foundation is planning to build a four-year Christian university before 1980."

"You've been checking up on me," Wayne said.

"Just as your Mr. Hodges has been asking questions about the Ten High Corporation. It's only good business." He shrugged his massive shoulders. "But I'm sure you know what needs to be known: I own Ten High. Ten High owns a controlling interest in Essex Records. You want to purchase Essex Records for a million and a half, and so you're sitting in my study."

Wayne nodded. He said calmly, "Is Essex worth that much?"

Krepsin responded with a soft laugh. "Ha! My boy, *you* made the offer. Is it worth that much to you?"

"Essex lost two hundred thousand last year alone," Wayne replied. "It's lost clout in the country-western music business, and Essex can't afford to lure in hit-producing artists. I want to pump new money into it, and start it all over as a gospel label."

"So I understand," Krepsin said quietly. "You're a very bright young man, Wayne. You have . . . a great insight, as well as a very special ability. Tell me something, now, and your answer will never go beyond this room: I've watched your television shows over and over, I've seen the expressions of these people who pass through—what do you call it?—the Healing Line." His head bent forward, jowls and chin hanging. "Are you *really* a healer? Or is it . . . trickery?"

Wayne paused. He wanted to get up and leave this room, get away from this strange house and this man with the black eyes. But he remembered that his daddy had told him to trust Mr. Krepsin, and he knew his daddy wouldn't tell him wrong. He said, "I am a healer."

"And you can heal any kind of sickness? Any kind of . . . *disease?*"

From a distance of time and space Wayne seemed to hear a whispered but accusing voice: *Do you know what you're doing, son?* He shut his mind on years of accumulated doubts that had haunted him in the night. "Yes."

Krepsin sighed and nodded. "Yes. You can, can't you? I've seen it in your face; I've seen it in the faces of those you've healed. You conquer the fading flesh and brittle bone. You conquer the filth of disease, and drive out the germs of Death. You . . . hold the power of Life itself, don't you?''

"Not me. God works through me."

"God?" Krepsin blinked, and then his smile was back. "Of course. You could have Essex Records, as my gift to your Crusade. But I'd prefer to stay on in a consulting position. I like the idea of going gospel. There's a lot of money to be made in it.''

Wayne frowned. For an instant he thought he'd seen something dark and huge standing behind Krepsin—something bestial. But then it was gone.

"I know you're tired from the flight," Krepsin said. "You and I are going to get along very well, Wayne, and we'll have plenty of time to talk later. Mr. Niles is waiting for you at the end of the corridor. He'll take you downstairs for some lunch. I'd suggest a nice afternoon steambath and then a siesta. We'll talk again this evening, all right?''

Wayne stood up, an uncertain smile on his face, and Krepsin watched as he left the room in his sanitary cotton slippers. Krepsin peeled off his rubber gloves and dropped them into a waste receptacle beneath the desk. "Plenty of time," he said softly.

47

"Here ya go," the cab driver said, and pulled to the curb. "You sure this is where you want to get out?"

"Yes sir," Billy told him; at least he thought it was the place. A crooked sign said Cresta Street, and the address on the small brownstone building was 1212. Across the street was a sad-looking little park with a rusty swing set and a few drooping trees; set around the park were other brownstone buildings and old two-story houses, many of which looked empty. The larger buildings of downtown Chicago loomed in the distance, filtered by gray haze.

Billy paid the driver—Four-fifty for a car ride? he thought incredulously—and stood with his battered suitcase in front of a wrought-iron gate and fence that separated 1212 from the other buildings. He didn't know exactly what he'd expected, but this place was far from it. The gate shrieked as he pushed through, and he walked up the steps to the front door. He pressed the doorbell and heard the faint sound of chimes.

There was a small round peephole in the door, and for a moment Billy felt himself being watched. Then locks began to click open—one, two, and three. He had a sudden urge to run all the way back to the Greyhound bus station, but he stood his ground.

The door opened, and standing within was a young girl, perhaps sixteen or seventeen. She had long black hair that hung almost to her waist, and Billy thought she looked Spanish. Her eyes were pretty and alert, but there was a trace of sadness in them. She glanced at his suitcase. "Yes?"

"Uh . . . this must not be the right place. I thought this was the Hillburn Institute?"

She nodded.

"Well . . . my name's Billy Creekmore, and I'm here to see Dr. Hillburn." He fumbled in his back pocket for the envelope and held it out to her.

The girl said, "Come in," and then locked the door behind him.

The interior was a pleasant surprise. Dark wood paneling gleamed with oil and polish. There were clean rugs on the shining hardwood floor, and an abundance of green plants added a welcoming touch. The tempting aroma of good food wafted in the air. A staircase ascended to the second level, and just to the left of the front door, in a high-ceilinged parlor, a half-dozen people both young and old watched television, read, or played checkers. Billy's entrance caused a pause in their activities.

"I'm Anita," the girl told him. "You can leave your suitcase down here, if you like. Mr. Pearlman," she said, addressing one of the men in the parlor. "It's your turn to help in the kitchen today."

"Oh. Right." The man put aside his *Reader's Digest* and went off through a hallway.

"Follow me, please." Anita took Billy upstairs, through a

series of well-kept dormitory-like rooms. There were doors marked *Testing Lab 1, Audio-Visual, Conference Room, Research Lab 1*. The building was very quiet, with pale green linoleum floors and tiled ceilings. Billy glimpsed other people moving about, several of them wearing white lab smocks. He saw a young woman about his own age coming out of a testing lab, and he felt a quick spark of attraction as their gazes met and held. She was wearing jeans and a blue sweater, and Billy saw that her eyes were different colors: one was a pale blue, the other a strange deep green. The young woman looked away first.

Then Anita led him around a corner to a door maked *Dr. Hillburn, Ph.D., Director*. Billy could hear a muffled voice within. The girl knocked on the door and waited. A moment passed. Then: "Come in." It was a woman's voice, carrying an inflection of annoyance.

Dr. Hillburn was sitting behind a battered desk in a small office cluttered with books and papers. The beige-colored walls were adorned with framed certificates and brass plaques, and a window looked out over the Cresta Street park. A green-shaded lamp burned atop the desk, which also held a blotter, a metal can with a collection of pencils and pens, and several pictures of people Billy assumed were her children and husband. Her hand was clamped around a telephone receiver.

"No," she said firmly. "I can't accept that. The grant was promised us last year and I'll fight for it right up to the capital, if I have to. I don't *care* that all the funds are tied up, and I don't believe that anyway! Am I just supposed to shut down everything and go out on the street? God knows we're almost on the street as it is!" She glanced up and motioned for Anita to close the door. "Tell the esteemed senator that I was promised matching funds, dollar-for-dollar. No! We've cut our staff down to a skeleton crew already! Ed, just tell him that I won't stand for any more foolishness. I'll expect to hear from you by tomorrow afternoon. Good-bye." She put the receiver down and shook her head. "It's getting so deep over in Springfield you need waders to get through! Do you know what's ahead of us on the budget agenda, Anita? Consideration of a grant for a study of litter patterns on the north beach! I ask them for fifteen thousand dollars to keep our programs going for another year, and—" Her clear gray eyes narrowed. "Who are *you*, young man?"

"My name is Billy Creekmore. You people sent me this letter." He stepped forward and handed her the envelope.

"Alabama?" Dr. Hillburn said, with obvious surprise. "You're a long way from home, aren't you?" She was a fragile-looking woman in a white lab coat, her eyes deeply set, alert, and very intelligent. Billy thought she was probably in her late forties or early fifties. Her dark brown hair, threaded with silver, was cut short and brushed back from her high, furrowed forehead. Though she had a gentle appearance, the sound of her voice on that telephone told Billy she could spit nails if angered.

Dr. Hillburn looked up at him for a moment after reading the letter. "Yes, we sent you this some time ago. I think I recall the correspondence we got from this friend of yours, Mr. Merkle. Anita, will you do me a favor please? Ask Max to go through the M files and bring me the letters from Mr. Reginald Merkle." She spelled out the name, and then Anita left. "Now. What can I do for you, Mr. Creekmore?"

"I've . . . come because your letter asked me to."

"I expected a reply by mail, not a visit. And besides, that was some time ago. Are you here in Chicago with your family?"

"No, ma'am. I'm here alone."

"Oh? Where are you staying, then?"

Billy paused, smelling disaster. "Staying? Well, I . . . left my suitcase downstairs. I thought I'd be staying *here*."

Dr. Hillburn was silent; she nodded and spread her hands before her on the blotter. "Young man," she said, "this is not a hotel. This is a workshop and research center. The people you probably saw downstairs, and those in the labs, have been invited here after long consultation. I know nothing about you, and to be perfectly honest I can't even recall why we wrote you in the first place. We write hundreds of people who don't answer us. Our labs certainly aren't as well equipped as those at Duke University and Berkeley, but we have to make do on the budget we get from the University of Chicago and small grants. That budget is hardly enough to continue our tests and research on the individuals we *select;* and certainly there's no room here for someone off the street."

"I'm not here off the street!" Billy protested. "I've come a long way!"

"Of course you have, young man. But I'm saying that . . ." She looked up as a middle-aged man in horn-rimmed glasses and a lab jacket brought in a file folder containing several letters.

"Thank you, Max," she told the man, and when he'd gone she put on a pair of reading spectacles and took several letters from the folder. Billy recognized Dr. Mirakle's spiky handwriting.

"What kind of place is this?" Billy asked her. "What goes on here?"

"Pardon? Don't you know?" She glanced up at him. "The Hillburn Institute is a death survival studies clinic, sponsored in part by the University of Chicago. But as I say, we . . ." She trailed off, engrossed in something she was reading.

"What do those people downstairs do?"

"They . . . they've had experiences with manifestations or spirit controls." Dr. Hillburn looked up from the letters and pushed the spectacles up onto her forehead. "Young man," she said quietly, "you evidently left your friend Mr. Merkle deeply impressed. The experiences he's written down here are . . . quite interesting." She paused, returned the letters to the folder, and said, "Sit down, won't you?"

Billy took a chair in front of her desk. Dr. Hillburn swiveled her chair around to stare through the window at the park, her face illuminated by pale gray light. She took her glasses off and put them in her jacket pocket. "Young man," she said. "What do you think of our city?"

"Well, it's noisy," he replied. "And everybody's running around so fast." He didn't tell her that he'd seen the black aura twice—once clinging to an elderly black man on the bus and once surrounding a young girl a few blocks away from the bus station.

"Have you ever been this far away from home before?"

"No, ma'am."

"Then you must feel the ability you have—whatever it is—is very special. Special enough to leave Alabama and come such a distance? Why did you come here, Mr. Creekmore? And I'm not talking about the letter. Why did you come?" She turned toward him again, her gaze sharp and watchful.

"Because . . . my friend, Dr. Mirakle, said I should. And because my mother wanted me to. And . . . maybe because I didn't know where else to go. I want to understand more of why I'm like I am. I want to know why I see things that other people don't. Like the black auras, and the entities that look like mist and carry so much pain, and the shape changer. My mother could see the same things, and her mother before her . . . and it's likely that my son or daughter will be able to, as well. I want to know as much as I can about myself. If I'm in the wrong place for that, tell me now and I'll leave."

Dr. Hillburn had been observing and listening to him carefully. She was a trained psychiatrist as well as a parapsychologist with two books on death survival studies to her credit, and she'd been looking for telltale signs of emotional instability: inappropriate gestures or grins, facial tics, a general irritability or melancholia. She sensed in Billy Creekmore only a genuine desire for self-knowledge. "Did you think, young man, that you could just present yourself on our doorsteps and we would offer easy answers for all your questions? No. I'm afraid that's not to be the case. As I say, this is a workshop; a damned difficult workshop, I might add. If there's any learning to be done, we learn together. But everything has to be verified through extensive tests and experiments. We don't deal in trickery here, and I've seen enough psychic fakers in my lifetime. Some of them have sat where you're sitting now. But sooner or later their tricks fail them.

"I don't know anything about you, except from what I've read in these letters. As far as I know, you don't understand a thing about death survival research. You may have a psi ability—though I'm not saying I'm convinced you do—but as far as I'm concerned it may only be a figment of your imagination. You may be a publicity hound. You may even want to disrupt the work we're trying to do here, though God knows we have enough disruptions. Do you believe you *can* communicate with the dead, young man?"

"Yes. I can."

"That remains to be seen. I'm a born skeptic, Mr. Creekmore. If you say a traffic light's red, I'll say it's purple, just for the sake of an interesting argument." Her eyes had taken on a shine. "If I decide you're worth being here, you might rue the day you ever walked through the gate. I'll throw every test I can think of at you. I'll take your brain apart and put it back together again, more or less as it was. In two or three days you'll hate me, but I'm used to that. You'll have a room the size of a closet to sleep in, and you'll be expected to work around here like everyone else. It's no free ride. Sound like fun?"

"No."

"Now you've got the idea!" She smiled cautiously. "Tomorrow morning at eight o'clock you'll be right here, telling me your life story. I want to hear about your mother, and the black auras and the

315

entities and . . . what was it? A shape changer? Indeed. Dinner's in fifteen minutes, and I hope you like Polish sausage. Why don't you go get your suitcase?"

Billy rose from his chair, feeling confused about the whole thing. It was still at the back of his mind that he should leave this place, and he had enough money for a return ticket home. But he'd come this far, and he could stick out whatever was in store for him for at least three days. He didn't know whether to thank the woman or curse her, so he left without saying a word.

Dr. Hillburn looked at her wristwatch. She was already late getting home, and her husband would be waiting. But she took the time to read Merkle's letters again. A pulse of excitement had quickened within her. *Is this boy from Alabama the one?* she asked herself—the same question she asked when any new subject came to the institute.

Is Billy Creekmore the one who'll show proof positive of life after death? She had no way of knowing, but she could hope. After a moment of reflection, she stood up and took her coat from a rack beside the desk.

48

Wayne Falconer's scream cracked the silence that had fallen over the Krepsin estate.

It was just after two o'clock in the morning. When George Hodges reached Wayne's bedroom—one of the few rooms in the strange house that had windows—he found Niles already there, pressing a cold washcloth to Wayne's forehead. Wayne was curled up on the bed, his eyes feverish with fear. Niles was still dressed as if he'd just stepped out of a business meeting.

"A nightmare," Niles explained. "I was walking along the hall when I heard him. He was just about to tell me what it was, weren't you, Wayne?"

Henry Bragg came in, rubbing his eyes. "Who screamed? Wayne? What the hell's . . ."

"Wayne's fine," Niles said. "Tell me your dream, and then I'll get you something for that headache."

Hodges didn't like the sound of that. Had Wayne gone through his Percodan and codeine capsules yet again?

In a halting voice, Wayne told them what he'd dreamed. It was a hellish vision of Jimmy Jed, a skeleton in a yellow suit gone green and rotten with grave dirt, screaming that the witch of Hawthorne had sent him to Hell where he would burn forever if Wayne didn't free him. When he was finished, a terrible groan came from Wayne's throat, and tears glittered in his eyes. "She knows where I am!" he whispered. "She's out there in the night, and she won't let my daddy come to me anymore!"

Bragg had gone a sick gray. Wayne's obsession with his dead father was getting worse, Hodges realized. For the past four nights, Wayne had been awakened with nightmares of Jimmy Jed and the Creekmores. Last night, he'd even sworn that he'd seen the Creekmore boy's pallid face grinning through the window at him. Wayne was coming to pieces, Hodges thought, right out here on the sunny Coast.

"I can't sleep," Wayne gripped Niles's smooth white hand. "Please . . . my daddy's rotted, and I . . . can't make him all right again. . . ."

Niles said softly, "Everything's going to be fine. There's no need for you to be afraid, not while you're in Mr. Krepsin's house. This is the safest place in the world for you. Why don't you put on your robe and slippers? I'll take you to see Mr. Krepsin. He can give you something to calm your nerves—"

"Now just one damned minute!" Hodges said angrily. "I don't like all these late-night 'visits' Wayne's been having with Krepsin! What's going on? We came here for a business conference and so far all we've done is hang around this crazy house! Wayne's got other obligations. And I don't want him taking any more pills!"

"Herbal medicine." Niles held Wayne's robe for him. "Mr. Krepsin believes in the healing power of Nature. And I'm sure Wayne will agree that you're free to go anytime you please."

"What? And leave him here with *you*? Wayne, listen to me! We've got to get back to Fayette! This whole thing is as shady as the dark side of the moon!"

Wayne tied his robe and stared at him. "My daddy said I was to trust Mr. Krepsin. I want to stay here for a while longer. If you want to go, you can."

Hodges saw that the young man's eyes looked blurry and dazed. His grip on reality was lost, Hodges knew . . . and just *what* kind of pills was Wayne being given? "I'm begging you," he said. "Let's go home."

"Jim Coombs is going to take me up in the Challenger tomorrow," Wayne said. "He says I can learn to fly it, no trouble at all."

"But what about the Crusade?"

Wayne shook his head. "I'm tired, George. I hurt inside. I *am* the Crusade, and where I go, that's where the Crusade goes too. Isn't that right?" He looked at Henry Bragg.

The lawyer's smile was tight and strained. "Sure. Anything you say, Wayne. I'm behind you one hundred percent."

"You gentlemen needn't stay up," Niles said, taking Wayne's elbow and leading him toward the door. "I'll see that Wayne gets his sleep. . . ."

And suddenly George Hodges's face reddened with anger, and he was crossing the room to clamp his hand on the other man's shoulder. "Listen to me, you—"

Niles twisted around in a blur, and for an instant there were two fingers pressing rigidly against the hollow of Hodges's throat. Hodges felt a brief, dizzying pain that almost buckled his knees, and then Niles's hand dropped to his side. A low fire burned in the man's pale gray eyes. Hodges coughed and backed away, his heart pounding.

"I'm sorry," Niles said. "But you must never touch me like that again."

"You . . . you tried to kill me!" Hodges croaked. "I've got witnesses! By God, I'll sue you for everything you've got! I'm getting out of here right now!" He stalked past them and out of the room, his hand pressed to his throat.

Niles glanced back at Bragg. "Will you see to your friend, Mr. Bragg? There's no way for him to leave tonight, because the house is kept sealed by hydraulic pressure on the doors and the first-floor windows. I reacted hastily, and I regret it."

"Oh . . . sure. Well, no harm done. I mean, George is . . . kind of upset."

"Exactly. I'm sure you can calm him down. We'll talk in the morning."

"Right," Bragg said, and managed a weak smile.

Augustus Krepsin was waiting in his huge bedroom one floor up and on the other side of the house. When Wayne had first seen it, he'd been reminded of a hospital room: the walls were an off-white, with a blue sky and clouds painted on the ceiling. There was a sunken living area with a sofa, a coffee table, and a few leather chairs. Persian rugs in soft colors covered the floor, and track lights delivered a delicate golden illumination. The large bed, complete with a console that controlled lighting, humidity, and temperature and contained several small closed-circuit television screens, was surrounded with a plastic curtain like an oxygen tent. An oxygen tank and mask were mounted next to the bed.

The chess game was still on the long teak coffee table, where it had been left the night before. Krepsin, dressed in a long white robe, sat over it, his small eyes pondering options as Niles brought Wayne in; he was wearing his cotton booties and surgical gloves. His bulk was stuffed into a specially supported Angus steerhide chair.

"Another nightmare?" he asked Wayne after Niles had left. "Yes sir."

"Come sit down. Let's pick up the game where we left off." Wayne took his chair. Krepsin had been teaching him the fundamentals of the game; Wayne was losing badly, but the knights and pawns and rooks and whatever-they-weres took his mind off the bad dreams.

"They can be so real, can't they?" Krepsin said. "I think nightmares are more . . . true than ordinary dreams, don't you?" He motioned toward the two pills—one pink, one white—and the cup of herbal tea that was set in front of Wayne.

Without hesitation Wayne swallowed the pills and drank the tea. They helped relax him, helped smooth out the throbbing pain in his head, and when he did sleep, toward morning, he knew he would have wonderful dreams of when he was a child playing with Toby. In those drug-induced dreams everything was bright and happy, and Evil couldn't find its way into his head.

"A little man fears inconsequential things, but only a man of great character feels true horror. I enjoy our talks, Wayne. Don't you?"

He nodded. Already he was feeling better, his brain clearing, all the musty cobwebs of fear drifting away in what felt like a fresh summer wind. In a little while he would be laughing like a small boy, the worries and responsibilities faded away like bad dreams.

"You can always judge a man," Krepsin said, "by what makes him afraid. And fear can be a tool, as well; a great lever that can move the world in any direction. You of all people must know the force of fear."

"Me?" Wayne looked up from the board. "Why?"

"Because in this world there are two great terrors: disease and death. Do you know how many millions of bacteria inhabit the human body? How many organisms that can suddenly become malignant with disease and leech themselves into human tissues? *You* know how frail flesh can be, Wayne."

"Yes sir," Wayne said.

"It's your move."

Wayne studied the inlaid ivory board. He moved a bishop, but had no particular plan in mind other than to capture one of Krepsin's black towers.

Krepsin said, "You've already forgotten what I've told you. You must keep looking over your shoulder." He reached across the board, his face like a bloated white moon, and moved the second of his black rooks to capture Wayne's last bishop.

"Why do you live like this?" Wayne asked. "Why don't you ever go outside?"

"I do go outside, occasionally. When I have a trip scheduled. Forty-nine seconds between the door and the limousine. Forty-six seconds between the limo and the jet. But don't you understand what floats in the air? Every plague that ever ravaged across cities and countries, destroying hundreds and thousands, began with a tiny microorganism. A parasite, riding a sneeze or clinging to a flea on a rat's hide." He leaned toward Wayne, his eyes widening. "Yellow fever. Typhus. Cholera. Malaria. The Black Plague. Syphilis. Blood flukes and worms can infect your body, drain your strength, and leave you a hollow shell. The bubonic plague bacillus can lie dormant and impotent for generations, and then suddenly it can lay half the world to waste." Small droplets of sweat glimmered on Krepsin's skull. "*Disease*," he whispered. "It's all around us. It's outside these walls right now, Wayne, pressed to the stones and trying to get in."

"But . . . people are immune to all those things now," Wayne said.

"There is no such thing as immunity!" Krepsin almost shouted.

His lips worked for a few seconds before he could speak. "Levels of resistance rise and fall; diseases shift, parasites mutate and breed. Bubonic plague killed six million people in Bombay in 1898; in 1900 it broke out in San Francisco, and the same bacillus that causes plague has been found in the ground squirrel. Don't you see? It's *waiting*. There are cases of leprosy in the United States every year. Smallpox almost spread into the United States in 1948. The diseases are still out there! And there are new bacteria, new parasites evolving all the time!"

"If disease could be controlled, so could death," Krepsin said. "What power a man would have! Not to have to . . . fear. That would make a man godlike, wouldn't it?"

"I don't know. I've . . . never thought about it that way." Wayne stared at Krepsin's bulbous face. The man's eyes were fathomless pools of ebony, the pores in his flesh as big as saucers. His face seemed to fill the entire room. Warmth coursed through Wayne, and a feeling of safety and belonging. He knew he *was* safe in this house, and though he might have nightmares sent by the witch-woman, she couldn't get in at him. Nothing could get in at him: not pressures or responsibilities or fears, not any of the diseases of real life.

Krepsin rose from his chair with a grunt like a hippo rising from dark water. He lumbered across the room, drew aside the plastic curtain ringing his bed, and pressed a couple of buttons on the command console. Instantly images appeared on the three video-tape screens. Wayne squinted and grinned. They were video tapes of his television show, and there he was on the three screens, touching people in the Healing Line.

"I've watched these again and again," the huge man said. "I hope I'm watching the truth. If I am, then you're the one person in the world who can do for me what I want." He turned to face Wayne. "My business is very complex and demanding. I own companies from L.A. to New York, plus many in foreign countries. I make a phone call, and stocks do what I want them to. People do anything to get close to me. But I'm fifty-five years old, and I'm susceptible to diseases, and I . . . feel things slipping away. I don't want that to happen, Wayne. I'll move Heaven—or Hell—to keep things as they *are*." His black eyes burned. "I want to keep death away from me," he said.

Wayne stared at his hands, clenched in his lap. Krepsin's voice echoed inside his head as if he were sitting within a huge cathedral. He remembered his daddy telling him to listen hard to what Mr. Krepsin had to say, because Mr. Krepsin was a wise and just man.

Krepsin put his hand on Wayne's shoulder. "I've told you my fear," he said. "Now I want to hear yours."

Reluctantly at first, Wayne began. Then he told more and more, wanting to get it all out of him and knowing Mr. Krepsin would understand. He told him about Ramona Creekmore and the boy, about how she'd cursed both of them and wished his father dead, about his Daddy's death and rebirth, how she was making him have nightmares and how he couldn't get her face, or the demon boy's, out of his mind.

"She . . . makes my head hurt," Wayne said. "And that boy . . . sometimes I see his eyes, staring at me like . . . like he thinks he's *better* than me. . . ."

Krepsin nodded. "Do you trust me to do the right thing for you, Wayne?"

"Yes sir I do."

"And I've made you feel comfortable and safe here? And I've helped you sleep and forget?"

"Yes sir. I . . . feel like you believe me. You listen to me, and you understand. The others . . . I can tell they're laughing at me, like up on the Tower. . . ."

"The Tower?" Krepsin asked. Wayne rubbed at his forehead but didn't reply. "I want to show you how sincere I am, son. I want you to trust me. I can end your fear. It would be a simple thing. But . . . if I do this thing for you, I'll soon ask you to do something for me in return, to show me how sincere *you* are. Do you understand?"

The pills were working. The room had begun to slowly spin, colors merging together in a long rainbow scrawl. "Yes sir," Wayne whispered. "They should burn in the fires of Hell forever. *Forever*."

"I can send them to Hell, for you." He loomed over Wayne, squeezing his shoulder. "I'll ask Mr. Niles to take care of it. He's a religious man."

"Mr. Niles is my friend," Wayne said. "He comes in at night and talks to me, and he brings me a glass of orange juice just before I go to bed. . . ." Wayne blinked and tried to focus on Krepsin's face. "I . . . want some of the witch's hair. I want to hold it in my hand, so I'll know. . . ."

The huge face smiled. "A simple thing," it whispered.

outside. He remembered his daddy telling him to listen hard to
what Mr. Kneppin had to say, because Mr. Kneppin was a wise and
just man.
Wayne put his hand on Wayne's shoulder. "I've told you my
plan," he said. "Now I want to hear yours."

49

Indian summer had lingered late. The blue evening light was
darkening as yellow leaves stirred on the trees and a few of the
dead ones chattered on the roof of the Creekmore house.

Ramona turned up the lamp wicks in the front room as darkness
gathered outside. A small fire burned in the hearth, her chair
pulled up so she could warm herself near it—she followed the
Choctaw custom of building little fires and stepping close, instead
of the white man's belief in making a bonfire and standing back.
On a table next to her a lamp burned, a metal reflector behind it,
so she could read for the third time the letter she'd gotten from her
son today. It was written on lined notebook paper, but the envelope
had Hillburn Institute and the address in nice black print up in the
left-hand corner. Billy had been in Chicago for almost two weeks,
and this was the second letter he'd sent. He described what he'd
seen of the city and told her all about the Hillburn Institute. He'd
had long talks with Dr. Mary Hillburn, he'd said, and also with the
other doctors who worked on a volunteer basis.

Billy said he'd met some of the other people, but many of them
seemed withdrawn and kept to themselves. There was a Mr.
Pearlman, a Mrs. Brannon, a Puerto Rican girl named Anita, and
a scruffy-looking hippie named Brian; all of them, it seemed, had
had an experience with what Dr. Hillburn termed "theta agents"
or "discarnate entities." Billy also mentioned a girl named
Bonnie Hailey; she was very pretty, he'd written, but she stayed
apart from the others and he saw her only infrequently.

He was taking tests. Lots of tests. They'd punched him with
needles, wired electrodes to his head and studied squiggles on
long pieces of paper that came from the machines he'd been
connected to. They'd asked him to guess what kind of geometric
shapes were printed on something called Zener cards, and he was

keeping a diary of his dreams. Dr. Hillburn was very interested in his experiences with the shape changer, and whenever they talked she took everything down on a tape recorder. She seemed more demanding of him than of the others, and she'd said that she looked forward to meeting Ramona sometime. Next week there would be hypnosis sessions and sleep deprivation, not something he particularly looked forward to.

Billy said he loved her, and that he'd write again soon.

Ramona put his letter aside and listened to the wind. The fire crackled, casting a muted orange light. She'd written a reply to Billy and had mailed it this afternoon. It had said:

Son, you were right to leave Hawthorne. I don't know how things will turn out, but I have a lot of faith in you. Your Mystery Walk has led you out into the world, and it won't end in Chicago. No, it'll go on and on, right to the end of your days. Everybody's on their own kind of Mystery Walk, following the trail of their days and doing the best with what life throws at them. Sometimes its mighty hard to figure out what's right and wrong in this mixed-up world. What looks black can sometimes really be white, and what appears like chalk can sometimes be pure ebony.

I've been thinking a lot about Wayne. I drove over there once, but his house was dark. I'm afraid for him. He's pulled toward you, just like you are to him, but he's scared and weak. His Mystery Walk might've led him into teaching others how to heal themselves, but it's been warped now by greed and I don't think he can see his path clearly. You may not want to stomach this, but if ever in your life you can help him, you have to. You're bound by blood, and though the Walk took you off in different directions, you're still part of each other. Hate's easy. Loving's damned hard.

You know what's a greater mystery than death, Billy? Life itself, the way it twists and turns like a carnival ride.

By the by, I think I catch a little peacock-strutting when you talk about that Bonnie girl. I know she must be special if you've taken a shine to her.

I'm very proud of you. I know you'll make me even prouder. I love you.

She picked up the lamp and went to the bedroom to get her needlepoint.

Catching her reflection in a mirror, she stopped to examine

herself as she combed out her hair. She saw more gray hairs than dark, and there were so many wrinkles in her face. Still, there remained deep in her eyes the awkward girl who'd seen John Creekmore standing across the barn at a hoedown, the girl who'd wanted that boy to hold her until her ribs ached, the girl who'd wanted to fly above the hills and fields on the wind of dreams. She was proud that she'd never lost that part of herself.

Her Mystery Walk was almost over, she realized with a touch of sadness. But, she thought, look at all she'd done! She'd loved a good man and been loved by him, had raised a son to manhood, had always stood up for herself and had done the painful work her destiny demanded. She had learned to take life for good or bad, and to see the Giver of Breath in a dewdrop or a dying leaf. She had only one pain, and that was the red-haired boy—the image of his father—that J.J. Falconer had named Wayne.

Unsettled wind whooped around the house. Ramona put on a sweater and took her needlepoint to the fireside, where she sat and worked steadily for over an hour. There was a prickling sensation at the back of her neck, and she knew it wouldn't be very much longer.

Something was coming through the night. She knew it was coming for her. She didn't know what it would look like, but she wanted to see its face and let it know she was not afraid.

In the mirror she'd seen her own black aura.

She closed her eyes and let her mind drift. She was a child again, running wild and free across the green meadows in the heat of a summer sun. She lay down in the grass and watched the clouds change shape. There were castles up there, with fleecy towers and flags and—

"Ramona!" she heard. "Ramona!" It was her mother, calling from the distance. "Ramona, you little dickens! You get yourself home now, you hear?"

A hand brushed her cheek, and her eyes flew open. The fire and the lamp's wick had burned very low. She'd recognized that touch, and she was filled with warmth.

There was a knock at the door.

Ramona rocked on in her chair a moment more. Then she lifted her chin, stood up, and approached the door; she let her hand rest on the latch for a few seconds, then she took a deep breath and opened it.

A tall man in a straw cowboy hat, a denim jacket, and faded

jeans stood on the porch. He had a grizzled gray beard and dark, deep-set brown eyes. Behind him there was a glossy black pickup truck. He chewed on a toothpick and drawled, "Howdy, ma'am. Seems I took a wrong turn up the road a ways. Sure would appreciate it if I could get some directions and maybe a glass of water. Throat's kind of—"

"I know who you are," Ramona said, and saw a little shock and unease register in the man's eyes. He wasn't a real cowboy, she'd seen, because his hands were too smooth. "I know why you're here. Come in."

He paused, the smile slipping off his face. He saw that she *did* know. Some of the power seemed to drain out of him, and under her firm gaze he felt like a bug that had just crawled from beneath a rock. He almost called it off right then and there, but he knew he couldn't take their money and run; they'd find him, sooner or later. After all, he was a professional.

"Aren't you coming in?" she asked, and opened the door wider.

He took the toothpick out of his mouth, mumbled, "Thank you," and stepped across the threshold. He couldn't look her in the face, because she knew and she wasn't afraid and that made it unbearable for him.

She was waiting.

The man decided he'd make it as quick and painless as possible. And that this would be his last one, God help him.

Ramona closed the door to shut away the cold, then turned defiantly toward her visitor.

ELEVEN

The Test

50

A muffled cry burst from Billy's throat, and he sat up in the darkness as the cot's hard springs squealed beneath him. His mind was jumbled with terrors. He switched on the lamp and sat with the blanket around his shoulders as rain crashed against the window.

He couldn't remember the details of the nightmare, but it had to do with his mother. And the house. Sparks flying into the night sky. The awful face of the shape changer, glowing dark red with reflected light.

Billy got out of bed and trudged into the corridor. On his way to the men's bathroom he saw a light on downstairs, in the parlor. He descended the stairs, hoping to find someone he could talk to.

In the parlor, a single lamp burned. The television was on, silently showing a ghostly test pattern. And curled up on the sofa, lying beneath a brown raincoat with patched elbows, was the girl with different-colored eyes. Except her eyes were closed now, and she was asleep. Billy stood over her for a moment, admiring the dark auburn of her hair and the beauty of her face. As he stared, she flinched in her sleep. She was even prettier than Melissa Pettus, he thought, but she seemed to be a troubled person. He'd found out from Mr. Pearlman that she was nineteen and her family lived in Texas. No one else knew anything about her.

Suddenly, as if she'd sensed him in the room, her eyelids fluttered. She sat up so abruptly he was startled and stepped back a pace. She stared at him with the fierce concentration of a trapped animal, but her eyes looked glazed and dead. "They're going to burn up," she whispered, in a barely audible voice. "Cappy says they will, and Cappy's never wrong—"

Then Billy saw her gaze clear, and he realized she'd been

talking in her sleep. She blinked uncertainly at him, a red flush creeping across her cheeks. "What is it? What do you want?"

"Nothing. I saw the light on." He smiled, trying to ease her obvious tension. "Don't worry, I won't bite."

She didn't respond, but instead drew the coat tighter around her. Billy saw she still wore jeans and a sweater, and either she'd gotten dressed after she was supposed to be in bed or she'd never been to bed at all.

"Doesn't look like there's much on TV," he said, and switched it off. "How long have you been in here?"

"Awhile," she replied, in her distinctive Texas drawl, topped with frost.

"Who's Cappy?"

She flinched as if he'd struck her. "Leave me alone," she said. "I don't bother folks, and I don't want to be bothered."

"I didn't mean to disturb you. Sorry." He turned his back on her. She was surely a pretty girl, he thought, but she lacked in manners. He had almost reached the stairs when she said, "What makes *you* so special?"

"What?"

"Dr. Hillburn thinks you're special. Why is that?"

He shrugged. "I didn't know I was."

"Didn't say you were. Only said that Dr. Hillburn thinks so. She spends a lot of time with you. Must think you're important."

Billy paused at the bottom of the stairs, listening to the noise of the rain hammering at the walls. Bonnie sat with her legs drawn up defensively to her chest, the coat around her shoulders; there was a scared look in her eyes, and Billy knew she was asking for company in her own way. He walked back into the parlor. "I don't know why. Really."

A silence stretched. Bonnie wouldn't look at him. She stared out the bay window into the icy storm.

"It's sure been raining a lot today," Billy said. "Mrs. Brannon says she thinks it'll snow soon."

Bonnie didn't respond for a long while. Then she said softly, "I hope it keeps rainin'. I hope it rains and rains for weeks. Nothin' can burn if it rains like this, can it?" She looked at him appealingly, and he was struck by her simple, natural beauty. She wore no makeup, and she looked freshly scrubbed and healthy but for the dark hollows under her eyes. Not enough sleep, he thought.

He didn't understand her comment, so he didn't reply.

"Why do you always carry that?" she asked.

And it was only then that he realized he held the piece of coal gripped in his left hand. He must've picked it up when he left his room. He was seldom without it, and he'd explained its significance to Dr. Hillburn when she'd inquired.

"Is it like a good-luck charm or somethin'?"

"I guess so. I just carry it, that's all."

"Oh."

Billy shifted his weight from foot to foot. He was wearing pajamas and a robe and slippers provided by the institute, and even though it was well after two in the morning he was in no hurry to return to bed. "Where are you from in Texas?"

"Lamesa. It's right between Lubbock and Big Spring. Where are you from in Alabama?"

"Hawthorne. How'd you know I was from Alabama?"

She shrugged. "How'd you know I was from Texas?"

"I guess I asked somebody." He paused, studying her face. "How come you've got one blue eye and one green?"

"How come you've got curly hair if you're an Indian?"

He smiled, realizing she'd been asking as many questions about him as he had about her. "Do you always answer a question with a question?"

"Do you?"

"No. I'm only part Indian. Choctaw. Don't worry, I won't take your scalp."

"I wasn't worryin'. I come from a long line of Indian hunters."

Billy laughed, and he saw from the sparkle in her eyes that she wanted to laugh, too, but she turned away from him and watched the rain. "What are you doing so far from Texas?" he asked.

"What are you doing so far from Alabama?"

He decided to try a different tack. "I really think your eyes are pretty."

"No, they're not. They're different, is all."

"Sometimes it's good to be different."

"Sure."

"No, I mean it. You ought to be proud of the way you look. It sets you apart."

"It does that, all right."

"I mean it sets you apart in a good way. It makes you special.

331

And who knows? Maybe you can see things more clearly than most folks."

"Maybe," she said quietly, in an uneasy tone of voice, "it means I can see a lot of things I wish I couldn't." She looked up at him. "Have you been talkin' to Dr. Hillburn about me?"

"No."

"Then how'd you know about Cappy? Only Dr. Hillburn knows about that."

He told her what she'd said when she was startled out of sleep, and it was clear she was annoyed. "You shouldn't be creepin' around, anyway," Bonnie told him. "You scared me, that's all. Why'd you come sneakin' down here?"

"I didn't sneak. I had a nightmare that woke me up."

"Nightmares," she whispered. "Yeah, I know a lot about those."

"Haven't you been to bed?"

"No." She paused, a frown working across her face. She had a scatter of freckles across her cheeks and nose, and Billy could envision her riding a horse under the Texas sun. She was a little too thin, but Billy figured she could take care of herself just fine. "I don't like to sleep," Bonnie said after another moment. "That's why I was down here. I wanted to watch TV and read as long as I could."

"Why?"

"Well . . . it's just because I . . . have dreams sometimes. Nightmares. Sometimes they're . . . really awful. If I don't sleep, I won't see them. I . . . was even going to go out for a walk tonight, until it started rainin' so hard. But I hope it keeps on rainin' like this. Do you think it will?"

"I don't know. Why's it so important to you?"

"Because," she said, and gazed up at him, "then what Cappy's been showing me won't come true. Nothin' can burn like what he's been making me see."

The tone of her voice bordered on desperation. Billy sat down in a chair, prepared to listen if she wanted to talk.

She did, and Billy listened without interrupting. The story came hesitantly: when Bonnie Hailey was eleven years old, she was struck by lightning on the stark Texas plain. All her hair burned off, her fingernails turned black, and she lay near death for almost a month. She recalled darkness, and voices, and wanting to let go; but every time she wanted to die she heard a clear, high childish voice tell her no, that letting go wasn't the answer. The voice urged her over and over to hang on, to fight the pain. And she did, winning by slow degrees.

She had a nurse named Mrs. Shelton, and every time Mrs. Shelton would come into the room Bonnie would hear a soft ringing sound in her ears. She began to have a strange recurring dream: a nurse's cap rolling down a flight of moving stairs. A week later, Bonnie found out that Mrs. Shelton had tripped on an escalator in a Lubbock department store and broken her neck. And that was the start of it.

Bonnie called the strange, high voice in her head Cappy, after an invisible playmate she'd had when she was five or six. She'd had a lonely childhood, spending most of the time on the small ranch her stepfather owned near Lamesa. Cappy's visits became more frequent, and with them the dreams. She foresaw suitcases falling from a clear blue sky, over and over again, and she could even read a nametag and a flight number on one of the cases. Cappy told her to tell somebody, quickly, but Bonnie's mother had thought it was utter foolishness. Two planes collided over Dallas less than a week later, and suitcases were strewn over the plains for miles. There had been many other incidents of dreams and hearing what she called Death Bells, until finally her stepfather had called the *National Star* and they'd come out to interview her. Her mother was horrified at the attention that followed, and in came in a flood of crackpot letters and obscene telephone calls. Her stepfather wanted her to write a book—oh, just make it up! he'd told her—and for her to go on tour talking about the Death Bells.

Bonnie's parents had split up, and it was clear to Bonnie that her mother was afraid of her and blamed her for the divorce. The dreams kept coming, and Cappy's voice with them, urging her to act. By this time, the *National Star* touted her as the Death Angel of Texas.

"A psychiatrist at the University of Texas wanted to talk to me," Bonnie said, in a quiet, tense voice. "Mom didn't want me to go, but I knew I had to. Cappy wanted me to. Anyway, Dr. Callahan had worked with Dr. Hillburn before, so he called her and made arrangements to send me up here. Dr. Hillburn says I've got precognition, that maybe the lightning jarred something in my brain and opened me up to signals from what she calls a 'messenger.' She believes there are entities that stay here, in this world, after their bodies have died . . ."

"Discarnates," Billy offered.

"Right. They stay here and try to help the rest of us, but not everybody can understand what they're trying to say."

"But *you* can."

She shook her head. "Not all the time. Sometimes the dreams aren't clear. Sometimes I can hardly understand Cappy's voice. Other times . . . maybe I don't want to hear what he's saying. I don't like to sleep, because I don't want to see what he shows me."

"And you've been having dreams just recently?"

"Yes," she said. "For several nights now. I . . . I haven't told Dr. Hillburn yet. She'll want to hook me up to those machines again, and I'm sick of those tests. Cappy's . . . shown me a building on fire. An old building, in a bad part of town. The fire's fast, and it's . . . it's so hot I can feel the heat on my own face. I can hear the fire engines coming. But the roof collapses, and I . . . can see people jumping out of the windows. It's going to happen, Billy. I *know* it is."

"But do you know where this building is?"

"No, but I think it's here, in Chicago. All the other dreams I've had came true within a hundred miles or so of where I was. Dr. Hillburn thinks I'm like . . . like a radar or something. My range is limited," she said, with a frightened little smile. "Cappy says they're going to die if I can't help them. He says it's going to start in the wires, and it's going to be fast. He keeps saying something that sounds like 'spines,' but I can't figure out what he means."

"You need to let Dr. Hillburn know," Billy told her. "Tomorrow morning. Maybe she can help you."

She nodded vaguely. "Maybe. But I don't think so. I'm so tired of being responsible, Billy. Why did it have to be me. *Why?*" When she looked up at him, there were tears glimmering in her eyes.

"I don't know," he said, and he reached out to take her hand as the rain flailed against the windows. For a long time they sat together, listening to the storm, and when the rain stopped Bonnie let out a soft, despairing whisper.

51

As Billy sat with Bonnie Hailey at the Hillburn Institute, the telephone was ringing at the Hodges's house in Fayette. George Hodges stirred, feeling his wife's back pressed against his own, and fumbled for the receiver.

It was Albert Vance, an attorney he'd met at a business conference in Fort Lauderdale the year before, calling from New York City. Hodges told him to stay on the line, nudged Rhonda, and asked her to hang up when he yelled from downstairs. He went down to the study, rubbing sleep from his eyes, and took the call. "Okay!" he shouted, and the upstairs phone clicked down.

He didn't want Rhonda overhearing. His heart was pounding as he listened to what Vance had to say.

"I had to go through red tape like you wouldn't believe," Vance said, in a northern accent abrasive to Hodges's ear. "Ten High owns a few companies here in New York, and on the surface they're as clean as polished glass. No IRS trouble, no union problems, no bankruptcies. They're real Boy Scouts."

"So what does that mean?"

"It means I had to dig five thousand dollars deeper, and I had to cover my tracks. That's why I'm calling so late. I don't want anyone in my office to know what I found out about Ten High . . . just in case."

"I don't understand."

"You will. Ten High may or may not be connected."

"Connected? With what?"

"The organized boys. Got the picture? I said may or may not be. They've insulated themselves pretty damned well. But the word I get is that Ten High has sunken its claws into the West Coast porno business, the garment trade, owns a sizable slice of

Vegas action, and controls most of the Mexican illegal-alien flow. Ten High is strong, prospering, and *lethal*."

"Oh . . . Jesus. . . ." Hodges's hand clenched around the receiver. Wayne and Henry Bragg were still out there! Wayne had missed a television taping, and now the Houston date had passed and still Wayne showed no intent of coming back to Fayette! God only knew what hold Krespin had on him! He said weakly, "I . . . Al, what can I do?"

"You want my advice? I'll give you a fifty-buck warning for free: keep your ass away from those people! Whatever's going on between them and your client, it's not worth being made into dog food over. Right?"

Hodges's mouth was numb. He said in a whisper, "Yes."

"Okay, that's it. Send me the money and a case of Jack Daniel's, I'll call it even. But listen to me, and I'm serious about this: you never called me to check into Ten High. I never heard of Ten High before. Got it? Those guys have very long arms. Okay?"

"Al, I appreciate your help. Thank you."

"Sleep tight," Vance said, and the telephone was hung up in New York City.

George Hodges slowly returned the receiver to it cradle. He was shaking, and couldn't find the strength to rise from his desk.

For all intents and purposes, the Falconer Crusade—the foundation, the scholarship fund, everything!—was in the grip of Augustus Krepsin, chairman of the board of the Ten High Corporation. Surely Henry Bragg could see what was happening! Couldn't he?

No, he thought bitterly. Henry was too busy lying around that pool and meeting the young girls Niles introduced him to. Palm Springs was all the things Henry had ever fantasized about, and he was hooked as deeply as Wayne!

Hodges reached for the phone again, and dialed 0. When the operator answered, he said, "I'd like to make a long-distance call please. To Birmingham, to the Federal Bureau of . . ." And then he tasted ashes in his mouth, because what could he say? What could he do? Wayne wanted to be out there. Wayne felt safe in that stone tomb, hidden from his responsibilities.

Those guys have very long arms, Al Vance had said.

"Yes sir?" the operator asked.

Hodges thought of Rhonda, and of Larry in his freshman year at

Auburn. *Long arms.* He'd seen Niles's eyes: the eyes of a killer. His gut lurched, and he hung up.

Things had been coming loose at the seams ever since J.J.'s death. Now the whole package was coming apart. Hodges feared what might be at its dark center.

But he had his family, his stocks and bonds. His house and money. He was alive.

Hodges rose wearily from his desk, and as he started across the room he thought he saw, through the picture window, a red glow in the sky when wind whipped through the trees. A fire? he wondered. In that direction lay Hawthorne. What could be burning?

Still, it couldn't be a very large fire. And it was several miles away. It would be put out. He'd find out what it was in the morning.

"God help me," he said quietly, and hoped he would be heard. Then he turned off the lights and climbed the stairs. He felt as if his soul had been scorched to a cinder.

52

"I'll be perfectly honest with you, Billy," Mary Hillburn said. She put on her reading glasses and opened a file folder that lay before her atop the desk. "I have all your test results right here, everything from Zener cards to biofeedback. You checked out just fine on your physical, incidentally."

"That's good to know." It had been several days since Billy's talk with Bonnie Hailey, and just yesterday morning he'd finished the last of the tests Dr. Hillburn had planned for him. It had been a long hypnosis session conducted by Dr. Lansing, and Billy had felt as if he were floating in a dark pool as the therapist tried to take him to different levels of consciousness. From the disappointment on Lansing's face, Billy could tell it had been a dismal failure.

That same disappointment, he saw, was in Dr. Hillburn's eyes. "Your psychological tests," she said, "are also positive. Your Zener card tests were about average, indicating no special ESP ability. You were cooperative in hypnosis, but Dr. Lansing reports no unusual or noteworthy reaction. Your dream diary shows no thread of continuity. You scored highest on the biofeedback session, which may indicate you have a more intense power of concentration than average. Other than that . . ." She looked up at him over the top of her glasses. "I'm afraid there's nothing in any of your tests that marks you as being more than just an ordinary, healthy young man with a high concentration potential."

"Oh," Billy said quietly. All that work for nothing? he thought. "Then . . . you don't think I can do what I say I can, is that right?"

"Take on pain from the dead? I really don't know. As I say, the tests—"

"They're not the right tests," Billy said.

She pondered that for a moment. "Perhaps you're right. But then, what would the proper test be, young man? Can *you* come up with one? You see, parapsychology—and death survival research in particular—is a very, very tricky enterprise. It's a fledgling science—a new frontier; we make up the tests as we go along, but even our *tests* have to be tested. We have to prove ourselves as being serious every day, and most scientists won't even listen to our findings." She closed his file. "Unfortunately, we have proven nothing. No proof of death survival, no proof of an afterlife . . . nothing. But still people come to us with sightings of discarnates. They come to us with precognitive dreams, with the ability to suddenly speak in different languages, or to play musical instruments that they had no prior experience with. I've seen individuals go into trancelike states and write in a completely different handwriting style. I've heard a little girl, also in a trance, speak in a man's voice. What does it mean? Simply that we have reached the edge of a new unknown, and we don't understand what lies before us."

Dr. Hillburn took off her glasses and rubbed her eyes. She was suddenly very tired, and she'd so hoped this young man from Alabama would be the one she was looking for. "I'm sorry," she said. "I don't disbelieve what you've told me about yourself and your family. Your friend Mr. Merkle was certainly convinced. But . . . how can we test that black aura you say you see? How can we test someone who feels he can calm the dead? I don't know. Until we come up with new, verifiable test procedures, we cannot. So I'm going to send your file around to some other parapsychologists. In the meantime . . . I'm sorry, but I've got a list of people waiting to come in. I'm going to have to ask you to vacate your room."

"You . . . want me to leave?"

"No, I don't want you to; but I'm afraid you'll have to. I can give you until the end of the week, and we'll put you on a bus back home. I'm hopeful one of the other parapsychologists who get your file can . . ."

Heat pulsed in Billy's face. He stood up abruptly, thinking of all the money he'd spent to come up here. "I'll leave tomorrow," he said. "And nobody has to see me off. I thought you were going to *help* me!"

"I said we'd put you through some tests. We have. I'm groping through the dark, just as you are, and I wish I had room for everyone here who has psi potential, but we don't. It's not that I don't believe in your abilities. But right now there's only your word for them."

"I see," Billy said, confused and angry. All this time, wasted! "I shouldn't have come up here. I was wrong, I know that now. You can't understand or help me, because you look at everything through machines. How can a machine know what's in my mind and soul? My mother, and her mother before her, never needed machines to help them do their work—and *I* don't, either." He glowered at her and then stalked out of the office.

Dr. Hillburn couldn't blame him. She turned her chair toward the window to look at the park in the gray midafternoon sunlight. She hated to let Billy Creekmore go, because she sensed something about him—something important that she couldn't quite understand. But she needed the space he was occupying, and that was that. She drew in a deep breath and turned to her next priority, Bonnie Hailey's dream diary. Bonnie was still having dreams about a burning building, and her messenger was still trying to impress a word on her. Something that sounded like "spines"? She reread Bonnie's latest dreams—all of them similar except for minor details—and then took a Chicago street map from a bookshelf behind her desk.

53

They came for Henry Bragg at a quiet hour, just before three in the morning, and turned on all the lights in his mirrored bedroom.

Niles was standing over the bed when Bragg got his eyeglasses on. "Mr. Krepsin would like to see you," Niles said. "You won't need to get dressed, just your robe and slippers will do."

"What's going on? What time is it?"

"It's early. Wayne's repaying a debt to Mr. Krepsin. It's important that you be there."

Niles and a sturdy blond bodyguard named Dorn escorted Bragg into the east wing of the house, Krepsin's private domain. In the week since George Hodges had been gone, Bragg had felt as pampered as a prince. He was getting a good suntan and becoming addicted to piña coladas. When the young girls that Niles introduced to him fawned over him, he conveniently forgot about his wife, children, his house and legal practice. He'd begun wearing a chain around his neck with his zodiac sign on it. He was doing his job: staying close to Wayne. If there just happened to be one hell of a lot of fringe benefits, was it *his* fault?

Niles pressed the button outside Krepsin's study. The doors unlocked, and Bragg stepped into the room. Track lights were aimed on him, and the mounted skeletons threw dark slats upon the walls. Krepsin sat behind his desk, his hands folded before him, his head in a pool of light.

Bragg had to visor his hand over his eyes because the light in his face was almost painful. "Mr. Krepsin? Did you want to see me, sir?"

"Yes. Step forward, will you?"

Bragg did. The feel of the Persian carpet under his feet changed. He realized he was standing on a wide piece of thin, clear plastic that had been laid down over the carpet.

"That's fine," Krepsin said. "Right there, if you please."

"What's going on?" Bragg grinned.

"Wayne?" Krepsin looked to his left, at the figure sitting in a high-backed chair. "Are you ready?"

It took Bragg a few minutes to recognize Wayne. The boy's face was pallid, haunted-looking. It had been several days since he'd last seen Wayne, and the boy looked like a stranger. Wayne held a small box in his lap and was rubbing something between his fingers. Was it . . . *hair?* he wondered.

"I don't know," Wayne said softly.

"What did I tell you before, son? You're either ready or not for your test."

"Hey," Bragg said, "is anybody going to tell me what's going on?"

Dorn was covering some of the skeletons nearest Bragg with clear plastic sheets. He moved a coffee table and chair to the far side of the room. Wayne sat staring at the hair in his hand; most of it was gray, and it had a luster that shone like starlight. He got a strange feeling from holding it. The Creekmore boy's face was fresh in his mind, and for an instant it didn't look evil at all. But then he remembered what his father had told him, about things of the Devil not always looking black as sin. "I'm ready," he said, and let Ramona Creekmore's hair slip back into the box. He could call it up from deep within, he *knew* he could. He rose to his feet, clenching and unclenching his fists at his sides.

"Let's begin," Krepsin said.

Before Bragg could turn, Dorn gripped his wrists and pinned his arms behind him. Bragg cried out in pain as Dorn held him so tightly he could barely breathe.

"Mr. Niles?" Krepsin said softly.

Niles had taken what looked like a set of brass knuckles from a black leather pouch. He slipped the weapon on his right fist, and Bragg whined with fear as he saw the wicked glint of broken razor blades studding the weapon's surface.

"Wayne!" Bragg screamed, his glasses hanging from one ear. "For God's sake, don't let them kill me!" He tried to kick out at Niles, but the other man neatly sidestepped. Niles gripped his hair and jerked his head back while Dorn increased the pressure on his lockhold.

And then Niles's arm swept outward in a blurred arc, across Bragg's exposed throat. Fountains of bright red blood leaped into

341

the air, jetting upon the plastic sheets. Niles leaped aside, but not in time: his gray suit was splattered with scarlet. Bragg's face had gone marble white.

"Let him go," Krepsin ordered. Bragg crumpled to his knees, his hands clasped around his throat, blood streaming between the fingers. Krepsin had clicked a stopwatch on when Bragg's throat was slashed, and the seconds were running; he inclined his head toward Wayne. "Now heal him," he said. "You have about three minutes before he bleeds to death."

Wayne had had no idea what the test was going to be. He was transfixed by the sight of all that blood.

"Please," Bragg whispered, and reached a gore-covered hand out for him. "Oh Jesus, oh Jesus don't let me die . . ."

"Hurry, Wayne," Krepsin urged.

Gripping the man's slippery hand, Wayne got on his knees beside him. Red tides rippled across the plastic. Wayne clamped his free hand over the gushing, ragged wound. "Be healed," he said, his voice shaking. "I . . . command you to be healed!" He tried to visualize the veins and arteries melding together as if by a cauterizing torch, but he knew it wasn't working. "Please," he whispered. "Please be healed!"

Bragg moaned hoarsely and fell on his side.

The stopwatch on Krepsin's desk continued to ticktickticktick.

Wayne felt trapped in rust. He *had* felt the healing fire when he'd touched Toby; he *had* felt it when he'd healed a little girl's numbed legs; he *had* felt it a hundred times in those old days, before he felt so pushed and squeezed and pressured to keep doing it day after day. But he couldn't pretend anymore, not with Henry dying in front of him. He had to find the blue fire again, and he had to find it fast. When he looked pleadingly up at Krepsin, he saw the man's impassive face like a huge chunk of eroding stone. Krepsin had put on a surgical mask.

"*Wayne* . . ." Bragg whispered.

He clamped both hands to the wound. "Be healed be healed dear God heal this man please heal him." He squeezed his eyes shut. It wouldn't happen! Where was the blue fire? Where was the power? "*Burn it shut!*" he shouted. Still nothing. He thought of the Creekmore witch, scorching in Hellfire. He thought of the Creekmore boy, still out there roaming the earth. One had been dealt with, the other must follow. "BURN IT SHUT!" he screamed, his mind turning toward revenge for the death of his father.

A faint jolt shuddered through his hands, like a spark plug misfiring. He was covered with blood and sweat, and as he concentrated he bowed his back and screamed for his daddy to help him heal Henry Bragg.

Spark plugs fired. Fired. Fired. "Yes, I command you to be healed! I command you to be heal—" a terrific pain suddenly ripped across his head. His brain felt as if it were about to explode. "BE HEALED!" he shouted, as blood oozed from his nostrils. His eyes bulged from his head.

Bragg's body writhed, his mouth opening in a moan.

Krepsin, breathing hard, began to rise from his chair.

Pain crisscrossed Wayne's head in savage waves. His hands, curled into rigid claws, were locked against Bragg's throat. A fire was coming up from his soul, sizzling through sinew and muscle and flesh. With it there was an agony that made Wayne throw back his head and shriek.

Krepsin thought he smelled charring flesh.

Wayne shook violently, the eyes rolling back in his head, as his hands convulsively twitched around Bragg's throat. The man's body was shaking too, his mouth making low gasping sounds.

And then Wayne fell backward as if thrust away by a physical force. He lay curled up on the bloody plastic. Agony throbbed through him like the vibration of a bass fiddle.

Bragg moaned, "Oh God help me . . . please help me . . . the pain . . ."

Krepsin released his breath in a hiss. The second hand of the stopwatch was sweeping past three minutes. "Check him," he rasped.

Niles bent over Bragg. "Pulse irregular. The bleeding's almost stopped. The blood's coagulated into a hard crust. I . . . I think the wound's sealed, Mr. Krepsin."

"*Hurts,*" Bragg whispered.

Krepsin's bulk leaned over the desk. "That man should be dead by now," he said. "He should be *dead!*" Breathing like a steam engine, he came around the desk and stepped onto the plastic film, avoiding the blood. "Get away, get away," he told Niles, who moved quickly aside. Very slowly Krepsin dared to bend forward and touch with one finger the hard crust of dried blood that had effectively sealed Bragg's wound. He drew his finger back as if it had been burned. "He's going to live," Krepsin whispered. Then, in a shout that seemed to shake the room: "*He's going to live!*"

Wayne sat up, staring blankly ahead as blood dripped from his nose. His head was full of black, consumptive pain.

"He's a healer," Krepsin breathed, his eyes wide and astonished. "He's a healer, he's a healer, he's a goddamned healer! I've found a healer!" He turned toward Wayne, one of his shoes sinking into a puddle of blood. "You always knew you could do it, didn't you? You never doubted it! Oh, I've looked for someone like you for such a long time, Wayne! You can heal anything, can't you? Cancers, fevers, plagues, *anything!*"

The son of Satan, Wayne thought through a haze of pain. Loose in the world. Mocking me. *I always knew I could do it.* Death deserves death. Send the demon boy to join the witch in Hellfire. *I always knew I could get it up!*

"My God, Wayne!" Krepsin was saying. "What a gift you have! I'll give you anything you want, anything in the world! You want to stay here with me, don't you? Here where it's safe, where nothing can get at you? What do you want, Wayne? I'll give you—"

"The demon boy," Wayne whispered. "I . . . want the demon boy dead. He's loose in the world, spreading death like a plague. Death deserves death."

"The Creekmore boy? Anything you want done, anything in the world. We know he's in Chicago, at the . . ." He couldn't recall, and snapped his fingers at Niles.

"The Hillburn Institute," Niles answered. The courier had come this morning, bringing a package containing snippets of hair and an envelope Travis Bixton had found in the Creekmore house. On that envelope had been the institute's address, and inside a letter from the Creekmore boy.

"Right," Krepsin said. "But that boy can't hurt you, Wayne. It was his mother you feared, wasn't it? And now that she's . . ."

"Dead," Wayne said, his haunted gaze burning toward the other man. "Dead dead I want the demon boy dead."

Krepsin glanced quickly over at Niles, then returned his attention to Wayne. "I want you to go back to your room now. Mr. Dorn will give you something to help you relax. Tomorrow you can go up in the Challenger with Coombs. All day if you want. Would you like that?"

"Yes sir."

Dorn helped Wayne to his feet. Bragg stirred and whispered, "Wayne, don't leave me."

"Henry's still hurting," Wayne said dazedly. "What's going to happen to him?"

"We'll see to Mr. Bragg. Go along now. And Wayne—you've passed your test magnificently!"

When Wayne had gone, Niles bent down beside Bragg and examined the throat wound as Krepsin raved on about Wayne's powers. Niles was fascinated at the way the blood had crusted; he'd never seen anything like this before. Bragg's bloodshot eyes were fixed on him. After a period of observation, Niles knew, Bragg would go into the incinerator. "What about the boy at that institute, Mr. Krepsin?" he asked.

"Wells won't have any problem with that, will he?"

"No sir." He stood up and stepped away from the body. "No problem. But aren't you curious about this Creekmore boy? He has some kind of hold over Wayne. Should we find out what it is?"

Krepsin recalled something Wayne had told him, in one of their first conversations: *The Creekmores serve the Devil, and they know all the secrets of death.* He narrowed his eyes and regarded Niles for a silent moment.

"Something about that boy and his mother has preyed on Wayne's mind for a long time," Niles said quietly. "What could it be? And could it be used to bind Wayne closer to you?"

"He'll never leave me," Krepsin said. "How long could a man live, Mr. Niles, if he cannot be touched by injuries or disease? A hundred years? Longer?" Then he said in a soft, dreamy voice, "Not to die, but to know the secrets of death. That would . . . make a human being godlike, wouldn't it?"

"The Creekmore boy," Niles said, "may know something about Wayne that you should know. Possibly we acted prematurely on the woman, as well."

"What's your advice, then?"

Niles told him, and Krepsin listened very carefully.

54

It was Billy's last afternoon at the Hillburn Institute, and he was packing his suitcase when he heard the scream from downstairs. He knew, almost instinctively, that it was Bonnie's voice.

He found her in the parlor, hugging Mr. Pearlman with tears streaming down her face. A few others were watching something on television. Billy stared numbly at the screen.

It was a nighttime scene of a blazing building, firemen wearing oxygen masks and scaling ladders to the upper floors as sparks exploded into the sky. The camera had caught pictures of people leaping to their deaths from the window.

". . . the scene at two A.M. at the Alcott Hotel in South Chicago," a female announcer was saying, "where a cigarette may have ignited one of the worst hotel fires in the past decade. Officials believe a smoldering mattress burst into flames just after midnight and fire spread rapidly through the structure, which has been used as a refuge for transients since 1968. Two firemen were overcome by smoke, and it's estimated now that over forty persons may have died in the flames. It may be days before the rubble is cleared away, and more victims may be buried beneath." The scene changed to an ugly dawn. The building lay in smoking ruins and firemen picked through the debris. "Stay tuned to WCHI's 'Eye on Chicago News' at five." And then the station returned to "The Wizard of Odds."

"It wasn't a cigarette," Bonnie said, staring at Billy. "It was the wiring. It happened just like I knew it would, and I couldn't stop it, I couldn't do anything. . . ."

"There's nothing you could have done," Dr. Hillburn said. She was standing at the foot of the stairs, and had seen the news bulletin. This morning she'd read in the paper about the fiery destruction of the Alcott Hotel, on South Spines Street, and had known that Bonnie's messenger had been right again.

"Yes there was. I could've told somebody. I could've—"

"You told *me*," Dr. Hillburn said. She glanced at Billy and the others and then her gaze returned to Bonnie. "I found Spines Street on a Chicago map. It's in a very bad area on the South Side, full of flophouses for derelicts. Two days ago I called the local police station and the fire department's prevention bureau. I explained who I was, and my conversation ended with, respectively, a desk sergeant and a secretary. I was told there were dozens of transient hotels on Spines Street, and an inspection of them all was impractical. You did the best you could, Bonnie, and so did I."

Forty people dead, Billy thought. *Maybe more, their bodies buried in the rubble. The Alcott Hotel, South Spines Street. Forty people dead*. He could envision them awakening from drunken sleep as fire roared through the corridors. They would've had no time, no chance to escape. It would have been a terrifying, agonizing way to die. *Forty people*.

Bonnie, her face strained and tear-streaked, took her coat from the closet and went out into the cold. She walked into the park, her head bowed.

"She'll survive," Dr. Hillburn said. "She's a fighter, and she knows I'm right. Billy, what time does your bus leave?"

"Four o'clock."

"Whenever you're ready, I'll drive you to the station." Dr. Hillburn watched Bonnie walking in the park for a moment, then started up the stairs.

Billy kept thinking about the Alcott Hotel. The raw image of people leaping from the windows was imprinted on his brain. What would his mother want him to do? He already knew; but he didn't know if he was strong enough for that many of them. He had two hours before his bus left. No, he should forget about the Alcott, he told himself. He was going home, back where he belonged.

Dr. Hillburn was about to enter her office when Billy said quietly, behind her, "I'd like to talk to you, please."

"Yes?"

"That hotel fire. All those people, trapped in there. I . . . think that's where I should go."

"Why? Are you presuming that just because there was fast and painful death, discarnates are present? I don't think that's a very valid—"

"I don't care what you think," Billy said firmly. "I know that

347

some souls need help in crossing over, especially if death came so fast they didn't have time to prepare themselves. Some of them—a lot of them, I think—are probably still in that place, and they're still burning up. They don't know how to get out."

"So what are you suggesting?"

"I want to go there. I want to see for myself." He frowned when she didn't respond. "What my mother taught me had to do with compassion, with feeling. Not with brainwaves or machines. They need me at that place. I have to go, Dr. Hillburn."

"No," she said. "Out of the question. You're acting on an invalid, emotional assumption. And I'm sure that what remains of the Alcott is extremely dangerous. While you're in this city, I feel responsible for you, and I won't have you walking around in a burned-out building. I'm sorry. No." And she went into her office and closed the door.

Billy's face was grim. He went to his room, put on his heaviest sweater, and tucked the rest of his money into a jeans pocket. A bus stop was two blocks north, he knew. He'd have to find the Alcott Hotel by himself. Anita saw him leave, but he spoke to no one. Outside, small flakes of snow were spinning down from an overcast sky, and the wind was frigid. He saw Bonnie out in the park and almost went over to comfort her, but he knew she needed to be alone, and if he paused he might lose the determination that was forcing him to the Alcott. He started walking north, and didn't hear Bonnie's voice when she looked up and called his name.

55

The bus doors hissed open, and Billy stepped onto the pavement in a chilly mix of rain and snow. On the corner was a rusted street sign that read South Spines. As the bus pulled away, Billy shoved his hands in his pockets and started walking into the wind, his teeth beginning to chatter.

For the last hour and a half he'd been transferring from bus to bus, heading deeper into Chicago's grim, gray South Side. He was almost at the edge of the city, and he'd ridden the bus to the end of the line. Rows of square, severe-looking buildings surrounded him, and on the horizon factory chimneys belched brown smoke. Metal shields were pulled down across storefront windows, and the reek of decay hung in the air.

Billy walked south, shivering. In the distance he heard a police car's siren, the wail strengthening and ebbing. The street was all but deserted. Around him snowflakes hissed as if falling on a hot griddle. From windows an occasional solemn face watched him pass.

After another block, he could smell charred timbers. The air grew denser, thick with a grayish brown haze that seemed to hang in layers. He heard an eerie chorus of police sirens, a noise that climbed the scales to a chilling dissonance. Billy could feel the hair at the back of his neck standing up.

The haze grew denser still, like a filthy fog. Billy walked into it, his eyes stinging.

And through it loomed his destination, a scorched five-story building with the letters ALL OTT HO remaining painted in dark red just under the rooftop, which had collapsed during the fire. Windows were rimmed with black, and rooms and narrow corridors had been exposed when part of the hotel's brick skin had slid down to the ground. Smoking rubble was piled up all over the street. A safety barricade, yellow sawhorses with blinking lights, had been set up to hold back a group of fifteen or twenty curious onlookers, and two police cars were parked nearby. Firemen in long brown canvas coats were picking through the debris. A group of men in scruffy clothes stood around a blaze in an empty oil can, passing a bottle back and forth. Parked across the street was a fire engine, its hoses snaking into the rubble.

Two firemen were digging something out. A third came over to help. The blackened shape they were trying to lift fell apart in their hands, and one of the men leaned unsteadily on his shovel as the group of drunks hooted and catcalled.

Billy's heart was pounding, the chorus of sirens making his skin crawl. He saw a couple of policemen moving around in the rubble. Something within the building cracked, and bricks fell from above, causing the officers to scatter.

And then Billy realized those weren't sirens he was hearing.

They were high, dissonant, eerie screams. Coming from inside the Alcott.

And he knew that he was the only one who could hear them.

"Got another one over here!" one of the firemen shouted. "Get me a bodybag, it's a bad one!"

Billy stared across the barricades into the blackened remnants of the lobby. Furniture had been charred into lumps. A tangle of pipes leaked dirty water, and a narrow staircase, warped by intense heat and the weight of water, ascended along a sooty wall. The screams drove themselves into his brain like spikes, and he knew there were too many. He couldn't handle them all, they'd kill him. He'd never tried to help this many, not at one time!

"Step back," a policeman told him, and he obeyed.

But he knew that if he didn't at least try, give it his best and strongest effort, he'd hear that terrible screaming in his mind for the rest of his life. He paused, waiting for the chance. I *am* strong, he told himself. I *can* do it. But he was trembling, and he'd never been more uncertain in his life.

The drunks started shouting at the firemen who were zipping a black form into a bodybag. The policeman hurried over to shut them up, his broad face reddening with anger.

And Billy slipped under the barricade, then into the Alcott Hotel's ruined lobby.

He ascended the stairs as quickly as he could, ducking low beneath twisted pipes and dangling timbers. The stairs groaned under his weight, and around him shifted a curtain of gray smoke. Above the sound of the ghostly screams he could hear restless wind roaring along the upper floors. As he reached the dank second floor, noises from the outside world faded away. He could sense the pulse of agony at the heart of the Alcott Hotel.

His foot plunged through a step; he fell to his knees, ashes whirling around him, as the entire staircase shook. It took him a moment to work his foot free, and then he forced himself upward. Cold sweat and soot clung to his face. The screaming spectral voices led him to the third floor; he was aware also of individual voices—low, agonized moaning, snippets of shouts, cries of terror—that he seemed to feel vibrating in his bones. The third-floor corridor was dark, puddled with ashy water, clogged with burned, unidentifiable shapes. Billy found a shattered window and leaned against it to inhale some fresh air. Down on the street, a white van marked WCHI THE EYE OF CHICAGO had pulled up to the barricade. Three people, a woman and two men—one with a camera unit braced against his shoulder—were having a heated argument with the cop while the drunks shouted and whistled.

The voices of the dead urged Billy on. He continued along the corridor, feeling something like a cold hand exploring his features as a blind man might. The floor groaned under his weight, and from above ashes shifted down like black snow. His shoes crunched on a layer of debris.

To his right there was a doorway that had been shattered by firemen. Beyond was a thick gloom of gray ashes. Billy could sense the terrible cold in that room, leaking out into the corridor. It was the chill of terror, and Billy shivered in its frigid touch.

Beyond that doorway, he knew, was what he had come here to find.

Billy braced himself, his heart hammering, and stepped through the doorway.

The voices stopped.

A pall of black ashes and smoke drifted around him. It had been a large room; he looked up, saw that most of the ceiling had collapsed in a morass of charred timbers. Water was still seeping down from above and lay a half-inch deep around the objects on the floor: charred rib cages, arm and leg bones, unrecognizable shapes that might once have been human beings. Around them, like black barbed wire, was a metal framework that had been melded together by intense heat. Bed frames, Billy realized. Bunk beds. They were sleeping in here when the ceiling collapsed on top of them.

There was a silence, as of something waiting.

He could feel them all around him. They were in the smoke, in the ash, in the burned bones and malformed shapes. They were in the air and in the walls.

There was too much agony here; it weighed heavily in the dense air, and terror crackled like electricity. But it was too late to run, Billy knew. He would have to do what he could.

But there was something else here, as well. The hair at the back of his neck stirred, and his flesh prickled. Hatred oozed from this room. Something in here seethed; something wanted to tear him to pieces.

A shape stirred in a far corner and rose up from the ashes, taking hideous form. It stood seven feet tall, and its narrowed eyes glittered like red beads. The shape changer's boarlike face grinned. "I knew you'd come," it whispered, in a voice neither masculine nor feminine, young nor old. "I've been waiting for you."

Billy stepped back, into puddled water.

"Oh, you're not *afraid*, are you?" The shape changer came out of the corner like a drift of smoke, its bestial gaze fixed on Billy. "Not you, no. Never afraid. You're strong, aren't you?"

"Yes," Billy said. "I am." And he saw a flicker of hesitation in the shape changer's gaze. He wasn't sure of the limits of the shape changer's powers—if indeed, there were any—but it seemed to him that as he got stronger, the shape changer grew more uncertain, more threatened. Perhaps, he thought, the beast couldn't physically hurt him in that demonic, elemental shape, but it could affect his mind, possibly make him hurt himself. If the shape changer ever devised a way to attack him physically, he feared he couldn't survive against such a hideous force.

The thing's form shifted, like a reflection seen in a rippling pond of stagnant water, and suddenly it looked like Lee Sayre. "You're a meddler," it said, in Sayre's voice. "Your family's full of meddlers. Some of them couldn't stand up to me, boy. Do you think *you* can?"

Billy didn't reply, but stood his ground.

Lee Sayre's face grinned. "Good! Then it'll be you and me, boy, with a roomful of souls in the balance! Think fast, boy!"

The floor creaked and pitched downward, dropping Billy to his knees in the water. It's a trick! he thought, as the floor seemed to sway precariously. An illusion, conjured up by the beast!

A blizzard of lighted matches swirled around Billy, burning him on the face and hands, sparking his hair and sweater. He cried out and tried to shield his face with his arms. A trick! Not really burning, not really . . . ! If he was strong enough, he knew, he could overcome the shape changer's tricks. He looked up into the matches that sizzled off his cheeks and forehead, and he tried to concentrate on seeing the shape changer not as Lee Sayre, but as it really looked. The blizzard of matches faded away, and the boar-thing stood before him.

"Tricks," Billy said, and looked up through the darkness at Melissa Pettus.

A fireball suddenly came crashing through the ceiling upon him, burying him in flaming debris. He could smell himself burning—a May Night smell—and he screamed as he tried to fight free. He ran, his clothes on fire, his mind panicked.

Before he reached the doorway, he stepped through a gaping hole in the floor that had been hidden by rubble.

As he plunged through, he caught a jagged piece of twisted metal bed frame that cut into his hand. His body hung halfway through the hole, his legs dangling twenty feet over a pile of timbers studded with blackened nails. His clothes were still on fire, and he could hear his skin sizzling.

"Let go, Billy," Melissa whispered. "It hurts, doesn't it? It hurts to burn."

"No!" he shouted. If he let go, he knew he'd fall to his death. The shape changer had wanted him to flee, had wanted him to step through this hole. Panic, terror, illusions, and insanity—those were the shape changer's most lethal weapons.

"Your mother's dead," Melissa's pretty face said. "The cowboy came and cut her throat. Your little house is a heap of ashes. Billy, your hand's bleeding—"

"Somebody up there?" a voice shouted from below.

"Let go, let go!" the shape changer, in Melissa's skin, said urgently.

Billy concentrated on the pain in his hand. His flesh had stopped sizzling. He turned his full attention to getting out of the hole. His clothes weren't on fire, weren't even scorched. He was strong, he told himself; he could resist the shape changer's weapons. Melissa's form began to fade away, and in its place was the boar. Billy climbed up and crouched on his knees in the water. What had the thing said about his mother? Lies, all lies! He had to hurry, he told himself, before the firemen found him in here.

There were scorched bones lying around him. A rib cage lay nearby. In the corner was a hideous, blackened form still wearing the shreds of clothes, its black skull-like head lolling.

Billy could feel them all around him, terrified and confused. They murmured and moaned, crowding around him to flee the dark power of the shape changer.

"No fear," Billy whispered. "Give up the pain, give up . . ."

"Get out of the dark place!" Jimmy Jed Falconer bellowed, his eyes blazing with righteous anger.

Something as soft as silk brushed Billy's face. A formless, pale bluish white mass had begun seeping out of the wall, reaching tentatively toward him. A second revenant hung in a corner like a spider web, clinging fearfully to the wall.

"You're not strong enough!" Falconer shouted. "You can't do it!"

"Give up the pain," Billy whispered, trying to mentally draw them closer. He squeezed his eyes shut, concentrating. When he opened them, he saw a third revenant drifting nearer, taking on a vague human shape, arms reaching to grasp for him.

"You have to leave this place," Billy said. "You don't belong here." And suddenly he shivered, as a cold white shape drifted over him from behind; it was as soft as velvet, and was so cold it made his bones ache. Two appendages that might have been arms enfolded him.

"No!" the shape changer thundered, reverting to the beast.

The revenant began to sink into him. Billy gritted his teeth as its human memories filled him; first the panic as the fire spread and the ceiling crashed down, then the agony of burning flesh. Then in his mind he saw a splay of cards on a table, a hand reaching for a bottle of Red Dagger wine, golden wheatfields seen from a speeding boxcar, dreaded policemen swinging clubs. Memories and emotions swept through him like leaves blown from dying trees.

Another form drifted closer, gripping Billy's hand and crawling up his arm.

Again, the agony of the blaze streaked through Billy's mind. Then a needle sinking into flesh. A thin woman standing in a doorway, cradling a child.

Billy shuddered and moaned from the intensity of the pain and emotions he was taking on. He saw dozens of white forms sifting through the room, rising from the heaps of bones and ashes. They were oozing out of the walls, some of them hurrying toward him, others still as frightened as little children and clinging to the corners.

"Let go of the pain," he whispered, as the forms clung to him. "No pain, no fear . . ." Images from other lives crackled through his mind: a knife fight in an alley, a bottle uptilted for the last precious drops.

"LOOK AT ME, BOY!" the shape changer shouted, and rippled into Fitts, standing with a python curled around his neck. "Your mother's dead, your mother's dead! The cowboy came and sheared her head!"

The revenants were all over Billy. Though they were weightless, the tonnage of the emotions they were shedding bore him to the floor, where he lay gasping on his side in ashes and water. He heard the shape changer roar, *"It's not over! It's not over yet, you'll see!"* but he closed his mind to the thing's taunts, mentally fixed on bringing the revenants into him.

The shape changer vanished. But, behind Billy, the charred corpse in the corner stirred. Its dead, burned-out eye sockets began to show a gleam of red. The thing moved, slowly, slowly, and started to drag itself toward the boy. One skeletal hand closed around a piece of metal, and lifted it to strike Billy from behind.

Burned bone cracked. The arm dangled uselessly, and as Billy turned to look over his shoulder, he recognized in the reanimated corpse's face the shape changer's red, hate-filled eyes. He lay immobile as the corpse crawled toward him, its mouth opening to emit a hoarse whisper through burned vocal cords; then the head lolled, ripping loose from the neck. The body shuddered and settled again into the ashes, as the shape changer gave it up.

Someone shouted, "Jesus Christ!"

And another voice, rising frantically, "Get the lights on!"

A stunning beam of light flooded the room. Some of the wraiths scattered away from Billy, fleeing the harsh illumination. Others floated above the floor, transfixed.

The fireman with his spotlight backed away, stumbling into the camera crew from WCHI, who were doing a doucmentary on firetrap hotels. The room was filled with strange white shapes, some of them vaguely in human form. "What the *hell?* . . ." the fireman whispered.

"Barry!" a tall woman with red hair said. "Film it!" Her eyes were wide and startled, and she was fighting the urge to run like hell from whatever those things were. The cameraman paused, stunned, and at once the woman switched on a power-pack strapped to his back. She lifted the video-tape camera from its mount on his shoulder, popped off the plastic lens cap, and started filming. Two intense lights attached atop the camera came on, illuminating every corner of the room. "Give me more cable! *Now,* damn it!" She stepped into the room, panning from corner to corner.

"Nothing there," the fireman was babbling. "Nothing there. Just smoke. Just—" And then he fled the room.

The camerawoman stepped over the boy passed out on the floor, jerked at the cable to make sure it wasn't snagged, and filmed a white shape with a head and arms as it fled into a wall.

56

When Cammy Falconer saw her son, she was amazed at how much older he looked. He was growing into a handsome man, but he was getting fat. He sat out at a table by the glass-enclosed swimming pool that was part of the Krepsin house, working on a plastic airplane model.

"Wayne?" Niles said quietly. "Your visitors are here."

Wayne looked up incuriously, and Cammy saw that his eyes seemed dead. She managed a weak smile as she stepped forward. "Aren't you going to say hello to your mother?"

"You've been smoking," Wayne replied. "I can smell it on your clothes." He glanced up at the husky, curly-haired man who stood a few paces behind her, and frowned. One of her boyfriends, he thought. He'd heard she had a lot of boyfriends out in Houston, where she'd moved after the Falconer Foundation had bought her a condominium.

"Wayne, this is Darryl Whitton," she said uneasily. "He plays for the Oilers."

"I don't like football." He concerned himself with putting together the fuselage of a Concorde. "How'd you find me?"

"Where you are isn't a secret." She glanced quickly at Niles, who seemed determined to stay around. "Can I be alone with my son, please?" Niles nodded in accordance, wished them a good visit, and returned to the house. "It's been a long time since I've seen you, Wayne."

"Did *they* send you?"

"No," she said, but she was lying. The Crusade people had called her and explained that they needed her help. Little Wayne was out in Palm Springs, they told her, and he didn't want to come home. Henry Bragg was missing, and George Hodges had quit the Crusade only a few days ago. Cammy inwardly shuddered when

Wayne looked at her; she feared he could see the lie through those scorched, haunted eyes.

Whitton, an affable lout, picked up one of the plastic pieces and grinned. "Mighty good job you're doin' there, Wayne. Your momma tells me you like . . ." And then the grin froze when Wayne's gaze fixed on him. Whitton cleared his throat, put the piece down, and ambled away along the edge of the large swimming pool.

"What's this all about?" Cammy asked. She was well tanned and obviously prosperous, and had broken out of the crystalline cocoon J.J. Falconer had spun around her. "Don't you want to continue the Crusade anymore?"

"They did send you, didn't they?"

"Wayne, you're the head of a multimillion-dollar corporation! And here you are, putting together kids' toys! Who is this Krepsin man, and why did he make it so hard for me to see you? I've called half a dozen times!"

"Mr. Krepsin is my friend," Wayne replied. "I'm resting. And you got in to see me, didn't you?" He concentrated on getting the wings done just right.

"Resting? For what?"

"The future," he said softly. "But you don't care, not really. You stopped caring after my daddy died. But I'll tell you about the future anyway. Mr. Krepsin is going to help me build a church, right out in the desert. It's going to be the biggest church in the world, and it's going to last forever. It's going to be built in Mexico, and Mr. Krepsin is going to show me where . . ." His voice trailed away, and he sat staring into space for a moment. "We can build our own television network, Mr. Krepsin says. He wants to help me, every step of the way."

"In other words, this man's got control over you."

He shot a dark glance at her. "You can't see the future, can you? I don't have any friends back in Fayette. They just want to use me. Back there I'm still Little Wayne Falconer, but here I'm *Mr. Wayne Falconer.* I can have anything I want here, and I don't have to be afraid of *anything.* And know what? They let me fly a jet. Night or day, whenever I choose. I take those controls and I fly over the desert and I feel so . . . so free. Nobody demands anything from me here."

"And what do you do for money?"

"Oh, I've had my bank accounts transferred from Fayette. I've got a new lawyer, too. Mr. Russo. We're going to put all the foundation money in a Mexican bank, because the interest rates are higher. So you see? I'm still in control."

"My God!" Cammy said incredulously. "You've handed over the foundation to a stranger? If the press finds out about this, you're through."

"I don't see it that way." He carefully squeezed plastic cement out of a tube, applying it to a tail fin. "Daddy doesn't either."

Cammy went cold. "*What?*"

"Daddy. He's come back to me, now that the Hawthorne witch is dead. He says what I'm doing is right, and he says he can rest in Heaven when the demon boy is dead."

"No," she whispered. "Wayne . . . where's Henry? Is Henry here with you?"

"Henry? Oh, he went on to Mexico."

Cammy realized her son was out of his mind. Her eyes stung with tears. "Please," she said. "Wayne, listen to me. I'm begging you. Please go back to Fayette. They can talk to you, and—" She touched his arm.

Instantly he jerked away, and the half-finished airplane scattered across the table and to the ground. "Don't touch me!" he told her. "I never asked you to come here!" His face reddened as he realized the model he'd worked so hard on was ruined. "Look what you made me do! You . . . you've broken it!"

"Wayne . . . please . . ."

"Get out!" he said angrily. "I don't want you near me!"

"You're destroying everything J.J. built. Don't throw it all away! You need help, Wayne! Please go back to Fayette, where they can—"

"GET OUT!" Wayne howled, rising to his feet. Whitton was hurrying over. "You Jezebel!" Wayne shouted, and tore away the necklace she was wearing. Pearls rolled across the ground. "You painted whore! You're not my mother anymore, so GET OUT!"

A glass partition separating the pool from the house slid open. Felix, the butler, looked out and then went to summon Niles.

Cammy stared at her son. He was too far gone now to be helped. She knew she'd never see him again. She touched a red welt across her neck where he'd scratched her. And it came out of her before she could stop it: "You're right, Wayne," she said in a quiet, firm voice, "I'm not your mother. I never was."

"Don't, Cammy!" Whitton said.

But Cammy's anger and disgust at what her son had become was pouring out of her. "I was never your mother," she said, and saw Wayne blink. "You spoiled little bastard! Jimmy Jed Falconer bought you, because he wanted a son to carry on the Crusade, and it had to be done quickly. Do you hear me, Wayne?"

Wayne was motionless, his eyes narrowed into slits and his mouth half open.

"He paid hard cash for you!" And then she shouted it for the world to hear: "Jimmy Jed Falconer was impotent! God only knows who your mother and father really were!"

Niles, who'd just come up behind the woman, grabbed Cammy's elbow. "I'll have to ask you to—"

"Get your hand off me!" She pulled away. "What kind of tricks are you people playing? Why don't you let Wayne go?"

"He can leave anytime he likes. Can't you, Wayne?"

The boy's eyes had frozen into chunks of blue ice. "You're a liar," he whispered to the woman. "I'm J.J. Falconer's son."

"Not by blood. There's a man who buys and sells babies. It was done in secret, and I was expected to go along with it. Oh, he loved you like you were his blood, and I tried my best, but I can't stand to see you throwing everything away like this!"

"*Liar,*" Wayne whispered.

"The visit is over," Niles said. "Felix, will you show these people to the door, please?"

"Go back to Fayette," Cammy pleaded. "Don't destroy J.J.'s lifework!" Tears filled her eyes. Whitton gently took her hand and they followed the Mexican butler. Cammy looked back only once, and saw the man named Niles put his hand firmly on Wayne's shoulder. "That was kind of cruel, wasn't it?" Whitton asked.

She wiped her eyes. "Take me to a bar, Darryl. The nearest damned bar you can find."

Niles watched them leave through hooded eyes. "Are you all right, Wayne?"

"I'm J.J. Falconer's son," the boy replied in a dazed voice.

"Of course you are." He recognized the shock settling into Wayne's face, and he took a plastic bottle of small white pills from his inside coat pocket. He shook out a couple into his hand. "Your sedatives, Wayne. Chew these up."

"NO!" The boy struck out at Niles's wrist, and the pills went flying into the swimming pool. Wayne's face was mottled and stricken. "I'm J.J. Falconer's son!" he shouted.

"That's right." Niles tensed, ready for anything. If the boy went out of control, there was no telling what he might try. "Of course you're his son," he said soothingly. "Now why don't you finish your model? They're gone now; they won't bother you again. I'll have Felix bring you a nice glass of fresh orange juice." The juice would be laced with Valium, enough to turn him into a zombie again.

"My airplane." Wayne stared down at the scattered plastic pieces. "Oh," he whispered, and a tear dripped down his right cheek. "It's broken. . . ."

"You can fix it. Come on, sit down." Niles led him to his chair. "What would you like to go with that orange juice?"

Wayne frowned, staring at the sun's reflection in the swimming pool. "Zingers," he said. "Vanilla."

"Remember, we leave for Mexico early in the morning. You'll need your sleep. Are your bags packed?"

"No sir."

"Felix will give you a hand with them." Niles hadn't understood all of what that damned woman had said, but she'd really given Wayne a jolt. Taped to the underside of the table was a voice-activated tape recorder about the size of a cigarette pack. Niles knew Mr. Krepsin would be interested in hearing it. He left the poolside.

Wayne had gathered up the plastic pieces when Felix brought out his orange juice and Zingers. He stuffed the cakes into his mouth after Felix had gone; the orange juice seemed more bitter than usual today. He didn't like it, so after one swallow he poured it into the pool and stirred away the color with his hand. Mr. Niles always insisted he finish everything that was put in front of him, and Wayne didn't want to get Mr. Niles mad. Then Wayne sat cross-legged on the edge of the pool, telling himself over and over again that the painted Jezebel had lied.

57

Billy Creekmore was watching *The House on Haunted Hill* on TV in his room at Chicago's Armitage General Hospital when Bonnie Hailey knocked softly at the door and came in.

"Hi," she said. "How're you doin' today?"

"Better." He sat up and tried to make himself presentable by running a hand through his unruly hair. His bones still ached, and his appetite had dropped to almost nothing. Sleep was a confusion of nightmares, and in the television's blue glow Billy's face looked ghostly and tired. He'd been in the hospital for two days, suffering from shock and exhaustion. "How about you?"

"I'm fine. Here, I brought you somethin' to read." She gave him a copy of the *Tribune* she'd bought down at the newsstand. "Helps to pass the time, I guess."

"Thank you." He didn't tell her that every time he tried to read, the lines ran together like columns of ants.

"You okay? I mean . . . are they treatin' you right around here? Everybody at the institute wants to come over, but Dr. Hillburn says nobody can come for a while. But me, that is. I'm glad you wanted to see me."

It was late afternoon, and the last rays of sunlight were slanting through the blinds beside Billy's bed. Dr. Hillburn had spent most of yesterday with him and had been there this morning as well.

"Did Dr. Hillburn call Hawthorne like she promised she would?" Billy asked.

"I don't know."

"I haven't heard from my mother for a while. I want to know if she's all right." Billy remembered the shape changer's mocking singsong: *Your mother's dead, the cowboy came and sheared her head.*

Bonnie shrugged. Dr. Hillburn had told her not to mention

Billy's mother. The owner of a general store in Hawthorne—the number Billy had said to call—had told Dr. Hillburn that Ramona Creekmore had perished when her cabin had caught fire in the middle of the night. Embers stirred by the wind in the hearth, the man had said. The place went up quick.

"I'm so tired," Billy said. Had a dark cloud passed over Bonnie's face, or not? His brain was still teeming with the emotions and memories he'd absorbed in the Alcott Hotel; he realized he had narrowly escaped death from the shape changer. The beast hadn't been able to crack his mind or erode his determination, but Billy shivered when he thought of that burned corpse dragging itself slowly through the ashes toward him. Had it been another mental trick, another assumed shape, or did the beast have the power to animate the dead as if they were grisly puppets? There had been utter hatred—and grim desperation—burning in those hollow eye sockets. When the shape changer had given up that husk of crisped flesh, the red glint of its eyes had extinguished like spirit lamps. And where was the beast now? Waiting, for another chance to destroy him?

They were going to meet again, somewhere. He was sure of it.

"Dr. Hillburn told me the people at the television station have a video tape," Billy said quietly. "They're keeping it locked in a safe, but they showed it to her yesterday. It shows everything. Me, the revenants in the room . . . everything. She said it shows some of the revenants being drawn into me, and some seeping into the walls. She said they're trying to decide whether to show the tape on TV or not, and they may do a documentary on the institute." He remembered the charge of emotion in Dr. Hillburn's voice as she'd told him other parapsychologists were going to want to see that film, and to meet him, and that very soon his life was going to change. He might not stay in Chicago, she'd said; Chicago—and specifically the institute—might be for him just the first step in a long, arduous journey. Dr. Hillburn's eyes had been bright with hope.

Pain stitched across Billy's forehead. His body felt like a damp rag. "I wonder if there's a piano somewhere around here," he said.

"A *piano*? Why?"

"I like to play. Didn't I tell you? There's a lot I want to tell you, Bonnie. About my family, and about something called the Mystery Walk. I'd like to show you Hawthorne someday. It's not much, but it's where I was born. I'll show you my house, and the high school; I'll show you the trails I used to wander when I was a kid. I'll take you to a place where a creek sings over the rocks, and where you can hear a hundred different birds." He looked up at her, hopefully. "Would you like that?"

"Yes," she replied. "I . . . I think I'd like that. A lot."

"It won't take me long to get well." His heartbeat had quickened. "I want to know the things that are important to you. Will you take me to Lamesa sometime?"

Bonnie smiled and found his hand under the sheet.

"Do you think a cowgirl could get along with an Indian?" he asked her.

"Yep. I think they could get along just fine."

Someone screamed from *The House on Haunted Hill*. It startled Bonnie, but then she laughed. It was a sound that warmed Billy's bones as if he were standing before a fireplace. Suddenly he was laughing too; then she leaned close to him, those strange and beautiful eyes luminous, and their lips gently touched. Bonnie pulled back, her face blooming with color—but Billy cupped his hand behind her head and this time their kiss was long and lingering.

"I'd better go," Bonnie said finally. "Dr. Hillburn wanted me back before dark."

"Okay. But you'll come back tomorrow?"

She nodded. "As early as I can."

"Good. Will you say hello to everybody else for me? And thanks for coming to see me. Thanks a lot."

"Get your rest," she said, and kissed him lightly on the forehead. At the door, she paused to say, "I do want to see Hawthorne with you, Billy. Very much." And then she left, while Billy grinned and stretched and dared believe that everything was going to be just fine.

She's dead, she's dead, the cowboy came and sheared her head.
I'll be waiting for you.

When a nurse brought in his dinner at five-thirty, Billy asked about finding a piano. There was one up on the fourth floor, in the chapel, she told him—but he was supposed to lie right there and get plenty of rest. Doctor's orders.

After she'd gone, Billy picked at his dinner. He paged through the *Tribune* for a while and then, restless and troubled, he put on the robe the hospital had provided and slipped down the hallway to the staircase. He hadn't noticed a heavyset Mexican orderly who'd been mopping the corridor outside his room. The man put aside his mop and took a beeper from his back pocket.

On the fourth floor, Billy was directed to the chapel. It was empty, and an old piano stood next to an altar with a brass crucifix. The walls were covered with heavy red drapes that would muffle sound, but he closed the chapel doors. Then he sat down at the piano as if gratefully greeting an old friend.

What came out was a quiet song of pain, made up of the emotions he'd drained from the revenants at the Alcott Hotel. It was dissonant at first, an eerie melody that advanced up the keyboard until the high notes sounded like strident human voices, but as Billy played he felt the terrors begin to leave him. Gradually the music became more harmonious. He ended only when he felt cleaned out and renewed, and he had no idea how long he'd been playing.

"That was nice," a man standing near the door said. Billy turned toward him and saw he was an orderly. "I enjoyed that."

"How long have you been there?"

"About fifteen minutes. I was out in the hallway and heard you." He smiled and came along the center aisle. He was a stocky man with close-cropped brown hair and green eyes. "Did you make that up yourself?"

"Yes sir."

The orderly stood beside Billy, leaning against the piano. "I always wanted to play an instrument. Tried the bass fiddle once, but I wasn't no good. My hands are too big, I guess. What's your name?"

"Billy Creekmore."

"Well, Billy . . . why don't you play something else? Go on. For me."

He shrugged. "I don't know what else to play."

"Anything. I've always liked piano music. Do you know any jazz?"

"No sir. I just play what I feel."

"Is that so?" He whistled appreciatively. "I sure wish I could do that. Go ahead, okay?" He motioned toward the keyboard, a smile fixed to his broad face.

Billy started playing, picking out a few chords, as the man nodded and moved around behind so he could watch the way Billy's hands worked. "I'm not really very good," Billy said. "I haven't practiced like I ought . . ." Suddenly he was aware of a sharp, medicinal aroma. He started to turn his head, but a hand clamped around the back of his neck. A wet cloth was pressed to his mouth and nose, stifling his cry.

"I like music," the man said. "Always have."

It only took a minute or two for the chloroform solution to work. He would've preferred to use a needle on him, but he didn't want it breaking off in the boy's skin. Anybody who could play a piano like that deserved some respect.

The Mexican orderly who'd been guarding the doors wheeled in a clothes hamper filled with dirty laundry. Billy was stuffed into the bottom, covered over with sheets and towels. Then the hamper was taken out and rolled along the corridor to a service elevator. A car was waiting outside, and a plane was waiting at an airstrip south of the city. Within ten minutes, Billy was asleep in the car's trunk. At the airport he would be given an injection that ensured he would sleep all the way to Mexico.

58

Moonlight shimmered on the swimming pool's surface. In his pajamas, Wayne switched on the underwater light, then slid the glass partition open and stepped into the poolhouse. He was trembling, and there were dark blue circles under his eyes. He'd tried to sleep, but what the woman had told him this morning had driven him crazy with doubts. He hadn't taken his sleeping pill before bedtime, and his nerves jangled like fire alarms; instead, he'd flushed the pill down the toilet because he'd wanted his mind clear, to think about what Cammy had told him.

The pool glowed a rich aquamarine. Wayne sat on the edge; he twitched with nervous energy, and his brain seemed to be working so fast he could smell the cells burning up. Why would Cammy have said that if it wasn't true? To hurt him? She was jealous of his power and stature, that was it. Yes. She was jealous.

His head ached. But hadn't he loved his "mother" at one time? he asked himself. What had made things change? How had they gotten so out of control? He raised up his healing hands and stared at them. Where was Henry Bragg? Waiting for them in Mexico?

All that blood, he thought. All that awful blood.

It hadn't been right to hurt Henry Bragg like that. Henry was a good man. But what kind of man was Mr. Krepsin, if he'd ordered that Henry be hurt?

His daddy had visited him in the night, and told him to trust Mr. Krepsin completely. But, Wayne thought, his daddy had tricked him because if he wasn't of J.J. Falconer's blood, then *whose* blood ran in his veins? And if his daddy had tricked him about that, if he'd failed to tell Wayne the whole truth, then could he be tricking him about Mr. Krepsin too?

A sudden clear thought rang in Wayne's head, a sharp peal of pain: My daddy is dead. I tried to raise him and couldn't, and I saw the coffin go into the ground. *He's dead*.

Then what came in the night, wearing his father's skin and yellow suit?

He was confused, his head a ball of pain breeding black thoughts. The witch was dead, and the demon boy would be dead soon . . . so why did he still feel Evil in the air, all around him, like one of the plagues Mr. Krepsin talked about? He trembled, clasping his arms around himself for warmth.

The witch was dead. There was no need to fear going home anymore. And Cammy was right; there was so much to be done to keep the Crusade going, just as his daddy—if J.J. had been his daddy—had wanted him to do. And only by returning to Fayette, Wayne realized, would he ever find out who his parents actually were. He stared blankly out across the water. So many decisions to be made; it was so *safe* here in Palm Springs, and what about the church to be built?

God help me, he prayed. Please help me decide what I should do.

The answer came to him with electric, painful clarity: he would not go with Mr. Krepsin to Mexico in the morning. He would return to Fayette, first to find out if that woman had been lying or not, and then to make sure the Crusade was in good shape because, no matter who had given him birth, he was a child of the Crusade as well, and now he must in turn take care of it.

And perhaps, he thought, in finding out who his parents were he would learn more about himself and the healing power that had shaped his life.

Yes. He would go back to Fayette in the morning.

He trembled and jittered, his nerves sputtering like raw fuses. He needed a Valium, he thought. No, no—his mind had to be sharp and clear when he went back home, so he could deal with all the problems. He was going to have to sweat all the Valiums, Dalmanes, and Tuinals out of his system. But fear throbbed through him, and he didn't know if he was strong enough to leave Mr. Krepsin and go back to that place where he would have to work and pray and preach and heal. It seemed there were so many problems, and so many people in the world who wanted his healing touch. And if he *really* healed them, if he reached down deep inside and brought up the cleansing power instead of prancing on a stage and pretending, in time the pain would tear him apart.

The voice came drifting into his head like a distant whisper: *Do you know what you're doing, son?*

"No," Wayne said, and shivered. "Oh God help me, I don't. . . ."

He leaned forward and put his hand into the water; it was comfortably warm. He sat for a moment listening to the noise of the desert wind outside the poolhouse, and a slight movement pulled his gaze toward a far corner. He thought something had shifted over there, like a haze of dark smoke, but now there was nothing. He stood up, took off his pajamas, and eased himself into the pool.

He slowly swam the pool's length. He was winded when he reached the deep end, and he treaded water beneath the diving board; then he reached up and gripped the board's edge, letting his body relax.

Water gurgled softly behind him.

A pair of purplish brown, rotting arms wound around his neck, like a lover's embrace. The foul odor of lake mud bubbled up. Black fingernails on skeletal hands playfully scratched at Wayne's cheeks.

He screamed, lost his grip on the board, and sank. Water flooded his mouth; he flailed and kicked, trying to get away from the thing that clutched at him. In the glare of the underwater light he saw a misshapen form with long black hair. Its bony arms reached for him, its purple rotten face pressed close, the lips seeking his. The thing kissed him, trying to plunge its bloated tongue into his mouth.

Wayne got his knee up against its chest and pushed it away. As he fought wildly to the surface, air exploded from his lungs. He swam frantically, tried to scream. Then he felt concrete underneath and he stood in water up to his waist; he turned toward the deep end, wiping hair and water out of his eyes, to see what had attacked him.

Water sloshed against the pool's sides. There was nothing in the deep end; nothing between him and the underwater light.

He whimpered softly, the breath burning in his lungs. *Nothing there,* he thought. *Nothing.* . . .

Something reached between his legs from behind, grabbing at his genitals. He gave a hoarse bark of fear and whirled around.

She was nude, too; but her breasts had decayed and fallen and Wayne could see the yellow bones of her rib cage through the slack, purple flesh. The gases in her body had long since swelled and exploded, and the skin hung down in putrid tatters. Her nose had collapsed or been nibbled away by fish; there was a hole in the center of her face. Her eyeballs were gelatinous, as yellow-white as pools of lake water about to break over her ruined cheeks. But her hair was the same: long and black and lustrous, as if the years of immersion had preserved it.

"*Wayne,*" the awful mouth whispered. There was a shattered place at the side of her head, where she'd struck a diving platform a long time ago.

He moaned and backed away, toward deeper water.

What was left of Lonnie's face grinned. "I'm waiting for you in Fayette, Wayne. I need you sooooo bad." She came closer, bits of her floating away in the water. "I'm still waiting, right where you left me."

"*I didn't mean to!*" he screamed.

"Oh, I *want* you to come back to Fayette. I'm so tired of swimmin', and I need my sweet lover boy back again. . . ."

"Didn't mean to . . . didn't mean to . . . didn't mean . . ." He stepped into deep water, sank, and heard himself scream underwater. He fought back to the surface, and now Lonnie was nearing him, holding out one purple claw.

"I need you, sweet thang," she said. "I'm waitin' for you to come home. I need you to heal me."

"Leave me . . . alone . . . please . . . leave me . . ."

He tried to swim away, but then she splashed behind him and her arms curled around his neck again. Her teeth nipped at his ear, and she whispered, "Let me show you what death is like, Wayne."

He sank as her weight became monstrous, as if she were made of concrete instead of rotten flesh and bone. She bore him deep. He opened his mouth; bubbles rushed from him, rising to the churning surface. They turned over and over, locked together as if in some hideous underwater ballet.

The light darkened. His cheek scraped against the bottom of the pool.

And then he was being pulled upward, wrenched to the surface, and dragged out onto the Astroturf. Someone turned him over on his stomach, and pressure squeezed the small of his back. Water streamed from his mouth and nose, and then he was throwing up his dinner and the three Zingers he'd eaten. He moaned, curled up on his side, and began sobbing.

"He'll be all right," Dorn said, stepping away from the body. His suit was soaked, and he glanced at Niles, who stood a few feet away with Felix. "What'd he try to do, drown himself?"

"I don't know." If Felix hadn't heard Wayne scream, Niles knew, the boy would be dead by now. When Dorn had leaped in, Wayne had been down in the deep water, struggling weakly as if trying to escape from something. "Bring me a canister of oxygen," he told Felix. "*Fast.*" The boy's body was almost blue, and he was shivering violently. "And bring a blanket, too. Move it!"

They covered Wayne with the blanket and cupped an oxygen mask to his mouth and nostrils.

The boy shuddered and moaned, and then finally drew a rattling breath. His eyes came open, bulging with terror. Tears slid down his cheeks. He gripped Niles's hands, his fingers digging into the man's flesh.

Niles said quietly to the others, "Mr. Krepsin doesn't have to know about this. It was an accident. Wayne went swimming, and he got water in his lungs." He looked up at them, his eyes darkening. "Mr. Krepsin would be very upset if he thought we almost let Wayne . . . hurt himself. Do you both understand? Okay, he's breathing fine now. Shit, what a mess! Felix, I want you to go to the kitchen and pour Wayne a *large* glass of orange juice. Bring it up to his room."

Wayne pushed the oxygen mask away from his face. "She was

369

here in the pool and she grabbed me and wanted me to die she's waiting for me she said she wanted me to know what death was like. . . ." His voice cracked, and he clung to Niles like a little boy.

"Help me with him," he told Dorn. "He's got to be ready to leave in the morning."

"No don't make me go back," Wayne moaned. "Please don't make me go back she's waiting for me in the lake she wants me to come back. . . ."

"He's flipped his fucking lid!" Dorn picked up the pajamas, his wet shoes squeaking.

"So what else is new? Come on, let's get him upstairs."

"Don't make me go back!" Wayne blubbered. "I want to stay with Mr. Krepsin, I want to stay and I'll be a good boy, I'll be good I swear I swear it. . . ."

As they reached the glass partition, Niles looked over his shoulder at the pool and thought he saw a shadow—a huge shadow, maybe seven feet tall, that might have been some kind of animal standing on its hind legs—in the corner where there should have been no shadows. He blinked; the shadow was gone.

"What is it?" Dorn asked.

"Nothing. Damn it, this door should've been locked!"

"I thought it *was*."

"Forever," Wayne said, the tears dripping down his face. "I want to stay here forever. Don't make me leave . . . *please* don't. . . ."

Niles turned off the pool's light. For an instant the rippling of disturbed water sounded like a high, inhuman giggle.

TWELVE

Inferno

59

Lizards scampered over rocks baking in the sun. A distant line of sharp-edged mountains shimmered in the midday Mexican heat. As Niles came out of the air-conditioned interior of Krepsin's concrete bunker twenty-five miles north of Torreon, he slipped on his sunglasses to keep from being blinded by a world of burning white.

Niles, immaculate in a khaki suit, walked past Thomas Alvarado's copper Lincoln Continental toward the concrete garage where a few electric carts were kept. Under a brightly striped canvas awning, Wayne Falconer was hitting golf balls out into the desert, where pipe-organ cactus and palmetto grew like a natural barbed-wire fence. Wayne had been urged to find something to do while Krepsin went over business matters with Alvarado, Ten High's Mexican connection.

Wayne hit a ball and shielded his eyes from the glare, watching it bounce across the rocky terrain. It came to rest about twenty yards from one of the observation towers, where a bored Mexican security man dreamt of a cold margarita.

"Nice shot," Niles observed.

Wayne looked up. His eyes were drugged from the extra Valium in his system, his movements slow and heavy. Since the incident at the swimming pool several days before, Wayne had needed careful watching. He fawned over Mr. Krepsin at every opportunity, and Niles was sick of him. Wayne's face was puffy with sunburn.

"I'm almost through with this bucket of balls," he told Niles, his speech slurring.

"Get another one."

"Mr. Krepsin says my church is going to be the biggest one in the world."

"That's fine." Niles walked past him, in a hurry.

"Are you going out there again?" Wayne asked, motioning with his golf club toward the little white concrete structure about a mile away from the main house. "I saw Lucinda go out there with some food this morning. I saw her come back. Who's out there, Mr. Niles?"

The man paid no attention to him. Suddenly there was the *whoosh* of the golf club, and a ball cracked off the garage wall and ricocheted dangerously close to Niles. He tensed and turned toward Wayne.

Wayne was smiling, but his face was slack and Niles sensed his belligerence. Niles had realized in the last few days that Wayne was jealous of his closeness to Mr. Krepsin. "You thought you could fool me, didn't you?" Wayne asked. "You thought you could put him right under my nose and I wouldn't know."

"No one's trying to fool you."

"Oh yes you are. I *know* who's over there. I've known all along!"

"Who, Wayne?"

"Henry Bragg." Wayne's smile stretched wider. "He's resting, isn't he? And that's why I'm not supposed to go over there."

"That's right."

"When can I see him? I want to tell him I'm sorry he got hurt."

"You'll see him soon."

"Good." Wayne nodded. He wanted to see Henry very much, to let him know what he was doing for Mr. Krepsin. Last night Krepsin had asked him to feel a lump in his neck because he was afraid it might be a cancer. Wayne hadn't been able to feel any lump at all, but said he did anyway, and that Mr. Krepsin would be just fine. "I've been having that nightmare again, Mr. Niles."

"Which one?"

"The one I have all the time. I thought I wouldn't have nightmares anymore, after *she* was dead. The snake and the eagle are trying to kill each other, and last night the snake bit the eagle in the neck and pulled it to the ground." He blinked, staring out at the horizon. "The snake's winning. I don't want it to win. But I can't stop it."

"It doesn't mean anything. It's just a dream."

"No sir. It's more. I know it is. Because . . . when the eagle dies, I'm scared something inside me—something important—is going to die too."

"Let's see you hit another ball," Niles said. "Go ahead, tee it up."

Wayne moved like an obedient machine. The ball sailed out toward another observation tower.

Niles continued to the garage, got in one of the electric carts, and drove out toward the white structure. A fly buzzed around his head in the heat, and the air smelled like scorched metal.

Niles rapped on the door. Lucinda, a short squat Mexican woman with gray hair and a seamed, kindly face, opened it at once. He stepped into a sparsely furnished living room where a fan blew the heavy air around. "How is he?" he asked in Spanish.

She shrugged. "Still sleeps. I gave him another shot about an hour ago."

"Was he coming out of it?"

"Enough to be talking. He spoke a girl's name: Bonnie. After this morning when he threw his breakfast all over the wall, I wanted to take no chances."

"Good. Mr. Krepsin wants to see him tonight. Until then, we'll just keep him under." Niles unlocked a slatted door across the room and stepped into a darkened, windowless bedroom with cinder-block walls. The boy was lying on the bed with a strap across his chest, though the precaution was hardly necessary; he was deeply asleep from the drug Lucinda had injected. The boy had been kept drugged since he'd been brought in on the private airstrip behind Krepsin's bunker several days before. Niles stood over him, felt the boy's pulse, hooked up an eyelid and then let it fall. *This* was the boy Wayne feared so much? Niles wondered. Why? What hold did this boy and his mother have on Wayne?

Niles said, "I'll call before I come to get him tonight. You might want to give him some sodium pentothal around nine o'clock. Just enough to keep him settled down for Mr. Krepsin. Okay?"

Lucinda nodded in agreement. She was as familiar with drugs as she was with fried tortillas.

Satisfied with Billy's condition, Niles left the white house and drove back to the bunker. Wayne had started on a new bucket of balls, chopping them in all directions.

The bunker's front door was metal covered with oak, and it fit into the concrete wall like the entrance to a bank vault. Niles pressed a little beeper clipped to his belt, and electronic locks disengaged. Disinfectant filled the entrance foyer, which led to a honeycomb of rooms and corridors, most of which were underground. As Niles closed the door behind him, he failed to notice the fly that circled quickly above his head and flew off through a faint swirl of air-cleansing chemicals.

He found Mr. Krepsin in his study, talking to Thomas Alvarado, a gaunt dark-skinned man with a diamond in his right earlobe. "Twenty-six?" Krepsin, wearing a white caftan and surgical gloves, was saying as he ate from a plate of Oreo cookies. "Ready to come across by when?"

"Next week. Thursday at the latest. We're bringing them in a truckload of uncured iguana hides. They'll have to bear the stink, but at least the *federales* won't poke their noses in."

Krepsin grunted and nodded. The cheap Mexican labor that Alvarado provided was used by Ten High in a number of ways, from the orange groves to the Sundown Ranch in Nevada. On the floor beside Krepsin's chair was a can of film, another gift from Alvarado, who owned a motion-picture studio that cranked out cheap westerns, horror films, and martial-arts gore-fests. "How is he, Mr. Niles?"

"Sleeping. He'll be ready."

"A secret project?" Alvarado asked.

"In a manner of speaking," Krepsin said. Behind his desk was a stack of newspapers, all carefully sprayed with disinfectant, carrying articles on Chicago's vanished "Mystery Medium" and photographs from a video tape that had been made in a burned-out vagrants' hotel. The boy's sudden disappearance from the hospital had fueled a controversy over the authenticity of that tape, and emotions were running high. Krepsin was intrigued, and wanted to know more about Billy Creekmore.

Krepsin had been explaining to Alvarado how the Falconer Crusade's assets were being transferred to Mexican banks, and how Wayne was fully in favor of the idea.

"But what about his own people? Won't they cause trouble?"

"It's not to their advantage to rock the boat, and that's what Mr. Russo is telling them right now. They'll still run part of the show and draw their salaries. Every penny donated to the Crusade will first go to Alabama. In time, we'll build a television center outside Palm Springs so Wayne can continue his network ministry."

Alvarado smiled slyly. "It's a bit late for you to become a man of God, isn't it, Señor Krepsin?"

"I've always been a man of God," he replied, chewing another cookie. "God's green, and he folds. Now let's go on to the next item of business, shall we?"

60

When an amber oval moon had risen over the stark mountain peaks and Wayne Falconer was asleep in his room, Niles and Dorn came for Billy.

Floating in the darkness, unaware of where he was or how he'd gotten here, Billy heard the lock click and thought it was the woman again. He was startled when the overhead light came on, blazing into his eyes. There were two men in suits standing over him. A strap cut across his stomach as he weakly tried to lift his head. He remembered a tray of food, and the way it had splattered against the wall. The woman with the needle had said some very nasty things to him.

"Mr. Krepsin wants him scrubbed," one of the men said.

The woman started on Billy with a soapy, rough sponge, and scrubbed him until blood was almost drawn. Billy had come to like the woman in a way, to depend on her. She helped him find the bedpan when he needed to go to the bathroom, and she fed him when he was hungry.

The strap was loosened.

The man who'd spoken put a finger against Billy's throat to check his pulse.

"Is Bonnie here?" Billy asked. "Where's Dr. Hillburn?"

The man ignored his questions. "We want you to stand up now. We've brought you some clothes." He motioned toward a chair across the room, and Billy made out a pair of yellow pants and a pale blue short-sleeved shirt. Something about the yellow pants jarred him—the color was familiar. From where? he wondered.

"Stand up, now."

Billy did, and his legs collapsed. The two men waited until he could stand up by himself. "Need to call my mom," Billy said.

"Right. Come on, get dressed. Mr. Krepsin's waiting."

Dazed and weak, Billy put on the clothes. He couldn't understand why they hadn't brought him any shoes. He almost cried because he had no shoes, and the pants were so loose they bagged around the thighs and hips. The shirt had a monogram: a scrolled W.

"These aren't my clothes," he said. The two men were blurred shapes in his fogged vision. "I went up to play the piano."

"Let's go."

The night was chilly. During a ride in a little car, Billy felt the cold wind in his face. Its chill helped to clear his senses a bit. He could see lights on towers that stood high off the ground. "Where is this place?" he asked the two men, but neither of them answered.

They approached what looked to Billy like a huge square of concrete. He almost fell twice on the flagstone walkway, and the man in the gray suit had to help him walk. Billy felt a coldness coming off the man, like a bitter frost.

And then he remembered the shape changer saying his mother was dead.

The memories came back in a rush: the hospital, the chapel, the man behind him pressing a strong-smelling cloth to his face. A distant memory of engines whining. The sun beating down on a runway, and on the horizon nothing but white desert. He tried to pull free from the gray-suited man, but he was held in a viselike grip.

Inside the concrete structure, Billy was made to put on a pair of cotton slippers. The air smelled like the hospital room. The two men led him along a hallway to a closed door, and one of them knocked on it. A voice said, "Come in."

They took him in and left him, and the door closed behind him.

Billy weaved on his feet, his vision blurring in and out. The largest man he'd ever seen was waiting in a chair before him, next to a table that held a lamp and a cassette recorder. The man wore a long white caftan trimmed in gold, was bald, and had small black eyes.

"Hello, Billy," Krepsin said, and put aside the file folder of newspaper clippings he'd been going through. "Please sit down." He motioned toward one of the two chairs that faced him.

Think! Billy told himself. He knew he'd been drugged, knew he was a long way from home. And knew also that he was in danger. "Where am I?"

"In a safe place. Don't you want to sit down?"

"No."

"My name is Augustus Krepsin. I'm a friend of Wayne Falconer's."

"Wayne Falconer? What's he got to do with this?"

"Oh, everything! Wayne asked that you be brought here. He wants very much to see you. Look here at what Wayne's been doing." He showed Billy the folder, full of clippings about the Alcott Hotel video tape. "He's been cutting these out. You're a famous young man, did you know that?"

"Then . . . Wayne's *here?*"

"Of course. He even loaned you his clothes. Come on, sit down! I'm not going to bite you!"

"What do you want with me? I was playing the piano. Somebody came up behind me and—"

"Just to talk," Krepsin said. "Just a few minutes of your time, and then we'll take you wherever you'd like to go." He offered a plateful of Oreos, Lorna Doones, and vanilla wafers. "Have one."

Billy shook his head. Everything was mixed up in his mind, nothing was clear. Wayne wanted to see him? Why? "The woman with the needles," he said, pressing a hand to his forehead. "Why'd she keep sticking me?"

"What woman, Billy? Oh, I imagine you've been under a lot of strain. With what you did at that hotel, I mean. You're in newspapers all across the country. Wayne's very interested in you, Billy. He wants to be your friend."

"No. I don't believe you." Exhausted, he sank down into one of the chairs. "I want to call Dr. Hillburn, tell her where I am."

"Of course you do. And you will. Tomorrow morning. It's late, and the telephone system here isn't very reliable. Wayne wanted you brought here—to Mexico—as his guest. I'm sorry if you've been under a strain, but—"

"Why didn't Wayne just *ask* me to come?"

"He did. Well, he asked Dr. Hillburn. Several times. But evidently that woman was resistant to your leaving Chicago. Perhaps some of the staff misinterpreted Wayne's request. Wayne's told me so much about you, I feel I know you already.

379

You and Wayne . . . you're alike in many ways. You're both well on your way in making a mark for yourselves—and you're both *special*, aren't you? He's a healer, and you're . . . blessed with a sight few other men ever know. To see beyond this world, and into the next. The pictures in those clippings aren't faked, are they?"

Billy didn't want to answer, but he was so sluggish and lazy it didn't seem to matter. "No, they're real."

"I knew they weren't faked. How could you fake something like that, in front of so many witnesses? No, no; you can see the dead, can't you? And you can speak to them?"

"Yes."

Krepsin ate another cookie; his black eyes gleamed with the desire to pick the secrets from Billy Creekmore's mind. "You've seen life after death, haven't you? And you can control the dead? You can speak to them and make them do as you please?"

"I don't try to control them. I try to help them. Why are you taping all this? Why's it so important to you?"

"It's just . . . this subject excites me. And it excites Wayne, too."

"What do you mean?"

Krepsin smiled. "You *really* don't see it, do you? You don't understand your own potential! What you've done up to now is important, but you can go much, much further. Oh, the secrets you could know about Death! The *power* you could hold! You could reach anyone on the other side, you could relay messages back and forth. People would pay a lot for that. You could find out where lost treasures were, you could bring back messages that would shock the world! You'd be a famous and powerful young man! Don't you see that?"

"No."

"Wayne does," Krepsin said quietly. "He wants you to join the Crusade, Billy. He wants you to tour with him."

"*What?*"

"Yes. Tour with him. Wayne would be the healer, and you would be the . . . the spiritual adviser! With all this publicity, it would be a simple thing! People would pay to see you summon the dead. Oh, they'd sit in awe of you, Billy! You'd have your own television show, and you'd speak to the dead right on the air before millions of people!"

Staring at the man, Billy shuddered inwardly. It would be like digging up graves so people could gawk at the bones, like a Ghost Show using real revenants, a hideous entertainment.

"Think of it!" Krepsin said. "You've only scratched the surface! You and Wayne, touring together! There are no secrets that would be hidden from you. Billy, you'd even hold power over the dead!"

Billy felt dizzy and sick. But he looked into the man's black eyes and saw the truth. The man wanted power over the dead himself. The man wanted to use him like some puppet in a sideshow, pulling in the paying customers with hints of dark mysteries. He couldn't believe that Wayne had any part in this! "No," he said. "I can't do that. I won't do it."

"And why not? Why *not?* Of course you may be afraid and reluctant now, but after you think about it—and after Wayne's talked to you—you'll see the light. Ever since I saw those newspaper articles—no, ever since Wayne told me all about you and your mother, I knew there was something special about you. I knew you had the power to—"

And then he stopped, a strangled whine bubbling in his throat. Billy stared at him. On Krepsin's hand a fly had landed.

The man leaped up with a scream, knocking over the chair and table as he tried to get away from the thing. He batted wildly at the air as the fly buzzed around his head. In his mind he was back on the refugee ship that had brought him and his family from Greece, and he was seven years old and watching the flies crawl over his parents' stiffened corpses as fever killed half the people aboard.

Krepsin's eyes bulged from their sockets. The fly had touched him. Disease had broken through his barriers. Rats chittered in the ship's hold, his parents' bodies moldering and full of maggots. He screamed with pure terror as the fly danced across his cheek, and he fell to his knees.

Billy stood up and waved the fly away from his face. The men would be coming back for him, he knew, and they'd take him back to the woman with the needles. Danger was here, all around. He had to shake off the dizziness, had to find a way out of this place! He turned the doorknob and stepped out into the empty corridor as Krepsin shrieked again behind him.

He started along the corridor, trying to remember how he'd come in. Krepsin's voice echoed behind him. Billy broke into a run, stumbled and fell, then got up and ran again. The walls around him seemed to breathe, as if he were caught inside a huge beast that was trying to consume him.

And then he turned a corner and abruptly stopped.

A young man with electric-blue eyes and a shock of curly red hair was standing in his pajamas less than ten feet away, in front of an open doorway. He had frozen when he saw Billy. The sweat of a nightmare sheened his sunburned cheeks.

"*Wayne?*" Billy said.

Wayne's mouth hung half open. His eyes were glazed and dull with shock.

Billy took a step toward the other boy, and saw Wayne cringe. "What have they done to you?" Billy whispered. "Wayne? What have they—"

A hand gripped his shoulder. Niles wrenched upward on Billy's arm to keep him from running. Krepsin was still screaming like a madman.

Wayne was pressed against the wall. He had seen that they had even provided the Hawthorne demon boy with *his* clothes. They had brought him here and hidden him in the white house, and they had given him his clothes! "You said I was safe," Wayne whispered to Niles. "You said as long as I stayed here, I was—"

"Shut up, goddamn it!" Niles told him.

"Wayne, they brought me here!" Billy said, the pain clearing his head. "They're trying to use me, Wayne, just like they're trying to use you!"

Niles said, "Wayne, I want you to get dressed and pack your bag. Do it quickly. Mr. Krepsin wants to leave here in fifteen minutes."

"*Demon,*" Wayne whispered, as he huddled against the wall.

"Get ready to go! *Move!*"

"Kill him for me," Wayne said. "Right here. Right now. Kill him like you had the witch killed."

Billy almost got free with a sudden burst of strength, but Niles pinned him tighter.

And then Wayne knew the truth. "You did bring him here," he said, tears in his eyes. "Why? To hurt me? To make me have nightmares? Because," he moaned softly, "that boy's evil . . . and Mr. Krepsin is *too?*"

"I won't tell you again to get your fat ass moving!" Niles said, and forced Billy back along the corridor, toward where Krepsin was babbling about returning to Palm Springs because there was disease in the bunker.

It was all a trick, Wayne realized. They'd never really been his friends; they'd never really wanted to protect him. They'd brought the demon right to his door! Everything had been a trick to get the Crusade!

It was all clear to him now, and his mind crackled with wild currents. Maybe they'd even brought Billy Creekmore here, he realized, to *replace* him.

Even his daddy had tricked him and wasn't his daddy. He'd been tricked and lied to from the very start. Had been told Keep healing, Wayne, keep healing keep healing even though you don't feel the fire anymore keep healing. . . .

His mind was cracking. The snake was winning.

But not yet! He was still Wayne Falconer, the South's Greatest Evangelist! And there was one last way to destroy the corruption that had surrounded and finally trapped him. He wiped the tears from his face.

The eagle might still destroy the snake.

61

Jim Coombs took the Challenger to sixteen thousand feet. He checked his instruments and turned on the automatic pilot. Below the jet, as indicated by a downward-tilted radar mechanism set in the nose, was a rough terrain of desert and mountains. A scan of the weather ahead showed clear skies. The takeoff and landing were the skillful parts of flying the Challenger; now, with the jet flying itself and visibility almost perfect, Coombs could sit back and relax. He'd been awakened in his quarters at the jet hangar about half an hour earlier, and told by Dorn that Mr. Krepsin wanted to go back to Palm Springs immediately. Krepsin was a nervous wreck back in the passenger section; the man had waddled aboard wearing his white caftan, his face as pale as milk, and had started sucking at an oxygen mask as soon as he'd strapped in. Niles and Dorn were even more quiet than usual. Wayne was silent and brooding, not even bothering to answer when Coombs had spoken to him. And there was another passenger aboard, as well: the dark-haired boy that Coombs had flown down from Chicago. The boy had a hard, shiny look in his eyes, something between fear and rage and probably a bit of both. Coombs didn't know what was going on, but for some reason he was very glad he wasn't that boy.

Coombs yawned, still weary from his interrupted sleep. They'd be in Palm Springs in a couple of hours.

From his seat at the middle of the plane, Billy watched Krepsin's chest heaving as the huge man breathed through an oxygen mask. Krepsin sat toward the front, where he had plenty of room; his breathing sounded like that of a man in agony. Abruptly, he reached out and drew the clear plastic curtain around his seat, cutting himself off from the rest of the cabin. Niles sat sleeping just behind Billy, Dorn across the aisle. Across from Krepsin, Wayne sat like a statue.

What had they done to him? Billy wondered. How had these people gotten control of the Falconer Crusade? There had been madness and terror in Wayne's eyes, and Billy feared his brother was beyond help. But still, somehow, he had to try. He saw that, too, as part of his Mystery Walk—breaking through the barrier of fear that kept them apart, that had put Wayne on a twisted path leading into the clutches of Augustus Krepsin. His mother—*their* mother—was probably dead. Wayne's madness had wanted it done, and Krepsin had obliged. Fear and hatred had been Jimmy Jed Falconer's legacy to his adopted son.

And now Billy recalled something his mother had told him: that Wayne wouldn't be able to recognize true Evil when it reached out for him. That Wayne might be *his* weak link, that the shape changer might be able to work on Wayne to get at Billy. He leaned his head back, squeezing his eyes shut. What would she want him to do now? When he opened his eyes, he saw Wayne looking back at him over his shoulder. They stared at each other for a long moment; Billy thought he could feel electricity passing between them, as if they were batteries feeding off each other. Then Wayne rose from his seat and came back along the aisle, averting his gaze from Billy.

"What is it?" Niles asked him, when Wayne had prodded him awake.

384

"I want to go up to the cockpit," Wayne said. His eyes were glassy, and a pulse beat rapidly at one temple. "Can I?"

"No. Go sit down."

"Mr. Krepsin always lets me," Wayne told him. "I like to sit up front, where I can see the instruments." One side of his mouth hitched up in a slight sneer. "Mr. Krepsin wants me to be happy, doesn't he?"

Niles paused for a moment. Then he said irritably, "Go on, then. I don't care what you do!" He closed his eyes again.

"Wayne?" Billy said, and the other boy looked at him. "I'm not your enemy. I never wanted things to be like this."

"You're going to die." Wayne's eyes flared, two hot bursts of blue. "I'm going to make sure of that, if it's the last thing I do. God's going to help me."

"Listen to me," Billy said; it was burning to come out of him. He had to tell him, right now, and he had to make him understand. "*Please*. I'm not evil, and neither is . . . was my mother. Didn't you ever wonder where your healing power came from? Didn't you ever wonder, why *you?* I can tell you why. Don't turn away! Please! The Falconers weren't your real parents, Wayne. . . ."

Wayne froze. His mouth worked for a few seconds, and then he whispered, "How did you know that?"

"I know, because my mother—*our* mother—told me. I'm telling you the truth. Ramona Creekmore was your mother, Wayne. John Creekmore was your father. You were born the same day as me: November 6, 1951. Jimmy Jed Falconer bought you from a man named Tillman, and he raised you as his son. But it wasn't because our parents didn't love you, Wayne. They did. But they wanted you to have a good home, and they had to—"

"Liar!" Wayne said in a strangled voice. "You're lying, trying to save your own life."

"She loved you, Wayne," Billy said. "No matter what you did. She knew who you were from the first time she saw you, at the tent revival. But she saw you were being used, and she couldn't stand it. *Look* at me, Wayne! I'm telling you the truth!"

He blinked, touched his forehead. "No. Lies . . . everybody's lied to me. Even . . . my own daddy. . . ."

"You've got Creekmore blood in you. You're strong; stronger than you think. I don't know what they've done to you, but you can fight it. You don't have to let them win!"

385

Niles, who'd been dozing in his seat, stirred and told Billy to shut his mouth.

"You're going to burn in Hell," Wayne told Billy. And then he turned away, and walked toward the flight deck. He stood staring at Augustus Krepsin for a moment; Krepsin's eyes were closed, the breath rasping in and out of his lungs like a bellows. "You'll see," Wayne whispered, and then he stepped through onto the flight deck, where Jim Coombs sat half dozing in the pilot's seat.

Coombs yawned and sat up, quickly checking the instruments. "'Lo, Wayne," he said.

"Hi."

"Glad you came up. I was just about to ask you to sit in for me while I go to the john. We're on auto, you don't have to touch a thing. Pretty moon, isn't it?"

"Sure is."

"Well . . ." He stretched, then unstrapped his belt and stood up. "I'll be as quick as I can. Listen to those engines hum. Man, that can just about put you to sleep!"

"Yes sir." Wayne eased into the co-pilot's seat, fastened his belt tightly, and glanced over the instrumentation panel. Airspeed 431 knots. Altitude sixteen thousand. Compass showing a northwest heading.

"Good boy," Coombs said, and left the cockpit.

Wayne listened to the headphones, hearing signals floating through space from navigational beacons. He watched the control yoke, moving at the command of the autopilot. A sense of power thrummed through him, setting him on fire. He had them all now, right where he wanted them; he knew he couldn't let them take him back to Palm Springs. He'd failed the Crusade, failed in his healing mission, failed, failed. . . .

But now, up here in the sky, he could forget all about that. He could be in control. He lifted a trembling hand and cut off the autopilot.

"Don't do it, son." Jimmy Jed Falconer, in his bright yellow suit, was sitting in the pilot's seat; there was an earnest, concerned look on his face. "You can trust Mr. Krepsin; he cares about you, son. He'll let you do what you like with Billy Creekmore. *Anything* you like. But don't do what you're thinking. That'll . . . that'll ruin *everything*. . . ."

Wayne stared at him, then shook his head. "You lied to me. All the time. I'm not your son, am I? I never was. . . ."

"Yes you are! Don't listen to that shit! Listen to *me!* Trust Mr. Krepsin, Wayne. Don't do what you're about to try. . . ."

Wayne saw the frightened look in the man's eyes. It pleased him. "You're scared," he said. "You're scared to death, aren't you? Why? You're already dead. . . ."

"DON'T DO IT, YOU LITTLE FUCK!" Falconer's face began to crack like a waxen mask. One red, animalish eye glared out at Wayne.

In the cabin, Billy felt a cold chill and opened his eyes. The pilot was just moving past him, on his way to the bathroom at the rear of the plane. Billy jerked his head up and looked around, because he'd seen the thing that had made his heart hammer in his chest.

The pilot stopped and looked back, his forehead creasing. "What's wrong?" he asked uneasily.

Billy stared. The man's body was surrounded by a malignant purplish black haze; stubby, vaporous tentacles undulated around him.

"What're you looking at?" Coombs asked, transfixed by Billy's dark, intense gaze.

Billy turned his head and looked across the aisle at Dorn. The black aura clung to him like a shiny, dark skin. Niles's hand came over the seat and grasped Billy's shoulder. The hand was coated with the black harbinger of death. Niles's face, surrounded by the roiling black aura, thrust forward. He said, "What's your problem, kid?"

They were all about to die, Billy realized. And possibly himself, as well. The jet. Who was at the controls? Wayne? Suddenly Death's cold chill had filled the cabin. When Wayne had entered the cockpit, things had abruptly changed. Wayne was going to do it. Wayne was going to kill them all.

"NO! DON'T DO THAT, YOU LITTLE SHIT!" the thing in the pilot's seat roared. "DON'T DO IT!" Its J.J. Falconer mask had melted away, and now Wayne saw it for what it was: a bestial thing with flaring red eyes and the hideous snout of a wild, savage boar. Wayne knew he was seeing Evil for what it was. The thing made a garbled, babbling noise as Wayne gripped the control column, his foot finding the rudder pedals. Then he whipped the Challenger to the right and upward, at the same time throttling more fuel to the engines.

Billy heard the shape changer's roar an instant before the jet's

387

nose lurched upward; the plane veered over on its right side, its engines screaming. Billy's body pressed backward in his seat, the pressure so great against his chest he couldn't draw a breath. Everything that wasn't strapped or bolted down in the cabin—briefcases, glasses, bottles of Perrier—took dangerous flight, slamming and crashing against the bulkheads. Jim Coombs was jerked upward so fast he never knew what had happened; his head hit the cabin roof with a sharp sound of cracking bone, and his body stayed glued in place until the jet rolled over and leveled off. Then Coombs slithered into the aisle, his eyes open and his teeth clenched through the bloody stub of his tongue. His hands twitched as if he were trying to snap his fingers.

Billy gasped for air. The jet rolled suddenly to the left and went into a steep dive. A bottle of Perrier whirled past Billy's head and exploded against the wall. Krepsin was screaming through his oxygen mask. Dorn's face was marble white, his hands gripped deeply into the armrests of his seat; he was squealing like a child on a scary fairgrounds ride.

The thing in the pilot's seat shimmered like a mirage and dissolved. Wayne's face was set in a rigid grin, the flesh of his cheeks pushed back by the intense g-forces. Now he'd show them, he thought. He'd show all the liars. He laughed aloud and cut back on his airspeed, rolling the jet over; the Challenger responded immediately. A loose clipboard smacked him in the middle of his head; a pencil and paper clips danced around him. He pushed the control column forward, putting the Challenger into a shallow dive toward the dark plain below. There was a high whine of air around the nose cone. He watched the altimeter falling. Thirteen thousand. Twelve thousand. Eleven thousand. Ten.

"WAYNE!" Niles shrieked from his seat behind Billy. "STOP IT!" He started to unstrap his belt, but he saw Coombs's corpse folded over a teakwood table, blood leaking from the cracked skull, and he realized with a cold certainty that he was a dead man if he left the safety of his seatbelt.

Wayne grinned, his eyes filling with tears. Up here, at the throttle of this fantastic machine, he was in full control. He saw the altimeter reach four thousand feet, and then he whipped the jet off to the right. Airspeed fell dramatically; the control column shivered in his grip. He had never felt so free and full of power before in his life. The engines moaned; the entire plane began shuddering, straining to its limits. He couldn't breathe, and black motes danced before his eyes.

With an effort that almost tore his arms from their sockets, Billy unsnapped his belt. Instantly he was pushed over the top of his seat, almost into Niles's lap; he clutched at the seat in front of him, trying to pull himself toward the flight deck.

Wayne leveled the Challenger off and then threw it into a dive again. Billy was tossed like a cork inside the cabin; he rolled head over heels, trying to grab anything to steady himself. His chin cracked against a table; dazed, he tumbled forward. His left shoulder smashed into something, and white-hot pain filled him. Then he gripped the plastic curtain around Krepsin's seat; it ripped down, and through the haze of pain Billy saw feral fear stitched across Augustus Krepsin's pallid face.

At less than five hundred feet, Wayne wrenched back on the control column. The Challenger shuddered and leveled off; the altimeter read four-nine-two. He was aware of strange shapes on the landscape before him, bathed in amber moonlight; he pulled the throttles back, cutting airspeed. Something huge and dark and jagged passed to the right, barely fifty yards away.

Billy was at the flight deck, and Wayne looked over his shoulder with a half-snarl, half-grin.

And then Billy saw it; it loomed up, filling the windshield. Moonlight glinted off wind-etched rock. Wayne twisted around, and instinctively tried to lift the jet over the mountain peak they were almost upon. The Challenger shuddered, caught by an updraft. Then there was a banshee scream of ripping metal as the right wingtip was clipped by rock. The violent motion of collision threw Billy against a bulkhead; he heard bone snap, and then he was on his knees watching blood drip from his nostrils.

The underside of the fuselage scraped rock, splitting open like a sardine can; sparks and fire rippled along the seam, being sucked upward into the starboard jet engine. It exploded, first crumpling the starboard fuselage wall and then bursting through with the scream and whine of popping rivets. Red-hot daggers of metal impaled Niles from behind, going through him and into the seat Billy had left. A flying sheet of metal, rippling with flame, took off the top of Niles's head and splattered Dorn with brains.

Warning buzzers went off all over the instrument panel. The rear of the plane was on fire, the starboard engine gone, the starboard wingtip and ailerons mangled. The rudder wouldn't respond. Wayne saw the airspeed falling. They were going down, toward a wide flat plain rimmed with mountains. Fuses were burning, the cockpit filling with acrid smoke. The ground was coming up fast, a blur of amber-colored earth strewn with sparse vegetation.

Wayne had time only to cut the remaining engine's power. The jet hit, and bounced. Hit again. Dust boiled up, obscuring his vision. He was thrown forward and then backward, the belt almost squeezing him in two, and he lost his grip on the yoke. The jet ground forward on a sizzling sheet of sparks. It split in half, lost its wings, spun, and careened onward over a rough runway of pebbled desert. Wayne's head rocked forward, slamming into the yoke. The skeletal remains of the jet slid on a hundred more yards, then lay still.

Billy stirred from the floor of the flight deck, where he'd been pinned against the back of the pilot's seat. He saw that the cabin was a mangled mass of burning cables and furniture. Where the jet had cracked in half he could see out across the desert plain—for over three hundred yards there was a litter of burning debris and a trail of flaming jet fuel. The rear section had been ripped away. Through a haze of eye-stinging smoke, Billy saw that Krepsin's seat had been torn away, too. The man was gone.

He tried to stand. There was no feeling in his left arm; looking at it, he saw white bone gleaming at the severe break of his left wrist. A wave of pain and nausea passed over him, and cold sweat broke out on his face. Wayne moaned softly and began sobbing. In the remains of the passenger cabin, the carpet and seats were on fire. The plastic curtain that had hung around Krepsin's seat was melting. Billy forced himself up, cradling his injured arm against his chest. He grasped Wayne's shoulder and eased the boy back; Wayne's head lolled. There was a purple lump over his right eye, and the eye itself was swelling shut.

Moving as if in agonized slow motion, Billy unstrapped Wayne's seatbelt and managed to haul him from the seat. "Wake up, wake up," he kept saying as he dragged Wayne out through the burning cabin with his good arm. With the last of his ebbing strength, Billy half carried, half dragged Wayne as far as he could before his legs gave out. He fell to the ground, smelling his own burned flesh and hair. Then the long, terrible pain racked him and he curled up like a fetus against the oncoming darkness.

opening, the overwhelming web of blackness. The gryfon was starting it up, too. All it could do was stand and watch the gryfon's exaltation.

Vespin had come only from their hatching custom's view. The gorilla and humanoid life again, come railed up calling up his

62

He knew he was moving. Hurtling rapidly through darkness. He was in a tunnel, he thought, and soon he'd reach the far end. He wasn't hurting anymore. He was afraid, but he felt fine.

In the distance there was a sudden glint of bright, hazy golden light. As if a door were slowly being opened.

For him, he realized. For *him*.

It was the most beautiful light he'd ever seen. It was all the sunrises and sunsets he'd ever witnessed, all the golden sunny summer days of his childhood, all the colors of sunlight streaming through the multicolored leaves of an autumn forest. He'd soon reach that light, if he hurried; he desperately wanted to get there, to feel that warmth on his body, to bask in it and just let everything go. He was able to turn his head—or he thought he turned his head, but he wasn't sure—and looked back along the tunnel at what he was leaving behind. There was something back there on fire.

The door was opening wider, flooding the tunnel with that wonderful glow. He had to reach it, he knew, before it closed again. His forward progress seemed to be slowing . . . slowing . . .

The door was wide open, the light so bright it stung his eyes. Beyond the doorway was a suggestion of blazing blue sky, green fields, and hills and forest stretching on as far as he could see. There were wonders over there, a beautiful place of peace and rest. There would be new paths to explore, new secret places, new journeys to be made. Joy surged through him, and he stretched out his arm to reach the opening.

A figure stepped into the threshold. A woman, with long russet hair that flowed over her shoulders. He knew instantly who it was, and she looked at him with an expression of sadness and compassion.

"No," she said softly. "You can't give it up yet. It's too soon."
And the door began closing.

"Please!" Billy said. "Help me . . . let me stay!"

"Not yet," she replied.

He shouted, "*No!*" but he was already falling away from it, falling faster and faster as the door closed and the light faded. He sobbed and fought as he tumbled along the tunnel, returning to the place where pain waited to grip into him again. Memory ripped through him: Wayne at the controls, Krepsin screaming, the jet skidding along the ground while flames chewed at the cabin, a shriek of metal as the wings tore away, the final violent thrashing of the fuselage. . . .

He moaned and opened his eyes. Two dark forms that had been poised near his head spread their wings, making startled cries as they flew away. They circled overhead in the graying sky, then dropped down onto something about a hundred yards away.

I'm not dead, Billy thought. But the memory of the golden light and the beautiful landscape almost cracked his heart; his mother had been there, waiting for him, but had turned him away instead. Why? Because his Mystery Walk wasn't yet finished?

He braced himself with his right arm and tried to sit up. Pain pounded through his head, broken bones grinding in his jaw where his head had struck the table. Then he had forced himself into a sitting position, and he looked across the desert.

The first orange rays of the sun were slicing the sky over a line of purple mountains to the east. Small fires still flickered everywhere; a large section of the jet—the rear of the cabin and the tail—had burned itself out into a black mass of tangled metal. Debris was scattered for more than a mile. Billy watched sunlight explode over the mountains. The heat was already stifling; in another hour or so it would be unbearable, and there wasn't a scrap of shelter.

He heard a soft, shuddered moan behind him. With an effort, he turned his head and saw Wayne Falconer—his face swollen, his hair scorched, his clothes ripped and burned—lying about ten feet away, his back supported by part of a seat that had been blown out of the aircraft. There was crusted blood all over Wayne's face, and one eye was swollen shut. The other was deep-sunken, bright blue, and was fixed on the Challenger's strewn wreckage. The eye moved and came to rest on Billy.

Wayne whispered, "The beautiful eagle. It's dead. It's all torn

392

up and dead." A tear glittered in his eye, overflowed, and ran down his blood-streaked cheek.

Billy watched the vultures circle and swoop. A few of them were fighting over something that lay about thirty yards or so away—something twisted and charred black. "Do you know where we are?" he asked Wayne.

"No. What does it matter? Krepsin's dead; they're all dead . . . except *you*."

"Can you move?"

"My head hurts. And so does my side. But I landed her, didn't I? We were on fire, and I put her right down. What did we hit?"

"One of those, I think." Billy motioned toward the peaks with his right hand. "Somebody'll help us. They'll see the smoke."

Wayne watched the smoke rising. The sun painted his bruised face bright orange. "I wanted them all dead . . . but you, most of all. I wanted to die, too. I don't remember much after we hit the ground; but I remember somebody pulling me out of the flight deck." He turned his head, the single eye unblinking. "Why didn't you leave me there to burn?"

"I don't hate you," Billy said. "No matter what you think, I'm not your enemy. Krepsin was, because he wanted to own you— and he wanted to own me, too. They brought me here from Chicago, to make me do . . . awful things. If you hate me, it's because J.J. Falconer owned you, and he taught you how to hate."

"Daddy . . ." Wayne said softly. "He used to visit me, all the time. Late at night, just before I slept. But . . . he lied to me, didn't he? No, no; it wasn't my daddy. It was . . . something else, something that . . . looked like an animal. I saw it, in the flight deck, just before we went down. It was lying to me, all the time, making me think my . . . my daddy was still alive. And it told me to trust Mr. Krepsin, to stay with him and do whatever he wanted. They hurt Henry Bragg. They hurt him bad, and I had to heal him." Wayne lifted his hands and looked at them. "I just wanted to do good," he said. "That's all. Why was it always so *hard?*" There was pleading in his voice.

Billy slowly rose to his feet. He was still wearing the cotton slippers that had been issued to him at Krepsin's hacienda. The ground was a pavement of rough pebbles, interrupted here and there by gnarled growths of cactus and spikes of palmetto. "We've got to find some shade," he told Wayne. "Can you walk?"

"I don't want to move."

"The sun's still low. In a couple of hours it's going to be over a hundred degrees out here. Maybe we can find a village. Maybe . . ." His gaze passed across the rise of mountains that stood to the north, and he squinted in the fierce, hot glare. The mountains seemed to be only a mile or so away, shimmering in the heat waves. There were rippled outcrops of rock that might throw enough shade to keep them alive. "Up there," he said, and pointed. "It's not too far. We can make it."

Wayne balked for another moment, then stood up. He grasped Billy's shoulder for support, and something like a charge of electricity passed between them, stunning and energizing both of them. The pain seemed to drain out of Billy's body; Wayne's head was cleared as if he'd inhaled pure oxygen. Startled, Wayne drew his hand back.

"We can make it," Billy said firmly. "We *have* to."

"I don't understand you. Why don't you just leave me and walk away? Whenever I saw you and your mother, whenever I heard your names, I was afraid; and I was ashamed, too, because I *liked* the power I had." His face was agonized. "But I had to start lying about the healing, because I *couldn't* heal everybody. I had to make them think I could, or they wouldn't listen to me anymore. I wouldn't have the power anymore. Even when I was a child, I was lying about it . . . and I knew it. And somehow, you and she knew it too, right from the start. You could see right through me. I . . . I hated both of you, and I wanted to see you dead." He squinted up toward the sun. "But maybe it was because I hated what I was, and *I* wanted to die . . . I still want to die. Just leave me here. Let me rest."

"No. I don't know what Krepsin did to you, but you can get help. Now let's start walking." He took the first step, then the next and the next. The pebbles felt like glass under his feet. When he looked back, he saw that Wayne was following, but at a dazed, unsteady pace.

They passed through the wreckage. Puddles of jet fuel still burned. Cocktail napkins with *Ten High, Inc*. printed on them fluttered past on a hot breath of wind. There was a litter of burned cables, shredded seats, broken glass, and razor-edged sheets of metal. A headless body in a scorched suit lay draped over the crisp remnant of a black leather sofa. The vultures were at work, stopping only to eye Billy and Wayne as they passed.

They found Krepsin's a few minutes later. The massive body was still strapped in its seat, lying on its side in a thatch of sharp palmettos, which had kept most of the vultures away. Krepsin, the clothes almost all ripped away from his body, was covered with mottled bluish black bruises. The tongue lolled from his head, and his eyes protruded as if they were about to explode. The body was already swelling, the face, neck, and arms grown to even more freakish proportions.

Billy heard the thin, high screaming in his head; the noise grew louder and then ebbed. He said, "Wait," and Wayne stopped. The screaming was agonized, terrified; Krepsin and the others were still here, caught at the instant of their deaths. Abruptly, the screaming stopped as if it had been squeezed off. Billy listened, feeling a cold chill work through him. Now there was only silence.

Something was different, Billy thought. Something was wrong. The hair at the back of his neck was standing up. He felt danger here. *The shape changer*, Billy thought, and was suddenly afraid. *What had happened to the shape changer?* If it fed off the evil in Krepsin, Niles, and Dorn, might it not swell with hideous, consumptive strength?

Billy said, "Let's get out of here. Right now." He started off again. Wayne stared down at Krepsin's corpse for a moment, then followed.

Behind them, one of Krepsin's swollen, burned hands moved. The fingers crept down and worked the seatbelt loose. It shrugged free of the seat, and grinned with a mouthful of shattered teeth. Its face turned toward the figures who were walking fifty yards away; its eyes had changed, now burning red and animalish. The reanimated corpse crawled through the palmetto, muttering and chuckling. Powered by a surge of evil stronger than anything it had ever consumed, the shape changer rose slowly on its scorched, swollen legs. Its hands clenched into fists as it watched the figures walking away. This body was still strong, not like the others that had been torn to pieces and gnawed on by the vultures. This body could be used.

The thing prowled through the wreckage, getting used to the feel of its fleshy cocoon. It giggled and muttered, ready now to smash and crush and rip. Vultures squalled and flew away from the lumbering thing; it sought Niles's headless body, ripped open the coat, and dug a thick hand into the pocket. It brought out a leather pouch, tied with a drawstring. The prize inside wouldn't fit on the swollen hand; impatiently, the shape changer snapped off the first joints of the fingers and jammed the prize onto the stubs.

Sharp pieces of razor blades gleamed in the sunlight. It was the weapon that Niles had used to slash Henry Bragg's throat.

Krepsin's face turned toward the distant figures; the red eyes glared out as if through a bloated, bruised mask of flesh. Now it had human form—and superhuman, evil-charged strength—and it would show them it would not be cheated. The thing swung its arm in a vicious arc and grinned. *Now* it would show them both.

The corpse waddled after them, with murder flaring in its eyes.

63

The sun burned down relentlessly. Cradling his injured arm, Billy saw that he'd misjudged the distance to that range of mountains. They'd been walking for over thirty minutes, and still the cactus-covered foothills seemed at least another half-mile away. The mountains were boulder-strewn ridges of tortured earth, red rock shimmering in rising heat waves. He could see a few scattered caves, though; there were maybe twelve, most of them little more than shallow cracks. He was losing liquid in rivulets, his head pounding from the deadly weight of the sun. His feet, bruised and cut by the rough desert pavement, were leaving bloody prints.

Wayne staggered, about to pass out. His nose was bleeding again, the liquid attracting a horde of flies. His face felt like a sheet of hot metal, and as he lifted his gaze toward the sky his single eye saw the two vultures that were circling overhead. One for each of them, he thought, and almost giggled. One would get the dark meat, one would get the white. They were going to die out here. It would be soon, and it was no use to keep walking. They might as well just lie down right here and let the vultures go to work. He lagged behind Billy, then abruptly sat down.

Billy turned and stopped. "Get up."

"No. I'm hurting too much. It's too hot." He sucked in a lungful of searing air, and the pain in his side flared. He watched as Billy stepped back toward him. "Want me to heal you?" he asked, and grinned. "Want me to lay my hands on you and make you all right? Take a number."

"We don't have much farther to go. Come on."

He shook his head. "I'm burned out. There's nothing left." Wayne's eyes closed. "The snake's won," he said. "It's killed the eagle. . . ."

"What? What snake and eagle?"

"I see them in a dream, fighting. The snake bit the eagle, bit it right in the heart, and pulled it down from the sky."

Billy remembered how his eagle had clamped its beak down on the snake's head, how in his dream it seemed to be winning. "The eagle's smoke?" he said. "And the snake's fire?"

Wayne's eyes snapped open, his head cocked to one side. "How'd you know that?"

"What I told you on the plane, about your mother," Billy said, "was true. You have to believe me. There's still time for you to be strong; there's still time for the eagle to win."

Sweat dripped off Wayne's chin, making a dark puddle on the ground. "I always wanted to *fly*. But somehow I . . . always ended up crawling. I wish I'd known more about her. And about you, too. Maybe things would've been different. Go on, now. Leave me alone."

But Billy was looking out across the desert, toward the haze of black smoke where the Challenger lay. He saw the figure approaching, now about a hundred yards away. The mottled, bloated body waddled toward them, legs pumping in a frantic hurry.

Wayne peered over his shoulder, his vision blurring in and out. "Krepsin," he said hoarsely. "He's not dead. . . ."

The body was moving in a jerky pantomime of life; with each step, the head joggled from side to side as if the neck had been snapped. Its shoes stirred up puffs of dust. The shattered left shoulder made the arm swing like a fleshy pendulum.

No, Billy thought; that's not Krepsin. That's something wearing Krepsin's flesh, something hurrying now to catch them before they reached the foothills.

"Wait for me, boys!" the thing roared, a rasping voice forced through Krepsin's dead vocal cords. "I've got a present for you! Look, it's something shiny!" The thing bellowed and snorted, and swung its right hand in a quick arc. Billy saw sunlight glint off a metal object. "Wayne? Billy? Wait for me right there! *I'm coming!*"

The shape changer, Billy knew. Only now it wasn't playing games, wasn't shifting masks to confuse him and Wayne. It was wearing human flesh, muscle, and sinew; it was tracking them down, gobbling and snorting with glee. And in that form, Billy realized, no mental tricks were needed; it would tear them to pieces. "Get up, Wayne. *Hurry.*"

Wayne rose to his feet, wincing from the pain. Then he and Billy were hobbling away, trying to put distance between them and the thing. It shouted, "YOU CAN'T RUN! THERE'S NO-WHERE TO HIDE!" It tried to break into a run too, but the lumbering unwieldy legs collapsed and the shape changer fell to the ground. Sputtering with rage, it forced itself up again and moved onward.

The heat quickly slowed Billy and Wayne down. The behemoth stalked after them, keeping a steady pace.

"WAYNE!" the shape changer shouted. "He's trying to trick you! He's a demon, the son of Satan! He's trying to mix up your head! Can't you see me? I'm alive!"

"No," Wayne whispered, "you're dead . . . you're dead . . . you're . . ."

The voice changed, became feminine and softly seductive. "Wayne? I'm waiting for you at the lake! Want to go swimmin'? Don't run away, Wayne! Wait for me!" And then, thunderously, "I'LL KILL YOU, YOU LITTLE FUCK!"

"Don't listen!" Billy said.

"Billy?" the thing called out. "Do you know *who* you're trying to help? He had them kill your mother, Billy. Know how it was done? They cut her throat. They cut it right to the spine. Then your pretty little Hawthorne house was set on fire so everything would be ashes! He wanted to have *you* killed, too! Oh, he *dreamed* of killing you! GO ON, ASK HIM!"

"Don't look back," Billy told Wayne; his voice was choked with conflicting emotions.

They reached the foothills and began climbing. The terrain grew rockier and steeper. Behind them, the shape changer muttered and shouted and babbled, swinging its weapon back and forth with malicious glee. They climbed over sharp-edged boulders, the breath of pain hissing from between their teeth. They were slowing down as their strength burned away, but the shape changer was gaining ground. Black, stomach-wrenching pain hit Billy as his injured arm grazed an outcrop of rock, but he clenched his teeth to contain the scream. In another few moments their progress was slowed to a crawl; they left sweat stains wherever they touched, and bloody prints where Billy's feet had gripped rock. The caves were above them, less than fifty feet away over a torturous trail of jagged stone. Wayne looked back, saw the bloated thing grinning thirty feet or so beneath them as it clambered up. He recognized the weapon on its right hand.

"Running out of steam, boys?" the walking corpse called out, showing its mangled teeth.

Billy reached up with his good hand to climb onto a ledge. His feet slipped on loose stones, and he almost tumbled down, but then Wayne was pushing him up from below. He crawled upward, onto the ledge about six feet wide and exposed to burning sunlight. A large cave was twenty feet above, but his strength was gone. He lay panting with pain as Wayne crawled up beside him.

Wayne tried to drag Billy the rest of the way, but he was too weak to go more than a few feet. Sweat burned into his eye, blinding him for a few seconds; when he cleared his vision, Krepsin's dead face was rising over the ledge.

Wayne let go of Billy and kicked out at the thing. Bone cracked in the corpse's neck, and watery blood gushed from the nose, but it was still pulling itself onto the ledge. Wayne kicked out again, but the shape changer's arm swung to stop the blow. The razored weapon slashed into Wayne's ankle, scraping the bone. Wayne fell onto his injured ribs, curled up, and lay still with blood pooling under his leg.

"Two very naughty boys," the shape changer whispered as it rose on Krepsin's legs. "They must be punished."

Billy was transfixed with fear, too weak to even try to crawl away. The shape changer had them now. His Mystery Walk—and Wayne's, too—would end here, on a scorched slab of rock a hundred feet above the Mexican desert.

"You won't steal the food from my table anymore, you whelp." It lumbered forward, bloodied head lolling. "I'm going to take my time with you, I'm going to enjoy this. You remember what I told you, a long time ago? In that bitch's smokehouse? I said I'd be seeing you again. Oh, it's worked out just fine, hasn't it? The little ghost boy is about to see what Death is like from the other side; and I'll keep you screaming for a long, long time. . . ." It grinned, ready to feast on more agony, already drawing on Billy's fear to make itself stronger. It swelled with the terror and evil it had drawn from the dead men in the jet.

The shape changer gripped Billy's hair and thrust his head back, glaring into the boy's eyes. "First, a scalp," it whispered, raising its arm. "A scalp from an Indian."

And then Wayne grabbed the corpse's chin from behind, wrenching its head backward.

Jagged edges of bone ripped through the throat with a noise like tearing cloth. The immense football-shaped head was jammed backward, the shape changer's eyes were blinded by the sun. The head, now separated from the spine, hung back like a sack of flesh; the shape changer couldn't see. It turned upon Wayne, flailing blindly with the razored knuckles.

Wayne ducked the first blow, trying to balance on his good leg, but a backhanded swipe laid his cheek open and he staggered toward the edge. The shape changer danced with rage, striking at empty air, coming closer and closer to Wayne. Then Krepsin's corpse found him and they grappled, Wayne's hand closing around the thing's right wrist, trying with the last of his strength to hold back the razors. They were balanced on the edge, the shape changer unable to see forward, the ruined head hanging back over the corpse's shoulder.

Wayne lost his grip. The razors glinted, the swollen hand burying itself in Wayne's stomach.

Wayne caught his breath, felt warmth oozing down his legs. His vision hazed, but his brain was clear and for the first time in his life he knew what had to be done. The shape changer was making croaking sounds of triumph through Krepsin's ripped throat. Its hand twisted, driving the razors deeper into Wayne's stomach.

"NO!" Billy shouted, and tried to rise. He'd seen the death aura flare around Wayne; it undulated, shimmering a deep purplish black. Blood was streaming from Wayne's stomach, his face quickly bleaching.

But there was no fear in his unswollen eye. It caught Billy's gaze, locked, and then quickly shifted back to the struggling shape changer. This was the thing that had taunted him all along, that had tricked him by taking his daddy's form . . . and the form of a young brunette girl who'd never really existed at all, except in his own head. The hot pain that shot through his body was thawing rusted, cobwebbed gears in his brain. He wasn't afraid.

He could still learn to fly, he realized. *Yes.* There was still time to kill the snake!

Now! he thought. Do it *now!*

And he twisted himself off the ledge, taking Krepsin's corpse with him.

Billy heard the shape changer's mangled roar, and then they were gone.

The air was bright and blue and whistled around Wayne's ears. He was falling toward the surface of water, there in the Fayette Public Swimming Pool, and everything was all right. He had finally gathered the courage to soar from the Tower, and no one was laughing at him anymore. The water shimmered beneath him, coming up fast. He closed his eyes and saw the fighting shapes, the smoke-eagle and the fire-serpent. The eagle was mortally wounded, but it was still strong; it dug its claws into the reptile and gripped the burning spade-shaped head in its beak. With a triumphant cry, the eagle beat its tattered wings toward the sky and lifted the writhing snake up . . . higher, and higher, and higher, until the snake crisped into ashes and whirled away on the bright currents of air.

He would be all right now. He'd done the best he could, and he was ready to soar.

Billy heard them hit. Rocks cascaded down the mountainside, and then there was a long silence but for the noise of sliding grit. He crawled painfully toward the edge and peered over.

Wayne lay on his stomach forty feet below, his arms outstretched. Fifteen feet beyond him, Krepsin's corpse had exploded like a gasbag on impact with a truck-sized boulder.

Something dark and leprous rose like a mist from Krepsin, moving slowly toward Wayne's body.

"Get away from him!" Billy shouted. "GET AWAY!"

The wraith picked and probed at Wayne. But Billy had seen the twisted angle of Wayne's head, the torn ankle and a protrusion of bone through the other leg. For the shape changer, the body was useless. The mist rose, took on the murky appearance of the huge boarlike beast. Its red eyes blinked; it was stunned and confused, unable to strike physically at Billy again. Within it, Billy saw roiling ectoplasm—a spectral hand clawing at the air, a football-shaped head with an open, silently screaming mouth, another face that might have been Niles's mirroring shock and agony. The forms churned, slowly losing their clarity—as if they were being digested in the belly of the beast.

"You've lost," Billy said. "Now run. Hide. RUN!"

The thing glowered at him for a moment, clutching its clawed arms around its stomach; the souls it had snatched writhed in soundless pain.

It looked down at Wayne's broken body, and its hideous face rippled with a snarl of hatred and frustration. The boy had escaped, was now far beyond the shape changer's control. The thing began to fade, taking its prizes with it. Before it had drifted away completely it glared up toward Billy and said, "There'll be a next time." But the voice—a mixture of Krepsin's, Niles's and Dorn's—was weaker, and carried an undercurrent of what might have been fear.

"I'll be ready," he replied, but the thing had already gone, leaving a slight turbulence of dust and grit.

The air settled. The sun baked down, and the vultures began to gather.

Billy waited, his head bowed with concentration. He was certain that Wayne was gone. Wayne had found the tunnel, and was now on a different kind of Mystery Walk. He wanted to bury the body, but the rocks that had slid down over it would keep the vultures away for a while, and he knew he was too weak to climb down and then back again. He said a silent prayer for Wayne. The air was clear and untroubled. After another few minutes Billy crawled away and painfully climbed to the large cave just above.

There was no water, but the shade was deep and cool. Lizards scurried over the rocky floor, chasing small beetles. Billy crouched in a corner, ripped off the rags of his shirt, and fashioned a sling for his arm—not much, but it would serve to keep the bones from moving. He was full of fever, his head pounding with heat; if he didn't find liquid soon, he knew, he was going to die. He could let go; it would be easy to curl up and die, and so much pain would be avoided, but he knew his mother wouldn't want that. *He* didn't want it. He and Wayne had come so far from Hawthorne, both over twisted and treacherous ground—their paths had split early, their Mystery Walks leading them in such different directions, but at the end they'd faced the shape changer together. And Wayne had been stronger than the evil thing that had toyed with him for so long.

The fever was burning Billy dry. He was getting chills now, and he knew that must be a bad sign. He closed his eyes, concentrating on Bonnie, waiting for him in Chicago. He tumbled into sleep, escaping fever and thirst.

"Billy?" someone said quietly.

He stirred and forced his eyes open.

There was a figure standing in the cave entrance, silhouetted against harsh white sunlight. It was a little boy, Billy realized, but he couldn't see the face. A little boy? he thought. Out *here?* No, no; he was dreaming—hallucinating. The little boy wore a clean shirt and trousers, not a spot of dust or drip of sweat on him.

"Who's that?" Billy asked, his tongue so swollen he could hardly speak. "I can't see what you look like."

"It's *me!* You remember, don't you, Billy? It's me from a long time ago! We used to play together! Remember?"

"Who? I don't know you." *The shape changer,* he thought, and went cold. "Get away from me."

"I'm not trying to trick you. Honest. I want to help you, if I can. But you've got to help yourself, too. You can't lie there too much longer. You'll die."

"Maybe I will."

"But *why?* You've come a long way, Billy. You've . . . you've grown up. You helped me once, a long time ago."

"I want to sleep. Whatever you are, leave me alone. You can't hurt me anymore."

"I don't want to. I . . . know how bad it can be. It can be real bad here, but you can't give up. You can never give up, and you're not ready . . . not yet." The little boy watched him for a moment, his head cocked to one side in a way that Billy thought was familiar. Was it . . . no, no not *him.* . . .

"Leave here when it gets dark," the little boy said. "But watch how the sun goes down, so you can figure out which way is due west. That's the direction you've got to walk, right where the sun sets. There are others trying to help you, too, but sometimes it's not easy. You still think I'm trying to fool you, don't you? I'm not, I promise. You've got to start walking when it gets dark. It's going to be hard, but you have to keep going. Okay?"

"No. I'm staying right here until someone finds me."

403

"They won't," he said quickly. "You're a long way from where people are, Billy. You have to get out of here."

"Go away. Leave me alone."

"No; first you have to say you will. Okay?"

Billy closed his eyes. It was the shape changer, he knew, trying to make him lose himself in the desert. Trying to make him walk in the wrong direction and away from where the villages were.

"Do it, Billy. West, okay? Okay?"

The last plea hung in the air. When he opened his eyes again, he saw the cave entrance was empty. The fever was making him hear and see things. No, it was best to stay right here where he was cool and safe, where someone would eventually find the jet's wreckage. Surely someone would see the smoke!

But there was something lying in the palm of his right hand. He stared at it, his heart beating rapidly.

It was a piece of coal that had been covered with shellac so that the black wouldn't rub off.

He stood up, hobbling to the entrance. There were no prints but his own bloody ones in the dust. The fierce heat forced him back into the shadow, where he sat down again and clenched the coal tightly in his fist. Had he had the coal with him all the time? No, no; it had been left in Chicago, two thousand miles away. Hadn't it? He couldn't remember through the fire in his head. He put the coal in his pocket and waited for the sun to sink.

In deep blue twilight, Billy carefully descended over the rocks to where Wayne and Krepsin's corpses lay sprawled. A flurry of vultures sailed away; they'd already feasted on much of Krepsin. They'd been working on Wayne's back and legs, but hadn't marked the face yet. Billy took Wayne's shoes and squeezed his swollen feet into them. He sat for a few moments beside Wayne, then he aranged rocks over the body to keep the vultures away awhile longer.

He began walking westward; he stopped once to look back over his shoulder, where his brother's body lay. But his brother was gone, and there was no reason to mourn his passage to the other side. He wished he'd known more about Wayne, that they could've learned to understand each other. That they could've been friends, instead of two young men who'd walked separately, each seeking some kind of answer to the forces that had taken over their lives.

Billy left his brother's corpse, and went on.

He alternated walking and resting all through the long, chilly night. His feet were bleeding again, his broken wrist swollen to twice its size, but he had to keep going. Just before dawn, when he was exhausted and staggering, he climbed a small hill and came upon a squatter's cabin. The place was falling in, but inside there was a dirty mattress on the floor; on a table were plates with green-molded food not fit to touch, much less eat. But there was a coffee pot, too, and something faintly sloshed inside when Billy picked it up. He eagerly poured a few drops into the palm of his hand; the water was slimy and green and alive with bacteria. He took one of the plates outside, scraped it clean with coarse sand, and then brought it back in. He tore a square of his pants leg off and stretched it over the plate, then carefully poured the water through the cloth to catch the bigger clumps of green growth. What remained at the bottom of the plate—barely three swallows, brackish and stagnant—was quickly tipped into Billy's mouth. He wet his face with the damp cloth, and then he slept for several hours on the filthy mattress.

When he awakened, bright swords of sunlight pierced gaping holes in the rotting walls around him. He was feverish and very weak, his legs cramped into knots. His arm was a burning, leaden weight, the wound oozing yellow fluids. He shut his mind to the pain, and concentrated on Bonnie. He would show Hawthorne to her, and he wanted to see Lamesa, and he wanted to know everything about her from the day she was born. He hung her face up in his mind like a picture. He *would* get back to her.

He stepped outside the cabin and was jolted by a sudden shock.

About three or four miles away, sitting right in the middle of brown sand desert, was a large lake. It was surrounded by motels and restaurants with high signs that could be seen from the highway that passed about a half-mile from the cabin. There were cars and dune buggies on the road, and out on the lake Billy could see a sleek red speedboat pulling a water-skier. Palm trees waved in the streets of some resort town built around a desert spring. The entire scene shimmered in the heat waves; Billy stood motionless, expecting the whole thing to vanish suddenly.

He began to walk toward the mirage. On the highway a dune buggy swerved to avoid him, blasting its horn. He walked slowly down the center, being passed by cars and motorcycles and dune buggies. Some of the cars were hauling speedboats, and kids were hanging out the windows. The lake glittered like liquid gold in the strong sunlight.

Billy stood in the center of the highway and started laughing. He couldn't stop, even though his jaw was aching and he was so weak he was about to fall on his face. He was still laughing when a Mexican police officer on a motorcycle pulled up beside him and shouted something that included the word *loco*.

THIRTEEN

Home

64

They'd rented a brown Gremlin at the Birmingham airport, using Bonnie's driver's license, and had driven the two-hour trip to Fayette under a gray late-December sky. The southern winter had set in, a wave of cold air and rain had rolled down from the northwest scattering brown leaves before it. Christmas was two days away.

They passed a large sign, punctured by .22 bulletholes, that said WELCOME TO FAYETTE! HOME OF LITTLE WAYNE FALCONER, THE SOUTH'S GREATEST EVANGELIST! The second line, Billy saw, was being allowed to weather away. It would not be repainted. Home for Wayne's body was now a meticulously kept cemetery near the Falconer estate; he'd been buried next to his daddy, and there were always fresh flowers on the grave.

"I've never seen so many hills," Bonnie said. She'd noticed him wince, as if from an old injury, as they'd passed the sign. "Lamesa's about as flat as a flapjack. Are we gettin' near?"

"We'll be there in a few minutes. It's just past Fayette." There were still dark hollows under his eyes, and he needed to gain five or six pounds so his face would fill out, but he was doing much better. He'd been able to walk without crutches for the first time just a week before. There were a few lost weeks in which Billy had faded in and out, his body fighting against massive infection. His jaw was wired and was healing well, as was his left arm in its thick elbow cast. Dr. Hillburn had been straight with him: the doctors didn't know why he hadn't died out in that desert. The injuries he'd received in the crash had been severe enough to begin with, but the exposure and the infection from his broken wrist should have finished him off.

Dr. Hillburn hadn't replied when Billy told her that he *had* died, but had been sent back from the other side. And those people had been right, Billy said; it *was* beautiful over there. But he planned on sticking around here for a while longer, if Dr. Hillburn didn't mind.

Dr. Hillburn had smiled and said she didn't mind at all.

Later, Billy had asked about his mother. Dr. Hillburn confirmed what Billy already knew: Ramona Creekmore had died in a house fire of indeterminate origin. The cabin was almost a total ruin.

Bonnie stayed with him day and night, helping him with his grief. Now that he was safe, and his body was healing, his conflicting emotions about Wayne and the loss of his mother welled up out of him in agonized, bitter tears. Bonnie cradled his head while he cried. He had nightmares for a while, about the jet crash and the shape changer in possession of Krepsin's bloated corpse, stalking him and Wayne across the burning desert; they faded as his body and mind healed, though he'd broken out in a cold sweat when he and Bonnie had stepped aboard the plane from Chicago, their trip a gift from the staff and residents of the Hillburn Institute. The most difficult thing was snapping the seatbelt, and when the 747 bound to Atlanta had taken off, he'd closed his eyes and held tightly to Bonnie's hand. Once up in the air, though, his fear drained away—as he'd hoped it would—and he was even able to look out the window for a few minutes. The plane ride was much faster and more comfortable than the bus or the train, Billy's other travel alternatives, and he'd wanted to get back to Hawthorne as quickly as possible.

He'd told Bonnie fragments of what had happened in Mexico, but she knew it was hard for him to talk about it. She didn't want to push him; if and when he was ready to tell her, she would be there to listen.

Now they were passing through Fayette, and Hawthorne was only fifteen miles away.

Billy had turned twenty-one while still in a semiconscious state in the hospital. He was different now, he knew, from the person who'd left Hawthorne that first time to join Dr. Mirakle's Ghost Show. He saw his direction more clearly, and he was secure with his own place in the world. He'd fought his way, he realized, through a rite of passage that had begun when he'd stepped down into the dark Booker basement a long time ago; he was strong now, strong in his heart, and he knew that in his life the eagle was winning.

His Mystery Walk was pulling him onward, out into the world.

But first, before he could walk forward—to the University of California, Duke University, or even to Oxford in England, where parapsychologists had been studying the Alcott Tape and were eager to get Billy into their death survival research programs—he had to look back over his shoulder. There were good-byes to be said, both to people and to places.

The Gremlin rounded a bend, and Billy saw the old weather-beaten high-school building with its brick gym addition. There was a large, ragged scar in the football field, as if grass wouldn't grow where the bonfire had exploded.

Billy touched Bonnie's arm and asked her to stop.

The parking lot was empty, all the students out for Christmas holidays. Billy rolled down his window and stared out at the football field, his eyes dark with the memory of May Night.

"Something bad happened here, didn't it?" Bonnie asked.

"Yes. Very bad."

"What was it?"

"A lot of kids got hurt. Some of them were killed." He ran his gaze along the new fence, remembering the pain of his hands being ripped as the shock wave blustered past. He waited for a few minutes, listening to the sigh of wind out on the field. Pines swayed in the distance, and clouds seemed to skim the hills.

"They're gone," he said. "There's nothing here. Thank God. Okay. I'm ready to go."

They drove on, following the road into Hawthorne. When Billy saw the tangle of black timbers and the standing chimney where his house had once stood, his heart sank. The field was overgrown, the scarecrow sagging, everything gone to ruin. He didn't ask Bonnie to slow down, though, until they'd almost reached the lot where the decaying hulk of the Booker house had stood.

The rubble had been cleared away, and now a trailer sat on the property. It was there to stay, sitting on concrete supports sunken into the earth. A Christmas tree stood in a front window, white lights blinking. A little boy—who looked not at all like Will Booker—sat outside, roughhousing with a big brown dog that was trying to lick him in the face. The boy saw the Gremlin and waved. Billy waved back. There was warmth surrounding that trailer, and he hoped the people who lived there were happy. Hawthorne's "murder house" was long gone.

He heard the sawmill's high whine as they approached the

411

cluster of grocery store, gas station, and barbershop. A couple of farmers sat outside the gas station, watching with interest to see if the Gremlin would pull in. Someone was loading a sack of groceries into a pickup truck. A television flickered from within Curtis Peel's barbershop, and Billy saw figures sitting around the red glow of the old heater. Life was going on in Hawthorne at its own slow, steady pace. The world had touched it—there was a poster on a telephone pole that said NOW HIRING QUALIFIED LABOR. APPLY AT THE CHATHAM PERSONNEL OFFICE. WE ARE AN EQUAL OPPORTUNITY EMPLOYER—but the essence of life, easy and unhurried, would never totally change. Maybe that was for the best, Billy thought; it was comforting to know that some places in the world remained the same, though the people living in them grew and matured and learned from their mistakes.

"Would you stop here?" Billy asked, motioning to the curb near Peel's barbershop. "I want to go in there for a minute. Want to come with me?"

"That's why I'm here," she replied.

When Billy opened the barbershop door, the three men sitting around the heater looked up from their television show—"Let's Make a Deal"—and froze. Curtis Peel's mouth dropped open. Old Hiram Keller, as tough as leather, simply blinked, then returned his attention to Monty Hall. The third man, younger than the others, with curly brownish blond hair and a plump-cheeked face tinted red by the heater, leaned forward as if he were staring at a mirage.

"Damn my eyes!" Peel said, and stood up. "Is that . . . Billy Creekmore?"

"That's right." He stood tensed, ready for anything. He'd recognized the younger man, and saw Duke Leighton's eyes narrow.

"Well, I'll be a . . ." And suddenly Peel's face broke into a grin. He came forward, clapped Billy on the shoulder, and then, embarrassed by his own ebullience, stepped back a pace. "Uh . . . we didn't expect to see you back, after . . . I mean, we . . ."

"I know what you mean. I want you to meet my friend, Bonnie Hailey. This is Curtis Peel. That's Hiram Keller, and Duke Leighton."

"Howdy," Hiram said without looking up.

"I didn't figure you'd recognize me, Billy." Duke patted his

412

bulging beer-belly. "I guess I've changed a lot. You have, too. You look like you've been in an accident."

"Could be."

They were silent for a long moment. Then Curtis said, "Hey! You two young folks want a Coke? I've got some in the back, just as cold as they can be! No? Weather's turned for the worse, I hear. Supposed to get a hard freeze tonight. Listen, y'all take a chair and make yourself—"

"We're not staying," Billy told him. "I've come to visit the cemetery."

"Oh. Yeah. Well . . . Billy, that was a bad thing. A real terrible thing. The fire burned everything up so *fast,* and the wind was bad that night too. I . . . I'm sorry."

"So am I."

Peel turned and stared into Bonnie's face for a few seconds, seemingly entranced by her eyes. He smiled uncertainly, then looked back at Billy. "You need a haircut, Bill. Come on, get in the chair here and we'll fix you up. On the house, okay? I recall you used to like the smell of Vitalis. You still do?"

"No," he said, and smiled slightly at Peel's willingness to please. "Afraid not." He was aware of Leighton's unyielding gaze on him, and he felt anger begin to simmer.

"Well . . ." Peel nervously cleared his throat. "Most everybody's heard about you, Bill. You're a celebrity. I mean, I don't rightly understand what you've been up to and all, but . . . look here." He stepped next to the shelves of hair tonic, shampoo, and pomades and pointed to something mounted on the wall; he smiled proudly, and Billy saw it was a bulletin board. It was covered with newspaper clippings about the "Mystery Medium," and the Alcott tape, and pictures of Billy. "See here, Bill? I've been keepin' them. People come in here to read 'em all the time. You're a real celebrity hereabouts! And look up there on the wall. Recognize that?" He'd motioned to a framed needlepoint picture of an owl sitting on a tree limb; the features were a bright mixture of colors, the eyes so sharp and lifelike they followed you around the room. Billy recognized his mother's handiwork. "Fella from Montgomery came through here about a month ago, offered me a hundred dollars for it," Curtis said. He swelled his chest proudly. "I said no. I said it was done by a local artist, and you couldn't put any price on something done with as much feeling as that's got in it. Didn't I say that, Hiram?"

"Yep."

"I've got another one at home. It shows a mountain and a lake, and an eagle flying way up far in the sky. I think it's the prettiest thing I've ever seen. See, I've put this one where I can look at it all the time!"

Hiram suddenly stirred and regarded the picture. "Fine work," he said, lighting his corncob pipe and sticking it in his grizzled gace. "You'd go a far piece to find anything finer, I'll tell you that." He cocked his head and looked at Billy. "Your mother was full of magic, boy. She was a damned fine woman, and it took us a long time to realize it. Any woman who could run a farm like she did, and make pictures like that, and never complain 'bout her lot in life . . . well, I remember that night at the tent revival. Maybe we didn't want to hear what she said, but she had guts, boy. Looks like you've got *your* share too." He motioned with his pipe toward the bulletin board.

"*What* . . . ?" Billy managed to say. He was stunned, and he felt hot tears in his eyes. "You mean you . . ."

Duke Leighton started to rise. His gaze was baleful in the red light. When he stood erect, his back was hunched over; with his first step, Billy saw that he walked with a terrible limp, much worse than his father's. As he approached Billy, Duke seemed to grow smaller and paler and thinner. He saw Billy staring and stood in front of him, his lower lip trembling. "It happened just after you left. I was ridin' in the car with my dad. He was . . . he was drinking pretty heavily. He'd taken to drinkin' a lot since Mom died. Anyway, he . . . the car was going too fast, and we went off the trestle bridge. I just got cut up, but my dad was dead by the time the ambulance came." His face was set and grim. "About a week later, Coy Granger came to see me, and he said he'd seen my dad standing at the side of the road, right at the trestle bridge where the car had gone off. . ."

"Saw him myself," Hiram said quietly. "Plain as day. Plain as I can see you."

"My dad . . . couldn't leave." Duke's voice cracked, his eyes swimming. "I saw him, and I called out to him, and he looked like he was tryin' to answer but he . . . he couldn't speak. His . . . throat was crushed in the wreck, and he strangled to death. And when I tried to touch him, I felt so *cold*. Then he was gone, just faded away in an instant." He looked helplessly at Bonnie, then back to Billy again. "Who else could I go to?" he asked. "I had to help my dad!"

"And my mother freed him?"

"I saw her do it." Hiram puffed out a wreath of blue smoke. "We all did. She stood right there on the trestle bridge and opened up her arms, and we all saw Ralph Leighton with our own eyes." He set his jaw and grunted. "Damnedest thing I *ever* saw. And Ralph just . . . disappeared, just kinda eased away, I guess. Ramona fell down, and she had to be helped home. . . ."

"My wife stayed the night with her," Peel said. "She took care of her."

Duke wiped his face with a sleeve. "Sorry. I didn't mean to . . . act like a fool. I never believed in such a thing as spirits until I saw my *own* father standin' there, trying to call out to me. . . ."

"Sheer guts," Hiram said. "She did it in front of everybody who cared to watch. Oh, at first some laughed. But after it was over and done . . . wasn't *nobody* laughin' no more."

"I bought this picture from her soon after that," Peel said. "She didn't want to take the money. Said she had no need for it. But I made her take it. The very next night . . . well, that fire was so fast and windblown it was over before we knew it."

"I didn't know." Billy looked at all of them in turn. "She never wrote me about what happened on the trestle bridge."

"Maybe she figured you had your own worries." Hiram relit his pipe, clenched it between his teeth, and watched the game show again.

"I'm sorry about your father," Billy said.

"Yeah. Well, things hadn't been too good between me and him for a long time. He took me down to the Marine recruiting station in Tuscaloosa right after high school. I never went to college like I was supposed to. I went to 'Nam—another kind of college, I guess. I got into demolition, but I guess you heard. That's funny, huh? Me, in demolition?" He tried to smile, but his face was too loose and weary, his eyes too haunted.

"Funny? Why?"

Duke stared at him for a long moment. "You . . . you *don't* know, do you? Well, why would you? I came back from 'Nam in seventy-one with a shot-up hip and a Purple Heart. Then what I'd done kept eatin' at me, so . . . I went to the sheriff and told him. I served my time—one year on a two-year sentence. I've just been out since October. But I want you to know, Billy, that it was never my idea. I wasn't the one who came up with the idea. . . ."

"What idea?"

"The fireworks," Duke said quietly. "I thought you knew; I thought everybody knew. I was one of the boys who put all those fireworks in the bonfire. It was . . . supposed to be a joke. Just a joke. I thought it'd make pretty colors. I thought people would laugh. I swear, I never knew it would blow up like that. My dad found out about it, and he shipped me off to the Marines damned fast. I can't ever forget that night, Billy. I don't sleep too good. I can still, y'know, hear the sounds they made. Billy, you'd . . . you'd know if any of them were still there, wouldn't you? I mean, you could tell, and you could help them?"

"They're gone," he replied. "I'm sure of it."

But Duke shook his head. "Oh, no they're not. Oh, no." He opened his eyes and tapped a finger against his skull. "They're all still in here, every one of them who died that night. You can't help me, can you?"

"No."

"I didn't think so. I served my time, got out on good behavior. My dad pretended I was away, workin' in Georgia. Well . . ." He moved past Bonnie and took his hat off the rack on the wall. It was a gas-station cap. "I'd best get back to work. The gas won't pump itself. I thought you knew about all that, Billy. I surely did."

"They're gone," Billy said as he reached the door. "You don't have to keep them inside you anymore."

"Yes I do," Duke said, and then he opened the door—the little bell over it tinkled merrily—and he was gone.

"We were wrong about your mother," Peel said. "All of us were wrong. It wasn't evil. It never was, was it?"

Billy shook his head; his eyes were watering, and Bonnie pressed close to his side to support him.

"Terrible thing about that Falconer boy. Heard he died in a plane crash in Mexico, of all places. God only knows what he was doin' down there. I heard he went off the deep end, just gave up everything. . . ."

"Not everything," Billy said. "Just the things that didn't matter."

"Huh?"

"Nothing." He looked again at the needlepoint owl. It was a

416

beautiful picture, and would be seen by a lot of people. He couldn't think of a better place for it to be hanging.

Peel touched his shoulder. "Bill, I've got a fine idea! Why don't you and the little lady join my family and me for dinner tonight? I'll call her, and I guarantee you the finest fried-chicken dinner you ever put in your mouth! All right?"

"You got room at that table for me?" Hiram asked.

"Maybe we do. What the hell . . . *sure*. We got room for everybody! Okay, Bill? How about it?"

He smiled, glanced at Bonnie, and then nodded. "We'd like that very much."

"Fine! Let me get on the horn right now!"

"Curtis," Billy said as he moved to the phone, "I'm going to see my mother. She *is* in the cemetery isn't she?"

"Oh. Yes, she is. Don't you worry about a thing. We took care of her real good, Bill. You'll see."

"We'll be back." They walked to the door, and as Billy opened it he heard Peel say over the phone, "Ma? You're gonna have a real celebrity over tonight! Guess who's . . ."

"Sheer guts," Hiram grunted.

Fifteen minutes later, Billy was standing with Bonnie beside his mother's grave. His father was buried a few feet away. Pine needles covered the ground, and the chill wind whispered softly through the trees. Billy could smell pine sap: the aroma of life, waiting to burst free in April.

A stone marker had been planted at the head of Ramona's grave. It was fine cut, simple but proud. It gave her name, her date of birth and death, and underneath that, in expertly etched block letters: DAUGHTER OF HAWTHORNE.

Billy put his arm around Bonnie. His mother wasn't here, he knew; her body was, returning now to the earth as all bodies must, but her soul—that part of her that had made her very special—was somewhere else, still carrying on her Mystery Walk. And his would go on too, from this place and moment. He would meet the shape changer again, because it was part of the Evil that lived in the world, but he knew now that, though it couldn't be totally destroyed, it could be *bested*. The eagle could win over the snake. Courage could win over fear.

A few tough stalks of goldenrod grew in the brush a few feet from Ramona's grave. Billy picked some, scattering the yellow wild flowers over the earth. "Flowers for the dead," he said, "and for the living." He gave Bonnie the remaining stalk, and saw her strange and beautiful eyes shine.

They stood together, as the clouds moved overhead in a slow and graceful panorama of white and gray. Snow flurries began to spin before the wind, clinging to their hair and eyelashes, and Billy remembered the infant step of his Mystery Walk—when he and his father had left the cabin to walk in the snow and had passed the Booker house. Now he had someone else to walk beside—someone who could understand him and believe in him, as much as he in her.

"I knew you'd come back," Bonnie said. "I knew it. You left the piece of coal, and I didn't think you'd leave without it. I kept it by my bed all the time, until one morning when I woke up and it wasn't there. I had a dream that night. . . ."

"About what?"

"You," she replied. "And me, too. We were . . . together, and we were old. We were tired, but it was a good tired, like you've done a hard day's work and you know you'll have a peaceful sleep. I don't know where we were, but we were sitting in the sun and we could see the ocean. We were holding hands." She shrugged, a blush creeping across her freckled cheeks. "I don't know, but . . . after that dream, I knew you'd be all right. I knew you'd come back. Funny, huh?"

"Why?"

"It's the first dream I ever had that I wasn't afraid of," Bonnie said.

It was time to go. They walked down the hill to the car and got in. His Mystery Walk was about to carry him—and possibly Bonnie as well—far away from Hawthorne, he realized. Life and Death were part of the same puzzle, part of the same strange and miraculous process of growth. He hoped someday to work in the parapsychology labs himself, to go to school, to study as much as he could; he wanted to help others understand that Death wasn't an ending, and that Life itself was a wonderful mystery full of chances and challenges.

"Have you ever wanted to see England?" he asked her.

"Why?"

He smiled faintly. "Dr. Hillburn told me there are supposed to be more haunted houses in England than in any country on earth."

They drove away from the cemetery. Billy looked back over his shoulder, through the snow's thin white curtain, until the marble marker was out of sight. So much to be done! he thought. So much to be learned!

Billy turned his attention to the road that stretched out ahead, out of Hawthorne and into the world. And he would carry with him his mother's words of courage:

No fear.

About the Author

Robert R. McCammon majored in journalism at the University of Alabama. After graduation, he worked at various jobs before being hired by *The Birmingham Post Herald*, where he was employed when he began writing BAAL, his first novel. After its publication he left the newspaper to write full-time. His other novels include THEY THIRST, BETHANY'S SIN, THE NIGHT BOAT, USHER'S PASSING, and STINGER. He lives in Birmingham, Alabama, with his wife, Sally, a first-grade schoolteacher.